THAT MELVIN BRAY

THAT MELVIN BRAY

MARGARET McBRIDE

abbott press®

A DIVISION OF WRITER'S DIGEST

Abbott Press books may be ordered through booksellers or by contacting:

Abbott Press
1663 Liberty Drive
Bloomington, IN 47403
www.abbottpress.com
Phone: 1-866-697-5310

Because of the dynamic nature of the Internet, any web addresses or links contained in this book may have changed since publication and may no longer be valid. The views expressed in this work are solely those of the author and do not necessarily reflect the views of the publisher, and the publisher hereby disclaims any responsibility for them.

Cover Image by Christine Kerrick

ISBN: 978-1-4582-1212-2 (sc)
ISBN: 978-1-4582-1280-1 (hc)
ISBN: 978-1-4582-1211-5 (e)

Library of Congress Control Number: 2013918254

Print information available on the last page.

Abbott Press rev. date: 03/29/2018

TABLE OF CONTENTS

I dedicate this book to
the great pretenders—fake it till ya make it;
the children whose parents are AA (alcoholic and absent);
and
Dale, a.k.a. Lee the Lion, for her awesome courage;
her bright light is a beacon for us all.

IN THE FALL OF 2010, I received a copy of *The Shack,* from my niece, Tina Putman, encouraging me to read it. I did read it and that little book touched my heart and changed my life. It was the impetus for my first book, *That Melvin Bray.* Thank you, Tina!

For the first year, the only ones who knew I was writing a book were my granddaughter, Michah Bering, her younger brother, Weston and my darling husband, Dan. I had sworn them all to secrecy and somehow they made it until the second year, at which time I released them from their promise. Thank you, my dears!

That second year, my cousin Reenie DaCosta, my sister-in-law, Karen Seibert (keep a light on for us, KK), and dear friends, Lindy Byrne and Angela Cotton formed "The Okra Book Club". We would all meet periodically at Lindy's house in Atlanta, to discuss the merits of my story while keeping me focused and on track. What a team and what fun we had! Thank you seems so inadequate, but each of you knows my heart.

Special thanks to my dear friends, Gail Giorgio and Kim Stiles, who also know what's in my heart, as they both have known me for a long time and are well-known authors, and of course could relate to the path I was on and were so helpful to me all along the way.

A special note of thanks to artists, Christine Kerrick and Emily Johnson for their contributions through their incredible artistic talents. Hallelujah!!

To my daughter, Mia Bering and my son Tyce Miller, thank you for being who you are and for loving me. You make me very proud. Your love, guidance and encouragement while I was writing this story kept me going. A super big thanks goes out to all the other cheerleaders in my wonderful family, near and far, you know who you are!

Major kudos to Katrina Arnim and Katherine Montgomery, two exceptional women who have been with me throughout most of this humbling, four year endeavor. Their expertise in their specific fields coupled with their patience, guidance and love kept me believing in myself. Thank you from the bottom of my heart!

To my first real friend, Phyllis McCubbin, thank you for always being there!

Last, a huge thank you to and in memory of my wonderful Mother, Mallie Mae McBride, who definitely knows my heart. I love you, Mother.

CHAPTER 1

My Little Biddy
April 3, 1953

Remember to look through the windshield and not the rearview mirror,
because you've already been there.
>   —*Lea Shaver, an ex–Miss Texas*

IT WAS MY FAVORITE TIME OF YEAR and a perfect, cool, crisp fall afternoon in 1989. Lizabeth had joined me on the cozy little patio behind her office. The golden leaves of this Indian summer were swirling all around us, gently falling to the ground. The warmth from the heat of the chiminea created a toasty, serene respite for us.

"Hey, you know what we need?" she asked.

"Yeah, a hot, giant java," I answered. She called out to Paula, her assistant, to fill our special order.

"Wow, we've been hit by the fall, Magg-Pie, and it doesn't hurt a bit! I was hoping you were going to show up for this particular visit. I'm really glad to see ya!"

"I know—me too. It's just that when you came out to Austin to visit me in June, you kept insisting I come to Boston this fall and talk about family stuff. Being a shrink and all, you know all too well that most of us are in therapy because of our families! I'm surprised you don't hear about more calls to 911 saying, 'Help me! I'm in a family. Get me outta here!' For me, therapy is like a really easy game show where the correct answer to every question is 'Because of my father.'"

"Well, Maggs, 'features alone do not run in the blood; vices and virtues, genius and folly, are transmitted through the same sure but uneven channel'— so saith Hazlitt," she explained.

"He would saith that, huh? Well then, I choose the part about genius and virtues myself, and neither of those is of my father, I assure you, Dr. Benis, MD!"

1

"Sarcasm sounds good on you, Maggs. You should try it more often; it's good for the soul."

"Well, I've spent so much of my life consumed with *him* and all the what-ifs that I've developed a chronic case of misfit such that I'm not quite comfortable in my own skin. As you know, I pretend a lot. I feel like I'm somebody I don't know anymore. Maybe I do need that personality transplant you promised after all! I even joined a book club just to get a discount on self-help books because that's all I've ever bought. There was one I read about a woman who cured her cancer with positive thinking. Shoot, I don't have enough *real* happy thoughts to get rid of a pimple. Then I read this other article that said the symptoms of stress are eating too much, impulse buying, and driving too fast. Are they kiddin'? That's my idea of a perfect day!

"Seriously, though, I'd just love to remove this cloak of dishonor he imprisoned me in so long ago, ya know? You told me once, 'Whether you think you can or you think you can't, you're probably right.' I'm still working on that one. Since I saw you last, Lizzy, I've been so apprehensive. Ya know how you can dread something and yet be excited about it at the same time—the fear of finally facing it and the unknown?"

"Hey, Maggs, I know exactly what you mean, and that's precisely how I felt about my first kiss. Now, maybe I should, but I don't even remember my first kiss. However, I do remember the first *good* kiss!"

"Oh Miss Priss, you're too much." I laughed.

"Well, I just want you to finally make peace with your past, Maggs, so you won't screw up the rest of your blessed life."

"Ya know, somebody told me once that true blessedness is a good life and a happy death," I answered.

"Well, I'm all over that one, which brings me to this one: it's never too late to have a happy childhood, but the second one is up to *you* and no one else, Maggs. It's *not* Mission Impossible either.

"The recovery of lost innocence is amazing to behold and can be likened only to a loving mother taking in the sweet breath of her newborn for the very first time. It's the feeling of springtime. 'Hope springs eternal,' as they say, dear, and despite having been through so much yourself, you possess a beguiling innocence and always wish to help others, especially if it's to offer that hope. I caution you, though, Maggs—you just can't live your life acting against your will, for someone else's desires. You're just too damn nice!" She stopped abruptly.

"Hey, hey now, don't be goin' round tellin' that—I'm tryin' to live it down.

Hummm, and that's not Hazlitt—that's *Lizzy*. Where do you get all these little pearls of wisdom anyway?" I asked.

"Maggie, you of all people know what was required for me to get that little MD after my name: four years of undergrad, four years of med school, and, finally, four more years of psychiatry residence training. And after all that, I have to put up with being called a *shrink*." She pouted.

"Oh, boo hoo, poor Dr. Shrink, MD, and all *I* had to do was play for four years in undergrad and then two years in grad school, having fun learning to draw and paint like Picasso, right? And for just six years, I got *three* letters to your *two*! Yeah, MFA: mighty fine artist—that's my degree. I'm pretty smart for an ole girl from a little one-stoplight town, or was it two?" I boasted.

"Well, let's face it, my dear master of fine arts, since I can't draw a straight line with a ruler and couldn't tell you who painted what, when, where, or why, I really do admire you for your career choices and all you've accomplished in your cultured world of art. You've done quite well for yourself, and I'm damn proud of you! Heck, I'm proud of both of us!

"I'm not complaining. I knew my choices would require a long, tough haul, but I figured I was just the one to do it, and I thank my dear mother for planting the seed very early on. Ya know, she used to tell me if anyone ever asked me to play doctor, I was to tell them I have to wait until I grow up. Maggs, we both know that I too am pretty smart for an ole girl, so I did exactly as dear Mother advised. I waited until I grew up to play doctor. Ah, think about it, Maggs; I can't remember ever making a mistake. I thought I did once, but I was wrong. Heck, as far back as I can remember, I thought why not be the kinda woman that when your feet hit the floor each morning, the Devil says, 'Damn, she's up!'

"Yeah, Maggs, we're vetted, baby—nothing to do with horses either! We're certified, bonafied, and masterfied—wouldn't you agree?"

"Yep, but you left out petrified, Doc. Ya know the last thing I wanta see on your mantel is the first prize award for Best Dried Arrangement," I added with a little of that sarcasm she had spoken of earlier.

"Oh, you may be right; that's awful! Okay then, let's start with *you*, Maggs. From the *outside*, your life has always resembled a woman who has been living the American dream. You were born; you grew up, went to fine schools, and achieved your professional goals. Plus, along the way, you got married and had two great kids."

"Heck, it sounds to me like you're describing the four stages of life. And just for the record, Lizzy, I had those two great kids so they could grow up and have all the things I couldn't afford, and then at some point, I'm gonna move in with 'em—don't tell 'em, okay? I *have* learned, though, what the four stages of life that really count are. One, you believe in Santa Claus. Two, you don't believe in Santa Claus. Three, you are Santa Claus. And four, you look like Santa Claus. I rest my humble opinion, Dr. Benis."

"Funny, but I'm serious, Maggs! Let's face it—all this breeding, brains, and beauty, and still I'm over forty and single with no kids and two cats, but at least I do have the knowledge to figure out why. I mean, let's face it—I'm a head-case doctor already. So what's *my* problem? Hey, maybe I'm not ready to know my own truth yet. Actually, that probably has more to do with a book I read way back in my Learning How to Be a Shrink 101 class titled *The 10 Best Ways to Prevent Divorce: Don't Get Married*," she teased.

"Oh, come on, Lizzy. I know for a fact you've had at least *one* serious relationship in all these years, and it stunned me when *you* did the walkin'," I challenged.

"Well, I gave him the best six months of my life," she moaned.

"Hold on now, Miss Benis—if I remember correctly, you and Eric were an item for over five years, dearie, right?"

"Gosh, how time flies when it's draggin' by, huh, Maggs? In Eric's case, he was the kind of man who thought *no* was a three-letter word. It took me a while to realize the only person he could ever be in love with was the one he saw in the mirror several times a day! He was so self-absorbed that if he *could* have fallen in love with me, we'd have been a triangle! You remember how I met Eric, Maggs?"

"Yeah, seems like you used one of your famous, scary lines on him, right? Wasn't he hittin' on ya at some fancy soiree?"

"You got it, sister, sorta. I was actually out with some colleagues of mine celebrating the director's birthday. I excused myself to go to the ladies' room, and on my way back to the table, he strutted past me doing that peacock puff he was so good at, remember? Then, all of a sudden, we're walking side by side, and as he pointed to my table, he said, 'You know, instead of eating that birthday cake over there, you should be jumping out of it. Are you married?' I'm thinking, *Hey, pretty good line, you fast smooth-talker you—haven't gotten that one yet.* I stopped in my tracks, looked him right in the eyes, shook my head, and said, 'No, I'm not married; someone's gonna have to get me pregnant first.' I guess he liked the idea of becoming a father, because that was the beginning of a long and eventually unfulfilling relationship for both of us. *I* loved him without a doubt, and *he* loved him without a doubt. And the father thing—well, let's just say he must have figured out the triangle thing. Ya know—him, him, and me? He just wouldn't have had any love left for a child. Another thing I should have noticed about Eric was that he never went fishing—not once. In my book, *real* men fish, Maggs, right? Oh sure, I guess marriage can be fun some of the time; trouble is, you're married all the time. If Eric and I had gotten married, next thing ya know, I'm running an ad in the newspaper: 'Wedding Dress for Sale. Worn once, by mistake. Call Lizabeth.'

"But enough of Eric and me; let's get back to *you*! Introspection and self-analysis is a good place to start with one's self—wouldn't you agree, Magg-Pie? However, in your *self's* case, *I'm* here to help with the analyzing. Are ya scared?"

"Hey, Doc, I know you're teasing—somewhat, anyway—and I appreciate the constructive criticism. And by the way, that's an oxymoron; there's praise, and then there's criticism—and they're *not* the same. I guess the next thing you're gonna tell me is that I'm suffering from balanced insanity. Am I close, Dr. Shrink? And if I am, then yeah, I'm scared."

All of a sudden, I could hear that scary music from *Jaws* pulsating in my brain. Fortunately, though, attentive Paula appeared just then and graciously served us giant, piping-hot javas and left us to our agenda. As we sat there in contemplative silence, sipping our brew and taking in the peaceful serenity of the moment, the sun was slowly calling it a day. Then, suddenly jarring the calm with a verbal invitation of sorts, the sound of Lizzy's voice brought me back to reality.

"Okay, Maggs, I appreciate all your objections, but the debate is finally over, babe, so what d'ya say we pull out those old sepia tones, pack your bags for the guilt trip, and head on down memory lane? Just sit back, relax, and tell the good doctor aaaaall about it."

Jaws music again interrupted my thoughts. Feeling paralyzed and noting the creep of fall's evening chill settling into my gut, I took a deep breath, and we were on our way to revisit my distant childhood and my long-guarded and repressed secrets.

Daddy and his buddy Melvin Bray left the mill on that Good Friday afternoon about three o'clock with the ink on their paychecks barely dry. First stop was Charlie's Place. The local liquor store known as Charlie's sat about twenty miles to the county line and just "one toke over the line, sweet Jesus." The county we lived in was still dry and would remain so for another fifty years.

It had been raining for three days, making the long dirt 'n' gravel—mostly dirt—road leading up to our old two-story rented farmhouse even more challenging. The road was dotted with holes and deep ruts as a result of time, weather, and neglect, so the rain just made it worse.

I was standing on the front porch with my two little sisters, Lainey and Fay.

It was a special day for lots of reasons. Mother worked six days a week in the textile mill about five miles from our house. Sunday was the only day we could actually wake up with her and spend all day long enjoying the full extent of her wonderfulness. She worked Monday through Saturday from 3:00 p.m. to 11:00 p.m.; they called that the second shift back then.

During the school year, Aunt Lucy would come over about noon each day and stay with us until four thirty, when my five older siblings would arrive home from school courtesy of the county school bus. Daddy was supposed to be home by three thirty each day, but Mother didn't trust him to come straight home from work. Aunt Lucy would never leave until my oldest sister, Lu, got home with the rest of the kids. Then Lu would pretty much take over the duties of both Mother and Daddy until Mother got home each night.

Lu was short for Luverta, and boy did that aggravate her! She hated the name Luverta with a passion. Who wouldn't? She never told any of us why, but I figured it out as I grew older. Anyway, Lu was fifteen years old, there was nothing she couldn't do, and she wasn't afraid of anything or anybody. She loved Daddy very much, and he was the only one who could make her cry. And sometimes he did.

The reason that day was so special was that Mother had the day off because it was Good Friday. Having been taught the Easter story, I sort of understood what the word *good* meant in that context, but I had my own meaning: it was Good Friday because my mother was home with me, not at work; the Easter bunny was coming to my house the next night; *and* I had a brand new baby biddy, which, as you know, Lizzy, was slang for a baby chick. The Easter bunny had dropped the biddy off at my house early just for me while I was sleeping the night before! As Mother told me, this was very unusual for the Easter bunny to do, but he knew how much I wanted and needed that little chick. She told me it was my responsibility to take care of that tiny little biddy and make sure no harm came to her. I guess I was just about the happiest little girl in the whole wide world!

I felt the rain on my sweet little face as it blew off the huge, old oaks nearby onto the porch, where I stood watching Daddy and his buddy Melvin Bray. They zigzagged their way up the dirt drive, attempting to dodge the muddy holes. When one is drunk, one may zigzag naturally. However, when you pile on rain, mud, deep ruts, and a somewhat large automobile, to the one who is inebriated, the driving part may become impossible, and that's what happened. They had just made it to the old well, when the Chevy became mired and stuck in the mud. We called it the old well because we had a new well much closer to the house, and Mother had asked Mr. Jennings, our landlord and owner of the property, to close up that old well. He had dismantled all but the brick and mortar that stood above the ground, but he hadn't quite ever finished the job.

I saw Daddy get out of the car, his arms waving up and down—probably cussing like a sailor, as Lu would say. He got back in the car, and then Melvin Bray got out and went behind the car to push. Daddy had his window down so he could look through the rearview mirror and yell instructions to Melvin Bray at the same time. It didn't take long until the two of them gave up and started walking up the muddy dirt road toward the house.

Mother, who was a notably handsome five-foot-five woman in her early thirties with a complexion as pure as her heart and naturally wavy golden-brown hair that rested comfortably on her proud but weary shoulders, just stood there observing all the commotion as she held the good-natured, fat, 'n' sassy baby Fay on her hip. Watching her as she planted kisses on baby Fay's little head full of soft ginger-colored curls, I sensed a change in Mother's playful spirit as Daddy approached the screen door. Mother moved away from the door and guided the sweet and innocent three-year-old Lainey and me back into the kitchen, and it wasn't long before Daddy was marching through the door. Once inside the kitchen, it was obvious he was dripping wet and swearing at Mother. Melvin Bray stayed outside on the porch as if he were enjoying the rain. I think he was.

CHAPTER 2

That Melvin Bray

The first rule of holes: when you're in one, stop digging.
—Molly Ivins, lively liberal columnist

I DON'T REMEMBER ever hearing Melvin Bray raise his voice or say even one bad word, unlike Daddy. He was quite shy and pleasant. He seemed more comfortable out on the front porch and seldom came inside. He must have felt Mother didn't like him. Well, I say, who could blame her? The only time she ever saw him was when he came to the house with Daddy, and of course alcohol was always involved. They stayed only long enough for Daddy to upset Mother and us kids, and then they would drive off to party land, and we might not see Daddy for days.

I never heard Mother say an unkind word to "that Melvin Bray," as she always referred to him. She would invite him in and offer him food, and she was always very kind to him. That was Mother. She treated everyone with kindness because she was simply a wonderful human being. But I pretty much understood That Melvin Bray's discomfort, because in her heart, Mother was a little uneasy about him, and he felt it.

One of her great lines was "You're judged by the company you keep," and while I'm at it, another great line of hers was "All a poor girl's got is her reputation." I'm pretty sure she made that one up all by herself since she had a slew of girls to rear, and boy did we hear that one a lot!

But there was just something about That Melvin Bray that made Mother a little uneasy. He was about twenty-five, I guess—tallish but not as tall as Daddy, lanky, and boyishly handsome, with a head of wavy dark hair. And when he smiled, although he seldom did, he exposed a dimpled grin with naturally straight white teeth. He'd been keeping company with Daddy for about two years, ever since they'd met while working together at the Collins Hosiery Mill.

Since That Melvin Bray didn't have a car, Daddy was quite convenient for him, because most mornings, Daddy would drive over to his little community about fifteen miles from us and take him back home after work. The truth was that Daddy needed a drinkin' buddy, and That Melvin Bray needed wheels because his uncle didn't allow him to drive his car very often. Yeah, they were the perfect pair. Supposedly, as Daddy told Mother, That Melvin Bray was doing his father a favor by coming down from Virginia to live with his sick uncle. The sick uncle was That Melvin Bray's daddy's brother.

And the no-car thing turned out to be a no-license thing. Apparently, That Melvin Bray had "lost" his driver's license somewhere along the way.

When he was at the house with Daddy, though, I guess he got Mother's vibe, and that's why he mostly hung out on the porch so much instead of coming inside, even when it rained. She told Daddy That Melvin Bray was awfully shy.

As I think about it now, I would call him *painfully* shy. Heck, he probably had a split personality, and we wouldn't have liked either one of 'em if we'd really known him.

Daddy went out on the porch, and then he and That Melvin Bray walked out a little ways to the woodshed as the rain kept pouring down on them. Our house was heated by big potbelly woodstoves, and Mother cooked on a woodstove, too. My oldest brother, P. C., had the honor of chopping wood every day year-round, and the woodpile would be as high as the sky sometimes. We stored the wood in a small shed with a roof that hung over a bit to shield the wood from bad weather. Daddy and That Melvin Bray both smoked, and the woodpile was their favorite hangout.

Mother wouldn't allow smoking in the house. She didn't allow drinking in the house either, for that matter. Actually, she didn't really allow Daddy's drinking or smoking at all, but she couldn't stop him either. So he did both his smoking and drinking out at the woodshed. Rain or shine, that's the way it was.

I watched through the kitchen window as the two of them, mostly Daddy, were going on about something. He was always giving orders to his shy friend.

It was gray outside even though it wasn't that late in the day, probably due to all the rain. I continued to watch as Daddy pointed down the driveway toward the car, which was still stuck in the mud near the old well, where they had left it earlier.

It was still raining hard, and That Melvin Bray started out alone, walking down that muddy dirt 'n' gravel—mostly dirt—road toward the car. He made it to the old well and stopped in his muddy tracks. He leaned over, and it looked as if he were digging himself out. It was still pouring rain, so I guess the hole just got deeper as the heavy rain continued to pound. He must have remembered the first rule of holes, because he stopped digging, stood upright, and leaned against the old well to get a better grip so that he could support himself. He was trying to pull himself out of the mud one leg at a time, but he slipped and fell back down in that muddy mess.

"Mother, That Melvin Bray is stuck in the mud just like the car. What a big mess!" I stammered as I turned away from the window, explaining the scene to Mother. She walked over to the window to see for herself, and as we both looked out the window together, the rain began to beat harder on the old tin roof, and the wind began to howl.

"Well, Magg-Pie," Mother responded, "it's raining so hard I can't see much of anything, honey. I'm sure he's gotten himself out of that big mess, and he's probably headed on down to the big road to hitchhike home. It's raining so hard I'm sure someone will pick him up in no time. There's really not much we can do to help him out there, sweetie."

Daddy entered the kitchen all wet and shouting for his playmate. His soaking-wet jet-black crew cut really didn't do him justice. However, his movie-star good looks made up for it. If only his personality and behavior had matched those good looks! Apparently, he had sent That Melvin Bray to get his liquor bottle out of the stuck-in-the-mud car, and that's what That Melvin Bray was doing when he got stuck in the mud himself.

Mother asked Daddy to stop yelling and told him that she hadn't seen That Melvin Bray. Daddy stormed out of the house and came back inside a few minutes later. It was still pouring rain, which seemed to really irritate him because he was too drunk to make it to the car himself in all that rain in order to get his mean firewater. He went back outside on the porch in a loud rage, yelling for his missing sidekick.

Shortly, he came back inside, still in a rage, flaunting his drunken arrogance. Mother pleaded with him to calm down, and he picked up a chair and threw it across the kitchen. She still had baby Fay on her hip, and the chair grazed Fay's little foot on its way to the other side of the room. The baby started crying, and Mother immediately instructed me to take Lainey into the living room, sit on the couch, and stay there. So that's what I did.

As I sat with Lainey on the couch, I could hear Daddy saying mean things to Mother. He told her she was the cause of all his problems.

Daddy was a well-built, strong, handsome six-foot-two man. When he was drunk, he was a well-built, stronger, mean, ugly six-foot-two son of a bitch. That's what Lu said anyway, and Lu was always right.

Just then, I heard the old school-bus brakes as they came to a grinding, screeching halt way down on the main road in front of our house, and I was sure glad to hear it, too! It was a pretty good ways for my three sisters and two brothers to run in the rain—through the big yard and up to the house. The bus driver would usually bring them up to the house on rainy days, but I guess he could see the old Chevy stuck in the road, so that was that.

Lainey and I jumped off the couch and ran over to the window and watched all five of our older siblings as they played in the rain and raced each other up to the porch. All were totally soaked but couldn't have cared less. I opened the front door, locked eyes with Lu, and, in one long breath, shouted, "Daddy hit baby Fay with a chair, and Mother made Lainey and me sit on the couch, and the car and That Melvin Bray got stuck in the mud!" Lu was old for her age of fifteen years due to the heavy responsibilities imposed on her—mostly because of Daddy's lack of responsibility. Lu was already physically attractive in every way, but she didn't seem to be aware of it in any way. She was a slender five-foot-five tomboy with long yellow pigtails attached to a perfectly oval-shaped head and matching pretty face, which was sprinkled with a few freckles across the tops of her rosy cheeks. She could have been the center of any Rockwell painting.

Lu led the way through the front door and headed straight for the kitchen, telling P. C. to keep the rest of us in the living room. P. C. was the second in line under Lu, and the older and more sensitive of my two older brothers. Lu knew what was going on and marched with her fearless courage straight to Mother.

By then, Daddy had managed to turn over the kitchen table and pull the dish cabinet off the wall, and somehow the refrigerator was standing in the center of the room. Mother quickly handed baby Fay to Lu and urged her to take the baby, Lainey, and me immediately over to Mrs. Brown's, which was across the road from our house. Then Mother told P. C. to take the rest of the kids upstairs to the boys' room, to close the door, and to stay there! Lu followed Mother's request with urgency, and before we knew it, Lu, with baby Fay on her hip, Lainey, and me were all standing at Mrs. Brown's front door. Lu knocked a few times, and the door opened. The nice and pleasant Mrs. Brown took one look at us and instantly her sweet smile turned upside down. I guess we all looked pretty pitiful, like the wet and homeless, certainly not the bold and beautiful. She graciously opened the door and invited us in.

Lu told her the situation at our house, and Mrs. Brown quickly grabbed the baby from Lu's hip to her own. She told Lu to tell Mother she was happy to help and not to worry about us. So there was Mrs. Brown with three little extras aged five, three, and thirteen months. She had one son, Danny, who was eight going on nine if you asked *him*. Of course his mother knew exactly what to do—after all, she was a mom.

Mrs. Brown and Mother had a few things in common. They both were mothers, were married, and went to church every Sunday. That was about it.

Mrs. Brown didn't work and had only one child. Her husband didn't drink; he owned a business, and they owned their home. She felt sorry for Mother and didn't like Daddy one little bit.

As Lu was leaving, Mrs. Brown told her to tell Mother she was welcome to come over with the rest of the kids and stay at her house until things were better over there. Lu promised she would deliver the message and started out the front door. The last thing she said to Mrs. Brown was something about "Please feed the kids; I'm sure they're hungry." As the door closed behind her, I knew in my little heart that Lu would make everything right. After all, there wasn't anything Lu couldn't do.

Mrs. Brown had Danny pull out his old high chair from the hall closet. She set it up at the kitchen table and put baby Fay in it. She sat Lainey and me in chairs at the table on one side, and Danny sat across from us on the other side. By then, it was probably close to five thirty, and everyone was hungry.

Mrs. Brown had been preparing their dinner as usual when we had shown up at her front door. She reached into the refrigerator and got out a few items and placed them on the counter. She had the ketchup bottle in her hand and was having trouble getting that yummy red stuff out of the bottle. I loved ketchup!

While she struggled with the bottle, the phone rang, and Danny jumped up to answer it. Danny told his daddy, "Hey, Mom can't come to the phone; she's hittin' the bottle!" Mrs. Brown grabbed the phone from Danny and informed Mr. Brown that supper was almost ready but that she was dealing with an unexpected situation. I remember her whispering into the phone, saying something like "That crazy alcoholic across the road is scaring his family to death again, and you better come on home."

She hung up the phone and talked baby talk to Fay. Fay laughed at her, and I thought Mrs. Brown would probably like to have a little baby around to play with since Danny was so old. I mean, he was almost nine!

Danny eyed his mother as she played with Fay, and he told her that babies were too much trouble. Mrs. Brown asked him how he knew that, and he told her that baby Fay had told him. Mrs. Brown chuckled and looked at him with a little grin.

"Well, Danny-Boy, I know some eight-year-olds who can be way too much trouble too sometimes—especially when they try to hide their broccoli in a glass of milk." Danny just gave her a little impish smile and deliberately changed the subject.

"Hey, Mom, did you know no matter how hard ya try, you can't baptize a cat?" He was such a boy.

"Drink your broccoli, young man" was his mother's reply.

Fay was getting sleepy and needed a nap, I'm sure. Naps—the best way to ruin a kid's day! Everything could be going just great, and then Lu or Ali would shout, "Okay, nap time! Hit the floor, you babies!" They'd spread a buncha quilts 'n' pillows on the floor and make us lie down for a nap. What a way to ruin a kid's day!

Mrs. Brown fed us and asked us if we wanted anything else. I told her, "No, thank you. We're all just full as a tick."

Mrs. Brown laughed and took Fay out of the high chair, placed her back on her hip, and told Lainey and me to follow her into the bathroom. She gave us each a little bath in the sink, or a "bird bath," as Mother called it. We were quite used to that. Since we didn't have indoor plumbing, obviously there was no need for a bathtub. Our kitchen had a big basin-like sink where a small, round tub lived, and that's where we did the dishes. Mother or one of my older siblings would fill the tub with water to wash the dishes and then take it out the back door, empty it, and refill it with fresh water for rinsing the dishes. Talk about all the luxuries of home. But all in all, it could have been worse.

Mr. Jennings, who owned the house, had just finished digging a new well right outside our back door by the pear trees. Before that, we had had to walk quite a ways down the dirt driveway to the old original well, where the car and That Melvin Bray had gotten stuck in the mud. It was no fun at all hauling buckets of water from the old well up to the house.

It was amazing how we lived back then, and *why*.

On many occasions, my brother Paddy, who was only a year and a half older than me, said he must have been switched at birth at the hospital. He said there was no way he would have chosen to live in a family with a mean daddy who made his family live the way we had to live. Paddy believed in everything but accepted little without discerning scrutiny. He was just your normal, adorable, average-sized seven-year-old boy, but he was way too cute for a boy, as he had long dark eyelashes and sparkling, inquisitive brown eyes that always needed answers. Mother would smile and remind him that he was born at home, not the hospital. Sorry, Paddy—there went *that* theory. She would also explain the importance of making the best of our situation, and regardless of what we *didn't* have, we were to do our best with what we *did* have. It was Mother's mantra. Paddy would just tell Mother, "Yes, ma'am," until the subject came up again—and it always did.

13

Lu had thrown some clothes together for us, and as Mrs. Brown was getting her three little girl guests ready for bed, there was a loud knock on the front door. Mrs. Brown raised her voice a little to say, "Come in." There was no such thing as locking your doors out there in the country. And at that time, lots of families didn't have a telephone either—tractors for sure, but not necessarily a phone. We didn't have either one.

Ole Man Jennings, as Daddy called him, owned the land and house we lived in, and he had *two* tractors. He let us live on his property for "free." All Daddy and P. C. had to do was plow his gardens, mow his wheat pastures, take care of his chickens, collect all the eggs every day, keep all the fences standing and the cows in 'em, and paint the house and barn when it was time. I think that covers it.

Every Saturday evening, P. C. and Paddy would chase down three chickens for our Sunday dinner. That was quite a sight to see, too! First, they'd pick out the three biggest hens and chase 'em all over the place. Once they caught 'em, they'd put 'em in the woodshed by the woodpile. One by one, Paddy would take a chicken out of the shed and hold it on the big wood stump, a.k.a. the chopping block, and P. C. would chop off the poor chicken's head. Once the boys had done the fateful deed, they'd take the lifeless birds to the back porch and put 'em in a small washtub. Lu would oversee the plucking part. She, along with prissy Ali, who was eleven and third in line under P. C., and Lee, the ferocious lioness at nine, would sit around the tub and pluck out the feathers. Once the plucking was done, Lu would take the chickens into the kitchen, wash them, put them in a pot, cover them, and store them in the refrigerator for Mother.

First thing on Sunday morning, while Mother and Lu made breakfast, Mother would cut up the chickens and fry them before we all went to church.

On Monday mornings, when Mr. Jennings would come to collect his eggs from the barn, he would always ask Mother, "How was Sunday's chicken dinner?" Mother was always polite and thanked him for the chickens. He would say, "Glad to do it, Miss Lillian!"

I heard P. C. calling Mrs. Brown from the front door. Lainey and I followed her as she walked out of the bathroom and toward P. C. with Fay on her hip. He told her that Mother had sent him over to check on the little ones. He winked at me as he told Mrs. Brown that hopefully Daddy would wind down and maybe fall asleep soon and everything would be all right. In other words, hopefully Daddy would pass out, allowing peace to be restored at the Chillton house.

Mrs. Brown asked if she should send Mr. Brown over, but P. C. said, "No, thanks." Mrs. Brown was well aware of the situation and was troubled. Even I could see that. She patted P. C. on the shoulder and turned on the porch light for him as he walked down the steps and back out into the rain. Mrs. Brown felt sorry for him. He was thirteen but still too young to carry the burden of the sins of his father on his small but proud shoulders. I yelled out to him, saying, "Take care of my little biddy, P. C.!"

"It's bedtime, little ones," Mrs. Brown said, and off we went into a pretty room with two beds. She put baby Fay with me in the big bed and Lainey in the smaller one. We said our prayers, and she hugged and kissed us and then tucked us in under the covers. She told me she would leave a little light on so that she could come in and check on us during the night just in case we needed her.

She left the room but left the door cracked just a little. Fay fell asleep right away, and then Lainey. I was the oldest, so I had to stay awake until they both were asleep. That was the way Mother had taught us—the oldest took care of the youngest.

As I lay there, I could smell the clean, sweet fragrance of the sheets and pillows. The bed was comfortable and soft; I knew it just *had* to be the same kind of dreamy bed that beckoned sweet dreams for a fairy-tale princess.

My last thought was of my sweet little biddy and how I would get to hold her the next day when I went home to my house. I fell asleep to the sound of the pouring rain.

Maybe it was Good Friday after all.

CHAPTER 3

Tornadoes and Tears

If you can't make up your mind, "What the hell" is usually the right answer.
—Ellen Reid Smith, businesswoman

THE NEXT MORNING was quite different for me. First, I woke up in an unfamiliar but wonderful bed with baby Fay in my arms. That had never happened in my whole five years of life! She was still asleep. I listened for the rain, but it had finally stopped. I glanced around the room, and Lainey was still asleep too.

I remembered that it was Saturday, and the Easter bunny would come that night. Again my thoughts went to my little biddy, and I was excited.

Wonderful, familiar smells twirled around my head. *Oh, yummy—bacon, eggs, and coffee and probably biscuits too!* I loved those smells. I was too little to drink coffee, but I sure loved the smell of it! Mother would let Lu have coffee sometimes but not often.

I slipped out of bed and peeked out the door and down the hall. The coast was clear. I could hear voices coming from the kitchen. It sounded like Mrs. Brown and Danny. Where was Mr. Brown? I took a few steps down the hall and stuck my little head in the next room. I saw someone lying in the bed with the covers pulled over his head, the way P. C. always slept. *Oh, that must be Mr. Brown, and I better be quiet,* I thought. I then noticed what looked like a whole mouth full of teeth sitting in a glass right by the bed. I gasped and thought, *Gosh, the tooth fairy will never believe this!*

I hurried back to the bedroom and lay back down on the bed by Fay. Lainey was awake, just lying there gazing around the room. She slid out of her bed and climbed up under the covers with Fay and me. Fay woke up and immediately asked for Mama. She wasn't used to being without Mother when she first woke up in the mornings. She was a little fussy, but Mrs. Brown walked in at that moment and lovingly came over to the bed and took her. That seemed to be just what Fay needed.

16

"Come on, girls; let's go have some breakfast," she said. Lainey and I got off the bed and followed Mrs. Brown to the kitchen, where Danny was already seated at the table. I helped Lainey get into her chair. Mrs. Brown put Fay in the high chair, and I sat down in mine; we were all exactly where we had been the night before at dinner.

Mrs. Brown went straight to her work and presented each of us with a hot breakfast, just what I had imagined from the smells in the bedroom earlier. I thought, *Yummy! She sure cooks good food good—just like Mother!*

The phone rang, and Danny jumped up to get it, but Mrs. Brown told him to sit down and finish his breakfast.

She walked over to the counter and picked up the phone. She told the caller, "Yes, this is Mrs. Brown. Three of the children are here and just fine. We're having breakfast. No, the oldest daughter brought them over last night.

"No, he's not up yet, but I can wake him. What happened? Where is he now? Yes, I've seen that fella before, but I didn't see him yesterday.

"No, I don't know him at all; I've just seen him over there now and then when he's with Mr. Chillton, and I believe they work together at Collins Hosiery.

"Yes, sir—sad but true. This is *not* the first time something like this has happened over there at that house!

"Yes, sir, I'll wake him and send him over right away!"

Mrs. Brown hung up the phone and told Danny to stay at the table and watch after us kids. She left the kitchen for a few minutes and headed down the hall to the room with all those teeth sitting in a glass for the tooth fairy. She returned in a flash, sat down next to Fay, and finished feeding her while Danny, Lainey, and I continued eating.

A few minutes later, Mr. Brown walked in with a big smile on his face and said good morning to all of us.

He went over to Danny, playfully mussed his thick, curly red hair, and then leaned down to hug him. Danny giggled and willingly returned the hug.

Danny was quick to tell his daddy about a dead robin he had found outside by the porch that morning, and he wanted his daddy to help him bury it after breakfast. Mr. Brown told him the robin probably had gotten confused in the rain and flown into the side of the house. "Yeah, that's probably what killed him, Daddy," Danny agreed.

Mr. Brown said, "Maybe Maggie would like to help you bury the bird, because I've got to go somewhere important right away and probably won't be back for a while."

"Okay, Daddy. Me and Maggie'll bury that robin," Danny assured him.

Mrs. Brown handed Mr. Brown a big cup of coffee and a bacon biscuit. He thanked her and playfully patted her on the top of her head, smiling that big smile of his. "I'll be back soon as I can, Mookie," he said as he headed out the back door. Her real name was Mary, but Mr. Brown always called her Mookie.

"You be careful, Rob," she called out to him as the screen door closed behind him.

"Maggie, if you're finished eating, go get dressed, and if you like, you can help Danny bury the robin."

I jumped up with a big "Yes, ma'am, Mrs. Brown," and then I quickly got dressed and was back in the kitchen in no time.

Danny took me out the back door and around to the side of the porch, where he had placed the poor dead robin. Danny was holding his small Bible in one hand and an old shoe box in the other, which Mrs. Brown had given him to put the bird in. He had me look around for important items, such as twigs, acorns, and little, shiny rocks, to put in the box with the little bird so that he wouldn't be lonely. I thought it was a good idea too. Danny dug a hole to make ready for a "proper burial of the deceased," as he put it.

He was a lot like me and my brothers and sisters. We all had to go to the Baptist church every Sunday morning for Sunday school and then Sunday service after that. In the summertime, the first week outta school, we all went to Vacation Bible School. Miss Cherry was Pastor Meyers's daughter, and she taught Bible school every summer. She brought homemade fudge and Kool-Aid every single day to Bible school. We sure had fun, too!

Danny knew an awful lot of Bible verses for an eight-year-old going on nine; that's what Mother told Mrs. Brown one time at church. "Oh, he loves to learn Bible verses," Mrs. Brown told Mother. Danny also loved animals and funerals. That kid would bury anything he found that even came close to looking like it was dead. He thought that was the right thing to do.

He positioned me next to him by the freshly dug hole and instructed me to clasp my hands under my chin and bow my head. He did the same. Animal funerals were serious business to Danny; plus, he insisted on using only the most appropriate words. So with reverent dignity, he intoned his version of what he thought our preacher, Pastor Meyers, would say at a funeral.

Then he opened his Bible, lowered his head, and spoke loudly. "I will read Leviticus 14:5: 'And he shall kill one of the birds in an earthen vessel over the running water,' and glory be unto the Faaaather, and unto the Sonnnn, and into the hole-he-gooooes." He bent down, gently placed the box in the hole, covered

18

it with dirt, and then explained in one long breath, "This was the Bible verse about a bird dying after he hit the side of a house while it was raining."

Then I remembered what Mr. Brown had said earlier about how the bird had probably died, and it made sense to me—sort of. Danny sure did know his Bible verses, and this was not his first funeral. We left the grave site and went back inside to report our good deed to Mrs. Brown.

Several years later, I would come to know how profound that Bible verse really was that day, as it related to my home and family. Leviticus 14 refers to "the cleaning of the house."

Lu stood in the kitchen with Fay on her hip, talking with Mrs. Brown. Mrs. Brown had already dressed Fay and Lainey. I was glad to see Lu. Mrs. Brown hugged Lu and told her we were welcome to stay on with her if necessary.

Lu thanked her and told her that she and Mr. Brown had done enough and that she'd be glad to do some ironing or cleaning for Mrs. Brown anytime at all. Mrs. Brown was busy putting on our jackets as she said, "Lu, you're a good girl, and you've got your hands full. You just help your mother and know that Mr. Brown and I are here if y'all need us for anything, and you tell your mother that for me." She kissed us all and opened the front door for us.

Danny-Boy came up behind his mother, reached around her, and yanked on my jacket. As we exchanged glances, he looked at me seriously and said, "Thanks for helping me with the funeral."

I stared back at him, nodded just as seriously, and then headed down the front porch steps with Lainey's hand in mine.

As we walked down Mrs. Brown's driveway toward the big road to cross over to our muddy driveway, Lu began to explain to me in her own way why we had had to stay at Mrs. Brown's. She told me the story of Dr. Henry Jekyll and Mr. Edward Hyde. In hindsight, I guess she felt that as a five-year-old, I might be better able to understand Daddy's alcoholism through that depiction.

Just for the record, I've seen every Jekyll and Hyde movie ever made, and Lu was emphatically correct in her comparison with the transformation in Daddy when under the influence of alcohol. He really did turn into a monster; and later on, he would become known as "Lee's monster."

We kept walking, and Lu continued to explain that Dr. Jekyll was good, but when he drank his potion, he became Mr. Hyde and was very bad, and that's what happened to our daddy when he drank alcohol. He started out being good like Dr. Jekyll, and then he drank his alcohol and turned into something mean and angry, just like Mr. Hyde. She said Mother didn't like Daddy to drink alcohol, but he wouldn't listen to Mother when he was Mr. Hyde. She assured me that Daddy loved us but couldn't seem to stop drinking the alcohol "potion." I told her if Daddy really loved Mother and us, he wouldn't *ever* drink alcohol.

Lu also told me she thought Daddy needed to go to a hospital to learn how to stop drinking alcohol, and then we could all be a happy family. She said she loved Daddy, but she didn't *like* him at all when he drank alcohol and became Mr. Hyde.

As we were approaching the house, all wet from the soggy, overgrown grass, Mr. Brown walked out of our house and onto the porch. I was surprised to see him at our house, since he had told Danny he couldn't help bury the robin because he had "to go somewhere important."

Unusual for him, he had a somber look on his face as he walked down the steps to meet us. He picked up both Lainey and me in his big, strong arms, and he headed back up the steps to the porch. Lu still had Fay on her hip as she followed us into the house.

When we got inside, I couldn't believe my eyes. It looked as if a tornado had torn through the inside of our house. The outside looked pretty bad too. *A violent, whirling wind must have blown through our house because of all that rain,* I thought. Everything was turned upside down. It reminded me of the place Daddy would take us when his old Chevy broke down and he needed to find some part to fix it. He called it the junkyard, and that's exactly what our house looked like—that old junkyard!

I saw a deputy walk into the house with a look on his face as if he couldn't believe his eyes, saying under his breath, "What the hell?" Mr. Brown went over to him and guided him toward the kitchen and continued to talk quietly. I noticed another deputy in the kitchen with Mother and P. C., but I didn't see Daddy or That Melvin Bray anywhere. I already knew That Melvin Bray had gotten a ride home, because Mother had said he would.

Mr. Brown had put Lainey and me down, and Lu quickly took Fay and us upstairs to our room. Fortunately, the tornado had not made it up the stairs. Lee and Paddy were sitting on the floor, playing our favorite card game. We called it War. Well, we were definitely in a war zone. They were glad to see us.

Paddy said, "Did you see what Daddy did?"

"Uh-huh. What the hell! I thought it was a tornado!" I said. Lu put her hand gently across my little mouth and told me not to talk like that. I told her, "I don't like Daddy either, and where's my little baby biddy?" She looked as if she'd seen a ghost.

"The biddy!" she yelled. She put Fay in the playpen, grabbed my hand, and hurried me down the stairs. P. C. had made a little house for my biddy out of a small cardboard box. He had put sawdust on the bottom so that she'd be comfortable and had placed two little mayonnaise jar lids in there too, filled with food and water. Lu went to the den, where the biddy box was supposed to be.

As we tramped through Daddy's path of wrath, Lu carefully guided me around the strewn furniture and broken glass from a large mirror. She parked me safely against the wall and began to search under everything for the tiny baby chick. We both saw the corner of the biddy box underneath a small table that was turned over on its side. She moved the table out of the way, and then I saw her bend down to pull the biddy box free. Her head drooped slightly as she leaned over the small box, but she remained silent.

I carefully stepped over the tangled mess and walked up behind her. I could see my little biddy lying in the box. She wasn't moving. "Is she dead?" I asked.

"Yes, Magg-Pie. I'm afraid she is," Lu whispered.

I sat down beside Lu. She reached in the box and picked up the lifeless little biddy in one hand and put her other arm around me. I saw tears trickling down her face—those tender tears that humanize the soul, the messengers of unspeakable love. I knew she cried tears for me and tears for my sweet little biddy.

Mother said tears were the safety valves of the heart and were released when too much pressure was laid on it. Daddy would make fun of Mother when she cried, and she'd say, "Well, what would a woman do if she couldn't cry?"

There were times she seemed to cry a bunch, and of course, now I know that was because she had a bunch to cry about.

I had seen Lu cry only one other time before that day. It was the time when Lu, P. C., and I were down at the barn gathering eggs for Mr. Jennings; all the other kids were up at the house.

I saw Daddy walking down the path from the woodpile, puffing on a Lucky Strike with his rifle in one hand and a big, old, rusty Luck's Pinto Beans can in the other. He was headed out to the clearing in the field behind the barn. He yelled out for P. C., and P. C. reluctantly walked out to the clearing where Daddy stood. I watched as Daddy handed the old can to P. C., and as the two of them walked toward the center of the clearing, P. C.'s shoulders dropped.

All of a sudden, I felt a chill run up my little spine, and I yelled for Lu. She knew Daddy had come down to the barn, but she had not seen what was about to take place. I might have been only five, but *I* knew, and it scared me. Lu heard me, stood up from the henhouse, and looked at Daddy and P. C. She too knew immediately what was about to happen. She ran out to the potential killing field and spoke with Daddy.

I couldn't hear what she said, but I could hear Daddy's voice, and he was arguing with her. His voice got louder and louder. I walked away from the barn, toward the newly formed gun club so that I could hear them better. Daddy wanted P. C. to hold the old can in his hand, and Daddy was going to use the can as his target. Lu was trying to reason with Daddy, reminding him that he had been drinking beer in the woodshed and that this stunt could be very dangerous. Daddy told her that P. C. was just a big sissy, and he wanted to teach P. C. a few things.

Lu must have thought she was losing the argument, because she immediately fell to her knees at Daddy's feet, wrapped her arms around his legs, and began crying and begging him not to make P. C. hold that damn can. Daddy told her to stop it and to take me and go back to the house. She wouldn't budge, and clinging to his legs, she kept right on crying and begging him to let her hold the can instead of P. C. Daddy grabbed the can from P. C., threw it on the ground, turned around, and walked back to the woodpile. He never said a word.

Lu raised herself up from her crouched position on the ground and put her arms around P. C. and held on to him for a minute. With his head hung down in undeserved shame, he began to cry. They didn't speak; they just started walking on up to where I was standing. P. C. put one arm around me, and then we all went back inside the barn and finished our chores. I don't know what the hell I was doing just standing there as if I weren't standing there, but I do know Lu probably saved P. C.'s life that day. Thank you, Lu!

This brutal and senseless death of my little biddy broke Lu's heart. When I saw her tears, I was sad, and I told her not to cry, 'cause Danny could help me with the little biddy's funeral. I hugged her real tight, but that seemed to make her cry even more. She held me close in her arms as she whispered how sorry she was. We were both trying to comfort each other. She still had my little biddy in one hand as she helped me up off the floor with the other.

We carefully stepped over all the broken glass and furniture. As we wove our way through the remnants of the tornado, all I could think about was the junkyard and another funeral. *What the hell!* I don't think I said it out loud, because I knew Lu wouldn't like it.

Lu took me and my little biddy back upstairs, and we shared our sad story with Lee and Paddy. When they saw my poor little biddy, Lee instantly blamed Daddy. "He just killed that sweet little thing; he's a monster," she yelled.

"Calm down, Lee," Lu told her.

Lee was very close to Mother. We all were, but Lee seemed to have an almost fierce mother-lion protector-type relationship with her. When she was a toddler, Lee would actually roar like a little lion when she got frustrated. Although Lee was just nine, she had already made up her mind that anyone who made her mother cry was her enemy.

Daddy made Mother cry a lot, so Lee had no use for Daddy, and she was not—and never would be—a daddy's girl. She always referred to him as a monster and kept her distance from him. Daddy knew how Lee felt about him, too. Lee was a good daughter and stood for justice. That's what Mother always said.

My family referred to Lainey, Fay, and me as "the three least ones." Being the youngest, we were too young to know all the Chillton family business and the kind of daddy we had. From Paddy at seven to Lu at fifteen, with Lee, Ali, and P. C. in between, there were obviously several years of unhappiness in our family that had preceded the three least ones.

Lee was furious and took my little biddy from Lu and ran down the stairs to find Mother.

"Hey, bring my little biddy back," I yelled. "I gotta take her to Danny's for her funeral!"

CHAPTER 4

The Cleanup

It's not the having, it's the getting.
—Elizabeth Taylor, actress, philanthropist

THERE WAS A LOT GOING ON DOWNSTAIRS, but the three least ones and Paddy remained upstairs, safe and out of the way. Lee was assigned to watch us, and after she reported to Mother that Daddy had killed my little biddy, Mother sent her back upstairs. She gave my little biddy back to Lu, and Lu promised me we would have a proper funeral for her the next day. "Tomorrow? Tomorrow's Easter!" I yelled.

"I know," Lu calmly replied with a smile. "But the funeral will have to wait until we clean up this junkyard, or the Easter bunny won't even be able to get in the house tonight!"

I guess I *had* said it out loud.

Fay had fallen asleep in the playpen, and Lainey was playing on the floor with her baby doll. Lee, Paddy, and I lay across the bed, and Lee began telling us the horrors of the previous night and that morning. She told us that after Lu had gotten back home from taking the three least ones over to Mrs. Brown's house, all hell had broken loose—that's exactly what she said.

Actually, I think Lee loved saying bad words. She said them with such intention, pretty much as Daddy did. Mother didn't say bad words. She didn't do anything wrong. However, I do remember hearing Lee tell Lu and Ali, "Mother should make Daddy leave us alone and never come back. He's a monster, and she's wrong to let him treat us so awful." I think Lee was right. So I guess that's the one thing Mother ever did wrong. But when ya think about it, Mother only loved Dr. Jekyll, not Mr. Hyde. She trusted Dr. Jekyll but was afraid of Mr. Hyde. I was too.

So that night, when Lu got back to our house from Mrs. Brown's, she and P. C. went into the kitchen to try to talk to Daddy.

24

Mother took Ali, Lee, and Paddy upstairs and closed the door to get them out of harm's way, hoping he would lie down and fall asleep.

Sometimes Lu was able to reason with him and had a lot of patience with him. I guess being the firstborn and having known Daddy when he was sober—Daddy hadn't really started to drink until I was born—had allowed Lu ten years of good memories with Daddy. Of all us kids, Lu was definitely his favorite.

On that night, though, Daddy was out of control, and Lu couldn't calm him down. If the car hadn't gotten stuck in the mud, he and That Melvin Bray would have left a long time ago. If only. Lee said that Daddy kept yellin' for That Melvin Bray and saying Mother had made his only friend leave, and that was why he was so angry with Mother. Lee said that Daddy was rantin' and ravin' like a madman. If his outburst hadn't been about That Melvin Bray, it would have been about somethin' else.

Daddy was one of those persons who got meaner by the ounce. Every swallow was like a drink of hell. He turned into the Devil. It was that bad and no worse. I mean, how much worse could it get? I'm just wondering—does it always have to get worse? Lee said Daddy just went crazy, and whatever he picked up came crashing down in a different spot.

Daddy was beginning to scare Lu and P. C., so they left him on the front porch in the pouring rain, yelling for That Melvin Bray. They went inside and sat down on the floor at the bottom of the stairs. Lu was worried that Daddy would try to go upstairs, and she was concerned for Mother. Mother seemed to only make things worse when Daddy was like that, as he seemed to enjoy upsetting her. Lu and P. C. stayed on guard in that spot at the bottom of the stairs until daylight. All the time they were sitting there, Daddy just stayed in monster mode, yelling and throwing anything he could get his hands on.

I remember Lee asking me, "Do you know the meaning of the word *monster*?"

"Yes, I do. It means a big, ugly, bad thing," I answered.

"Well, little girl, *Webster's* says a person is a monster if they are evil, uncaring, or a freak!" Lee had always called Daddy a monster since I could remember, so I figured she knew what she was talking about. Of course I understood exactly every word she said. She said Daddy was an evil freak. I had heard Pastor Meyers call the Devil that on Sundays many times. I guess you could say Daddy was the Devil. Could that be?

Lu loved him, Lee hated him, and I had to be somewhere in the middle. I guess I wasn't quite old enough to hate and feel anger yet.

Lee continued, relaying the events Lu had described to her. According to

Lu, she and P. C. fell asleep sometime during the night. When they woke up, they were still sitting back-to-back, leaning against the wall at the bottom of the stairs. They got up and walked through the house, expecting to find Daddy lying on the floor, passed out. He was not in the house. As they stumbled through the aftermath of destruction, they could easily see that everything we owned was pretty much destroyed.

They went outside and walked all around the old half-finished wraparound porch. No sign of Daddy. Then they walked out to the woodshed. No sign of Daddy.

They looked down the road toward the old well, where the car was still stuck in the mud. They made their way to the car and could see Daddy lying in the backseat asleep.

On a second glance, they checked the front seat for That Melvin Bray. He wasn't there. There was no sign of That Melvin Bray anywhere.

Lu and P. C. went back up to the house and upstairs to check on Mother, Ali, Lee, and Paddy. Mother was lying there with Paddy on one arm and Ali on the other. Lee said she had slept on a blanket by the door because she was also on guard. Upstairs was calm; everything was in its proper place. But at the bottom of the stairs, it was probably a glimpse of what hell looks like, because that was where the Devil monster had been the night before.

Lee said Lu woke them, and they all got up and went downstairs once Lu told Mother that Daddy was asleep in the car. Mother asked Lu if That Melvin Bray was in the car with him. Lu told her no and said that they had looked all over but hadn't seen him.

"Oh, he must have caught a ride home like all the other times," Mother concluded.

"Well, I hope he did hitchhike home, and if he knows what's good for him, he won't come back here! He's strange, and he has a sickening, sweet smell about him, Mother," Lee grumbled.

I thought to my little self, *Ooooh, what on earth does she mean by that?*

As we walked through the house, we saw nothing but destruction in room after room. Mother cried quietly. We hadn't had much before, and now we didn't even have that.

The "getting" business was what we Chilltons would be all about—again— for a while to come. As we were taking inventory, all of a sudden, Ali got really angry. Normally, she was calm and shy, but in that moment, she really came out of herself. Almost in tears, Ali said, "Mother, I'm sick and tired of having to keep on taking charity from the neighbors around here every time Daddy tears up the charity we had to take the last time he tore up everything around here! And Mrs. Brown tries to make us feel better by saying that it's *not* charity—that it's just a gift from one friend to another. But it *is* charity too!"

I remember Lee chiming in, saying, "Me too, and it's not right, Mother!" Mother didn't say anything to either of them. I guess she was having one of those real-life in-body experiences, and it wasn't a good one.

Daddy had even dragged the couch out onto the porch, and somehow it had fallen through one of the Daddy-designed holes in the old half-finished wraparound porch. One end of the couch was lying under the porch, and the other end was sticking out and up in the air. It was filthy and soaked from all the rain. He had also destroyed the couch pillows, and the front yard looked a lot like either a foam-rubber processing center or a junkyard. All the pillows were ripped apart as if Daddy had sought to annihilate all things in his destructive, drunken path. This time, he had taken out his anger on all those poor cushions. He had totally destroyed the couch and the cushions in his angry rage. What a sight!

We also had Daddy to thank for the altered condition of the porch. Surprise, surprise! There were gaping holes in the big wraparound porch where the wooden planks were missing. The Chillton kids had to get used to hearing Mother and Aunt Lucy warn, "You kids remember to be careful on that old half-finished wraparound porch." The porch was just another one of Daddy's many projects he had started but never finished.

Ali and Lee told me that someone at the Fancy Gap Curb Market had told Daddy there was probably gold under our old house—I mean, Mr. Jennings's old house. Well, that's all it took to get Daddy's non-Mensa brain set in motion. Mr. BB, one of the men Daddy gambled with, owned a metal detector. So Daddy bet Mr. BB he could win that gadget in a poker game. They gambled, and sure enough, ole Chill, as they called Daddy, won the metal detector, and all it took was his whole paycheck that week. He could have bought a brand new one for a whole lot less! Mother was furious, but Daddy believed that he was on his way to becoming a millionaire and that soon money would be the least of our problems! Oh yeah, Daddy was the man! He and That Melvin Bray started pulling up the wooden planks from the porch, and by the time they were finished, half a dozen were missing here and there all around the porch. There was plenty of room for them to jump down from the porch to the dirt below. They hit the switch on his trusty metal detector, and the latest get-rich-quick scheme was just a hummin' along! In a couple of weeks, there were gaping holes all around the porch, and dirt was everywhere. While there was an awful lot of stuff down there in that dirt, there was not even one tiny, shiny little speck of gold. Shoot, there went the trust fund!

The porch remained in disrepair for some time to come; however, I must say that hide-and-seek took on a whole new twist for the Chillton kids.

Mother would tell us, "Some people are rich, and some people have money." She could find the good in anything. Oh, my dear, sweet mother.

Mother, Lu, P. C., Mr. Brown, and the two sheriff's deputies were all gathered in the kitchen, discussing what to do about Daddy, who was still sleeping it off in the car. Apparently, this whole thing was a case of déjà vu all over again for them, because just two years before, Daddy had done this exact same thing, but I had been too young to remember any of it. Once again, the sheriff came out to the house and picked up Daddy, and off to jail they went.

While he was gone, the neighbors were all very good to us and brought food, furniture, and whatever we needed to basically start over—again. They called it charity. Ali knew all about charity.

As the story goes, one Friday night, Daddy and That Melvin Bray got paid, went to Charlie's Place, and of course showed up at our house all boozed up. Daddy basically went into a rage and pretty much destroyed everything. That Melvin Bray stayed on the front porch and never lifted a finger to help one way or another, and then they left. Later on that same night, they had a wreck. Daddy, the usual designated drunk driver, was hurt pretty badly. I remember he had a perfect imprint of the old Chevy's steering wheel in his chest—one huge purple bruise in the shape of a '48 Chevy steering wheel—and he bragged about it. He stayed in the hospital for a week, went to jail for a week, and then came back home. Lucky us.

That Melvin Bray was thrown out of the car but hardly had a scratch. The state patrol officer at the scene of the accident made the typical comments about drunk drivers getting out alive when they should have been killed. I say *why*?

Several months later, it was Friday again, payday again, and the usual suspects were at it again. It just so happened that Mrs. Brown had sent Mr. Brown over with some things for Mother, and he had walked over from his house, so his car was not at our house. Daddy didn't know Mr. Brown was in the house. On the porch, as Mr. Brown was leaving, he ran into Daddy and his constant shadow, That Melvin Bray, as they were going into the house. It was obvious Daddy had been drinking again, and Mr. Brown simply walked back to his house and called the sheriff.

When the sheriff pulled up to the house, That Melvin Bray took off down the back road behind the barn and hitchhiked back to his sick uncle's, and we didn't see him again at our house for a few weeks.

However, between the time Mr. Brown left our house and the time the sheriff arrived, Daddy was throwing various objects—oh, what a surprise—and P. C. was hit with something and ended up with a broken arm and a three-inch cut on the back of his head. Of course Daddy denied having had anything to do with P. C.'s injuries. Although no one else had actually seen it happen, P. C. knew the truth. When the sheriff took Daddy to jail that night, they also took P. C. to the hospital to get his broken arm set and his head sewed up. Happy times.

So two years later at Easter, the Chillton family faced the same insanity again. Thank goodness no one was hurt this time. No *person* anyway—just my sweet little biddy.

The neighbors must have thought Lillian Fay Chillton was one pitiful human being to put herself and her children through all that again and again.

"Your children deserve a childhood, Lillian" was what I heard Mrs. Brown tell Mother at church one Sunday.

After a lengthy discussion with Mother in the kitchen, the dutiful Mr. Brown suggested she have the deputies take Daddy to jail and keep him there until the judge could force Daddy to go into some type of rehab center for his alcoholism. Either way, Mr. Brown pleaded with her to not allow Daddy to stay there with us.

I think Mr. Brown caused Mother to see that regardless of what her heart was telling her, Daddy was on a dangerous course and she needed to think of her children. Mother agreed. Daddy would be going to rehab. After hearing this news, Lee and Ali jumped up 'n' down, hugging each other joyously. You'd have thought they'd just gotten new dresses.

The two deputies went down to the car by the old well, woke up Daddy, and walked him to the police car, and off to the jailhouse they went. Mr. Brown told Mother he was going back to his house to call some folks to help with cleaning up the tornado, and he said Mrs. Brown would be over right away with some food for us. He patted Mother on the back gently and told her not to despair. She returned the kindness with a grateful smile and reached out for his hand to caress it warmly. She seemed to have the "what can't be cured must be endured" syndrome. And then there was poor Ali, who, much to her chagrin, was about to receive yet a little more charity.

Sorry, Ali.

CHAPTER 5

Ricky

The Lord gives and someone else takes.

—Author unknown

"HEY, SLOW DOWN, SPEEDBOAT. I don't know about you, but I need a break! This is really some heavy and unexpected stuff," Lizzy whined.

"Thou shalt not whine, so stop your complaining, Dr. MD. I'm the tricked-out soul who's had to live this dark comedy," I said, whining right back at her.

"Yes, I hear you, but I'm starving, and some food would sure lift my spirits! Let's get some dinner and talk about *me* for a while," she joked.

"Fine, fine. I know how important your food is to you, dear. Let's eat!" I laughed.

"Hey, the way I look at it, after forty, a woman has to choose between losing her figure or her face. My idea is to keep the face and remain seated. It's a no-brainer since my profession requires that I spend way over fifty percent of my time sitting. You know, actually, skinny people irritate me! Especially when they say things like, 'You know, sometimes I just forget to eat.' Now, I've forgotten my keys, my mother's maiden name, and my address, but I have never forgotten to eat. You have to be a special kind of stupid to forget to eat, right, Maggs?"

"That's probably true. However, since you've always been a skinny little thing, weight has never been an issue for you. You just wanta get outta here 'cause ole memory lane's getting to ya, huh, Doc?" I teased.

"Oh sure, Maggs—that's it, sure. Don't forget that I'm the one with the big brain when it comes to the brain. Remember, I'm the fixer. Nothing scares me, Magg-Pie, but that's not to say that ole memory lane's not pretty scary. Just let me run in and check my e-mails, and we'll head out for some dinner. Then you can get back on that scary road, and we'll see who screams first, okay?" she concluded with confidence as we both walked back inside the office from the patio.

It was about eight o'clock in the evening, and Paula had long since left for the day. I amused myself by browsing around the oh-so-Lizzy office. It was beautifully decorated—very spacious yet warm, inviting, and quite disarming.

I guess that's what a psychiatrist's office is supposed to do—disarm one, right?

As I looked around at the walls, I studied several pieces of art that I had done for Lizzy over the years.

Entering the reception area just outside Lizzy's office, on the main wall, I couldn't help but notice a large, elegantly framed piece that I hadn't seen on my last visit to Boston. At first glance, I thought it was a page from a famous Shakespearean play or such, so I began reading it.

The Diary

For my birthday this year, I purchased a week of personal training at the local health club. Although I am still in great shape since being a high school cheerleader over twenty-five years ago, I decided it would be a good idea to go ahead and give it a try. I called the club and made my reservations with a personal trainer named Jock-O, who identified himself as a twenty-six-year-old aerobics instructor and model for athletic clothing and swimwear. Friends seemed pleased with my enthusiasm to get started. The club encouraged me to keep a diary to chart my progress.

MONDAY

Started my day at 6:00 a.m. Tough to get out of bed, but found it was well worth it when I arrived at the health club to find Jock-O waiting for me. He is something of a Greek god, with blond hair, dancing eyes, and a dazzling white smile. Woo-hoo! Jock-O gave me a tour and showed me the machines. I enjoyed watching the skillful way in which he conducted his aerobics class after my workout today. Very inspiring! Jock-O was encouraging as I did my sit-ups, although my gut was already aching from holding it in the whole time he was around. This is going to be a fantastic week!

TUESDAY

I drank a whole pot of coffee, but I finally made it out the door. Jock-O made me lie on my back and push a heavy iron bar into the air; then he put weights on it! My legs were a little wobbly on the treadmill, but I made the full mile. His rewarding smile made it all worthwhile. I feel *great*! It's a whole new life for me.

WEDNESDAY

The only way I can brush my teeth is by laying the toothbrush on the counter and moving my mouth back and forth over it. I believe I have a hernia in both pectorals. Driving was okay as long as I didn't try to steer or stop. I parked on top of a Geo in the club parking lot. Jock-O was impatient with me, insisting that my screams bothered other club members. His voice is a little too perky for that early in the morning, and when he scolds, he gets this nasally whine that is very annoying. My chest hurt when I got on the treadmill, so Stupid-O put me on the stair monster. Why the hell would anyone invent a machine to simulate an activity rendered obsolete by elevators? Dumb-O told me it would help me get in shape and enjoy life more. He said some other crap too.

THURSDAY

Wack-O was waiting for me with his vampire-like teeth exposed as his thin, cruel lips pulled back in a full snarl. I couldn't help being half an hour late—it took me that long to tie my shoes. He took me to work out with dumbbells— *he's* a dumbbell. When he was not looking, I ran and hid in the restroom. He sent some skinny witch to find me. Then, as punishment, he put me on the rowing machine—which I sank.

FRIDAY

I hate that jackass Jock-O more than any human being has ever hated any other human being in the history of the world—stupid, skinny, anemic, anorexic little aerobics instructor. If there was a part of my body I could move without unbearable pain, I would beat him with it. Lame-O wanted me to work on my triceps. I don't have any triceps! And if you don't want dents in the floor, don't hand me the darn barbells or anything that weighs more than a sandwich. The treadmill flung me off, and I landed on a health-and-nutrition teacher. Why couldn't it have been someone softer, like the drama coach or the choir director?

SATURDAY

Satan left a message on my answering machine in his grating, shrill voice, wondering why I did not show up today. Just hearing his voice made me want to smash the machine with my planner; however, I lacked the strength to even use the TV remote and ended up catching eleven straight hours of the Weather Channel.

SUNDAY

I'm having the church van pick me up for services today, so I can go and thank God that this week is over. I will also pray that next year I will have the wisdom to choose a gift for myself that is fun—like a root canal or a hysterectomy. I still say if God wanted me to bend over, He would have sprinkled the floor with diamonds!

Author Unknown

This anecdote fell right in line with our "skinny" conversation earlier, and I was laughing so hard that I distracted Lizzy. She closed her laptop, stood up, chuckled, and said, "Yeah, that's a keeper. Somebody sent it to me in an e-mail a while back, and I printed it out and had it framed. It's definitely an icebreaker, because most of my patients are women and, of course, can relate to the diet and exercise thing. They come in here all uptight and bummed out and read that little disarming ditty while they're waiting, and it actually changes their mood."

"Well, it sure disarmed *me*, lifted *my* spirits, and increased *my* appetite too! Just reading it was a workout; now *I'm* starving." I laughed.

"Well, thank God, Maggs, 'cause these active hunger pains of *mine* are two minutes apart now, and we've gotta get *me* to the restaurant!" she moaned.

"Okay, drama queen, in that case, should I call a cab?" I mocked.

She ignored me, and we headed for the door and out to her almost-new white Benz. She was a certified car junkie. Her knowledge about high-performance vehicles amazed me. She was probably some famous, awesomely cool race-car driver in a previous life. Nah.

She was successful in her practice and could afford her heart's desire, but she couldn't bring herself to pay the sticker price on a new car. Every other year, she would wait until the new cars hit the lots, and then she would go trade in on the previous year's new model. Her behavior confused me. She was quite frugal, and I was certain she had gotten that from her father. She always made me laugh, and I've never met anyone like her—ever. She was totally sweet, silly when necessary, and real when it counted. Ya know that saying about throwing the mold away? They did. I've also heard that "love is blind, but friendship is clairvoyant." It's true.

"Hey, Maggs, let's go spend some Benjamins, baby! I know this superb little Italian bistro that just opened a couple of months ago. They serve the best expensive wine in town!"

"Best Expensive Wine—is that their house label? Okay, let's move out, Lizzy-Girl!"

As we sped off in her oh-so-cool convertible Benz, her long blonde hair blew in the breezy night air, and I had bittersweet flashbacks of the first time I met little Miss Sarah Lizabeth Benis.

It was the first day of school in September 1953, and we were on the playground. She was six and a half, and I was about to turn six at the end of the month. Yeah, it was only a six-month difference, but she made a big deal about it—that is, until we reached forty. Well, of course we couldn't possibly have known back then, playing on that playground together for the first time, what life would bring to us.

Before I knew it, we were pulling into the parking lot at the restaurant and up to the valet parking sign. The young man opened Lizzy's door, and I got out on my side. She handed him the keys, he handed her the valet ticket, and we walked inside the restaurant.

The host seated us at a perfect little dimly lit corner table adorned with a small vase of fresh fall flowers. Lizzy always ordered the wine for us and never missed. We both loved pinot noir no matter what we ate. The wine came, we toasted each other, and as usual, she was right, because the wine and the restaurant she had chosen were both simply perfect for our mood.

"Okay, what do ya call a smart blonde, Maggs?"

"Oh, here we go with the blonde jokes again, huh, Blondie? Okay, I'll bite—what?" I answered.

"*Bite*? That's good—a golden retriever! Blondie yourself, silly!" She chuckled.

"All right, what did the blonde say to the doctor when she found out she was pregnant?" I asked competitively.

"Oh yeah, sure, she said, 'Are you sure it's *mine*?'"

"Oh, you think you're so smart, don't ya? You must have that know-it-all disease," I picked at her.

"There's no such thing as the know-it-all disease, Blondie." She winked.

"Really, *you* should know," I replied.

"Ha-ha, you got me there, Maggs. Okay, last blonde joke for the two hungry—not dumb, just hungry—blondes, 'cause we gotta order dinner. So did you hear about the Chinese couple that had a blonde baby?"

"No, I didn't. What about 'em?" I said, playing along.

"They named him Sum Ting Wong," she answered.

"Funny—very funny, my dear. So when are ya gonna take this blonde act on the road?" I quizzed her playfully.

"Sorry, but the world is simply not ready for me, Magg-Pie, so I'm just gonna keep my day job," she assured me.

"Well, you *are* the brainy blonde of the two, so I'll trust your judgment on that, and just for the record, I think you made the right call, Doctor," I teased.

She insisted we order a fabulous meal, way more than we could eat, but vowed nothing would go to waste because she would, of course, request a doggie bag for leftovers. "Okay, that's fine, Dr. Freud—I mean Frugal—but you're paying," I said. She just sipped her wine and ignored me.

We recounted the last time we had been together. She had come out from Boston to attend the opening of my new gallery in Austin. We had been going back and forth between Boston and Austin for years and did our best to get together every three or four months or so.

During that last trip to Austin back in the early spring, she had made me promise to come spend a couple of weeks with her in the fall. She had said she was concerned about me and had suggested one of her specialties at the family rate. I had asked her what she had in mind. "Oh," she had said, "funny you should bring up the *mind*, 'cause I'm thinking about performing a cleansing of your mind's *soul*," she answered.

"Yikes, what's that—a basic lobotomy or just a personality transplant?" I had stammered.

She had always been bossy, sassy, and right—for the most part. I was none of those things—for the most part. I guess that was the part that caused us to get along so well—for the most part.

We enjoyed every minute of our time together that evening—the meal, the wine, and the always-interesting conversation, which was just what we both needed.

As usual, Lizzy told me about her latest most interesting and challenging patient. This practice was something we had done since she first opened her practice several years ago. She would give me the specifics surrounding the case—using code names, of course—and then I would come up with my own diagnosis.

Over the years, we had also developed our own code names for each other. I would refer to her as Holmes, and I got to play Doctor, as in Watson. I became a pretty good Doctor myself—without the pay, naturally. Actually, our little game was uniquely interesting and challenging, and we both enjoyed it immensely. It was all in fun. We really never did want to grow up.

This new case was different, though, and Lizzy was busting to tell me about it. She was quite intrigued and knew I would be also, and once again, I must admit that the Lizzy-Girl was right.

"Do you remember when we were in the first grade and had just met for the first time at Grace Chapel School?" she asked.

"Yes, dear, of course," I said, rolling my eyes.

"Okay, do you remember that little boy who was kidnapped on the army base in that little community next to us that same year?" she asked.

"Oh gosh, yes, I do remember, because he was our age, wasn't he?" I answered.

"He was actually *my* age almost to the day! Remember, you're six months *younger* than me, little baby!" she mocked in her usual bossy tone, and she stuck her tongue out at me.

See what I mean—*older*, wiser?

"They looked for him for years, Maggs, and to this day, they've never found a trace of him or who took him!" she explained.

"So what does that little boy have to do with your new patient?" I asked.

"Well, my dear Watson, my new patient is his mother—her code name is the Mother—and I'd say she's about twenty years older than us, Maggs.

"So in 1950, her husband was reassigned from New Jersey to that army base not far from us in Grace Chapel. They had one child, Ricky, who was three at the time, and then three years later, when Ricky was in the first grade, same as us, he was abducted. They had just celebrated his sixth birthday, and a few days later, the day before Valentine's Day, he just disappeared. The Mother relived her horror story for me in our first meeting.

"It was right after school let out that sunny but chilly February afternoon in 1953, and all the little army brats who lived on the base rode the school bus home every day. The bus let them all out together just inside the base gate, and the mothers or babysitters would meet the kids at the bus, making sure everyone got home safely. The Mother was right there as usual, waiting for Ricky at the bus stop. The two of them walked on down to their house, went inside, and had a little snack as usual.

"That day was a special afternoon snack, though, because it was Friday, and the next day, Saturday, was Valentine's Day. The Mother had made Ricky's favorite chocolate cupcakes with red icing for his little Valentine's Day party they had planned for the next day. So for his after-school snack that day, he got to be the taster, just to make sure the cupcakes were good enough for his party. The Mother and Ricky also exchanged early Valentine's cards as they enjoyed their cupcakes together.

"After their snack, Ricky reached into the back pocket of his Levi's and pulled out his small plastic wallet, with the mini Buster Brown metal button he had pinned to it. He opened the wallet and carefully placed his mother's colorful little valentine behind his favorite baseball card. He loved his mom, but that baseball card was his most prized possession. He quickly closed the wallet and returned it to its proper back pocket.

"He had gotten a really cool Buster Brown kite for his birthday and was anxious to get outside and get it airborne while there was still a little wind left in the breezy air that afternoon. He grabbed the kite off the back porch as he hustled on outside to play in the fenced backyard. So, in essence, this day was basically just like any other day, nothing really unusual—that is, until about a half hour later, when the Mother went outside to make sure Ricky still had on his coat and hat, and then she discovered he was gone," Lizzy concluded.

"Oh, you're right, Holmes—that *is* a horror story. What now?" I moaned.

"Well, it's my learned opinion, Dr. Watson, that when the Mother went outside to check on Ricky, it was that very moment that marked the beginning of the end of the Mother's life. She would never, ever be the same. Her heart was broken, and it would never mend. She won't *die* of her broken heart; she just wishes she could.

"Remember, Maggs, the news of Ricky's disappearance even impacted *our* little town, and everyone was filled with fear and disbelief and full of anger too. The inconceivable fact surrounding the scene was how someone could have taken Ricky from the backyard without climbing over the six-foot fence to get him, and then both the kidnapper *and* Ricky would have had to go back over the fence to get *out* of the yard, since there were no gates located anywhere on the fence. The only way anyone could get into the backyard was by going through the house and out the back door.

"Ricky was a small six-year-old child and couldn't climb the six-foot-high fence without help. In addition to that, all those little houses were like row houses—very close to each other. So how could this have been achieved in broad daylight without someone seeing some*one* or some*thing* odd or strange? Unless, of course, it wasn't a stranger and therefore didn't appear odd or strange at the time.

"The Mother did say that once she realized Ricky was not in the backyard, she ran back into the house to see if he could have possibly come back inside the house and gone out the front door without her hearing him, because she was in the back bedroom, ironing and listening to the radio. She checked the front door, and it was, in fact, still locked from the inside, just as it always was. She immediately checked all the windows to ensure they were down and the latches locked.

"Obviously, this became a very high-profile case. The fact that this child was the son of a military man and had disappeared from military property forced the weight of the military to be added to the investigation. Early on, the FBI joined the search, along with local and nearby law enforcements.

"It was as though Ricky had simply disappeared into thin air, without a trace of evidence to assist authorities in their massive search to find him *or* the hideous child thief. The search went on for quite some time, to no end or closure. To this day, she has no explanation for what actually happened to her little boy, Maggie. However, she does have recurring nightmares of what *might* have happened to him."

"So how did the Mother end up here in Boston in *your* office?" I asked.

"Well, the Mother and the boy's father had no other children, and a few years after Ricky disappeared, they moved to Boston in an attempt to begin a new life. The years dragged by with cruelty, and the Mother just couldn't seem to come out of her tragically imposed life sentence of despair. Finally, her personal physician here in Boston referred her to me," she explained.

After many years of practice in Boston, Lizzy's professional peers had nicknamed her the Fixer, and she never let me forget it.

I knew she was good, and she knew she was good. In fact, I was considering having a little plaque made for her that would say something like "To save time, let's just assume I know everything."

She had made quite a name for herself, specializing in adult psychiatry, and was acclaimed for her approach to the unconscious mind using medical hypnosis therapy.

Shoot, that's probably what she's got planned for me, I thought. *What!*

Anyway, she told me she had a difficult time dealing with her own issues around loss every time she saw the Mother.

Lizzy knew loss up close and personal. Actually, loss was our common denominator, and we shared it to the very cores of our beings.

"So give me the specifics, Holmes—what's the Mother expecting from you?" I asked.

"That's what's so intriguing with this case. It's not the specifics per se. The first time I looked into her eyes, she pulled on my heartstrings. I can't explain it, Watson. This is something different. I haven't figured out the *why* yet, but I'm certain Ole Man Fate has a hand in this. And since I don't have the gift of prophecy, I'll do what I always do: trust my instincts. Don't forget: I don't make mistakes—not *big* ones, anyway," she assured me.

"No, dear, I'll not forget. Uh, and would ya pass me a slice of that humble pie?" I replied.

"I'm not kidding, Maggie! There's a plot here that's plenty thick!" she proclaimed.

"You must be serious; you called me Maggie. Okay then, Holmes, what's your next move?" I asked.

"I've asked her to begin a journal and write down everything she can remember about her life, starting with the day she got married," she explained.

"Why *that* day?" I asked.

"*That* day? Elementary, my dear Watson. That day was the beginning of both her greatest joys and sorrows. 'The Lord gives, and someone else takes,'" she answered solemnly.

The waiter interrupted us as he asked politely, "Would you ladies care to see a dessert menu?"

"We would indeed, and thank you very much," Lizzy replied with a big, grateful smile as she gracefully took the menu from him. I tightened my lips and squinted at her from across the table as she sorta glared back at me. "All right, we'll *split* something! It's the weekend—come on," she begged.

"Fine, then it better have chocolate in it, with a side of Dom Pérignon." I smiled back at her.

We finished our double double-chocolate mousse, which was practically piled to the ceiling with whipped cream; slowly downed the champagne; got the doggie bag; paid the check; and, just like Elvis, left the building. We didn't realize it, but we'd been there over three hours.

The valet had already brought the car around and was waiting for us. He hopped in and started the engine to warm the car, as the clear fall night air had gotten quite chilly. Lizzy palmed him some cash, and we headed back to her house for the weekend.

She liked convenience and order in her life, and so did I. She had it, I didn't, and I wanted it. We were both pretty pooped and both willingly accepted the award of Party Pooper Duo—for that night only, of course. The evening curtain was drawing near as the champagne, compliments of dear Dom, was delightfully taking us to another place. By then, all we wanted was to lie down, close our eyes, and have a glorious, sweet dream. Tomorrow was another day, and I wasn't about to even contemplate my impending family-rate specialty she had promised me on this trip. *Somebody help me!*

Good night and thank you, Mr. Pérignon!

CHAPTER 6

The Privileged Character

Death is not the worst evil, but rather when we wish to die and cannot.
—Sophocles, Greek playwright

I AWOKE TO Lizzy's a cappella version of "The Eyes of Texas."

"You call that singing?" I laughed.

"Well, I've been up for hours, and you're just laid up in here like some skinny, spoiled celebrity! No wonder you look so damn good for an old heifer; you sleep half your life away, Maggs. Get up and smell the coffee, girl!"

Just then, I rolled over, and there stood sweet Lizzy with my favorite morning drink: a hot, giant java! *No offense, Mr. Pérignon,* I thought to myself. *I need you to put me to sleep and java to wake me up. That's my motto.* "Oh my gosh, I have a headache throughout my entire body. This is the first time I've been up this early since the last time I've been up that late. And *you*—you are simply the best!" I sat up and praised her gleefully.

"Well, aren't you the right one today—so far, anyway," she agreed in her sassy tone. "Hey, you know this stuff's a drug, don't you?" she asked playfully.

"Nah, coffee's not a drug; it's a *vitamin,* silly," I argued.

"Yeah, when pigs fly, it is," she mocked. "You should have a little of my tea once in a while—now, that's some gooooood stuff!"

"I sure do love you, Lizzy-Girl," I jokingly swooned.

"Yes, darling, and I love you too. Why couldn't at least one of us have been a lesbian?" she teased.

"Yes indeed—she's a funny, gentle little soul, she is," I mused back at her. "By the way, whose lips did that first good kiss belong to anyway? Was it that cute little dirty-mouthed Barry Snyder in the fifth grade?" I asked.

"You know it was, and he was soooo cute I couldn't stand it! But boy did he cuss like a sailor. Hey, maybe Lee took cuss lessons from Barry! He couldn't stay out of trouble either, remember, Maggs?"

"Yes, I do, but I'd forgotten that until this very moment. What fun times—at least some of 'em, anyway. Ya know, sometimes I refer to the past as the good ole *bad* days, and other times I think of it as the bad ole *good* days. Is there a difference, Dr. Benis, MD?" I wondered aloud.

"Well, we'll just have to ponder that one a little, huh? For now, though, I've got to eat something before I faint! I've got some bagels and goodies in the kitchen, so come on, Magg-Pie—get a move on!"

"And another thing—why couldn't at least one of us have been a smoker? And preferably me since I'm the one who's always hungry. Maybe smoking would curb my appetite; isn't that what they say?" She laughed.

"Oh brother, now that does bring back another memory from ole memory lane I'd like to forget," I said as we headed out to the kitchen.

"Which part—the hungry part or the smoking part?" she asked.

"The smoking part," I answered.

"Okay, have another giant cup of vitamins, and tell me about it while I toast these bagels," she urged.

"Well, this was the fall of 1954. School had just started, and we were in Miss Brownie's third-grade class. Remember her, Lizzy? She was such a good teacher for little kids. She brought us brownies every Friday for recess, so early on, we nicknamed her Miss Brownie. She must have thought it was clever, because she allowed us to call her that all year long. She was especially good to you and me. When I think back on it, she probably was one of Pastor Meyers's earthly angels sent straight from heaven just to look after you and me that sad, bad year.

"Anyway, the haunting memories of the smoking fiasco are pretty cruel. It was, of course, a Friday afternoon after school. It had to be payday because Chill, a.k.a. Monster Daddy, was carrying on as in previous times—he'd just gotten paid and had gone straight to Charlie's Place to get his big bag of bad. He was just shameless—that's all. You'd think after all that had just happened to our family, he would have at least tried to *act* like a decent human being. I mean, really! But if you're not a decent human being, I guess you're not gonna *act* like one, except in the movies, huh?"

I remembered the day as if it were yesterday.

⚬ఇ

Aunt Lucy was trying to sell her little house, and we were going back and forth between her house and the big house. She simply didn't take any crap off Daddy, so when he came home struttin' 'n' crowin' like a rooster with alcohol on his breath, she just flat-out told him to take his sorry fanny back where he came from—and right then.

Lee chimed in with "And don't let the door hit ya on your way out, or we'll call the sheriff!" Thank ya, Lee. Daddy knew Aunt Lucy would do it with no hesitation.

Aunt Lucy and Mother were twins, but they were very different. Oh, they both had beautiful hearts for sure, but Aunt Lucy was not as passive or forgiving of Daddy's cruelty as Mother was. Growing up, Aunt Lucy had always had health problems and didn't even get to finish high school. However, she was blessed with an awesome load of common sense, drive, and integrity. Being sickly, as they called it, probably aided her in trying harder to succeed at whatever she attempted. What a challenging slice of life she was cut. She never complained once, and she loved Mother and us kids with all her heart. We were damn lucky to have her, too.

Anyway, Daddy left in the old Chevy, and we all were relieved. Later on that evening, Aunt Lucy needed a few things from her house and wanted to run by the Fancy Gap Curb Market on the way back. She told us we were gonna make special cookies with ice cream later that evening, and we were all excited. She was so good to us. So Aunt Lucy and the girls left, and P. C., Lee, Paddy, and I stayed at the house.

The Chillton family was having a pretty rough time, and we all were just going through the motions and trying to cope one day at a time. What a hell of a time. Aunt Lucy and the girls hadn't been gone fifteen minutes before we heard a car coming up the drive. To our shock and dismay, it was Daddy, and P. C. was out on the porch smoking a cigarette.

P. C. had been sneaking smokes for a few days. He was struggling to cope with his sorrow, and smoking was one way of dealing with it, I guess.

Unfortunately, Daddy didn't deal with anything, because he let his alcohol do his negotiating for him. I had heard P. C. say countless times that he would never grow up to be like Daddy.

P. C. was named after Daddy, Charles Phillip Chillton III, and early on, everyone called him C. P. When he was ten, though, he came home from school one day and, outta the blue, told Mother he had changed his name from C. P. to P. C. Mother asked him why, and he told her he would much rather his name be short for Privileged Character than short for Charles Phillip.

Mother was well aware of the sadness in P. C.'s heart regarding Daddy. Once he had told her that he wished to die because Daddy didn't love him. So Mother, in her loving way, agreed to the name change, and P. C. it was. From that day forward, P. C. had his new name, with a new meaning that worked for him, and that made him happy.

Daddy must have seen P. C. out there smoking on the porch when he drove up, and we could hear him yelling at P. C. about it. Daddy had started smoking when he was thirteen. P. C. was already fifteen, so what was the big deal anyway? Back then, smoking was *in*, baby! Remember the phrase "smoke 'em if ya got 'em"?

Yeah, Daddy was the perfect role model—not to follow.

But actually, he *was* great at teaching his children what *not* to do, and only time would tell if a monster's offspring would thrive or strive with such angry blood running in their veins.

The monster got out of the car, walked over to the porch and up the steps, and headed straight over to where P. C. was standing. Without hesitation, he immediately started shoving and pushing P. C. while cursing at him. P. C. was not a fighter and for good reason: he was afraid of Daddy.

Lee dashed out the door with Paddy and me right behind her.

"Death is not the worst evil thing you can cause me, Daddy," P. C. shouted through his tears. Daddy slugged P. C. right in the face and knocked him off the porch and onto the ground. He was three times as big as P. C., and when he was drunk, he had the strength of an angry gorilla—and he acted like one too. We knew we had to do something before he really hurt P. C.

"You dirty bastard, leave him alone," Lee yelled at Daddy. She sure did love to cuss. She must have kept *The Cuss Book* hidden under her pillows. She was on the porch and ran over to Daddy and pushed him with all her might. He certainly didn't expect *that*, and it caused him to lose his balance, and he fell backward off the porch and onto the ground. "Now you know how it feels, don't ya? How do *you* like it, you *monster*?" Lee raged. "Get up, P. C.! Get up!" She kept screaming at P. C., but P. C. didn't move.

About that time, Daddy got up off the ground and headed toward P. C., but Paddy and I ran after Daddy and started pushing and pulling on him, begging him to stop.

We didn't know it at the time, but P. C. was really hurt and couldn't get up. He must have hit his head and blacked out when he landed on the ground after Daddy's vicious attack. Paddy and I were just little kids and weren't very big or strong, but we detained Daddy long enough for Lee to get P. C. up and on his feet. She was almost carrying P. C. as she frantically struggled across the front yard toward Mrs. Brown's house. Paddy picked up a pretty big rock by the porch and threw it at Daddy. The rock hit Daddy right upside his head and knocked the livin' tar out of him, and he fell to his knees. Paddy and I ran like lightnin' and caught up with Lee to help her with P. C. We made our way through the

44

yard and across the main road to Mrs. Brown's. Poor Mrs. Brown—what did she ever do to deserve *us*?

Well, we must have looked like little rabbits running lickety-split through that yard. Once again, the Chillton kids were on the run, fleeing their crazy, drunk father. We made it to Mrs. Brown's, we climbed those oh-so-familiar steps in the dark, and we banged on her front door. We were all afraid Daddy might be right on our heels, but we didn't dare slow down to look back.

Mrs. Brown turned on the porch light and opened the door. I'm sure she knew it was us even before she opened the door, because we were all yelling and screaming at the top of our lungs. When she saw P. C., she immediately reached for him and assisted Lee in getting him inside the house. We didn't know what she had seen, because it was dark and we were too busy running for our lives. It was about seven o'clock in the evening, but Mr. Brown had not gotten home yet, and Danny was on a weekend Boy Scout camping trip. Mrs. Brown put her arms around P. C., walked him into the first bedroom, and then helped him lie down on the bed. She looked him over thoroughly and told us we had to get him to the hospital. She made Lee sit by him at the bed and press a cold compress on his face and mouth. We couldn't tell if his teeth were missing or not—there was too much blood—but it looked like it.

Poor, sweet P. C.—he was such a good boy and had never hurt a soul. Daddy was so cruel to him. It seemed that every time Daddy drank, he targeted P. C. with his uncontrolled anger. That psycho!

Mrs. Brown ran to the kitchen and called Mr. Brown to come home immediately and help her with us. Actually, she wanted him to be there to watch out for Aunt Lucy and the girls. We all figured Daddy would be pretty mad once he got off the ground after Paddy hit him with that rock. Mrs. Brown told Mr. Brown we were going to head to the hospital but weren't leaving until he got there, for Aunt Lucy's sake. We all got in her car, and she drove down to the end of her driveway, where we waited. Fortunately, there was no sign of Daddy anywhere. Mr. Brown arrived shortly and stayed by the road to flag Aunt Lucy down so that she wouldn't go back to the house and possibly be in harm's way.

When we got to the hospital, Mrs. Brown saw to it that P. C. was seen immediately. Mrs. Brown and Lee went into the ER with him. Paddy and I sat out in the little waiting room. It was probably close to two hours before Mrs. Brown and Lee came to get us and told us P. C. would be staying overnight in the hospital. He was going to be fine, but they needed to watch him through the night because he had a concussion from hitting his head in the fall after Daddy's near-fatal blow. We asked if his teeth had been knocked out, and Mrs. Brown said yes, but a special type of tooth doctor would be coming to see him in the morning, along with another special doctor for the cuts on his face and mouth. Apparently, he had a bad cut under his right eye, and his top lip and gums were all ripped up. The doctors in the ER knew that surgery was imminent and didn't want to do anything but keep P. C. calm until the surgeon could look at him first thing in the morning.

Paddy and I wanted to stay with him, but Mrs. Brown said there was no need. She said the doctor had put P. C. to sleep for the night, and P. C. wouldn't know if we were there or not. She was so kind and made us feel a lot better.

In the car on the way to the hospital, Lee had given Mrs. Brown a blow-by-blow account of the havoc Daddy was once again wreaking on his children. Once Mrs. Brown got P. C. into the emergency room and told Dr. Fitzpatric what had happened, he had the hospital call the sheriff's office. They would be going out to pick Daddy up and take his butt to jail. Thank you, Dr. Fitzpatric!

When we got back to Mrs. Brown's house, Aunt Lucy and the girls were all there with Mr. Brown. He told us the sheriff and a deputy had in fact come over and taken Daddy away. Mrs. Brown told Mr. Brown that Dr. Fitzpatric had had the hospital call the sheriff's office to report the incident after she explained what had happened to P. C. Mr. Brown said he figured that's what had happened, because he and Aunt Lucy had decided to wait until we got back from the hospital to make a decision about Daddy, so they weren't the ones who had called the sheriff.

Mrs. Brown then gave Aunt Lucy the good, the bad, and the ugly news on P. C. Aunt Lucy thanked the Browns, and then we left and went home. When we got home, Aunt Lucy told us all we should save the cookie party for a special homecoming for P. C., which is exactly what we did.

As it turned out, Aunt Lucy insisted that Daddy be taken back to the "alcoholics' hospital," as she called it, for several months as a result of that evening.

"So what happened to P. C.?" Lizzy said, interrupting my thoughts.

"Well, bright 'n' early the next morning, Aunt Lucy and the young fight club members—Lee, Paddy, and I—all got in the car and headed to the hospital to meet with the doctor. Aunt Lucy wasn't about to allow anyone to do anything to P. C. without talking to them first."

I thought back to that terrifying morning.

When we got to the hospital, the doctor was already in P. C.'s room, examining him. Poor ole P. C. looked like hell. Both eyes were black, and his face was so swollen that he hardly looked like himself. Both his lips were all cut up, but his top lip looked really scary. He was feeling no pain though—thank you, Dr. Drugs!

When we first walked into P. C.'s room, I think he saw the look of horror on our faces. He tried to tell us it wasn't that bad, that he was gonna be fine. That was P. C. for ya—selfless, just like Mother. He was never thinking of himself. There he was, with those big, fat, broken lips and missing two front teeth, and yet he was determined to reassure *us*.

He raised himself up on his pillow and mumbled, "Well, that's the last damn cigarette I'll ever smoke!" We all just busted out laughing, including the doctor.

Then the doctor and Aunt Lucy stepped outside the room, leaving "the Wild Bunch" to relive their almost-successful getaway from the night before. Paddy told P. C. that P. C. was gonna owe him big-time since he had single-handedly slain Daddy, as David had Goliath, to give P. C. time to get up and start running after Daddy hit him. Paddy added that the rock he'd thrown at Daddy had been a little bit bigger than David's pebble. We all cheered P. C. and told him we would be his servants for as long as he needed us, but not to overdo it. We were all laughing and feeling sorry for P. C. at the same time.

Aunt Lucy came back in the room and told us what the doctor had suggested for P. C.'s recovery. The operation would fix two cuts on his face, repair both lips and the upper gum, and replace the two top front teeth. Aunt Lucy was most concerned with the healing and scarring process. The doctors expected the physical recovery time to be several months, but they insisted that P. C. would have a full recovery with only minor visible scarring.

Sadly, there was no way to determine the *emotional* scars, as only time would reveal those. On the way home from the hospital, Aunt Lucy told us not to fret, because P. C. was in good shape for the shape he was in.

"You know," Lizzy interrupted, "from what I've heard so far, you kids lived in hell! I don't remember you ever telling me any such tales about your father in all these years, Maggs. I do understand now, though, why my mother always insisted you come to *my* house when we got together. Why, I don't remember ever going to play at your house even once, Maggs!"

"Oh Lizzy dear, you ain't heard nothin' yet. I've got all shades of darkness hidden away deep inside my heart. Are you sure you wanta keep headin' down nightmare lane—I mean, memory lane? It's not too late to turn back, ya know," I offered.

"No way, José, but hell's bells, girl—it's no wonder I've sensed apathy in you for some time now. Our trip down memory lane is just you painting another Dorian Gray for me; let's call it *The Ugly Truth*, shall we? I'm getting the *real* picture now, though, Maggie, and *The Honest Truth*, in spite of the major role you had in *The Horror Movie of Your Past*, is that you can rise above it all and fly—high!

"Actually, Maggs, I do know a little about flying myself and how it can affect you in the most positive ways. I remember the night my grandma Bubbee died. I was actually lying right next to her in bed with my arms around her. I had accepted she was leaving me, but my heart was still breaking. You of all people know what she meant to me, Maggs.

"Daddy came in the room and asked me if I was all right. I told him no but said I would be; I just wanted to stay with her for a little while. He came over to the bed, kissed Grandma Bubbee and me, and then respectfully left us in each other's arms. I fell asleep from fatigue and grief.

"When I woke up, I still had my arms around Bubbee, but I felt so light, and this supreme, heavenly, happy feeling swept over my entire body. It was the most incredible feeling; I really can't justly describe it. As I lay there, still hugging Bubbee in this euphoric state, I remembered a wild dream about flying I had just had.

"In the dream, I watched myself rise up, out of my body. When I got up to the ceiling, I looked back down and saw myself still lying in the bed with Bubbee. I'm certain I was out of my body and just logically accepted it as real. I continued to rise and went through the ceiling and onto the roof in a state of flight—not fright, but *flight*. Once I was on the roof, I could feel the chill in the air as I gradually moved angelically through the air. I was *flying* and gazing down upon my house, my yard, the trees, and the neighborhood—I could see everything!

"The curious thing about all this was that I instinctively knew and trusted that this was indeed happening right then and there. I have no idea how long I hovered over the neighborhood, but at some point, I returned to the bed with Bubbee in the exact same way I'd left it.

"As I lay there nestled snuggly next to her frail little body, describing the jubilant feeling of flying to her, I realized her breathing had changed, and it was very faint. I was calm, though, and well aware of what was happening. I was certain Bubbee had had a hand in arranging my flight schedule that night. We loved each other so much and, on a soul level, were keenly tuned in to one another. She was well aware of my feelings about her leaving, and we both knew it was time for her to go. She knew I had accepted it.

"I sat up in the bed, took her hands in mine, and told her I was just fine, to 'go on already.' That was our little thing, remember, Maggs? Then the very last thing I said to her was 'Thanks for getting me on that flight, Bubbee; it was outta this world, and I'll never forget it as long as I live. You're the best, and I'll see you in the next world. Tell Mother I love her.'

"To use your words, Maggs, 'it was incredible—simply incredible'!

"So, in a desperate time, if one can simply take flight—or rise above it—the circumstance can definitely change for the better. Obviously we can't always do it Bubbee-style, but maybe we could fashion it after her, at least psychologically.

"In your case, Maggs, you just have to spread your *imaginary* wings and start flappin', little girl! You know, keep on doing that *pretend* thing you do so well and pretend you can fly high above all your shady darkness—at least until you arrive at the door of forgiveness. Forgiveness is about not letting negative feelings spoil your life, girl. You've got to reprogram the way you think about things and reassess the circumstances of your situation. No doubt you've been hurt, but only your subconscious knows just how deep the pain of that hurt goes. Once you've accomplished this, believe me, you *will* fly, and from that day forward, the Great Pretender can finally use that Get Out of Jail Free card and never look back!

"Granted, I admit I'm saddened and shocked to hear of these memories, Maggs, but I'm *not* shocked at your strength and courage. You *are* your mother's daughter!

"And that pretending thing you've done all these years—well, I have my own interpretation of that, and I call it the Fake It Till You Make It Challenge. This has been your coping method for most of your life. It appears your subconscious has been guiding you all this time to protect you until you can take care of yourself in a conscious, healthy way.

"Now the time has finally come for you to stop hating your father and just forgive him already! You and that hatred fella have become best friends, ya know? If you harbor ill will or anger toward someone, even when justified, your emotional unhappiness will bind you like a pair of handcuffs. I'm not saying your father doesn't deserve to be hated—shoot, I was feeling pretty hateful myself as I listened to you relive all those frighteningly awful images of him. And I'll tell you right now, it's not the easiest thing to do; forgiving even the smallest debt can be a huge mountain to climb for some, and sadly, some just can't do it for one reason or another. I've seen people filled with such hatred that they actually *live* to hate. That kind of hate is a sad sickness of the soul. And there's nothing on Earth sadder than a sick soul, my dearest friend, because it will literally suck the life out of you.

"So *forgiveness* is the new word of the day, okay? Are you listening, Maggs?"

"Yeah, yeah, I hear ya; ya don't have to skywrite it. However, I do believe we got a dual problem here, Dr. MD. I don't think my problem is with the forgiveness part; it's the forgetting part that I fear is gonna get in my way. So I guess I really am gonna require at least a *partial* lobotomy, right? You know, for the part of my brain that does the forgetting? I'm actually sorta serious, too."

"Oh bro-thuurr! Okay, Maggs, over the next few days, you can just relax and try not to conjure up any demons about forgiving and forgetting. This process is definitely going to take a little longer than I thought, but I *am* the Fixer, and I'm more than 'sorta' serious!"

"Fine, I'm all yours, Doc, and I was careful to pack an extra change of clothes."

"Shoot, it sounds like you may need a whole new wardrobe before I'm through *changing* you," she teased with a wink. We laughed, but we both also knew she was right about me being screwed up. Carrying the heavy burden of my childhood experiences involving my father had deeply affected me, and I had followed in my mother's footsteps by marrying an alcoholic myself. I also had married an abusive, self-absorbed, emotionally unavailable man—a man just like my father. It had taken me ten years to realize that I was not my mother and that my two children and I deserved better—a lot better. The Great Pretender had faced reality and gotten herself a divorce.

And considering all that forgiveness talk, I didn't doubt for one minute that just maybe, in addition to a personality transplant, I might need a heart transplant, too! Oh man! Well, at least Lizzy hadn't threatened to ship me off to the convent. Heck, that would be one more frightening experience—me sitting in one of those straight-backed wooden desks, the nuns smacking me with a ruler as they forced me to constantly play Truth or Consequences. I saw that 1940s movie *The Song of Bernadette*, starring Jennifer Jones. Oh, the humanity! Yeah, like I needed *that*. Hey, I *knew* the truth; I just couldn't *get* to it. 911! 911! 911!

We finished our bagels 'n' cream cheese and decided to shower and get dressed. I told Lizzy to hit the shower while I put the dishes in the dishwasher. A few minutes later, I pressed the start button and headed down the hall to the shower myself. As I was undressing, I noticed a Post-it note stuck to my vanity mirror. It read simply, "If the heart truly forgives, there's nothing to forget." There was a big cursive *L* with a little heart at the bottom of the note. I got it, loud and clear. Sometimes the written word can be far from silent.

I showered and got dressed, and on my way back to the kitchen, I noticed Lizzy in her office, checking her voice mail. Our plan for the day was to check out the annual fall festival in the little nearby community known as Niceville. No kidding. This was the twenty-fifth anniversary of the Niceville Fall Festival. Niceville was founded in the mid-1700s, and the area was known for a number of museums offering modern and classical art, among other things, but the art was of special interest to me, of course. I had been to this festival with Lizzy several times in the past, and we always had a great time. I was certain this year's festival would be just as much fun. I went on into the kitchen and waited for Lizzy to finish up in her office.

"Are you ready to hit the road? I'm hungry!" she whined.

"Of course you are, and thou shalt not whine," I said as we headed for the back door to the garage. I pressed the garage-door button on the wall as we stepped down into the garage. The garage door began to rise, and we got in the convertible, backed out of the garage, and headed out to the scenic parkway toward the lovely little town of Niceville.

"I've been waiting on this festival for a whole year now, ya know?" she mumbled under her breath.

"Yeah, sorta like you do every year, year after year?" I questioned her.

"Exactly!" She came back at me with pure vigor. Yep, she was hungry.

The constantly winding roads kept us alert and forced us to take notice of the magnificent beauty along the way. The fall trees were on fire with vibrant shades of yellow, orange, and red. We had the top down, and the exhilarating, brisk wind sent exciting chills up my spine. The peace and solitude I felt in that same moment were beyond words. The silence was truly golden, and I honestly felt as though my world were on top of the world. I was quite certain I was very close to heaven, and I wanted to hold on to that glorious feeling as long as possible. Was I flying?

"What ya thinkin' 'bout there, little Magg-Pie?" Lizzy asked playfully as she broke the purity of the silence I was so enjoying.

"Heaven," I answered.

"Hey, I want in," she replied rather pleadingly.

"You're already there, my dear—just look all around ya," I assured her. As she took a deep breath, the wind forced her to pull several strands of her long golden hair out of her eyes. She was rounding the curves with ease and the expertise of an experienced driver at Daytona. The sunlight was brilliant, and as I sat there watching her, I realized just how heavenly she looked as the autumn sun touched her blonde hair. *Maybe we are in heaven; it sure ain't Kansas,* I thought to myself.

We arrived at the festival and parked the car, and Lizzy couldn't have been happier.

"Hey, let's go check out the first food gazebo, okay, Maggs?" Naturally, the first thing out of her mouth was how to get something *in* her mouth.

"Lead the way; I'm right behind ya, piglet," I assured her. There was no stopping her anyway, 'cause she was on a life-or-death mission for sure!

Fortunately for Lizzy, about every fifty feet or so, we ran into another little food gazebo with an abundance of incredibly superb cuisine. I was pretty sure the food was the number-one reason she refused to miss this festival each year. That girl sure did love to eat.

In addition to the wonderful food and the museums, there were all kinds of interesting exhibits and arts and crafts—unique keepsake items, most created locally, with expensive price tags. Lively entertainment was scattered throughout the park, including extravagant little marionette shows and vignettes from famous stage plays, which were really quite impressive and most entertaining.

The festival was truly a community effort, and there was also an abundance of really nice people in Niceville. There was even nice weather for the occasion; the sun was shining, and there was a slight, crisp chill in the air, delightfully assuring everyone that the explosive burst of fall color was in full arrival everywhere. As I looked around at all the glorious splendor I was about to enjoy, I felt the ache of a familiar, tense anxiety in the pit of my stomach. It hurt, and once again, I sought emotional refuge as the Great Pretender. It became clear to me that we had ourselves a perfect day going, and all I had to do that morning was get up, get there, and get happy—if only I could.

CHAPTER 7

Heeeeee's Baaaack

Be careful what you wish for; you just might get it.

—Proverb

AFTER THE FESTIVAL, we got back to Lizzy's about seven o'clock that evening and couldn't hit the couches fast enough. We were pleasantly exhausted and so full that we could hardly talk—well, maybe not *that* full. We each had bags of purchases from the festival and were excited to check them out and compare our unique little treasures.

Lizzy's favorite find was a small, exquisitely jeweled picture frame, complete with one of those generic, all-American Gerber baby photos.

My special item was a small, jeweled box with a secret, hidden bottom compartment. Did I say *hidden*? Yes, and the only way I knew it was hidden was because Papa had given a similar box to Paddy when we were little, and I recognized it right away. Papa had told Paddy it was a secret box—just for keeping secrets. "If you have a secret and you're 'bout to bust to tell it," Papa had said, "just write it down on a piece of paper and hide it in the secret box."

"Oh, what have we here, little Magg-Pie?" Lizzy playfully quizzed me as she reached for the box.

"Well, it just so happens that I have a secret box, Miss Smarty Pants!" I teased as I handed it over to her.

"Hmmm, interesting. Let's check it out and see if we can find any secrets," she said as she tried to open it. She fumbled with it for a few minutes and passed it back to me. "I give; *you* do the honors—smarty pants yourself, miss!" she said mockingly.

I took the box back and did my little magic, and it sprang right open.

"Wow, look here, Lizzy; we have a *secret!*" I said excitedly as I pulled a wrinkled, faded piece of paper from the little drawer.

"Open it! Open it! What does it say?" She jumped up with the excitement of a little kid and headed my way to see if we really had found a secret. I unfolded the small, yellowed paper carefully. The message was hand printed, obviously by a child. It read simply as follows:

Dear Mom,
I love you the most.
You are my valentime.
Happy Valentimes's Day.
SRL

"Oh, how sweet it is. What a darling valentine card, and notice how it's spelled. I sure hope SRL didn't keep that secret from Mom very long, right, Maggs?" Lizzy asked.

"Well, if the little secret keeper was anything like you and me, and his dear mom was anything like our dear moms, that secret wasn't kept very long at all!" I assured her.

Lizzy picked up her little jewel-framed Gerber baby picture and held it next to my little jeweled box and said, "Hey, look at the little jewels—they *match*!" I examined the frame and the box and agreed with her. As we looked at them more closely, we both agreed they could possibly be priceless antiques.

"Heck, Maggs, *I'm* the only antique around here that I know of; how 'bout you?"

"I'm with ya, but hey, I don't know nothin' 'bout no antiques, Miss Lizzy," I said.

"Well, next week we'll just take these little treasures to an expert who *does* know 'bout antiques, Miss Maggie. We'll find out exactly what we've found, if anything. What d'ya say to that?"

"I say yes, sir, ma'am, and yes, sir!"

"Okay, so much for secrets and antiques, Magg-Pie. How about we pick up where we left off yesterday, when we first started down memory lane—you know, that Easter weekend when the tornado hit your house?"

"Sure, I guess that's as bad a place as any to start," I lamented.

"You know, I'm recording all this, Maggs, so we won't be concerned if we get a little off track now and then. We'll find our way back to the sometimes-painful ole memory lane eventually, and I might add, it's proving to be just that," she confirmed as she hit the move-on-down-the-road button on the recorder.

"You're the doc, boss. After all that talk this mornin' about my personal protector, the subconscious, who knows? Maybe little SRL's not the only one with a hidden secret," I suggested.

"That's probably closer to the truth than we know, my dear. You just start embracing the new word of the day, okay, missy?" she instructed.

"Yes, sir, ma'am, I got it—*forgiveness, forgiveness*! So remember on that Saturday morning, the day before Easter, the sheriff and his deputies came and took Daddy to jail? Mr. Brown cautioned Mother about the possible dangers of Daddy coming back home after all he had done that Good Friday night, as well as all the previous times."

"I remember. I'm with ya, Maggs." She nodded.

"Well, fortunately, Mother took Mr. Brown's advice, and Daddy ended up in the hospital for alcoholics. Nowadays, we call that simply rehab. This made Lu very happy since she'd told me that's where Mr. Hyde needed to go to get help with his DPPs—drinking potion problems.

"Daddy spent a few weeks in jail; then the judge made him go to rehab for his drug-of-choice abuse. Of course, they didn't call it that either back then. Anyway, he stayed three months and came back home in late June of that year, 1953."

As I relayed the story to Lizzy, my mind took me back to June 1953.

If it hadn't been for Aunt Lucy, I don't know what we would have done. Between her, Uncle Rory, and Uncle Quinn, we didn't do without anything we really needed, and Aunt Lucy stayed with us quite a bit.

It was a Friday morning when Daddy was released from the hospital. Aunt Lucy came by and picked up Mother, and they went to get Daddy. Mother had taken the day off so that we could all be together on his first day home. Lu had stayed out of school to watch Lainey, Fay, and me while Mother and Aunt Lucy went to get Daddy. Lu was excited to see him. When he walked into the house, she went right up to him and hugged and kissed him. He held her tightly in his arms and then hugged us little girls.

Lu could always forgive Daddy, just as Mother could. Aunt Lucy was a different story, though. She didn't trust Daddy as far as she could throw him, as she told Mother on many occasions. All she had heard from Mother for the past three months was how Mother had prayed for Daddy to come home *well* and help her take care of the family. It didn't matter what anyone thought of Daddy; Mother was hopelessly heart *and* brainwashed. But Aunt Lucy had told her, "Be careful what you wish for; you just might get it." Mother would remind Aunt Lucy that the Lord worked in mysterious ways but was *always* working. She also reminded Aunt Lucy of the accident Lucy had suffered when they were little girls. The doctors had told Aunt Lucy she'd never walk again, but she had—and she was *still* walking.

About four o'clock in the afternoon that day, P. C., Ali, Lee, and Paddy all came home from school, probably more than anxious about the ensuing family reunion. P. C., Ali, and Paddy all hugged Daddy, but typical of Lee, she kept her distance. In many ways, she was much like Aunt Lucy, and she made no excuses for her behavior—ever. The following Monday, Daddy was able to return to his job at Collins Mill, and life became quite different for the Chillton family. It was better than tolerable—hallelujah—and on occasion, even Lee was somewhat human to Daddy—for Mother's sake, I'm sure.

Aunt Lucy, however, was a different story. No real surprise there. Over the years, I've learned that once you get on her no-count list, you just don't count!

September rolled around, and sadly, summer was ending and school was about to start. I was completely devastated. Ya had to be six years old before starting school. I was turning six at the end of the month, but much to my dismay, I was allowed to go ahead and start school that first week of September with all the other first graders.

There was no such thing as kindergarten back then, so I'd had zero preparation for what was about to happen to me. I was being forced to leave my mommy, and my world as I knew it was about to end. I wondered if there was any way possible to get out of this school dilemma I was forced to face.

"I later found out after meeting *you* that first day, Lizzy dear," I told her, "that it didn't seem to bother you at all. I was just so attached to Mother. I guess in your line of work today, Dr. Benis, MD, your diagnosis would be that I was suffering from separation anxiety, right?" I asked.

"No, actually you were suffering *with* anxiety from just the very *thought* of the separation, my dear," she explained.

"Well, I was about to do some serious suffering that first day, if you remember."

"Yes, I do, little Magg-Pie," she said softly with an incredibly affectionate smile.

"Well, I remember it as if it were yesterday, Lizzy! That's the way my feeble mind works. I remember the best and the worst."

"That's the way most minds work, dear, and it has nothing at all to do with *feeble*," she explained. "However, the mind does have its own way of protecting us from the worst, as you call it. The mind will file the very darkest, scariest, and most confusing memories so far away that it's as if they happened to someone else. In most cases, though, that hidden memory can haunt one for the rest of his or her life. It's as if you innately know or feel something is not quite right, and as time goes on, the memory becomes a heavy psychological burden that you have no idea how to lift off your heart and mind. That's why the good Lord created psychiatrists—ta da," she quipped as she stood up and took a little bow.

"I know that's what you think my problem is, right? I've got something hidden deep inside my subconscious, and consciously I'm afraid to let it out?" I questioned.

"Well, it doesn't take a brainy brain doctor like me to know you got a head problem, Maggie dear. However, in your case, your head problem is definitely connected to your heart, the connection to the new word of the day. Didn't you tell me just yesterday that you don't feel comfortable in your own skin? Not to mention the fact that you admit to keeping the self-help book industry in business and probably should buy stock in Deepak Chopra workshops?" she quizzed me seriously.

"I didn't say a word about Deepak Chopra; you made that part up," I protested.

"That's true, but either way, I feel certain I'm on the right track here, because I *get* it! The tension and resistance you feel tell me you're ready for this change. But for some time now, that little inner child has been kicking and struggling like a child refusing to take her bath, holding on to the stairway balusters at every turn. It's now time to stop, be still, and just go with the flow. It's the correct and healthy decision for you to make, Maggie—finally," she explained.

"Well, you're the Fixer," I said half mockingly.

"Yeah, lucky for you, I am! I'm certain the reason you're so resistant is that you truly have pretended for so long that all's well that your abnormal childhood has taken you into abnormal adulthood. Not unusual at all. You see yourself basically as normal. Consciously, though, you're confused and also even a little frightened about something, but you're unclear of exactly *what*. Now, here comes the subconscious part—it knows what to do, but your fears are standing in the way and blocking your higher self, which is your subconscious. But this is normal also, Maggs; trust me. We're going to get to that peaceful place within your heart and mind. I made you a promise, and I never make a promise I can't keep. Oh, and in addition to that, I figure you're worth it, you little baaaaby!" she lovingly teased. "For right now, though, let's go back to the first grade. You were just about to get to the part about *me* and when we first met," she added excitedly.

"Okay, it was the first day of school, and for the very first time, yours truly hopped on the school bus with the rest of the bus-ridin' Chillton kids. We got to good ole Grace Chapel School and got off the bus; Lu took me into the schoolhouse, and we walked hand in hand down the long hall to the classroom marked 'Miss Reddy.' Course I couldn't read yet, but that's what Lu read out loud to me when we stopped outside the door."

☙◗◖❧

"This is it, Magg-Pie."

"But I'm not ready yet, Lu," I whimpered.

"Magg-Pie, your teacher's *name* is Miss Reddy," Lu said. She chuckled, hugged me, and told me I was just a little homesick and to go on into the classroom. She reminded me that all the other kids were new too, just like me. With much reluctance, I let go of her warm, comforting hand and entered the Chamber of Horrors.

Once I got inside the classroom, I instantly reverted to infancy. I stood there and began to cry like baby Fay. Miss Reddy looked up and growled at me from behind her desk, asking, "What's your name?" I was too upset to speak. Miss Reddy loved scaring the daylights out of her students. She got up from her desk, walked over to me, and asked my name again. I tried my best to speak through my tears, but the only thing she could understand was the *Chillton* part. Paddy had been in her class just the year before and Lee the year before that. Fortunately, Lu, P. C., and Ali had escaped her clutches; they had all had Miss Frank in the first grade—those lucky dogs!

Miss Reddy proceeded to tell me that I had a choice to make. I could stop crying or go stand outside in the hall all by myself. I chose to stand in the hall all by myself. Heck, I didn't know any of the kids, and what I knew about Miss Reddy I sure didn't like.

I was thinkin' to myself, *What would Lee say at a time like this? "Oh no, I'm in hell. I can't take it anymore, and I just wanta go home to my mommy!"* So I stood out in that lonely hall all by my little self, leaning on the wall this way 'n' that, like a little wiggle-worm. It seemed like forever, and then the door opened. There she stood—ole Meanie Face. I could see flames shooting from her mouth as she ordered me to come inside and line up with the rest of the kids for lunch. Then she scolded me in front of everyone, saying, "You should act like your nice big brother Paddy. What happened to you?" That was it; I started cryin' all over again. Where's appendicitis where ya need it, huh? And what was she thinkin' anyway? She took me to my desk, sat me down, and told me to stay there till the rest of the children got back from lunch, and then the other students followed her out of the classroom without me—thanks a lot!

I sat there all by myself with my little head down on the desk, staring at the floor through my tears and runny nose. All of a sudden, I spotted a little cricket on the floor, and I was quickly distracted and began amusing myself with the little fella. He was jumpin' and crawlin' all over the place and was quite the performer. However, he had obviously made a potentially perilous wrong turn when he had entered the War Room, where the poster person for the Uncle Sam Wants You sign resided. Looking back, I assume those signs were for the rising seniors, because they were posted all over the school. Well, they certainly weren't for little-baby first graders. What did I know about war? However, between Miss Reddy and my daddy, I was learning quickly.

Actually, Miss Reddy was much more suited for the military than for sweet, innocent little first graders. What was the school thinkin'? They sure weren't thinkin' of *me*. Miss Reddy was the worst first-grade teacher I could have ever had for my personality. I thought Daddy was bad. At least he had an excuse sorta, 'cause he could blame all his bad deeds on Mr. Hyde, but Miss Reddy was just a mean, angry old-maid schoolteacher. The key word there was *mean*. So I cornered that little cricket, took him to the window, and gently set him free. Oh man, was it his lucky day or what? Crickets were supposed to be good luck, and the worst thing someone could do was kill a cricket—everybody knew that! I was certain I was gonna have good luck that day, because I was also certain I had saved that cricket's life from the military firing squad mean ole Miss Reddy would have turned on him if she'd come back from lunch and found him in her barracks!

The other students returned to the classroom, and sure enough, my luck changed. Miss Reddy told me to get in line because we were going outside to the playground. Hallelujah, and thank you, little cricket! Out of fear for my life, I got up and scurried to the end of the line, and just like a little lamb, I followed the kid in front of me.

It was only five hours into the first day of school, and I hadn't made a good impression so far. No one really wanted to hang out with the little crybaby; they all seemed to keep their distance when we got to the playground. I sat down at a little wooden picnic table under a giant oak tree. I took a deep breath and felt there just might be hope for me after all. I sat there quietly, enjoying the laughter of the other kids.

☙❧

"That's when you walked over to the table and sat down beside me," I told Lizzy. "You didn't say anything at first. You just handed me that big red apple.

"'Here, I know you're hungry; eat it. I'm Lizzy.'

"Pretty straightforward, huh, bossy?

"'Thank you. I'm Magg-Pie,' I said timidly as I took the apple, and then I took a quick bite.

"'What kind of a name is *that*?' you asked with just a hint of judgment.

"'That's the one I like,' I answered while chewing that first bite.

"'Well, what's the one you *don't* like?' you quickly responded.

"'Maggie Ann,' I answered—rather meekly, I'm sure.

"'Okay, I like it. Magg-Pie it is,' you stated firmly. 'Are you sick or something?' you said, continuing with the questioning.

"'Yes, just a little,' I said.

"'What's wrong with you?' you quizzed sympathetically.

"'Well, Lu said I'm just a little homesick.'

"'Is that why you cry?' you asked kindly.

"'That's what Lu said, so I guess so,' I answered.

"'Who's Lu, anyway?' you asked in that bossy tone of yours.

"'She's my biggest sister,' I said proudly.

"'Oh, I don't have a sister,' you stated sadly as you hung your little head.

"'Really? I have *five* sisters,' I boasted as I waved five little fingers in the air at ya.

"'That must be *very* nice,' you said as you looked up at me with a sweet smile.

"With that smile, in that moment, I knew in my heart this was just the beginning of a beautiful friendship, as they say, Doc. Okay, and maybe that big, juicy red apple helped a little.

"Right about then, we were interrupted by children's public enemy number one: mean ole Miss Reddy. In that military style of hers, she began shouting orders for the platoon to once again line up and march back to the barracks pronto! That's how *I* remember it, anyway.

"I made it back to class without shedding one little tear. You think the fact that you held my hand all the way back to the classroom made any difference, Lizzy?

"Later that afternoon, Lu came to the classroom to walk me to the bus. You rode a different bus, so we did our 'see ya tomorrow' thing and went on our merry little separate ways." I smiled at the recollection and then continued to reminisce.

⚬₪₪₪⚬

Lu and I got on our bus and sat near P. C., Ali, Lee, and Paddy. She asked me how my first day had gone. I told her all about mean ole Miss Reddy, and

Lu's concern was obvious. She asked me if I would like school if mean ole Miss Reddy wasn't there, 'n' I said, "Well, I think I'm probably just wastin' my time anyway, 'cause I can't read, I can't write, and she won't let me talk, but I *did* meet my best friend, Lizzy, today!" She smiled and told me I had done just fine and that Mother was going to be very interested to hear all about my first day at school.

I didn't know it, but Lu told Mother all about mean ole Miss Reddy and how upsetting my first day at school was. This news disturbed Mother, so she had one of the older kids go over to Mrs. Brown's and call Aunt Lucy to come over the next morning and drive us to school. Mother had never learned how to drive. Early the next morning, Aunt Lucy showed up at the house.

When we got to school, Lu took me to "the barracks" and told me to go sit down at my desk and be good. She added that she was certain I was going to have a better day that day and said she would see me after school. At that moment—unbeknownst to me, of course—Mother was at the other end of the hall, sitting with our principal, Mr. York, discussing Miss Reddy, and after that day, a much nicer version of Miss Reddy came to the classroom every day. Talk about a personality transplant! Life was good. Thank you, Mother!

I remember later that same year, close to Christmas, my family was all home together on Sunday after church, decorating the tree.

Daddy was actually outside on the back porch, replacing all the wooden planks that he and That Melvin Bray had taken out when they were experiencing the gold rush—or, in their case, the rush for *no* gold—under the porch.

There was a knock at the front door, and Mother went to answer it. She opened the door, and a man walked inside. He turned out to be That Melvin Bray's sick uncle. He told Mother that his nephew had not been home or back to work since he had gone off with Daddy from work last Easter. Mother told the uncle that we all thought he had hitchhiked home that Friday night because the car had gotten stuck in the road and they couldn't move it in all that rain.

She went on to tell him all about Daddy, the house, the jail time, and the several months of rehab. She added that Daddy had gotten his job back at the Collins Mill but had never mentioned his nephew, nor had his nephew ever been back to our house since that Good Friday night. The story this man told Mother didn't quite match the story Daddy had told Mother about That Melvin Bray. This sick uncle was That Melvin Bray's daddy's brother; however, the supposedly sick uncle wasn't sick at all.

The uncle explained to Mother that about three years ago, he had agreed to let That Melvin Bray come live with him and his wife in the little community next to Grace Chapel as a favor to his brother. Apparently, as the uncle put it, That Melvin Bray had gotten into some trouble with the law in Virginia, where he lived with his family. So That Melvin Bray had come south and moved in with the uncle. The first thing he had done was get a job at the Collins Mill, where he had met Chill.

The uncle had never met Daddy, but according to his nephew, Chill was his only friend, and his nephew had described Chill as a righteous dude. Well, he didn't use those exact words, but the uncle did in fact come to our house thinking Chill was a hardworking, churchgoing family man.

Of course, Mother had just enlightened the uncle regarding righteous ole Chill, and the uncle now knew that his nephew had told him only what he thought the uncle needed to hear about his new best friend, Chill, but in fact, Chill was a flaming alcoholic; I'm sure that was comforting.

The uncle explained that he felt responsible for his nephew and that neither he nor anyone else in their family had seen or heard from That Melvin Bray in all that time. They were all concerned, especially the father in Virginia, who had asked the uncle to check with Chill, since apparently he was the last one to see That Melvin Bray.

They thought Daddy might have knowledge of where That Melvin Bray had gone, or if maybe he had a girlfriend. About that time, Daddy came in the back door and into the living room. Mother introduced Daddy and the uncle, and Daddy confirmed all that Mother had told the uncle. The uncle handed Daddy a phone number to call, should Daddy hear from That Melvin Bray. He thanked Mother and Daddy, and then he left.

Apparently, That Melvin Bray had lied to both Daddy and his uncle, because his uncle was not sick and his best friend was no saint.

Christmas came and passed, the 1954 New Year's bell rang, and life continued quietly for the Chillton family. The important thing was that Daddy wasn't drinking and had actually been a decent—for *him*—human being for over six months, and it had nothing to do with the movies. Mr. and Mrs. Brown didn't have to hold their breath every time someone knocked on their front door, and Mother, Aunt Lucy, and the Chillton kids got a huge break too. Last but not least, dear Ali was officially out of the charity business.

It was all good. Thank you, Jesus!

CHAPTER 8

The News Is Out

It's like finding a needle in a stack of needles.
—Harry Joiner, executive recruiter

"FIRST GRADE WAS ROCKIN', and you and I were inseparable," I told Lizzy, continuing the story. "Mother would actually let me spend the night with you at your house from time to time. I'm pretty sure your mother and daddy were, as you suggested, well aware of my daddy's wicked past, because you never stayed at my house even once.

"I believe that since you were an only child, your mother really nurtured our friendship right from the beginning, remember? And, of course, both our mothers were delighted for us and had developed a friendship of their own. Remember that time in the second grade when we made that list of all the things we had in common and why we were such good friends? The signed 'Limited Edition 2/2 List.' I actually still have a faded copy of it somewhere. It went something like this: We both were girls. We were the same age, at least six months out of the year. We went to the same school. We mostly went to the same church, but sometimes you had to go to a synagogue. We had the same number of letters in our real names. We both loved our mothers to infinity and back.

"We sure were cute and silly, too, weren't we, Lizzy? The key word there is *we*. That first grade started something really good, huh? You found someone to boss around without gettin' married, and I found yet another sister—only this one was a princess! You told me very early on that your name in Hebrew meant 'princess,' and I was so impressed.

"Before we knew it, it was early June, and we were so excited because we were about to experience the last day of the first grade! Could life be any better? For the most part, Miss Reddy and I suffered each other quietly after that first day. She wanted Paddy; I wanted Miss Brownie. Miss Reddy gave out headaches and ulcers; Miss Brownie gave out brownies and joy.

"We were really looking forward to summertime. We were going to

Vacation Bible School together, and who knows what else! You were so lucky having a swimming pool in your neighborhood, and I was going to get to go swimming with you over the summer.

"Yes, you had it made, kiddo! But I was glad for ya, believe me. You know the saying '*Mi casa es su casa*'? In our case, we just reversed it, and I sure loved going to *your* casa!

"We did in fact have a wonderful summer that year, didn't we?

"We both went on trips to visit our grandparents the week of July Fourth. We went to the O'Malleys' and visited Papa and Miss Libby and, of course, *all* the O'Malley clan. Papa had gotten remarried to Miss Libby several years after he and Grandma divorced. Aunt Lucy always went with us to Papa's, which made it even more fun. Your family went to visit your daddy's parents up north.

"Hey, that's another thing we forgot to add to our in-common list: we both went to our grandparents' for July Fourth each year. Make a note of that!" I laughed and then grew more serious as I remembered the rest of that summer.

ᑲᴥᒧ

When my family got back from Papa's after the Fourth of July, That Melvin Bray's uncle came back to our house, but this time, he brought his brother, That Melvin Bray's father from Virginia. Daddy sat out on the front porch and talked with them for quite a while. When they left, Daddy showed Mother a photo that the father had given him. It was a large color picture of his son, and the man in the photo looked exactly as That Melvin Bray looked in real life. Mother appeared to study the picture as she walked back to the kitchen and put it in a drawer.

It had been over six months since the uncle had been to our house that first time at Christmas, and they still had not seen or had any contact with That Melvin Bray. The father had decided to hire a private detective to try to find his son. He was going to go to the Grace Chapel sheriff's office to ask the sheriff to distribute the photos and get the news out throughout our little town. He had already gone to the Collins Mill and done the same thing. Daddy suggested he also take some photos up to Charlie's Place, because everybody up there knew That Melvin Bray. The father and uncle both agreed that was a good idea.

On that day, Mother told Daddy that she had always had an uneasy feeling about That Melvin Bray and that finding him was going to be like finding a needle in a stack of needles. But if he wanted to be found, she said, he'd show up somewhere sometime.

Not long after that, the sheriff made a visit to the house to talk to Daddy about That Melvin Bray. He told Daddy that a fella up at Charlie's Place thought he'd seen That Melvin Bray sitting in a car with a woman in the parking lot at Charlie's, but the fella hadn't actually talked to That Melvin Bray. Until then, I believe the sheriff thought Daddy had something to do with That Melvin Bray's disappearance. He couldn't be sure if Daddy was actually clueless or compliant. Or maybe he thought the two of 'em had cooked up some scheme to leave town, with That Melvin Bray leaving first.

Anyway, the sheriff quizzed Daddy for any other information he might have had that could possibly assist him in his search for That Melvin Bray. The sheriff left, and that was pretty much the end of it. We never saw the uncle, the father, or That Melvin Bray again. I figured his father probably found him or that he joined the army—couldn't have hurt.

CHAPTER 9

The Surprise

Destiny is not a matter of chance, but of choice.
—*Ralph Waldo Emerson*

"**SCHOOL STARTED,** and you and I were so excited," I told Lizzy. "We were all grown up now. We thought, *Second grade, here we come!*

"We were so lucky, too. First, we got in the same class again, and then we got that wonderful Miss Baldwin! She was the complete opposite of Miss Reddy, thank the Lord! Instead of kickin' butt and takin' names that first day of school, Miss Baldwin started our day with chocolate milk and cookies. Life was so goooood, remember? She and Miss Brownie were perfect teachers for little ones, weren't they, Lizzy? We settled into second grade without a hitch.

"October came, and the excitement of Halloween was all over school, as it should be. The week before Halloween, Dixieland Acres, where you lived, always had a party in the community playhouse for all the little kids and then a hayride. You and your mother picked me up at my house that Saturday, and we had the most fun two little girls could ever have!" Little did I know, more exciting times were to come.

⁊⊙⊙⊙⊙⊙⊙⊙⊙

The next morning, at the breakfast table at my house before we all started getting ready for church, Mother said she had a surprise for us, explaining, "We're going to have another baby!"

I don't remember the various reactions around the table, but I do remember Paddy jumping up and yelling, "Number nine—oh boy! I hope it's a *boy*!" Aunt Lucy was there, of course, since she always picked us up for church on Sundays.

Daddy didn't go to church with us but once in a blue moon. Even though he wasn't drinking anymore, he still had a hard time with faith and the faithful, so he just stayed home on Sunday mornings. I think you call that a case of *shame on him.*

I'm sure Aunt Lucy already knew Mother was pregnant. After Mother made her announcement, Aunt Lucy had a solemn look on her face and simply reminded us all that we'd need to be more mindful of Mother and make an extra special effort to help out more at home. Of course, Lainey and Fay got a pass on the chores 'cause they were still too little for the labor force; however, I did teach Lainey how to string beans over the next few months. I never was much good at that myself.

That same day, though, when Aunt Lucy dropped us off at home after church, her parting words to Mother were "It's not a matter of chance but of choice, Lily." I figured that was some kind of grown-up code talk, but once I deciphered it, I figured that Aunt Lucy wasn't too happy about Mother's surprise.

Christmas was approaching, and we were all feeling the excitement and joy of the season. The little town of Grace Chapel was all about Christmas! All the decorations were up and lit all over town, and some evenings, Daddy would even take us ridin' around town to see the lights when it got dark. Hopefully, *he* would see the light, I thought.

The tree we had that year at our house was so big that it required a ladder just to reach halfway to the top. I can remember all us kids, including little Fay, hanging something on that tree all at the same time. We had a ball decorating it.

"Hey, now, there's a good memory, Lizzy-Girl," I said.

Mother was the happiest then that I could remember. Aunt Lucy was so good to her and took her on a special shopping spree as her Christmas present that year. To say we were poor was an understatement. The fact that there were eight children, fathered by an alcoholic gambler who had never contributed much to Mother's income, just added to the level of poverty we experienced. It didn't have to be that way and shouldn't have been that way, but it was that way.

We all had each other, though. Other than that, nobody had anything really, but we all had plenty of nothin' together, so no one felt left out. With eight children, Mother seldom got anything new, because there was always a kid who needed something more, and pretty soon, there'd be nine.

Needless to say, Aunt Lucy's little shopping trip was a real treat for Mother—actually, for both of them. Aunt Lucy delighted in giving to Mother, and Mother's delight was simply in spending time with Aunt Lucy. The twins were as different as night and day in some ways, but they loved and protected each other fiercely. Merry Christmas, Mother!

CHAPTER 10

Lillian Fay O'Malley

A mother is she who can take the place of all others
but whose place no one else can take.
—Cardinal Mermillod

IN MARCH 1955, when the Chilltons celebrated Easter, it had been exactly two years since Danny and I had buried my little biddy in his backyard, next to his dead robin. It was a good thing Danny had let me help him bury the robin that day, because it had prepared me for my little biddy's funeral, which had been the very next day. The Lord does work in mysterious ways.

I remember that Easter Sunday when Lu took my little biddy and me over to the Browns' house and asked Mrs. Brown if Danny could officiate. Mrs. Brown was sad about the little biddy but delighted at the prospect of closure for me, and she knew Danny would be excited to officiate the formal farewell services for the newly departed little biddy. When Danny walked into the kitchen and realized what was going on, he was in heaven (right along with his robin and my little biddy) at the thought of getting to perform another funeral so soon. It was no surprise to anyone that Danny grew up to be a minister. I can't confirm this, but I'll bet funerals are his specialty.

Two years later, in March of 1955, our Easter Sunday was a far cry from that sad prior Easter Sunday. We had no funerals to attend or perform, neither animal nor human, thank God!

The next Friday, Daddy went to work that morning and Mother that afternoon, as usual. When we all got home from school, Aunt Lucy was there with Lainey and Fay, waiting for us, as usual. When Aunt Lucy left, we all went about our usual routines. About six o'clock that evening, Lu mentioned that Daddy must have stopped off at the Fancy Gap Curb Market on his way home.

Unlike today, you couldn't just pick up your cell phone to let someone know you stopped at the grocery store and were going to be a little late getting home. There wasn't anything we could do, but I'm certain Lu and P. C. were concerned

68

and wondering where he was and what condition he'd be in if and when he did get home. Yeah, what a way to live.

Ole Chill finally got home about nine thirty that night, and much to no one's surprise, he was drinking. Two years of sobriety down the hatch.

Paddy, Lainey, Fay, and I were all upstairs in bed. P. C., Ali, and Lee were watching the little black-and-white TV, and Lu was sitting at the big, round kitchen table, working on a school project. She was a junior in high school and was very focused on her grades because she was determined to go to college after she graduated. Lu was startled when she saw Daddy and realized he was drinking.

P. C. heard Daddy and went into the kitchen to confirm his own suspicions. The minute Daddy saw P. C., he grabbed P. C.'s arm and headed toward the back door. Lu, in her premeditated calm, asked Daddy where they were going, and Daddy told her he wanted to take P. C. for a little ride. Lu suggested Daddy take P. C. the next day, because she really needed P. C. to help her with her school project. Of course, Mr. Hyde had a better plan and told Lu this couldn't wait and her project would have to wait until the next day. That's all it took for Lu to get up out of her chair, walk over to Mr. Hyde, take P. C. by the hand, and slowly back him away from the danger zone. Then she looked Mr. Hyde straight in the eyes of hell and told him she would go with him but P. C. could not. Mr. Hyde looked down at the floor, stood there for a moment, let go of his grip on P. C., and told Lu to forget it.

Then Mr. Hyde stomped out of the house, got in the Chevy, and sped away like Richard Petty at the Charlotte Speedway.

P. C. looked at Lu, gave her a little smile, sighed, and said, "That's two." Lu knew exactly what he meant; he was referring to the last time Lu had saved his life, on that awful day down at the barn with the old, rusty Luck's Pinto Beans can.

Ali and Lee came into the kitchen, and P. C. recounted the whole scene for them. They immediately began working on our escape route, should Mr. Hyde return that night. We all had learned to expect the unexpected from him when the potion was involved.

"Well, at least Mother only has a few weeks to go before she can take her maternity leave from work, and then she'll be home with us all the time," Lee said.

"So what? She can't do anything with him; he's as bad to her as he is to us." P. C. sighed.

Lu was quiet. She was so disappointed in Daddy.

By then, it was a little after eleven o'clock, and they heard a car coming up the old dirt drive to the house.

"Damn him—he's back!" Lee the Cusser yelled.

Lu went to the kitchen window and peeked through the curtain.

"No, it's not him; it's Mother," she said.

They opened the back door and watched Mother as she got out of her ride's car and walked up through the pear trees toward them.

"What's wrong?" Mother asked.

"It's Daddy," Lu told her, and then she began to verbally paint a Dorian Gray picture of what had just happened with the moral leper, Mr. Hyde.

Daddy didn't make it home again until that Sunday afternoon. While he looked like one of the homeless under the old Rock Store Bridge, thankfully, he was sober. He didn't talk to any of us but instead went upstairs and straight to bed. Mother followed him upstairs and closed their bedroom door.

She came back downstairs a few minutes later and handed Lu the car keys. She told P. C. and Ali to round up us kids. Apparently, Daddy had lost his paycheck in a poker game. He told her he was sorry and promised he'd get it back. *Yeah, sure ya will, big man.*

We all got in the car, and Mother gave Lu the directions to a little brown house in the woods. When we got there, we saw several cars casually parked around the yard among the trees. Mother had been there once before with Daddy to pay a gambling debt. Lu parked the car, Mother and P. C. got out and walked up to the front door, and Mother knocked. A few minutes later, she knocked again. The door opened, and a really big, burly bearded man in overalls was standing there.

It was obvious Mother was pregnant, and he glanced over and saw all of us all packed in the Chevy, which he knew belonged to Chill Chillton. He recognized Mother, smiled politely, and asked her what he could do for her. She was very calm and resolute as she told him she needed him to give her Chill's paycheck back. He looked at her and P. C. and then glanced back over at the car once more. He had a serious look on his face and told Mother he would be right back. He closed the door, and Mother and P. C. just stood there.

A while later, Big Burly came back to the door, and he handed Mother Daddy's paycheck—a big, whopping $120. But back then, that amount of money went a long way, as Mother would say. She took the check from BB, looked at it carefully, and looked back at BB. She smiled at him and thanked him, and then she and P. C. walked back to the car. They got in, Lu started the engine, and we went straight home.

We found Daddy still asleep—oh, happy day—and he didn't get up until the next morning for work. Hey, just another lovely Sunday afternoon at the Chilltons'.

A few weeks later, a Saturday morning in mid-April, Lu and Ali were busy in the kitchen, making breakfast. Mother was upstairs resting because she was still working every day, and at six and a half months pregnant, she was beginning to tire more easily. She had planned to continue working for six more weeks because we certainly needed the money.

Daddy and P. C. were outside with Mr. Jennings, working on the old barn. Aunt Lucy had come over and was upstairs with Mother, and they were playing with Fay, who had just turned three. Lu asked Lee to go outside and call Daddy and P. C. in for breakfast. Lee, Paddy, and I set the table, and Aunt Lucy came downstairs with Fay. We all gathered at the big, round table in the kitchen, and Aunt Lucy told us that Mother would be down shortly and we should go ahead with breakfast.

Daddy didn't waste any time, because he said he needed to get back outside with Mr. Jennings. He ate quickly and then went back outside to his chores. The truth was that he knew Aunt Lucy had his number—and had for years now— and she made him uncomfortable. Good.

Daddy had instructed P. C. to come back outside after breakfast and finish his work. We all sat there at the table, talking and laughing with Aunt Lucy. She had a great sense of humor, and she knew how to lift our spirits no matter what the situation—in spite of Daddy.

Mother entered the kitchen and smiled as she visually rounded the table, taking inventory of her not-so-wild bunch. P. C. jumped up and pulled a chair out for her. She sat down at the table with us, and we all proceeded to eat, laugh, and basically just have a good time together. It was a perfect Hallmark moment; there was a lot of love floating around us that morning. It was a good thing that Daddy had gone back outside earlier.

Apparently, Daddy's recent paycheck caper and "oops I fell off the wagon and I can't get up" weekend had had a profound effect on Mother. As I think back now, I believe that the fact that she was pregnant again caused her for the first time to really see Daddy for what he had become, and she was noticeably indifferent to him. It wasn't what she said to him but, rather, what she *didn't* say to him.

⌀﹏⌀

"Today we call that estranged, right, Dr. Shrink, MD?" I said to Lizzy. "Back then, we called it a good sign. Finally!" After interjecting this bit of psychoanalysis, I continued.

⌀﹏⌀

Approximately a month later, on a warmish mid-May Friday evening, we were all at home and excited because it was Mother's last day to work for a few months. She was then seven and a half months pregnant, and we were all looking forward to her being at home with us, getting some much-needed rest, and preparing for the arrival of child number nine.

About eight o'clock that evening, Aunt Lucy showed up at the back door. She had noticed Daddy's car was gone and realized he wasn't at home. She asked, "Have you seen or heard from your daddy?" We told her he had not come home from work. It was eight o'clock on a Friday—a payday—and there was no sign of Daddy; that could mean only one thing.

Aunt Lucy asked Lu and P. C. to sit down in the kitchen with her, and then she asked Ali to take the rest of us into the living room. She then explained to Lu and P. C. that Mother's supervisor at the mill had called her and told her Mother had gotten sick at work and had been taken to the hospital. Aunt Lucy went on to say that she had gone straight to the hospital and met with Dr. Cheek, and he had told her that Mother had started bleeding. Although she had lost a lot of blood, he felt she and the baby were out of danger. However, Mother would need to stay in the hospital for a few days until the doctor was certain he had the problem under control.

Aunt Lucy explained that she had asked the doctor exactly what the problem was, and he had told her he was certain it was a condition known as placenta previa. He'd gone on to explain that the situation was more common in women who had had previous pregnancies, especially those with scarring of the uterine wall due to previous pregnancies. In some cases, severe bleeding or hemorrhaging could occur in the beginning of the third trimester. Dr. Cheek was concerned because labor sometimes started within several days after heavy bleeding.

Dr. Cheek was the same doctor who had delivered me, Lainey, and Fay, in that order and in that very hospital, and Aunt Lucy knew him very well. He was just a good ole country doctor, but she trusted his judgment. He was fond of Mother too, and he knew all about Daddy.

I'm sure he felt sorry for Mother. Who didn't?

Anyway, the point was that Dr. Cheek was not going to take any chances with Mother. He had told Aunt Lucy he planned to stay at the hospital all night just in case Mother needed him. He had also told her about Dr. Godial, who had been on call in the ER when Mother had first arrived at the hospital that afternoon. Apparently, that day was Dr. Godial's first day at Grace Chapel Regional Hospital. According to Dr. Cheek, Dr. Godial might have saved

Mother's life that day, because when Mother had first arrived at the hospital in the ambulance, she had already lost so much blood that she needed a blood transfusion immediately. Dr. Cheek had assured Aunt Lucy that he and Dr. Godial would stay with Mother.

Aunt Lucy was concerned for Mother, and she wasn't about to put up with any nonsense from Daddy under those circumstances. She had Lu and P. C. pack some bags for everyone, and we all went to her house for the night. When we got there, she called Dr. Cheek, and he told her that Mother was still sleeping and that her condition was the same. We all played a few games, took baths, and then went to bed.

The next day was Saturday, and Aunt Lucy and P. C. got up early and went to the hospital, which was about fifteen miles away. The rest of us stayed at Aunt Lucy's. We were safe from Daddy there because Daddy never went to Aunt Lucy's house—ever.

Mother was awake and excited to see them when they walked into her room. She told them that after eight babies, she ought to know how to do this baby thing! They laughed and agreed with her. She said that both Dr. Cheek and Dr. Godial had already been in to see her that morning, and even though she felt just fine, they wanted her to stay there a few more days.

Mother was in a great mood and wanted Aunt Lucy and P. C. to help her choose the name for baby number nine.

Being twins, Mother and Aunt Lucy had perfect names, I thought. Lillian Fay and Lucy Mae suited them to a tee. When Fay had been born, Mother had insisted on naming her after Aunt Lucy. However, Aunt Lucy had thought Fay should be named after Mother since she would be the last Chillton baby. Obviously no one was planning on a number nine. Oops.

Well, the twins compromised, and Fay, baby number eight, was named after *both* of them. The birth certificate read Lucy Fay Chillton, and she would go by Fay, after Mother. So now they had to consider the name for baby number nine. The twins and P. C. tossed ideas around, and after little conversation that morning, P. C. told us that Mother and Aunt Lucy had agreed that if number nine was another girl, she'd be named after both of them again. The birth certificate would read Lillian Mae Chillton, and she'd go by Mae, after Aunt Lucy.

So be it. Mother teased P. C. and asked him to spread the word—no more Number Nine! We all had referred to the baby as Number Nine for so long that I think Mother was a little concerned the poor little thing would get stuck with the name. She was probably right too, because all but one of us had a nickname, and that was Fay.

Actually, I think Number Nine woulda been a pretty cool nickname, especially if he or she grew up to be a double-naught spy.

Aunt Lucy noticed Mother was tiring and insisted they leave. She promised Mother she would bring us all back for a little visit that evening before supper.

As promised, we all went back that evening and had such a good time. Aunt Lucy had bought Mother two beautiful nightgowns for after the baby was born, but she insisted Mother put one on while we were all there together that evening. Mother was pleased, because she was still wearing one of those little blue-and-white ensembles, compliments of the hospital.

We all know how haute couture hospital gowns are—not.

Aunt Lucy asked us all to step out in the hall so that she could put the new gown on Mother. When we came back into the room, Mother was smiling that beautiful smile of hers, and the delicate, lacy bridal-white gown made her look like an angel.

Paddy stared at her and playfully asked, "So where are your wings, Mother?"

She smiled, pointed to a door next to her bed, winked at him, and said, "Sweetheart, they're hanging in that little closet."

He looked over at the closed door and then smiled back and asked, "Are you the *queen* of angels, Mother?" Off-the-charts adorable—that was Paddy.

I've probably forgotten more than I'll ever know, but the memory of that special evening with Mother, Aunt Lucy, and all my siblings, including Number Nine (I mean Mae), is a memory I'll cherish for the rest of my life. I've relived it many times over the years.

We all hugged and kissed Mother good night, and Aunt Lucy told her we'd come back after Sunday church the next day. We left the hospital and went back to Aunt Lucy's house.

We all got up the next morning, had breakfast, got dressed, and went to church, as usual. Before we left the house, though, Aunt Lucy called her nurse friend, Tina, at the nurses' station on Mother's floor to see how Mother was doing. Nurse Tina told her that Mother and the baby were doing well, and Aunt Lucy was relieved.

After Sunday school was over, we all sat in a pew in the chapel, waiting for Pastor Meyers. I was thinking about Mother and began to miss her. Sunday was the only day Mother didn't work at the mill and the only whole day she got to spend with us kids. It was Sunday, but Mother wasn't there. I was alone in my thoughts and missing her.

The last thing Mother would do on Sunday mornings as we headed out the back door to get in the car with Aunt Lucy was stop by the mirror hanging on the wall behind the kitchen table. She'd stand there in front of the mirror with her small, creamy rouge compact and apply a little color to each cheek. Then she'd dab the tiniest little bit on her lips and step back from the mirror to get a better look, making sure she hadn't applied too much. Once satisfied, that was it. Mother was all made up and ready to go. What a glamour queen. Well, she was definitely Paddy's queen of the angels. I didn't know it back then, but as I watched her every Sunday in that mirror, I was creating a lovely memory.

The church sermon that Sunday was very interesting. Even *I* paid attention. Pastor Meyers was in rare form and was wearing a white robe. He usually wore a dark gray pin-striped suit, so I guess his new look was what caught my eye in the first place.

I looked around the sanctuary and noticed Danny-Boy sitting between Mr. and Mrs. Brown. He was sitting on the edge of his seat—listening earnestly for some new verses to use at his next funeral, no doubt. I'm sure the white robe had gotten his attention as well.

Pastor Meyers guided us to Colossians 1:16–17 and Job 38:4–7. He performed his version of the Easter play—a one-act, one-man show. He was acting as an angel in heaven. He explained that angels had specific jobs to do and that God created angels to minister to and for God. The message was very interesting to me.

Then Pastor Meyers took off the white robe, and there he stood in his usual dark gray pin-striped suit. He then referred the congregation to Psalm 91:11, Matthew 18:10, and Luke 15:1–10. He explained he was still an angel, but he represented an angel on Earth this time and was now dressed in his earthly suit. These earthly angels, he said, were messengers from God also and were here on assignment from God. They were able to come into our world, walk as humans, and do as humans. We would not see wings on these angels, but they were still angels. God sent them to Earth to help us in times of need and desperation.

The point of the sermon was that we are to be careful how we treat each other here on Earth, because these earthly angels see and report back to God, as they have watch and charge over us. Pastor Meyers ended the sermon with Hebrews 13:2, saying, "Remember to welcome strangers, because some who have done so have entertained angels without knowing it." Pastor Meyers then finished his sermon and released the congregation from the pews.

It seemed to me that everyone was especially nice and kind to each other on the way out of church that Sunday. Pastor Meyers must have felt good about his angel sermon, because he was smiling extra big as he greeted each of us on our way out of the church. He did his job quite well that day. Surely God and the angels were smiling too.

That Sunday sermon was the only sermon I can actually remember of all the Sundays I spent at church throughout my childhood; but in hindsight, I know why. Amazing, those angels!

Departing the church, we all walked one behind the other through the churchyard toward the car; Aunt Lucy was in front, looking like a mama duck with all her little ducklings trailing behind her. As we walked, the Browns came over, and Mrs. Brown asked Aunt Lucy if Mother was all right. They were concerned because they hadn't seen any movement at our house since Friday, and it was now Sunday. Aunt Lucy told her about Mother, and Mrs. Brown said they would go by the hospital to see her after Sunday dinner. We called the midday meal back then "dinner" instead of "lunch," and we called the last meal of the day "supper." Oh well, no matter what we called mealtime, we never missed one. Thank goodness!

Aunt Lucy asked the Browns if they had noticed Daddy at the house, and Mr. Brown said they hadn't seen the car there the whole weekend.

No surprise there, huh?

We said our good-byes and were off to the hospital. Between the angels and Aunt Lucy, we were all on a natural high and were excited about seeing Mother. Life was good for the Chillton kids.

We got to the hospital and took the elevator to the fourth floor, which was for mommies and babies. A big Shhhhh sign hung right outside the elevator. We all sat in the waiting room while Aunt Lucy went in first, 'cause she didn't want us to wake Mother in case she was sleeping. Dr. Cheek and two nurses were in the room, attending to Mother. She *was* asleep—in a deep, deep sleep. She was in a coma.

When Aunt Lucy reentered the waiting room, the big smile she had left us with had turned upside down. In her usual calm demeanor, she told us the doctors were with Mother and we would just make ourselves comfortable and wait there to hear from them. Over an hour passed before Dr. Cheek came out to talk to us. Aunt Lucy, Lu, and P. C. got up and walked out into the hall with him.

A few minutes later, they came back in, and Aunt Lucy suggested we all go out and get something to eat. We hadn't eaten since breakfast, so that sounded like a great idea. She knew what she was doing, as usual. We left the hospital and went to that little cafeteria-style restaurant a block from the hospital and had a nice Sunday dinner.

As we were finishing our desserts, Aunt Lucy explained the sad truth to us.

Mother was very sick, and the doctors were doing their best to help her. Aunt Lucy shared that sometimes things happened that we had absolutely no control over and we were left with the job of dealing with the outcome. She said we were all going to do what Mother would want us to do.

Lee interrupted and asked what Mother wanted us to do. Aunt Lucy told her, "Your mother wants us all to do what we *always* do—our very best."

As Aunt Lucy talked, tears welled up in Lee's eyes but wouldn't let go. She choked them back and turned her head away from us.

That's when it hit me. I saw an image of my wonderful mother lying up there in Aunt Lucy's beautiful white lace gown, looking like one of Pastor Meyers's angels in heaven—with wings!

I had that same awful feeling in my tummy that I'd had the first day of school when I'd had to leave Mother. Only this time, I knew she might have to leave *me*. I was so overwhelmed with sadness that I put my little head down on the table to cry. Lu was sitting by me with Fay on her other side. She put her arm around me and mussed the back of my head. No one spoke, not even Aunt Lucy.

We left the restaurant, and Aunt Lucy drove us back to her house because she knew the hospital was no place for the little ones. She did intend to take Lu and P. C. back with her to the hospital for her own personal reasons—probably because they were the oldest and deserved to know the truth, whatever that might be. Ali and Lee were to keep busy with the younger children, and Aunt Lucy promised to call us from the hospital. Lee begged Aunt Lucy to let her go with them too. I guess Aunt Lucy could read Lee's heart and respected her emotional plea, because she agreed to let her go with them. Once again, Aunt Lucy, along with the Chosen Three, left for the hospital.

As they were walking into the hospital, the Browns were walking out. They had kept their promise to go see Mother that day. When they had gotten to her room, Dr. Cheek had explained Mother's condition. They also knew Dr. Cheek well since he'd delivered Danny-Boy.

Mrs. Brown was crying, and Mr. Brown and Danny were visibly upset as well. Mr. Brown told Aunt Lucy to call them as soon as she had any news at all. Aunt Lucy asked him if he would keep an eye out for Daddy.

At that point, Daddy didn't even know Mother was in the hospital.

Mr. Brown said he would go over to the house to see if Daddy was there; then he put his arm around Mrs. Brown, and Danny led the way out of the hospital. Once they were out of sight, Aunt Lucy and her young but mighty-courageous Chosen Three went to Mother's room. They found Dr. Cheek standing right by Mother's bed, and her condition was the same—she was still in a coma. Aunt Lucy asked Dr. Cheek if she and the Chosen Three could all sit in the room with Mother together. Dr. Cheek reluctantly agreed and then had a large recliner brought to the room to aid in their comfort. He was a devout Christian and had told Aunt Lucy in private that Mother was in God's hands now. She repeated those words to Lu and P. C. but not to Lee.

The hours passed, and the evening dragged on later and later. Dr. Cheek and Dr. Godial came in and out several times before Lu, P. C., and Lee, all three spooning in the big recliner, finally fell asleep from concern and fatigue. The last thing Lee saw was Aunt Lucy standing by Mother's bed, holding her hand.

Here's Lee's story of what happened next, and to this day, she swears by it.

Lee lay there on the recliner between Lu and P. C. half awake, not half asleep. The room was dark except for the moonlight peeking through the slats of the window blinds, and a heavenly glow surrounded Aunt Lucy, who was still standing by the bed, holding Mother's hand. Then Lee realized it was not Aunt Lucy with Mother; it was Dr. Godial. She kept watching as Dr. Godial gently lifted Mother from the bed. Mother was awake and smiling at him, and now both of them had the moonlit glow all around them. They were holding hands and seemed to be floating upward toward the ceiling—Dr. Godial in his pure-white doctor's coat and Mother in her pure-white lace gown. Lee tried to speak but couldn't. She tried to move but couldn't feel her body. As she looked at the clock on one of Mother's monitors, the time was 3:33 a.m. She was aware of what her eyes were telling her. Then she felt an intense warmth running through her entire body from head to toe, which she described as "indescribable." Then the room went completely dark.

The Chosen Three awoke to Aunt Lucy's soft but firm voice. They looked around and noticed the room was empty except for the four of them. She asked them to get up because it was time to go home. They left the hospital in silence; the Chosen Three were all half asleep, not half awake, and Aunt Lucy was wide awake and overcome with grief. There was no conversation for several miles, and then Aunt Lucy pulled into the parking lot at Grace Chapel Baptist Church and parked the car. She asked the Chosen Three to come into the chapel with her, where they all sat down. And then Aunt Lucy began to tell them precisely what had unexpectedly happened to Mother.

She explained that after Fay was born, Dr. Cheek had advised Mother, Aunt Lucy, and Daddy of the possible serious health risks if Mother were to become pregnant again. Mother had already delivered eight babies, was over thirty-five, and was a high risk for placenta previa. She should have been resting in bed for the last few months, but instead, she had been working a very physical job six days a week at the mill. Shortly after she got to work on that Friday morning, she began to bleed internally, but she did not know anything was wrong until she collapsed hours later. By the time she arrived at the hospital, she was already in serious condition due to the hemorrhaging, and Dr. Godial had to administer a blood transfusion. Shortly afterward, she went into premature labor. Since she was only about seven months pregnant, Dr. Cheek and Dr. Godial were able to stop the labor with medication, and Mother's condition appeared to stabilize. However, she went into labor again, and the doctors determined that the baby was in distress and performed a caesarean to save the baby—our precious little girl Mae.

Both Mother and baby Mae were holding their own. At three o'clock in the morning, after surgery on Mother, Dr. Godial and a nurse rolled Mother back to her room. Aunt Lucy stayed with Dr. Cheek and a pediatric nurse as they performed all the necessary newborn procedures for baby Mae before they could officially put the little newborn in the nursery. Baby Mae weighed exactly five pounds and was going to be fine. Dr. Cheek left the nursery to go to Mother's room to check on Mother's condition. A few minutes later, convinced that baby Mae was not in any danger, Aunt Lucy left the nursery and headed down the hall to Mother's room to find Dr. Cheek and a nurse standing by Mother's bed. Mother had passed away. She was gone.

By then, it was 3:40 a.m., and the nurse told them that Dr. Godial had buzzed her from Mother's room at 3:33 a.m. and asked her to come there immediately to stay with Mother until Dr. Cheek could get there from the nursery. He had told the nurse he had another emergency to attend to. The nurse and Dr. Cheek had arrived at Mother's room at the same time and walked into the room together. When Dr. Cheek had checked Mother's pulse, he had known she was gone; just then, Aunt Lucy had entered the room. When Aunt Lucy realized Mother was at peace, she leaned down and whispered to Mother that baby Mae was just perfect. Then she gently kissed Mother on her beautiful, angelic cheek for all of us and told her we would see her in heaven and asked her and the other angels to keep watch over all of us.

While I don't know this for sure, probably what happened next was this: in Aunt Lucy's wisdom, she asked Dr. Cheek if they could move Mother out of the room immediately so that she could wake the Chosen Three and get them out of the hospital before telling them about Mother. I am quite certain that there was no way she was going to wake them from their sleep and let them see Mother like that without preparing them first.

Aunt Lucy had always been good on her feet and always thought of everything!

Afterward, Aunt Lucy went on to explain to the Chosen Three that she knew no one else could take the place of our dear mother but that she would always do her best for all of us. Aunt Lucy was tearful and emotional, and as she stopped to gather herself, Lee jumped in and gave them a vivid, descriptive account of what she had personally experienced in Mother's room at 3:33 a.m. There was absolutely no doubt in Lee's mind that she was supposed to go with them to the hospital that night. Aunt Lucy agreed and told her that obviously God had chosen Lee to have the joy of a worldly vision of Mother going on to heaven with her earthly angel, Dr. Godial. Lee's vision was a great comfort for them all, but it didn't prevent the weeping that took place in the chapel that sad and tearful day.

On a happier note, though, later that evening, Lee told Paddy that Mother officially had her angel wings now and that he also had a new baby sister. Somehow the news of both seemed to comfort him.

Meanwhile, back at Aunt Lucy's house, it was now about seven thirty in the morning on that dreadfully devastating Monday morning, and the Chillton kids were busily involved in their regular morning routines. Ali was making breakfast, Paddy was setting the table, and I was helping Lainey and Fay get dressed. We still had two more weeks of school, so it was business as usual for the Chillton kids.

As I came into the kitchen with Lainey and Fay following close behind, the back door opened, and Lu, the bravehearted leader of the Chosen Three, entered the kitchen first, with Aunt Lucy one step behind her. No one spoke, but it was obvious that something was horribly wrong. Aunt Lucy closed the door and walked over to Fay, bent down, took her up into her arms, and then sat down with her at the breakfast table. Now poor Aunt Lucy had to tell the rest of us about Mother's death. As she began to tell us about Mother's passing, the heavy sadness in that room was just too much to bear. We were all sobbing and holding on to each other, except for Paddy.

I guess he was in an even greater state of shock than the rest of us, because he wasn't crying at all. At first, he asked Aunt Lucy what she meant about Mother being *gone*. "What do you mean 'gone'? Gone where? Do you mean she's gone and never coming back to me?" He was consumed with questions and asked one right after another. It was as if he thought if he asked the right question, he'd get the one answer he so needed. Of course, that answer would never come, because no matter how many questions he asked, Mother was in fact gone forever and was never coming back to him—not in *that* life, anyway.

Aunt Lucy just sat there holding Fay, answering each one of Paddy's questions as honestly as she could.

"I'm paralyzed!" Paddy shouted as he paced around the room.

"You're not paralyzed; you're traumatized!" Lee explained.

Lee never could pass up an opportunity to keep it real.

"Well, whatever I am, it feels so bad. I can't live without my mother," he tearfully blurted as he ran into Lu's open arms and then begged her to give him the right answer. She held him in a tight, consoling embrace as he came to the realization that he would have to accept the fact that his mother was gone and he would never feel her sweet kisses on his little face again—except in his dreams and, of course, in his own fond, heartfelt memories of her.

Each of our hearts was broken and filled with despair. Life was over. I thought I was gonna die, and I *wanted* to die right then! I wasn't by myself either.

Oh sweet Lord, what a deliriously sad day.

Aunt Lucy, obviously tired and shocked, sat there with little Fay, gently rocking her back and forth while surrounded by the tearful brood of eight grieving Chillton children, allowing each of us all to weep and feel the depth of our tragic loss.

Thank you, Angel Lucy—I mean, *Aunt* Lucy!

A short while later, Aunt Lucy got up from the table, still holding Fay, and silently retreated to her bedroom and closed the door behind her.

Lu, still holding Paddy, took over for Aunt Lucy with the rest of us, because she knew Aunt Lucy had several phone calls to make. She also desperately needed to cry for her own loss.

The first call was to Dr. Cheek at the hospital to check on the baby and Mother. Baby Mae was doing well except for a little jaundice, so Dr. Cheek wanted to keep her in an incubator for a few hours each day for the next five days at least. He also wanted to get her comfortable with her formula before she left the hospital. He assured Aunt Lucy that baby Mae was in no danger and that he was personally in charge of her care. This was obviously a great relief and comfort to Aunt Lucy.

I mean, really, could she possibly have had just one more thing to handle that day? Her twin and only sister had birthed a baby and died, and just like *that*, she had inherited nine kids, including a newborn. She sure wasn't going to leave it up to our daddy to take proper care of us! What the hell?

Thankfully, Dr. Cheek had seen to the necessary arrangements with Hughes Funeral Home, and they had already taken Mother to prepare her for the funeral, which would take place on Thursday.

That's one Thursday I'll never forget.

The next call was to Mrs. Brown, and Aunt Lucy told us later how Mrs. Brown had broken down into tears and wept for all of us when she had heard the sad news about Mother. But of course she instantly rose to the occasion to help by insisting that she come over and pick up Lainey and Fay, as both were simply much too young to be exposed to all the confusion and grieving going on. She also told Aunt Lucy that Mr. Brown had gone over to the Chillton house, but Daddy was not there.

Aunt Lucy then called Collins Mill to see if Daddy had made it to work that morning and told his boss there was an emergency in the family and that she needed to get in touch with him. His boss told her Daddy was there, and he said he would have him call her right away.

Next, she called Principal York at the schoolhouse, told him the sad news, and explained that obviously the Chillton children would not be at school the rest of the week.

As soon as she hung up the phone, it rang, and it was Daddy. She didn't tell him about Mother but did tell him she had all us kids with her and that if he knew what was good for him, he'd get his sorry ass over to her house immediately.

Dear Aunt Lucy had a lot of love and compassion in her but not one ounce for Daddy, not even then—perhaps especially not then!

CHAPTER 11

The Twins

God doesn't give you the people you want; He gives you the people you NEED ... to help you, to hurt you, to leave you, to love you and to make you into the person you were meant to be.
—Unknown

IN 1928, twins Lillian Fay and Lucy Mae O'Malley were born. They had two older brothers, Rory and Quinn. Rory was eight years older and Quinn six, so basically the twins only had each other as playmates since their brothers were much older. Papa and Grandma O'Malley separated when the twins were only four years old. Grandma left the children and Papa and went back to her family to live with them. Grandma O'Malley—Mae, as she was known—was a beautiful woman but was in fragile health.

Papa, a.k.a. Jesse O'Malley, was a tobacco farmer, and Rory and Quinn stayed with him and the twins and worked the tobacco fields with him until their late twenties, when they both got married and started families of their own. While growing up, they lived a meager life way out in the country and, typical of that time, had no running water in their farmhouse; instead, they drank water from a spring about a quarter mile from the house.

At age five, the twins contracted typhoid fever from the spring water. This disease was serious, of course, considering the times and the limitations of medical treatment. The twins were sick for over a year but finally recovered. However, Lucy was not as fortunate as Lillian, and she would suffer various health issues for the rest of her life.

To make Lucy's life even more challenging, another incident occurred shortly after they turned seven. She and Lillian were in the house one evening, cooking dinner for Papa and the boys, who were outside chopping wood and hauling water from the spring.

Yep, I said *cooking.* To say they all had a pretty hard life was a big, whopping understatement!

Anyway, a large pot of water and potatoes was boiling on the old woodstove, and Lucy was standing by the stove, reaching for another pot nearby, as Lillian was setting the table. Somehow the pot of boiling water fell over onto Lucy. She was scalded from her knees down to her little toes. Lillian ran out and got Papa and the boys. Rory and Quinn wrapped Lucy in a blanket, and they all jumped in Papa's old truck and drove thirty miles to the nearest hospital. Lucy was in pretty bad shape. During her recovery, she endured several skin grafts on both legs, and she didn't walk again for over a year. She spent eight months in the hospital, and Grandma O'Malley and Lillian stayed at the hospital with her as much as possible.

Apparently, Grandma was from a well-to-do family, and Papa just didn't fit into their plans. Grandma's family hadn't taken it very well when Papa and Grandma had run off and eloped, and it hadn't been a shotgun wedding either! They had been just eighteen. Fifteen months later, Rory had been born, and two years later, Quinn had been born.

During the next five years, Grandma had gone back and forth to her parents' because of her frail health. The doctors had advised her not to have any more children; however, at twenty-six, she had become pregnant again, and the twins had been born. When the twins were four years old, she had gone back to her family for good, leaving the boys and the twins with Papa. The twins had to grow up fast under some incredibly harsh circumstances.

Grandma O'Malley died of heart failure before she was fifty. I didn't remember her at all. I knew her only through her beautiful photos and through Mother's, Aunt Lucy's, and the older kids' memories. I wasn't even a year old when she died.

One disturbing part of their upbringing was that the twins—my mother, Lillian, and Aunt Lucy—had a mother, my grandma O'Malley, who was born into a family of considerable means. However, apparently Grandma's parents didn't feel any responsibility toward her four children, their own grandchildren! They stood by and watched them live in squalor-type conditions and endure great hardships, just to teach Grandma and Papa a lesson.

Shame on them! As it turned out, Mother got to go to school, but Aunt Lucy made it only to the seventh grade before quitting due to her chronic poor health. She absolutely loved school, and Mother was just as sad as Aunt Lucy when it became apparent that Aunt Lucy wouldn't get to continue school.

As life went on, however, what made Aunt Lucy different also made her exceptional. She suffered and toiled for years with various acute and serious illnesses, and she constantly endured chronic pain. All of her lifelong health conditions and suffering took a visible toll on her looks. She and Mother were born identical twins; however, as the years passed, there was not even one tiny little resemblance between the two of them. Mother was simply beautiful, and Aunt Lucy was pencil-thin and gaunt and looked twice her age. When she spoke, though, people were well aware of her presence, and she walked with such an air of confidence and grace that she demanded respect from all those she encountered. She would tease us kids sometimes by saying, "Remember what they say about judging a book by its cover: looks can be deceiving, because this little ole body is hiding one good-looking woman on the inside!"

Yes, she was definitely one tough little lady and simply refused to ever give up on anything—Chill excluded.

Disease and illness might have broken Aunt Lucy's body, but they sure didn't break her independent spirit. Somehow she could find the joy in the midst of some serious trials. She had an enormous respect for life and a willingness to simply *live*, which was an inspiration to us all. She and Mother loved each other something powerful, and there was a bond between the two of them that no doubt still exists today.

Uncle Rory and Uncle Quinn grew into fine men and married wonderful women and had children of their own. They loved their sisters dearly and were always kind and giving to them. I remember that Uncle Rory once came to visit us to talk to Mother about Daddy's troubling alcoholism and gambling. He told Mother and Aunt Lucy, "God doesn't give you the people you want; He gives you the people you *need*," and he explained why.

Papa remarried several years after he and Grandma divorced. Miss Libby, as we all called her, was kind and witty. She was thoughtful and loving to the boys and the twins, and she was crazy about Papa.

We spent the Fourth of July week with them every summer and had the time of our lives. Uncle Rory and Uncle Quinn and our young cousins would all come to Papa's, which made it even more fun for everyone. There was no television, just a radio. We had a great time workin' on the little farm, doing what they did every day from sunup to sundown. We picked and ate vegetables, milked the cows and drank milk, fed and rode the horses, fed the chickens and ate chicken, dried and chewed the tobacco, bailed hay and jumped in the hayloft, churned butter and ate butter biscuits, made and ate homemade peach ice cream, picked and ate watermelons, went fishin' and swimmin' in the pond, caught fireflies every night, and climbed every tree worth climbin' on that fifty-acre playground. We spent hours on those lazy summer afternoons just skimmin' rocks across the pond—shoot, Huck Finn had nothin' on us. We even had a game called June Bug. The first one to catch a june bug, tie a string to its leg, and get it airborne was the winner.

Now, let me tell ya—that ain't the easiest thing to do either; trust me. We killed more june bugs that way. Yes, I do recall the sweet smell of summertime! Those were the good ole *good* days. Talk about "Summertime, and the livin' is easy." What a way to live!

Papa remained a tobacco farmer until he died. He was a good, hardworking, sweet man who loved his children and their children with all his heart. Miss Libby was quite a bit younger than Papa, and for years after he died, she continued to speak of him as if he were still alive, and she never remarried.

What they experienced and shared was called true love in *my* book, and I didn't have to read a Barbara Cartland novel to confirm it.

CHAPTER 12

Charles Phillip Chillton II
"Chill"

*I think it must be written somewhere, that the virtues of mothers
shall be visited on their children, as well as the sins of their fathers.*
—Charles Dickens

CHARLES PHILLIP CHILLTON II had many names, depending on who was talkin' about him.

Mother called him Charles—if he was sober.

Lu called him Dr. Jekyll if he was sober and Mr. Hyde if he was drinking.

Lee called him Monster—sober or not.

The rest of us kids just called him Daddy.

Aunt Lucy referred to him as "your daddy," as in "Have you seen or heard from your daddy?"

Everyone else, including his siblings, referred to him as "Chill-out". Growing up, he had been intense, easily distracted, and always in a hurry. He couldn't seem to ground himself and had no inclination toward self-discipline.

As time went by, though, he would be known simply as Chill.

He was the oldest of seven children—three boys and four girls. He was named after his father, who was a minister.

Yeah, hard to believe *that*, huh?

His younger brothers, Weston and Harrison, also became ministers when they grew up. Granddaddy Chillton probably wondered where he had gone wrong when it came to Chill, but I say two out of three ain't bad, right?

Sometimes, though, the preacher's kids could turn out to be the wildest—like Buddy Allred in high school. That boy was just *full* of I don't know *what*, but he sure was full of it!

Granddaddy and Grandma Chillton were kind, gentle folks of modest means.

87

Like Grandma O'Malley, Grandma Chillton died before I was a year old, so I had no memories of her either, but Mother spoke of her often and loved her very much.

Daddy was the black sheep of the family. He was reckless and impetuous early on and wouldn't listen to anyone. He was movie-star handsome and confident. I think his looks went to his head, along with the alcohol, of course.

Granddaddy Chillton always told him that the good Lord had really blessed him, but he was too arrogant to appreciate it. Humility was not Daddy's strong suit, but Mother had enough for both of them, unfortunately.

When my parents met, Mother was only seventeen and he was almost nineteen. She was captivated by him, and she fell madly in love with him. They married within the year, and a year later, Lu was born. As with Papa and Grandma O'Malley, theirs was no shotgun wedding either. They were just young, in love, and in desperate need of a change in their lives.

Aunt Lucy begged Mother not to marry Daddy, but it was no use, so Mother insisted Aunt Lucy come and live with them once they were married and settled. Aunt Lucy agreed at the time, for Mother's sake, but changed her mind later, saying she felt she needed to stay with Papa.

The truth was that there was no way Aunt Lucy was going to live in the same house with Daddy. On a soul level, she knew him, but it would be a long time and several children later before Mother would know him.

Daddy joined the army right away and was gone only two years. The word was that he was given a medical discharge, but it was probably a typo and shoulda been a *mental* discharge. Sadly, those two years while he was gone were probably the best years of their marriage.

Of course, Mother had gotten busy right away having babies. I was the sixth baby and still an infant when Mother first went to work in the textile mill. Until then, Daddy was the breadwinner, if you could call it that, but all that changed when Mother got a job, leaving six children at home, including a six-month-old baby—me.

It was also at that time when dear Lu would start *her* new job as surrogate mother. That was probably why Lu and I were always so close. She really had to step in for Mother with me at six months old, and she truly was a surrogate mother to me.

Once Mother had a job with a paycheck, Daddy took full advantage of the situation—and her absence. Yeah, he was an alcoholic most of the time, and she was absent most of the time.

Daddy's philosophy was filled with presumption and delusion, and his reign of terror became scarier for the Chillton kids once Mother got a job. We moved from house to house. By the time I was four, the Chillton family had lived in eight different houses. Of those eight houses, I was lucky in that I lived in the last one for three whole years of my first four years on Earth.

However, prior to that, the Chillton family's problems were not alcohol-related but gambling-related instead. Daddy had returned from the army with an insatiable gambling habit. Which was worse: broke and sober, or broke and drunk? Obviously, Daddy chose the latter by compounding his gambling problem with drinking. As time would prove, he was a lousy gambler and a mean drunk.

The last house we lived in for those three years before we moved into Mr. Jennings's house was the only house we ever owned. We left that house because it burned to the ground.

I had a faint memory of standing across a road while the sun set, with someone holding my little hand, while I watched what appeared to be a giant fireball hovering in the sky, along with dark, billowy smoke fiercely dancing its way toward heaven.

Lu told me some years later that Daddy had burned the house for the insurance money. The insurance company couldn't prove it, though, so they had to pay the insurance claim. My parents paid off the mortgage, and the few thousand dollars left went to pay off a gambling debt to the local yokel, mobster types who were always after Daddy. Of course, that gambling debt was his whole motivation for the fire. Oh, the sins of the father.

We stayed with Aunt Lucy a few weeks, and then we moved into Mr. Jennings's house. It was there that I had my first vivid memory of Daddy the Alcoholic. It was that Easter weekend when I was five, the weekend when the tornado hit our house only and Daddy killed my sweet little biddy.

Thank you, Mr. Hyde, you monster.

CHAPTER 13

A Good Mourning

Hope says to us constantly, "Go on, go on," and leads us to the grave.
—Francoise de Mainenon, French queen

IT WAS NO TIME AT ALL before Daddy was knocking on Aunt Lucy's back door. She asked all of us to go into the living room while she told Daddy about Mother.

Ali picked up Fay, and we all did as we were told. Lu closed the door and turned on the television to distract us.

P. C. took Paddy out the front door and headed out to Aunt Lucy's vegetable garden in the side yard. I could see them from the living-room window. P. C. had his arm on Paddy's shoulder as they walked down the individual rows of Aunt Lucy's well-groomed little garden. At one point, they sat down and disappeared among the tall sunflowers. P. C. was a good big brother, and Paddy trusted him.

Lee took her broken heart into Aunt Lucy's room, threw herself across the bed, landed facedown in the pillows, and quietly began to cry her eyes out, just like a little baby. Lu went in the bedroom and lay down beside her, and eventually the little lion fell asleep from exhaustion.

Ali and I played with Lainey and Fay, and although the television was on, we could hear most of the conversation between Aunt Lucy and Daddy.

It was quite obvious that she was furious that Daddy had never gone home on Friday after work, nor checked on his pregnant wife and eight children, who had no phone and no car, for three days and nights. Adding fuel to the fire, since Friday, Mother had been rushed to the hospital and had delivered the baby and died, and Daddy had known absolutely nothing about it until Aunt Lucy had tracked his sorry ass down that morning.

Yep, he was the *man*.

Aunt Lucy also reminded him that after Fay was born, Dr. Cheek had warned him emphatically of the possible risks to Mother's health should she become pregnant again. It became crystal clear to Ali and me right then why Aunt Lucy had not been happy about Mother's surprise that Saturday at breakfast when she had made her announcement to all of us about Number Nine—I mean, Mae.

As Aunt Lucy continued, her controlled voice became increasingly anguished. It also became clear that she blamed Daddy for Mother's death, and she didn't stop until she had her say either. Aunt Lucy's restrained whisper became less controlled, and her voice grew louder and louder as she reiterated the long list of Daddy's many sins, including his shameless past and all the dreadful acts he had committed against Mother over the years; his blatant cruelty toward P. C., which had broken Mother's heart; and the way he had taken Mother's love, kindness, and forgiving heart for granted. She furthermore told Daddy that he was a sorry scoundrel who couldn't be counted on to take care of Mother and us kids and that if it hadn't been for Mother's two devoted brothers and her faithful, loving sister, Mother and the Chillton children—*his* children—wouldn't have even had food in the house on occasions. Aunt Lucy also lamented how Daddy had turned Mother into a baby machine and kept her pregnant for six and a half years of her young thirty-six years of life. Mother, Aunt Lucy pointed out, would never even get to watch those now-weeping children grow up, and the youngest Chillton child—Mae, a newborn infant still in the hospital—would never have the joy of her mother's sweet touch and adoring love, because Mother had sacrificed and given her own life to give life to baby Mae.

I couldn't see either of them, but Aunt Lucy's voice was strong and powerful. She was on a roll. She had so much anger bottled up inside her toward Daddy that I guess once she got started, she just couldn't stop. She had just lost the one person on Earth she loved and cherished more than her own life, and she blamed Daddy for that loss.

The last thing Aunt Lucy told Daddy was that he might as well have just put a gun to Mother's head and pulled the trigger. It would have been less cruel and way faster, she insisted, but instead, he had forced Mother to spend the last ten years enduring a slow death while suffering Daddy's cruelty and continuous selfish and destructive ways. Everything Aunt Lucy said was true—everything!

I felt he deserved every last morsel of anger she could dish out to him. Ali and I were just lying on the floor and listening to all this, and then she said something like "I can just imagine what the *Tribune* will write for Mother's obituary today":

> Mrs. Lillian Fay O'Malley Chillton went to heaven today. Her death was work-related. She worked six and a half years as a baby machine and died because she made too many babies. She was only thirty-six years young. She is survived by her sorry-ass scoundrel husband; eight now-weeping children, one newborn still in the hospital; two devoted brothers, Rory and Quinn; and her faithful, loving sister, Lucy.

Ali always spoke the truth as she saw it. I told her I liked it. We probably heard a lot more than we should have that day, but I don't know if it made much difference in the big scheme of things where Daddy was concerned.

Let's face it—we Chillton children never had any expectation of our daddy standing up to accept the Father of the Year award at the annual Grace Chapel banquet, but maybe our daddy would have been in the running for the World-Class Monster award.

No doubt Aunt Lucy would have won the Best Aunt award that day if there had been such a thing! Once it appeared Aunt Lucy had finally gotten everything off her chest, Daddy didn't really respond or say much of anything at all in his defense; actually, he never even raised his voice. Maybe he was in shock, but it was apparent who was in charge: Aunt Lucy.

Frankly, Aunt Lucy was probably the only person on Earth Daddy actually respected, or maybe she intimidated him. Either way, when Aunt Lucy spoke, Daddy listened. When she finished, he left.

Our daddy didn't say one single word to any of us kids, not even Lu. He just got in the old Chevy and drove off, just like any other day.

Just way too much responsibility for ole Chill, I guess—a dead wife, a new baby he hadn't even seen yet, and eight other children who had just lost their mother.

I can hear Daddy now: "Man, I need a drink!"

Ali and I made a bet that he'd go straight to Charlie's Place and that he probably wouldn't show up again until after Mother's funeral. Problem was, though, nobody would bet against us.

Aunt Lucy spent the rest of that mournful day calling all the relatives, including Uncle Rory, Uncle Quinn, Papa's relatives, and, of course, Miss Libby. Since Papa had passed away fewer than six months earlier, the news of Mother's unexpected death was really gonna hurt. Papa had suffered a stroke and had been in poor health, so his death had been somewhat expected. Mother's death, however, was going to be a real shocker. Talk about a blue Monday coming down.

It was almost noon when Mr. and Mrs. Brown arrived at Aunt Lucy's front door. They'd come to pick up Lainey and Fay, as Mrs. Brown had insisted. They had also brought two big boxes of food. Mrs. Brown must have hung up the phone with Aunt Lucy earlier that morning and started cooking immediately. You name it, she'd cooked it! Mr. Brown had even gone by the florist and picked up a lovely wreath and hung it on the front door. He had also taken one over to the Chillton house as well. Mrs. Brown also insisted on calling Pastor Meyers to set the funeral plans in motion.

Yep, no contest there—the Browns would receive the Best Neighbors award.

It seemed as if that day went on and on, but as always, Aunt Lucy just stayed the course. With the Browns' help, she completed all the necessary arrangements and notified all the relatives, including Daddy's family, of course. Mother and Aunt Lucy were close to all of Daddy's family, and they all loved the twins very much. As a matter of fact, Daddy's sweetest sister, who was also named Mae and was my favorite, had tried to convince Mother on several occasions to divorce Daddy. Mother!

At almost eight o'clock in the evening, the sun finally set on that dark blue Monday. Now we would all finally be forced to lie down, close our eyes, and pray it was all just a bad dream.

The sun came up bright and early on Tuesday, only to be dimmed by the realization that Mother's death had *not* been just a bad dream. Aunt Lucy got all the big kids busy with preparations, deciding who was wearing what to the funeral and taking care of any loose ends. She had Lu call Mrs. Brown to check on Lainey and Fay, and before eight o'clock that morning, Mr. Brown was knocking at the front door once again, with yet another huge box of hot food for breakfast, compliments of Mrs. Chef Brown. I wondered if Mrs. Brown ever put anything on her to-don't list—I doubted it. As the day went on, boxes of food and flowers with sympathy cards poured into Aunt Lucy's little house. Everyone was very kind, and Ali didn't object to this kindness; it wasn't charity.

Dr. Cheek called with an update on the baby and told Aunt Lucy that Mae was just fine. He also wanted to know how we were all doing and made Aunt Lucy promise to call him or Mrs. Cheek if she needed them for anything at all, and he meant it too. Later that afternoon, Mrs. Brown called and asked Aunt Lucy if it would be all right if she took Lainey and Fay to Belk's and got them each a new dress and shoes for the funeral, since they were going to stay with her until Thursday, the day of the funeral. Aunt Lucy knew how sincere Mrs. Brown was and how much she loved Mother and us kids. She told Mrs. Brown that she was welcome to follow her heart where Lillian's children were concerned and that she appreciated all of her and Mr. Brown's kindness. Those Browns were something else!

The daylight finally turned into darkness, and we hadn't seen a glimpse of Daddy since he had left Aunt Lucy's the morning before. We weren't really surprised, but we were disappointed. Well, maybe not Lee; she only expected his very worst. She didn't like disappointment, and she didn't like Daddy.

Wednesday rose with an early morning shower. I lay in bed and heard the tune "Rain, rain, go away; come again some other day."

Thank goodness it was only a shower. I actually loved the rain, especially when I was happy. If I'd had to choose, though, I preferred Mr. Sun on my less-happy days and Miss Rain on my happier days.

That day was much like the previous few. Aunt Lucy did her best to keep us busy and hopeful. After lunch, she and P. C. went to the hospital to visit with Dr. Cheek and baby Mae and tie up a few other loose ends in preparation for the funeral.

～～～

"Apparently, Lizzy dear," I told her, "your mother had called Aunt Lucy that morning, and they had arranged to meet at the hospital. Your mother wanted to visit with Aunt Lucy personally, and Aunt Lucy took her to see baby Mae in the hospital nursery while they were there together. You know, Aunt Lucy was also very fond of your mother.

"When Aunt Lucy and P. C. returned home, it was getting close to dinnertime. We were all in the kitchen, and Aunt Lucy told us she had visited with your mother at the hospital, and then she opened her purse and took out an envelope and handed it to me. Of course, it was the sweet little letter you had written me, telling me how sad you were because my mother had died. You added that you had discussed it with your mother, and the two of you wanted me to know that your mother would stand in for my mother anytime I needed her—ever. You had included a small photo that your mother had taken of us a few weeks earlier at your house. We were in full dress-up mode and had makeup on us from one end to the other—just two little girls without a care in the world. And yes, I do still have that letter and picture.

"Aunt Lucy told me how thoughtful that was of you and said that I was fortunate to have such a good friend. Thank you, Lizzy-Girl!

"We heard a knock at the front door, and P. C. answered it. He opened the door, and there stood your daddy with a huge box of food. Your mother had asked Aunt Lucy earlier at the hospital if it would be all right if they took care of dinner for us that evening, so Aunt Lucy wasn't surprised to see your daddy. She welcomed him in, and he sat the box on the kitchen counter. They chatted for a few minutes and hugged each other, and then he left.

"As the big Chillton kids got busy setting the table and laying out all the food, Aunt Lucy opened the card your mother had taped to the box; I still have that card too. Aunt Lucy read your mother's dear, sweet words aloud to us, crying softly as she read; we *all* cried.

"When Aunt Lucy first opened the card, a piece of paper fell out onto the floor. When she finished reading the card, she bent down and picked it up. Lu asked her what it was, and she smiled through her tears and told us it was a check for a thousand dollars. She said she could certainly understand why our mother had felt the way she had about your mother. She said she had been expecting the dinner, but she had had no idea about the money. We all sat down at the table; Aunt Lucy said the blessing, praising God and thanking Him for your special family specifically; and then we all enjoyed a wonderful meal.

"Afterward, we spent the rest of the evening much like the evening before— all together and all dreading the inevitable *tomorrow*.

"That Thursday in late May couldn't have been more perfect, remember, Lizzy? It was pleasantly warm because, off and on, the sun kept hiding behind the clouds, and there wasn't one dark cloud among them. An abundant assortment of unusually colorful May flowers filled the churchyard! I was certain Mother was sitting in heaven, smiling down on all of us.

"I figure when we die, no matter how many tears are shed on Earth by those left behind, there's just no way you can be sitting in heaven and be sad, right?

"The churchyard was also filled with many people. I had no idea we had so many relatives and friends. I was so glad to see *you*, Lizzy, and so happy when Aunt Lucy insisted that your family sit with us once we got inside the church. She felt the special bond that my mother had felt, and that was her way of accepting your family into ours. And actually, that was a pretty big deal, knowing Aunt Lucy," I said, and then I reflected on the funeral service.

⟋∞⟍

The deacons passed out printed programs for attendees to use to follow along with the service and to keep as mementos of the day—May 26, 1955—in honor of Mother. Aunt Lucy had the foresight to save one for all the Chillton kids. She gave me mine when I was eighteen, and I still have it tucked away in my Bible, marking Romans 8:14. Along with the program, we each also received a cardboard handheld fan with a beautiful, colorful scene printed on it.

Few churches had air-conditioning back then. We'd get a big box of new fans every spring, and that spring the fans had a beautiful angel with enormous wings on the front of it. I have that fan tucked away along with some other special little items of Mother's.

Pastor Meyers began the service at three o'clock that afternoon by welcoming everyone. "The Celebration of the Life of Lillian Fay O'Malley Chillton" was printed on the program. Eight of the nine Chillton children were wearily seated in front of him on the first pew with Aunt Lucy.

Pastor Meyers was especially aware of and sensitive to each of us Chillton kids, and he reverently acknowledged our presence by smiling lovingly and empathetically while deliberately nodding his head toward each one of us individually. Then he glanced down at his program, invited everyone to read along with him, and began Mother's celebration of remembrance with the following verses:

> At that time the disciples came to Jesus and asked, "Who is the greatest in the kingdom of heaven?" He called a child, whom he put among thee, and said, "Truly I tell you, unless you change and become like children, you will never enter the kingdom of heaven. Whoever becomes *humble* like this child is the greatest in the kingdom of heaven. Whoever welcomes one such child in my name welcomes me." (Matthew 18:1–5)

> People were bringing even infants to him that he might touch them; and when the disciples saw it, they sternly ordered them not to do it. But Jesus called for them and said, "Let the little children come to me, and do not stop them; for it is to such as these that the kingdom of God belongs." Truly I tell you, whoever does not receive the kingdom of God as a little child will never enter it. (Luke 18:15–17)

> For all who are led by the Spirit of God are children of God. (Romans 8:14)

Pastor Meyers then continued with his truth about Mother.

> Our Lillian was led by the Spirit of God. She was humble, not proud or arrogant, and always understood her place before

God. These are her blessed children here with us today. They were blessed to have had such a humble, childlike mother to love them—unconditionally. I saw her heal many of their skinned knees and broken hearts with just a gentle, tender hug and the simplicity and beauty of a little kiss on the cheek. Her time here has been short, but her memory, how she lived her life, and what she stood for will be everlasting!

An attitude of gratitude is very important. This is how Lillian lived each and every day—with an attitude of gratitude for everyone and everything in her life. She was the kind of person whom you could walk up to and engage in a conversation, and after chatting a bit, when you turned to walk away, you would hear her say something nice about you! She always looked for the good in everyone.

She was delightfully disarming, she was never too busy to offer a helping hand, and she always lifted your spirits. To tell you the truth, I can't even remember ever hearing Lillian complain—about anything! She was the voice of hope and was forever encouraging individuals to "Go on, go on" and to believe in themselves because God believed in them.

I guess you could say that Lillian was just too good to be true. I have often thought of her in that way. I have also thought of her in other ways—as a loving and patient daughter, sister, wife, mother, and friend. She lived all these roles with honor and grace, and today we're here in honor of that grace.

Personally, I have never met anyone as accepting of others as was Lillian. I am honored to stand here today before all of you, especially her devoted children, and humbly thank Lillian for her loving and patient friendship to me and my family for so many years. We *all* have been truly blessed to have had Lillian in our lives, and she will forever be in our hearts and minds as a role model for the Christian life we all should attempt to live. Lillian was not ashamed of the gospel. I refer you to the following verses: "For I am not ashamed of the gospel of

Christ: for it is the power of God unto salvation to everyone that believeth" (Romans 1:16) and "For God so loved the world that he gave his only begotten Son, that whosoever believeth in him, should not perish, but have everlasting life" (John 3:16).

Today, my friends, our Lillian is beginning her everlasting life and, as we read in Psalm 23:6, "shall dwell in the House of the Lord forever."

As Pastor Meyers spoke, I followed along with the printed words in the program and silently agreed with every single word. Mother was *all* those things and so much more. How were we all going to live without her?

Pastor Meyers finished by saying, "Lillian was indeed a Christian, and I believe the following Scripture is a perfect example of her faith and relationship with God: "In God have I put my trust: I will not be afraid what man can do unto me. Thy vows are upon me, O God: I will render praises unto thee. For thou hast delivered my soul from death: wilt not thou deliver my feet from falling, that I may walk before God in the light of the living?" (Psalm 56:11–13).

For some reason, at that very moment, I glanced at the clock by the door to the choir and noticed it was precisely 3:33 p.m. I was reminded of Lee's vision at the hospital—an omen perhaps?

It must have been, since I don't believe in coincidences; however, I do believe in miracles.

Pastor Meyers then closed the service with a prayer, and we all left the chapel to attend the burial service outside in the church cemetery.

While memorial services were going on, it was customary at our church for many of the womenfolk to prepare a seemingly never-ending meal, which would take place on the picnic tables in the churchyard right after the burial service. While that beautiful spring day lightened our broken hearts a bit, I'm certain that if even one little drop of rain had fallen during that day, I would not have been able to make it through that most difficult day. I have a rainy-day list, and funerals are not on it—ever! It was sure one sad day. But then, as I recall, it was also a day of love and laughter.

While we had just been with so many of the same relatives a few months earlier at Papa's funeral, it felt good to be with them all again. At the same time, though, it didn't seem right to be there without Mother. If only Mother could have been there with us.

While I knew she was there in spirit, at the young age of seven years old, the spirit just wasn't the same as the real thing. I wanted my mother back and in person. I wasn't ready to let her go—none of us were. It seemed so unfair that she had to leave us like that. She was so young, and we were so young.

While we were at the gravesite service, Daddy seemed to just appear out of nowhere. That was the first time I'd seen him since Aunt Lucy's house, and he didn't even sit with us in the chapel. That didn't sit too well with Pastor Meyers.

Yes, our daddy did not even sit with his grieving and distraught children on the day their mother was buried after a tragic and unexpected death. Give me a break.

Ali and I were standing side by side at the gravesite, and she nudged me, motioning for me to look straight across to the other side. I did, and there stood Daddy with some of his siblings. Ali and I had lost our bet 'cause he had made it to the funeral after all. We had known we had no more than a fifty-fifty shot when we made the bet anyway. It was the only bet we ever lost on Daddy—we were shocked.

Ali later said that Pastor Meyers spoke directly to Daddy about us kids and how much Mother had loved us. She said Pastor Meyers was probably hoping Daddy would take a hint and realize we had just lost our mother but still had our daddy. Ya know, a godlike message: "Get a grip, man!"

Unfortunately, we would all find out our daddy's response to Pastor Meyers's words of insight and observations about our dear mother in his funeral sermon soon enough.

Daddy just stood there with his head hung down as Pastor Meyers read some of the words of Harriet Beecher Stowe: "The bittersweet tears shed over graves are for words left unsaid and deeds left undone." Well, that certainly should have struck a conscience chord with Daddy—if he ever had one!

Who knows what was going on in that mind of his at the time! I actually felt sorry for him. I don't know why, because he sure didn't deserve it, especially after the conversation Ali and I had overheard between him and Aunt Lucy.

I would later come to realize that Daddy not only lost Mother that day but also lost his only other fan. That day, the day of Mother's funeral, was the day Lu stopped loving Daddy. He had gambled too many times with their love and had finally lost.

I told you he was a lousy gambler.

After our final gravesite good-byes to Mother, we left her final resting place and wandered over to the picnic area for the meet-and-greet-and-feast portion of the day. There were tables set up in a shady area a little distance from the grown-up crowd just for the little-folks crowd.

Our Sunday-school teacher, Miss Cherry, took charge of us and was wonderful in creating a more joyous experience, especially for all of the Chillton kids. For a lot of the children, including some of the Chillton kids, thankfully, this was the first funeral they had attended. Actually, Papa's had been my first funeral, and even though I had loved him very much, my heart hadn't ached all the way down to my toes, nor had I felt the same sense of loss as I did that day at Mother's funeral. I loved my mother so much that I found myself pretending she was still alive sometimes.

During that afternoon remembrance honoring Mother's short life, every once in a while, I noticed Daddy talking with one of his sisters or brothers and thought about how sad they all looked; there were no smiles or laughter among them. Upon reflection, I certainly understood how painful it was for them; they had all loved Mother too, and they knew what a poor husband and father their brother was. As I wandered among all the others, it appeared they all were affected during Mother's remembrance-of-life service. They were hugging one another as if Mother were right there with them. I believed she was—in spirit.

At one point during that afternoon, Pastor Meyers and Dr. Cheek came over to the even brighter side of Mother's remembrance picnic to visit with all us children. The two of them had grown up together, gone to college together, and come back to our little Grace Chapel community to work, live, and raise their families, and they were certainly two strong pillars of the community.

I admired that they always made time for all the children, and they never showed up without a pocket full of Bazooka bubblegum.

I asked Mother more than once if we could have all the bubblegum we wanted when we got to heaven. "Of course, honey; when you get to heaven, you can have *anything* you want," she would always say.

Shoot, Dr. Cheek had delivered most of the kids in our little town, and most of us went to Pastor Meyers's church. It was all just a little family affair. On that special day in honor of Mother, the two community pillars were especially attentive to the Chillton kids—and rightfully so, I suppose.

During the afternoon, I saw the two pillars chatting with Aunt Lucy, Mrs. Brown, and Lu, and that night at Aunt Lucy's as we all went to bed, Lu told us kids an awesome bedtime story.

She told us that while they had been talking that afternoon, Aunt Lucy had mentioned to Dr. Cheek that she intended to send Dr. Godial a personal thank-you note for all he had done for Mother. Dr. Cheek had told her that might be a little difficult to do, since he hadn't seen or heard from Dr. Godial since Mother's surgery and the birth of Mae. He had gone on to say that Dr. Godial had insisted that he personally would roll Mother back to her room after surgery and had asked Dr. Cheek if he would attend to the baby and then join him in Mother's room. Dr. Cheek had been shocked to find that Mother had died and that Dr. Godial was not there with her when he arrived at her room.

The nurse on duty had told Dr. Cheek that at exactly 3:33 a.m., Dr. Godial had buzzed the nurses' station from Mother's room and asked her to come to Mother's room immediately and stay with her until Dr. Cheek got there from the nursery. She said Dr. Godial had told her he had been called to the ER and repeated himself and instructed her to go to Mother and not leave her bedside until Dr. Cheek got there.

So once Aunt Lucy and the Chosen Three had left the hospital, Dr. Cheek had gone to the ER, looking for Dr. Godial to inform him that Mother had passed away, but Dr. Godial hadn't been there; it was as if he had simply vanished.

Right then, Pastor Meyers had jumped in and reminded all of them of his angel sermon from that very same Sunday morning, the same day as Mother's death. He had explained that he hadn't delivered an angel sermon in several years but had been led to do so for that particular Sunday, and now he knew why!

Aunt Lucy had responded by recounting the vision Lee had seen at precisely 3:33 a.m. in Mother's hospital room. Upon hearing that, Pastor Meyers had assured them that Dr. John Godial was none other than *Angel* Godial, sent here straight from heaven for the sole purpose of preparing Mother and then escorting her to heaven.

Needless to say, Lee's vision was further confirmation of Pastor Meyers's angel Scripture and Sunday sermon message, and no doubt Pastor Meyers, Dr. Cheek, and Mrs. Brown all felt even more blessed to have been a friend of Mother's.

When Lu finished the bedtime story, Lee chimed in with how Aunt Lucy had told her *she* was special to have been chosen to receive the gift of this holy vision. We were all thrilled for her and, I do have to admit, just a bit jealous too.

We've made Lee tell us the angel story at least a thousand times over the years, and each time she tells it, it's as if she's telling it for the very first time. She's still a great storyteller.

That night, we all sat there for a little while in our own little worlds, with visions of angels dancing in our heads. Aunt Lucy broke the silence when she entered the room with sweet good-night kisses for each of us.

"That was incredible; what a story!" Lizzy interrupted. "I can't believe you've never told me that, Maggie! It may have given *me* some comfort too, ya know?"

"Well, I'm truly sorry, Lizzy. I've never told *anyone* until now, and as far as I know, the others haven't either. Lee's vision was like a holy gift to all of us from Mother herself. Do you think maybe psychologically we coveted it in some way? Do you think that Mother wanted us to know she was in God's hands—literally—and that we were not to worry about her? I have no doubt that my mother chose Lee to receive that holy vision because she knew we wouldn't have the slightest doubt if we heard this unbelievable story from Lee, and of course she was right. Maybe that's why Lee was so insistent with Aunt Lucy that Sunday night when she broke down and begged Aunt Lucy to let her go with them back to the hospital. She didn't know *why* she had to go; she just knew she had to go. You know, it was Lee's vision that we all have clung to for many years—and still do, I guess. Maybe in some way, Lee's vision can still give you some comfort, Lizzy-Girl."

CHAPTER 14

Moola from Heaven

He is rich or poor according to what he is, not what he has.
—Henry Ward Beecher

WE AWOKE TO THE SOUND of knocking on Aunt Lucy's front door. Ali, Lainey, and I were in one bed, and Lu, Lee, and Fay were in the other. P. C. and Paddy were in the smaller bedroom down the hall from Aunt Lucy's room. It was almost daylight, and Aunt Lucy came in our room and quietly asked us to stay in bed and rest; we were all so exhausted that we couldn't move an inch anyway, let alone get outta bed. Apparently, Miss Libby, Uncle Rory, and Uncle Quinn had asked Aunt Lucy to let them bring over an early breakfast on their way out of town so that they could all visit a little in private before they had to head back home up the mountains that morning.

As it turned out, Uncle Rory and Uncle Quinn told Aunt Lucy that right after Papa and Miss Libby were married, they had changed the beneficiaries of Papa's insurance policy, which he had taken out several years earlier. Papa had just passed away in early February, and it had taken Miss Libby a few months to settle the affairs of his estate. She and the uncles had intended to make a surprise visit to Mother and Aunt Lucy the next week, but sadly, Mother's untimely death had brought them to town a week early. Originally, Papa had named his four children—the uncles and the twins—equally as his beneficiaries. However, when he and Miss Libby had gotten married, she and the uncles had asked Papa to change the policy so that Mother and Aunt Lucy would be the sole and equal beneficiaries.

As Miss Libby, the uncles, and Aunt Lucy sat around Aunt Lucy's modest little kitchen table, Miss Libby handed Aunt Lucy an insurance check for $118,123.88.

Just another day in the neighborhood, right?

Since Mother had died, Aunt Lucy would become the sole beneficiary of the policy. Can you say *simply incredible*? Oh, and by the way, there was no metal-detector gadget involved in *that* bag of gold. Just sweet Papa relaxing up there in heaven, showering all us down here with some much-needed moola!

⌘

"Now, Lizzy," I said, interrupting the story to add an interesting sidenote, "you and I both have heard the quote 'He is rich or poor according to what he is, not what he has,' agree?

"Well, I just don't believe Ali would agree with it, do you? This unexpected windfall was probably going to assure her she would never, ever, never again be forced to accept that most humiliating gesture she had come to know too well as charity.

"Oh, and ya know that spiritual numbers thing we've been intrigued by for years? Well, just for the record, I added up all the numbers in the amount of the insurance check and reduced it to the smallest number, which is five. According to Jo Jean Boushahla and Virginia Reidel-Geubtner's book *The Dream Dictionary*, in the fifth spiritual center of spiritual numerology, the number five means an immediate change with which it is associated, a symbol of reaching out, and 'Thy will be done' or 'Have thine own way, Lord.' The fifth spiritual center's strengths are associated with 'cooperativeness and peace of mind, subject to God's will.'

"Pretty interesting, Doc, and once again, no such thing as a coincidence— just another miracle, known as divine intervention. Thank you, Papa. Thank you, God!" I smiled and then focused my mind back on the story.

⌘

While still enjoying a cozy morning in bed, I felt a little tickle on my face and looked over and saw sweet Ali smiling at me. Lainey was still asleep lying between Ali and me, so we both carefully slipped outta bed, 'cause we didn't wanta wake her. Lee was still asleep in the other bed with her arms wrapped around little Fay. Obviously Lu had already gotten up and left the room. Ali and I quietly slipped out of bed and headed down the hall, following the voices coming from the kitchen, where Aunt Lucy, Lu, and P. C. were all sitting around the table.

They all had an S&H Green stamp book in front of 'em and were putting the stamps in the books. P. C. was licking his stamps, but the girls were daintily sponging theirs. Aunt Lucy never stopped collecting Green stamps, and we kids licked those stamps and filled those books till we left home. The heavenly windfall that landed in Aunt Lucy's sweet hands that day did little to change her wise and frugal nature. Oh, our lives definitely changed for the better—and I mean immediately—but Aunt Lucy was now all about planning for the futures of nine kids, and she had the means to do it.

When Aunt Lucy saw us enter the kitchen, she opened her arms and motioned for Ali and me to come over and give her a kiss. She was always so affectionate with us, just like Mother. Lu got up and made plates for Ali and me. Aunt Lucy told us all that her visit with Miss Libby and the uncles had been just wonderful, and she said that when Lee and Paddy got up, she would tell us all about it. While Ali and I were eating, she made a phone call to Mrs. Brown and asked her if she would like to meet us all at the hospital to check on baby Mae. Mrs. Brown was all for it, and Aunt Lucy set up a time for us to meet her at the hospital.

As I sat there, I had a feeling that something just wasn't right; then realized that I was looking around the room for Mother. It hit me like a ton of bricks that fewer than twenty-four hours before, we had all been at our mother's funeral.

Surreal—that was what the feeling was. Of course, I didn't even know there *was* such a word back then, but that was what the atmosphere was that morning—*surreal*.

Lee walked into the kitchen with Fay on her hip, Lainey trailing behind them, and then sweet Paddy bringing up the rear. Now, except for baby Mae, there we were, all together again—our new family. Immediately, the kitchen got busier, and plans for the day were set in motion. Aunt Lucy made the announcement that our top priority for the day was a trip to the hospital to see baby Mae and officially welcome her to the family. In spite of everything, we were all pretty excited. Aunt Lucy was the only one who had seen Mae.

Even though baby Mae was just four days old, we would have seen her by then if everything had gone as expected. One thing was for sure, though: this little baby number nine, baby Mae, would prove to be the most wonderful gift Mother could have ever given Aunt Lucy. And since Aunt Lucy had most often been the gift giver of the two for all those years, baby Mae's precious life would turn out to be the ultimate gift and make up for all the gifts Mother had never been able to give Aunt Lucy.

As fate would have it, the twins started out together, literally, like four minutes apart. Early on, one of them suffered horrendous hardships, missed out on perceived blessings and joys of a life she had dreamed of for herself, and basically lived in the shadows of the other's life. And, by the way, she did it with dignity. Then, thirty-six years later, all that changed. Aunt Lucy graciously accepted this precious gift that Mother had left for her and would be blessed in ways she could have only imagined but certainly deserved.

And on another note, the incomparable Mrs. Brown would prove to be the best godmother a little girl could have ever had! As the years would pass by, we Chillton kids would get the biggest kick outta watching Aunt Lucy and Mrs. Brown fuss over baby Mae. Danny-Boy was jealous at first, but then he too fell in love with baby Mae. Seriously, talk about abounding blessings and joys.

Thank you, Mother!

The welcome party, including Mrs. Brown and Danny, provided a loving visit for baby Mae, and then Aunt Lucy took us all out to eat. Mrs. Brown and Aunt Lucy argued about who was gonna pay, but in the end, Aunt Lucy won her over. As we were all walking out of the diner, we ran into Dr. Cheek's wife, who had come to pick up a sack lunch for Dr. Cheek. The women began talking about Mother, and Mrs. Cheek repeated her condolences as she hugged each one of us tenderly.

What came next was undoubtedly a dark, shaded blue event—the shade I *do not like*, the one that twists Ole Man Fate.

Mrs. Cheek asked the grown-up girls if they had heard about the terrible wreck at the Rock Store. Our busy morning so far had not included the local news, so the answer to that question was a big no. Mrs. Cheek, Aunt Lucy, and Mrs. Brown stepped away from us kids and quietly discussed the topic. The women hugged and said their good-byes, and then Aunt Lucy and Mrs. Brown ushered us outside and back into the car. Mrs. Brown returned to her car and then followed us back up to the hospital.

As we were driving, Aunt Lucy told us that there had been an accident at the Rock Store by Grace Chapel School sometime late the night before. She parked the car in the hospital parking lot, got out of the car, and reached in the backseat for Fay. She asked the rest of us to stay in the car and said she'd be right back. We watched as she and Mrs. Brown quickly walked back into the hospital, shaking their heads and chatting all the way to the main entrance.

Lee spoke up and said, "What in the world's going on now?"

Lu told her we would know soon enough, and then P. C. spoke up curiously: "What do ya wanta bet it's got something to do with Daddy?" No one responded. We just continued to sit there pondering the what-ifs, fearing Daddy's well-known villainous behavior in our own private thoughts.

It didn't seem too long before Aunt Lucy and Mrs. Brown came back out to the car. Aunt Lucy returned Fay to Ali's arms in the backseat, and Mrs. Brown lovingly bid us all good-bye until the next day, when we would meet again at the hospital to continue baby Mae's welcome party. On the way home, Aunt Lucy told us she and Mrs. Brown had found their good friend Nurse Tina at the hospital, and Tina had told them about the wreck. That day was quickly turning out to be the second worst day of my life.

⟨∞⟩

"As I would soon come to learn, Lizzy dear, after you, your mother, and your daddy left Mother's funeral, you all went on one of your dad's 'mercy missions,' bearing food and gifts to one of his employees who had been out of work due to a long illness. Y'all stayed and visited with him and his family for a while, and later that night on your way home, a drunk driver ran the four-way stop sign at the big intersection by the Rock Store. Your darling mother died later at the hospital, and you and your daddy remained in the hospital in pretty bad shape.

"At the time, I was in shock and disbelief as I wondered, *What next? You're kiddin', right?* That invisible darkest blue cloud had finally shown itself! I guess it was there all the time, waiting for that perfectly awful moment to appear, Lizzy; we just couldn't see it." I paused for a moment before allowing my memory to return again to that day.

⟨∞⟩

We got back to Aunt Lucy's house, and we all went inside. By then, it was late afternoon, and Fay had fallen asleep in Ali's arms in the car. Ali carried her into the house and laid her down in the small bedroom to finish her nap. The rest of us all just plopped down all over in the living room. Aunt Lucy sat down on the couch and leaned back with her head resting against the back of the couch. Lu offered her some iced tea, but she just shook her head. Aunt Lucy looked up at the ceiling and spoke softly of all our blessings. She reminded us that even though each one of us was experiencing a great loss, we must stay strong and remember that anything could happen to anyone at any time, usually when we least expected it. She went on to explain that those experiences were not always bad or sad things; many times they were wonderful blessings in disguise. Either way, we would have to keep things in the proper perspective and trust that God surely knew what He was doing at all times, no matter the circumstance. Aunt Lucy encouraged us to try to remember that no matter how bad things might appear in our lives, there was always something wonderful to thank God for.

Just then, P. C. rose up off the floor and asked, "What's wrong with dying anyway, Aunt Lucy?"

Aunt Lucy answered simply, "Because life is God's ultimate gift to us, honey, and we must treasure it." She knew that all too well. What a wise and honest soul she was.

Of course, I know now what she was referring to, but I didn't in that moment: within a few days, we had lost our mother, found another sister, found Papa's gold, and lost another wonderful friend—Lizzy's dear mother.

Aunt Lucy sat up on the edge of the couch and led us all in a loving prayer for Lizzy and her daddy right then and there. She started crying as she prayed, and that was all it took; once again, the Chillton kids were all weeping with Aunt Lucy, this time over the sudden and tragic loss of *two* dear mothers.

A little while later, Aunt Lucy got up and called Dr. Cheek at the hospital and got the full story on the accident. The drunk driver had run the stop sign at the intersection of the Rock Store and Grace Chapel School and then hit Lizzy's family's car head-on at a high speed.

Just one more gigantic loss to endure.

Lizzy's daddy was all messed up with internal injuries, broken ribs, and a broken arm, and Lizzy had to have emergency surgery to remove her spleen.

To make the situation even worse, we Chillton kids were all dreadfully certain that the drunk driver was our daddy. We hadn't seen him since the day before, at Mother's funeral, so it was more than possible. We so needed a break, and we finally got one when Dr. Cheek assured Aunt Lucy that the drunk driver was absolutely not Daddy.

Thank you, Jesus!

The Chillton kids would have to wait a while longer to find out the details of the wonderful visit Aunt Lucy had had with Miss Libby and the uncles earlier that morning. For the time being, we all had yet another funeral to attend. That night as I went to bed, I cried desperately for both Lizzy and myself. I promised Jesus the moon and stars if He would send our mothers back to us. Being just a little child, I forgot that Jesus already had the moon and the stars. My pained little heart was so heavy that I needed to manifest my own twin to help me carry the load, and there was no way I was gonna add *dead mothers* to our list of the things we had in common. No way!

CHAPTER 15

Mother's Mourning Out

Hush now precious, please don't cry, there comes a time when we all die.
I've not gone away, we're never apart, as I will always be in your heart.
— *Carol Matthews, author*

THE NEXT MORNING, at the breakfast table, Aunt Lucy asked P. C. to run out and get the *Tribune* off the front porch; it had been lying there since the night before. She wanted to see if there was anything in the paper about the wreck. Sure enough, the story was there. Dr. Cheek had been correct; the drunk driver was not Daddy. Not that Aunt Lucy had doubted Dr. Cheek, but I was sure it relieved her to see a confirmation in black and white. The driver was Joe Johnston, the *other* town drunk. I would never forget *him* either; he was still on my psychological hit list.

⟨⟩

"You know, I still have a copy of that newspaper article too, Lizzy. It's safely tucked away with all my other VIP papers-for-posterity file. Thank God, Lizzy, that article doesn't have my daddy's name in black and white as the sorry drunk who killed your mother! I swear, I don't think I could handle that, too, for the rest of my life. And according to you, it's obvious I haven't dealt very well with the fact that I've always blamed my daddy for killing *my* mother. Yeah, that would just be too damn much, even for the Great Pretender. No matter how far down I try to push it, I don't care what ya say, there's no way my subconscious is *that* deep! Is it?"

⟨⟩

As Ali poured Aunt Lucy another cup of coffee, Aunt Lucy sat straight up in her chair with a curious look on her face as she refocused on the newspaper. She mumbled the words aloud as she continued to read the article about the wreck. As if she were shocked, she started over at the beginning and read the article once more, this time out loud to the rest of us. The article concluded with the following: "Mrs. Benis was taken from the scene of the accident to Grace Chapel Regional Hospital, where she later died of her injuries at 3:33 a.m."

Well, Lee got it immediately and flipped out. "Read that again, Aunt Lucy!" she shouted. This time, Aunt Lucy read the article from beginning to end very slowly. We *all* got it that time.

Lizzy's mother and our mother had both died at the exact same time—3:33 a.m.—exactly four days apart and in the exact same hospital!

"I wonder if Dr. Godial was there to escort her to heaven," Lee said excitedly. No one answered. We all just sat there in a curious state of mind, once more envisioning a wonderful earthly life leaving us to go to an even more wonderful heavenly life.

"Maybe Mother was there to help Mrs. Benis too 'cause they were such good friends!" Lee added.

"Well, Lee dear, you may be right, honey," Aunt Lucy told her.

"Oh, I wish I coulda been there!" Lee proclaimed loudly.

⚬⚬⚬

"Are you serious, Maggie? Our mothers died at the *exact* same time?" Lizzy interrupted.

"Well, according to the hospital and the *Tribune*, they did. And as I mentioned, I still have that article," I assured her.

"Why don't *I* know all this?" Lizzy mumbled under her breath as if she didn't quite believe it.

"It's not that difficult to understand, Lizzy. Think about it. Your whole family was in that wreck. Your daddy couldn't do anything, not really. He had numerous injuries and was lucky he even got to go to the funeral. You didn't even get to go to your own mother's funeral! You had emergency surgery and stayed in the hospital for like three weeks! Your grandma Bubbee came and stayed with y'all for quite a while. There really was no reason for your daddy or you to know the significance of 3:33 a.m. as it related to the Chilltons and *our* mother.

"Also, keep in mind, we all had just buried my mother, and everything was happening so fast. Your family was in a state of mourning for *us* and certainly not expecting to be in a similar horrible situation yourselves less than twenty-four hours later! It was just life at its very worst, I suppose.

"Nobody made that drunk driver do what he did that day. *He* chose to drink and drive. *His* decision caused you to lose your dear mother at the ripe young age of eight, and I *hate* him, Lizzy!"

"He's dead, Maggie; you can stop hating him," she reminded me.

"Nope, I don't care if he *is* dead; I'm *never* gonna stop hating him," I announced to her vehemently.

"Oh, dearest, how quickly we forget. I'll remind you—can you say *forgiveness*, Maggie? Don't make me come over there," she warned in a rather serious tone as she looked straight through me.

I didn't realize it, but in that moment, I was quite angry and looking for a fight with somebody—anybody. Lizzy wasn't rattled at all; she just sat there in her usual I'm-in-charge-here demeanor and remained in her normal calm posture. However, she was both enthralled and awed by the news that our dear mothers had left us and gone to heaven at precisely the exact same time of day.

"Well, as I told you earlier, Maggs, had I known about the heavenly angel Dr. Godial and 3:33 a.m. back then, I'm certain that knowledge would have been comforting. However, I know it now, and that's what's important to me. Your dear mother and my dear mother had a destiny to fulfill—*together*, Maggie. And it's just quite possible that Joe Johnston was in fact an integral part of the fulfillment of that destiny.

"You're the one who said you couldn't have handled it if your daddy had been the drunk driver who killed my mother, right? So evidently, Joe Johnston was the infamous one to carry out the dastardly deed. The way I look at it, the destinies of all three of them were fulfilled that night. And actually, I do agree with you somewhat in that 'it was just life at its very worst' that day, as it brought even more pain and sadness for so many so soon after your mother's death. Remember, Maggie, Joe Johnston was also killed in that accident, and I'm certain someone somewhere loved *him*, right?" she asked me calmly.

"Yeah, sure, probably his dear mother, whom I doubt was taken from *him* at a young age by some damn drunk driver, but that's beside the point," I stammered defensively.

"Well, what is the point anyway, honey?" she asked tenderly.

"The point is that the man should not have even been driving in the first place, 'cause he'd been in several alcohol-related accidents and didn't even have a driver's license, so he had no business at all driving on that road that night, Lizzy!" I whined without breathing. "*His* decision, *his* will, *his* bad, Lizzy!" I finished dramatically as I frantically searched my mind for a peaceful spot to run and hide.

Lizzy was aware of my emotional state and intelligently threw in another

I-agree-with-you type of statement, which took the focus off the alcohol-related topic that had me so wrapped up I couldn't see straight.

"Yeah, Maggs, I'm with ya. I never added that to our list of things we have in common either, babe. Frankly, I like the way you and I have always chosen to handle our mothers' disappearing acts; they're just two girlfriends off together on a little vacation, having the time of their lives, and we'll see 'em later, huh, girlie?" she offered as she smiled that sweet Lizzy smile of hers, peeking into my heart while taking my emotional pulse.

"Look, Lizzy, all I know is that as kids, decisions were made by going 'eeny meeny miney moe,' and mistakes were corrected by simply shouting, 'Do-over!' In my heart of hearts, having to lose our mothers at such a young age just had to be a mistake, 'n' all I've ever wanted and still want to this day is a do-over!"

"Damn, Maggie, I wish it could be that easy, but we both know it can't. Come on now—calm down, and let's keep going," she encouraged. I wiped away my tears and continued reliving that day.

๑๛๛๑

Aunt Lucy got up from the table, folded up the newspaper, and laid it on the counter. She started clearing the table, and Ali and Lu pitched in. She got on the phone with Pastor Meyers and then Mrs. Brown to get some direction on how we could all help with Lizzy's mother's funeral and also to determine what we could do to help Lizzy and her father. Then she took the next half hour or so to finally tell us all about the wonderful visit the morning before with Miss Libby and the uncles. She seemed to need to tell us this news and just couldn't delay it any longer. I guess under the dire situation we were all facing, it was certainly good news, and she simply wanted us kids to understand how Papa's money was going to change our lives in a positive way. She was right. We had been on a scary roller-coaster ride for days, and she wanted it stop it right then. Yes, we needed to hear some *good* news.

Lainey and Fay were too young to understand what it all meant, but the rest of us understood well enough to know our lives were in for a big upgrade thanks to Papa's heavenly gold. However, no one or any amount of money was gonna bring our sweet mother—or Lizzy's—back to us. We were all just gonna have to learn to live with that, and that really hurt! Aunt Lucy went on to explain emphatically, "You children know not to say anything about our good fortune to your daddy, right?"

I was thinkin', *Heck, even baby Mae knows that, and she is only a week old. We all know. Mum's the word, Aunt Lucy.*

Aunt Lucy made her phone calls while we all got ready to head to the hospital to meet Mrs. Brown and visit baby Mae. When we got to the hospital, we went straight to the nursery and found Mrs. Brown adoring baby Mae and all the other babies through the big nursery window. Danny-Boy was standing with his face plastered to the nursery window, making the silliest funny faces at baby Mae. *All* the babies were enjoying his performance. I realized just then how a baby could change everything. Baby Jesus sure did!

⟨ᴍᴍᴏ⟩

"Apparently, Mrs. Brown had spoken to Nurse Tina earlier to find out the status of you and your daddy. You'd already had the surgery to remove your spleen, and your grandma Bubbee was with you in your room on the pediatric floor. Your daddy was on the adult-patient floor just above you. After we visited with baby Mae, Aunt Lucy took me to your room, hoping to brighten your spirits, and of course it did—you still didn't know about your mother, though. Your grandmother told us that your daddy was going to tell you a few days later, because you were just too out of it so soon after your surgery.

"We were so glad to see each other. It was so sweet. I doubt you remember much of this, 'cause you were drugged, but I remember it very well, missy. It was a short but sweet little visit and a wise move on Aunt Lucy's part. You made her promise to bring me back, and she told you we'd come every single day for as long as you were there. That made you very happy, Lizzy-Girl, and it made me happy too. I left you that first day with such a heavy little heart, though, knowing the worst was yet to come for you. I felt so sorry for you and your daddy.

"Aunt Lucy and I then returned to the nursery and rejoined the ongoing welcome party still in session. We stayed awhile longer and then left and went to the little diner for the midday noon, lunch, dinner—whatever meal we called it. While we all were sittin' around the large dining table, Danny-Boy held us kids in court with one of his impressive tales on virtue, and Mrs. Brown told Aunt Lucy about her conversation with Nurse Tina earlier at the hospital. Nurse Tina had given her some rather mysterious, odd news, she said. It was no secret around the hospital that Dr. Cheek had been trying to locate the mysterious, odd Dr. John Godial a few days earlier regarding Mother's death.

"We didn't know then, Lizzy, but of course know now that everybody knows everyone's business in small-town hospitals. It's like a big family; it's just the nature of it all. You have to work hard to keep a secret in a place like that. So of course the circumstances surrounding Mother's sudden death and this Dr. John Godial had spread throughout the hospital staff because of Dr. Cheek's persistence.

"Okay, here comes the odd part. Nurse Tina told Mrs. Brown that two other nurses told her they saw Dr. Godial in the hospital after your mother was brought in from the accident. One nurse saw him in the ER with your mother, and the other saw him in the OR with your mother. Both nurses told Nurse Tina there was no doubt about it; it was definitely him. These two nurses were the same two nurses who had seen Dr. Godial when my mother was in the hospital, first in the ER and then in the OR. They told Nurse Tina that they believed he was an angel.

"Now, remember, neither Nurse Tina nor these other two nurses had any knowledge of Lee's heavenly vision. Nurse Tina was just passing on this mysteriously odd, as she called it, information to her friend, Mrs. Brown. Mrs. Brown said she told Nurse Tina, 'Reeeally? Well, what d'ya know? It is mysterious—maybe not that odd, though. I suppose it's quite possible he's one of Pastor Meyers's angels who walks among us.' That suited Nurse Tina just fine. Being a member of our church, she was most familiar with Pastor Meyers's angels.

"We finished our meal and made our way out of the restaurant toward the parking lot. The grown-up ladies were still discussing your mother's funeral arrangements, based on information Aunt Lucy had gotten from your daddy and grandmother when we were at the hospital. We reached the cars, said our good-byes, and went our separate ways until the next time we would all be together.

"We got to Aunt Lucy's, and since it was Saturday, we all just busied ourselves with various activities, including preparing for Sunday church. The phone rang, and it was Pastor Meyers, who told Aunt Lucy that your mother's funeral would be on Monday at three o'clock in the afternoon—the same time as *my* mother's funeral. *That* didn't go on the list either."

∽〰〰〰〰∼

Aunt Lucy and Mrs. Brown got busy preparing food for the meet-and-greet-feast part of the funeral on Monday. At Aunt Lucy's, Lu and Ali helped in the kitchen, P. C. and Paddy went out to her little garden and did some weeding for her, and Lee and I entertained Lainey and Fay. Aunt Lucy had us all busy and drawing strength from each other at the same time. If we'd been a place on a map, we probably would have looked like a small island off to itself. We all already missed Mother so much that we couldn't even say the word *mother*.

Aunt Lucy could, but we couldn't. And, oh yeah, we still hadn't heard a peep or a growl outta Daddy. Daddy who? The Lord is good!

The Sunday morning sunlight brightly dancing through the blinds woke me. Fay was still asleep, lying between Ali and me. I reached across Fay and ran my fingers through Ali's hair. She had her back to me, but she was awake and rolled over, lifted her hand to her puckering, sweet lips, and blew me a little good-morning kiss. Lee and Lainey were still asleep in the other bed. Ali and I were whispering; then Lee opened her eyes and sat up in the bed. The three of us got up quietly, left the room, and headed down to the kitchen to hook up to our lifeline, the one 'n' only Aunt Lucy.

The boys, Lu, and Aunt Lucy were all there, just sitting around the table, chatting. Lu and P. C. had cups of coffee sitting in front of them on the table.

"Look at that, Maggie," Lee grumbled, pointing to their coffee cups. It was no secret that Lee wanted to drink coffee like the big folks.

"Now, Lee, you can have a little coffee too, honey. Come over here and sit down, and I'll make you a little cup, but it's going to be mostly milk and, like I said, a *little* coffee," Aunt Lucy said, consoling Lee. Well, that was all Lee needed to hear. She ran over to Aunt Lucy, wrapped her arms around her, and tried to pick her up; it was funny to watch. Aunt Lucy got tickled and reached down and picked up Lee instead. They kissed each other, and we all had a good morning laugh at the whole scene. Lee got her coffee and was one grateful gal.

To this day, other than me, I don't know anyone who enjoys coffee more than Lee.

Lainey and Fay came waddling into the kitchen, and that meant it was time to eat! We all got busy setting the table and serving one of Aunt Lucy's well-planned meals. After breakfast, we went to church, and the whole place was abuzz about the tragic wreck and Lizzy's family. Of course, Lizzy and her daddy were still in the hospital, and since Lizzy and her mother were members of our church, Pastor Meyers did a lotta praying that day for Lizzy and her daddy. Actually, *everybody* did a lotta praying for them that day.

Monday morning, a hard rain was coming down so heavily that it woke me. My first thought was, *Oh no, this can't be Monday! If it is, then it's a blue Monday, 'cause everyone knows funerals are not on my rainy-day list, let alone on a blue Monday. Why, that's just double sad.* I lay there trying to talk myself into having a better day sorta, and I actually did it! I accepted the fact that it was Monday, it was raining, and it was the day of the funeral. How does the song go? "Rainy days and Mondays always get me down." Yeah, that was it—a perfectly *good* bad song for the occasion. About that time, Aunt Lucy cracked open the bedroom door and softly announced breakfast was ready and that she had a little surprise for us too.

Okay, maybe it's not all that bad, I thought. I, like most little ones, could get distracted even from sorrow. Something sure smelled wonderful, and I was getting a little more motivated to hop outta that bed. Ali and Lainey were awake also by then, and the three of us slid outta bed and Zombie-strolled down to the kitchen. Lu and Lee were busy setting the table, and Fay was sitting in her little chair at the end of the table. P. C. and Paddy shuffled in right behind us.

Aunt Lucy wasn't kiddin'. She had a surprise all right, but there was nothing *little* about it. She'd made what looked to a seven-year-old me like at least five hundred pancakes with hot syrup, ten pounds of bacon, a henhouse's worth of scrambled eggs, at least a bushel of fresh strawberries 'n' cream, and gallons of orange juice and Welch's grape juice—P. C. and Paddy loved the grape juice. It was the "Breakfast of Chilltons." In other words, good-bye, blue Monday, and hallelujah!

"You children sit down now and eat," Aunt Lucy instructed with a big smile. "I want you to take your sweet time, too. It's going to be a long day, and we all know what we're in for, so let's just set our minds, hearts, and faces to the smiling position right from the giddyup, okay, everybody?" We all assured her we could and would.

Before she sat down with us, she asked Lee if she would like a little coffee with her cream. Lee picked up a little cup, smiled big, and said, "Yesss, ma'am, thank you, ma'am, Aunt Lucy!" Aunt Lucy knew how to handle Lee—that was for sure. Well, we ate and ate and ate. Talk about "full as a tick"!

⚬ⱮⱮⱤ⚬

"That expression is just so gross—*why* did we say that back then? Boy, what a way to start the day, though, huh, Lizzy?

"Aunt Lucy had the right attitude for the day, regardless of the rainy-days-and-Mondays factor. Apparently, she just wasn't having any of that blue-Monday crap that I had been so into earlier! Believe it or not, by the time we'd finished eating and gotten dressed, the rain had ceased, and Mr. Sun had come out and was doing his shiny thing all over the place. It was shaping up to be a wonderful day for your mother's celebration. Sounds like a fun thing—if only it had been, huh, Lizzy?

"The Chillton family welcome-party members would wait until after the funeral to visit with baby Mae and you at the hospital. It was your dear mother's celebration, and that would certainly take precedent and rightfully dictate that day for all of us.

"We arrived at the church about two thirty that afternoon, knowing you would not be there. Mrs. Brown, Mr. Brown, and Danny-Boy were standing right outside the giant double doors at the main entrance to the church, where Pastor Meyers and several other church members all stood greeting friends and relatives on your mother's side. Since her mother had passed away a few years earlier, your daddy's mother, the wise and wonderful Grandma Bubbee, stayed at the hospital with you. Your father's brothers had already gotten him from the hospital to the chapel; he was in a wheelchair down by the first pew, just under the pulpit, where Pastor Meyers would be standing shortly. Surreal—and déjà vu all over again!

"Ya know, Lizzy, if someone told me a story like this, I probably wouldn't believe 'em the first time around, would you? Being asked to believe all this is kinda unbelievable—think about it. The circumstances around my mother's death and then your mother's death—that scene is still quite vivid. Just a few days earlier, you, your mother, and your daddy were sitting on the second pew with the Browns, right behind my family, honoring my mother's life. Now, just four days later, the whole scene was reversed, and *my* family was sitting with the Browns, right behind *your* family, honoring *your* mother's life.

"How could that possibly be? It was too much—just too damn much. My heart still aches to this day, Lizzy—even right now—all the way down to my toes.

"But, hey, just for the record, your mother's life celebration was as loving and beautiful as my mother's. I remember specifically Pastor Meyers making reference to the fact that you were unable to attend your own mother's funeral due to your injuries in the car wreck. He recited a beautiful quote for your daddy to share with you, though, when the time was appropriate. He said your mother wanted you to know 'I've not gone away, we're never apart, and I'll always be in your heart.' I think that was it; I can't remember exactly, but I do remember it was profoundly perfect in that moment, and it sounded exactly like what your sweet mother would have said to you. It was just so her, so sweet.

"There was one huge difference, though, between the two celebrations. Granted your mother wasn't there—yes, in spirit she was, of course, I know—but as Pastor Myers brought to everyone's attention, *you* weren't there in *any* form. I've often wondered if not being there that day left you with any permanent scars. However, the way you deal with issues, so utterly logically, if the psychological truth is known, *I'm* the one who's wearing those scars.

Not that you asked me to—I'm just too damn nice. That's what you told me yesterday, remember?

"Say, speaking of smoking, I feel like *I'm* the one who should take up the habit—like right now! Ya don't happen to have a loooong, skinny cigarette stuck in a little secret-box drawer, do ya?"

"Well, actually, I do have some cigarettes around here somewhere. Not mine, of course, but if I find 'em, they're mine. Let me see now … Oh, here they are—in this little cigarette case. Well, of all the places for cigarettes to be, really! Okay, I got 'em, Maggs. Let's go out on the patio and light up, and I'll even join ya! Nobody's the boss of us; we can smoke 'em if we got 'em, right?" Lizzy teased with a playful attitude in spite of all the funeral talk.

"Well, I was half kiddin', but why not?" I agreed.

"Hey, let's open a bottle of pinot too, Maggs! Aren't cigarettes much better if you're drinking?" she asked with enthusiasm.

"Yep, it's true. The awful taste of the alcohol masks the awful taste of the cigarette, making the whole process a little less awful. Personally, as you know, Lizzy, I love to smoke; I just had to give it up for Lent," I added.

"*Lent*? Liar! Okay, I'm getting the wine; you light us up," she instructed as she walked back inside to get the wine out of the cooler.

It seemed the visit back to the two-mother-funeral chapter on memory lane had hit an old, raw nerve. It was just a little bit much for me, and Lizzy got it; I needed a break. She *was* the doctor, right?

As I waited for her to get back with the wine, I realized that I really wasn't alone on my little trip. Whether Lizzy realized it or not, she and I were walking hand in hand down the shared memories of memory lane.

It might sound selfish, but I was comforted by that.

Ummmm, what's happening to me?

Lizzy walked back out to the patio with two sweaters, a couple of towels, and a tray with a bottle of pinot noir and two perfectly ballooned long-stemmed wine glasses.

By then, I was lying all stretched out in the chaise by the pool, with a long, skinny cigarette in each hand, puffin' on both.

"Well, Maggs, it's after midnight, and there's a chill in the air; I say we don the jackets, throw in the towels, and watch 'em swim around till they sink while we proceed to get our groove on." She laughed. "And give me my cigarette!" she added.

"That's the best advice I've heard all day long, Dr. Benis, and here, take your cigarette—what's left of it," I teased.

We proceeded to do some serious drinkin' and thinkin'—my most vulnerable state of mind. Over the next few hours, we covered a lot—I think. Thank goodness Lizzy was recording it all, 'cause we sure weren't gonna remember it.

One thing's for sure: we did a lotta laughin', 'cause my face was hurting when I woke up. Of course, maybe that was from all that puckering I did, smoking all those damn cigarettes!

At one point, Lizzy offered an apology: "Sorry I had to pull that knife on ya, Maggs, with all that forgiveness business earlier, but you gotta get that hate outta your heart!"

Do I dare ask? Is she right about this? Is she right about everything?

Nobody's right about everything, right?

CHAPTER 16

Parlez Vous Francais?

If you get a second chance, grab it with both hands. If it changes your life, let it. Nobody said life would be easy. GOD promised it would be worth it.
                                                            —*Author unknown*

SOMETIME IN THE MIDDLE OF THE NIGHT, we must have made our way to bed and fallen in. I woke up fully clothed, lying horizontally across the bed; my dry, parched mouth tasted like at least a carton of the stale, crumpled Lucky Strikes Daddy stuck between two planks in the old woodshed for safekeeping. Pretty bad—trust me.

That seemed to be the worst of it, though. I was certain I hadn't destroyed the house or blown up the pool Chill-style. That's what *he* was always faced with when he woke up from alcohol: destruction. Fortunately, alcohol didn't turn *me* into a monster. However, I hadn't touched one little toe on the floor yet; I just continued to lie there, coaxing myself to try it. My concern was with a get-up-and-throw-up vision of myself, so I wasn't in too big of a hurry.

Before I could move a muscle, in waltzed Miss Priss. "*Bonjour, mon amie!* Oh, aren't we the peak of chic this morning? It's fine, though, since there's no dress code for the first seating. Come on—I'm serving a fabulous breakfast out on the patio, *mon amie.* Come on. Get up; it's a beautiful day!" She hummed the whole invitation as she waltzed back out of the bedroom. I was a little surprised she didn't skate in. That Lizzy—what a performer!

"Okay, if you're saying we're still *alive*, then I'm comin'. I'm comin'—hang on!" I made a big effort to hum my reply back at her. I placed one foot on the floor and then immediately felt the need to grab my head. *Oh yeah, there you are, mean ole hangover.* I rose to my feet and Frankensteinishly lumbered out to the patio to find confirmation of Lizzy's "fabulous breakfast" claim. The closer I got to the door leading to the patio, the louder the music got.

Was it real or just in my head? I wasn't familiar with the tune, but it was quite lovely. I stopped for a moment to listen and realized it was in French—no

120

wonder. Lizzy spoke fluent French and had been to France several times. She and I had even visited Paris and the south of France together a few years ago, when I'd been invited to speak at a gallery event at the Louvre. I kept walking toward the door, thinking, *What is she up to now?* and then stepped out onto the patio and—voilà—we were back in Provence!

At first I thought, *Oh wow, now I'm having one of Mother's in-body experiences, and thankfully, it's a very good one.* Lizzy was obviously trying to outdo Aunt Lucy with this "Breakfast of Blonde Bingers." In other words, gooood-bye, mean ole hangover!

One thing's for sure, though: I had gone to bed in Boston and awakened in France. The ambience of it all was simply perfection—the music, the elegant table setting, the food, the food, and the food. It was fabulous, and Lizzy had been right—again.

"Maggs, if you can't find something you like here, then just sit down and watch *me* eat!" she said as she stuffed her mouth with strawberries 'n' cream and somehow handed me my hot vitamin-java at the same time. Thank you, Mademoiselle Doctor!

"When on earth did you do all this, *mon amie* Lizzy? This is breathtaking!" I proclaimed loudly.

"I guess all that damn nicotine wired me and kept me from sleeping; of course, I thought that second bottle of wine would for sure knock me on my fanny, but maybe the nicotine absorbed the wine for me and kept me from sleeping. Shoot, I don't know—what am I, a pharmacist? No, that's not it; it does start with a *p*, though, right?" she asked without taking one breath and, yes, totally wired, obviously from the nicotine and no sleep.

"Yeah, you're that *other p*—for *psychiatrist*. Oh, and no more nicotine for *you*, Nicky, ya hear me?" I playfully chided.

"Funny, Maggs—real funny," she mumbled with a mouth full of cheese soufflé.

"Well, I don't know how you did it, but for what it's worth, I'm impressed to infinity and back, Lizzy-Girl. May I please have the croissants and confiture?" I asked as I reached out to take the dish from her.

"Man, what a day, what a night, and, yeah, what a mornin'! I agree with ya, Magg-Pie; I've simply outdone myself. And do you realize that in the last twenty-four hours, we've covered some serious past, little sister?" she asked me as she took a big gulp of straight lemon water. "Okay, let's see now: alcohol, tornadoes, biddies, beatings, babies, best friends, charity, children, grandmothers, grandfathers, gold, God, monsters, mothers, moola, uncles, aunts, angels, the Fourth of July, families, funerals, forgiveness. Have I left anything out?" she asked amusingly.

"I don't think ya mentioned my daddy, did ya? Oh, maybe he's a subtitle under 'alcohol,' yes? That's certainly where he belongs!" I replied ardently.

"Your daddy is all over this, dear! He's what this whole thing is about, Maggs, and frankly, I sincerely believe you're just a little angry with your dear mother as well. Oh, you aren't consciously, but you are, dearest!

"If you'll remember, Ali and Lee certainly were. As a matter of fact, they were quite outspoken at times, questioning your mother as to why she didn't stop the madness and make him leave, right?" She stopped, waiting for my reply.

"Yep, once again, you can see the forest for the trees, Dr. Shrink. It's hard, but I must admit that over the years, this has been a debatable topic for the Chillton siblings. Of course, Lainey, Fay, and Mae are excluded since our memories are not theirs. They were just too young. Mae was the lucky one, except for losing out totally on Mother, of course. But she didn't have to experience the wrath of Daddy either. That was definitely a good thing! Yeah, she really was the lucky one. She hates him only because the rest of us do, but hating vicariously is just not the same. That kind of hate can't destroy you, can it, Dr. Shrink?" I asked seriously.

"Maggie, any kind of hate can destroy one," she explained.

"Oh, there you go again with the *Maggie*. Are we rollin'?" I asked curiously.

"Yes, we're *recorrrrding*, Maaaaggie," she said mockingly.

"Oh brother. Okay, Miss Serious, do me a favor 'n' pass me somethin' from your side of the table, will ya? How 'bout some of those crepes?" I politely requested.

"I'll trade ya the crepes for the *croque*, Madame Eggs and Ham," she negotiated as she passed my request over to me.

"You've been eating this entire time! Where in the world do you put all this food, Mademoiselle Lizzy?" I asked as I returned the favor.

"You know, I've often thought about this myself; plus, you and I have always teased about my voracious appetite, right? Well, the only thing I can come up with is the fact that very early on in my childhood, my father belonged to a small group of Jewish men at the synagogue who were the most prominent members of the congregation. They founded this special Funds for Families Organization, a.k.a. the FFO, which provided food, housing, clothing, and other necessities to needy families in Jerusalem. I heard many stories from my father and mother about all the starvation and strife the children there had to endure, how sinful it was to see the amount of waste all around us here, and how blessed we were. As a result of this important childhood lesson and parental perspective to be mindful of others less fortunate, I guess I developed a taste for food and material things in the name of appreciation but, at the same time, out of a fear of not having enough myself. My kind of head stuff, huh, Maggs?

"Well, little sister, I had no intention of ever going hungry or without. I didn't want to even imagine what life was like for the children over there, and I certainly didn't want to be one of them. It sounds so selfish, but I didn't feel selfish; I felt sad.

"You know I've been willing to work hard for every single thing I wanted in life and have intended to share whatever I have with them, as did my father. After med school, I joined my father at the FFO, and I am an active member to this day.

"Now, to answer the 'where do I put all this food I eat' part of your original question—well, it beats me! I have a love affair with food and eat like there's no tomorrow, and somehow I still resemble someone who's probably hungry—not anorexic, just hungry.

"An old Jewish proverb my wise and wonderful grandma Bubbee used to say repeatedly to me was 'As you do, so will be done to you.' That's the Jewish version of the Christians' Golden Rule: 'Do unto others as you would have them do unto you.' Right, Maggs? Well, either way, I don't want to be hungry or go without, nor do I want anyone else to suffer," she finished as she reached for an extra crepe filled with ricotta cheese and blueberries.

"I agree with ya, Lizzy. Your concern for the children in Jerusalem way back then just got to ya, and your delicious love affair with food, as you so wisely described it, developed in a psychological way, I suppose. And no, you weren't selfish. You were just a little child, dealing with a scary-to-you dilemma in your own way, just like you do everything else in your life—your own way. Pass me those crepes, will ya? I rest my humble opinion."

"Hey, listen to you. *You're* shrinking *me*! Thanks, that was some good insight, Maggs; I appreciate it. Here's your crepes, dear—eat up. I'm actually getting full as a tick," she said with a laugh.

"Oh, *fermez la bouche*! So gross, mademoiselle! Yuck, and thanks for that memory while I'm still eating!"

We pretty much devoured enough food for two and a half FFO families that morning. It was amazing and pretty scary at the same time. I kept on praising Lizzy for her stellar performance, not to mention her abundant, incredible array of delectable delicacies. It was truly a Julia-and-Jacques presentation straight from Provence, and she accomplished it all while I slept. That Lizzy—what a performer.

As we sat there at the table in the cool fall morning sunlight, I went on and on about the morning she had provided for us, and she was about to say something like "Oh, it was nothing, Maggs. I couldn't sleep, so I just threw a bunch of stuff together. Really, it was my pleasure; no big deal, dear, blah, blah, blah," when suddenly she was interrupted by two fellas in white coats pushing a large steel cart onto the patio from the side gate.

As they headed toward us at the table, Lizzy got up and motioned for them to join us. She greeted them and thanked them graciously for the beautiful morning they had provided us. Once they began to clear the table and load their cart with china, silver, crystal, and linens, Lizzy left the table to them and ushered me over to the pool to reclaim our chaise lounges, where we had stayed until the wee hours just a few hours earlier.

As we approached the pool, I noticed the towels we had thrown in the night before resting on the bottom of the pool, just waiting to be rescued. As Lizzy parked herself in the first chaise, I caught a glimpse of her eyeing me with one of her impish little grins and one eyebrow arched slightly higher than the other.

I hadn't said a word yet, but I had noticed a big white truck parked on the street by the side gate with "Bon Appétit Catering" painted on the side of it. I started laughing. By the time I made it over to her, she was lying on the chaise, laughing her butt off at me.

"I had ya going, Maggs, didn't I, ole girl? Ya know I did."

I lay down on the chaise next to her and joined in the laughter. Yep, she had gotten me. "My, what a morning after. Sneaky, *Nicky*—you just never cease to amaze me, ya know that?" I said.

"Thanks, little Magg-Pie. I did want to surprise you this morning and start our day with unexpected pleasures. Last night got a little heated, although it was all good and going in the right direction toward healing. I'm hopeful our little visit to France this morning was deliciously therapeutic as well. It sure worked for me, Maggs! By the way, I can't believe you actually thought I prepared all that food. Have you forgotten that I serve four meals only—frozen, microwavable, takeout, and, occasionally, catered? I'm into the joy of food, certainly not the *Joy of Cooking*. Ya know, 'Nobody said life would be easy. God promised it would be worth it.' I rest my humble opinion!"

"*Oui*, Mademoiselle Benis—as always, God is right. That touch of France was worth it indeed! Yep, ya had me goin', but frankly I don't care *who* did the cooking. I'm with you, ole girl; my joy was in the eating as well, and man, was that some gooood eatin'! Ya think you could get those folks back out here for dinner tonight, *s'il vu plait*?" I asked in my best French.

"*Oui*, madame. That's not a bad idea, but maybe we should try some other country for dinner—maybe a little farther south? You know, like in 'way down south in Dixie'?" she questioned in song.

"Well, that's definitely another country, but sure—I'm in, Boss Hogg," I agreed.

"That'll be fun, Maggs! We'll get to enjoy the kind of cooking we grew up enjoying. I'll have to find the perfect place. One with a unique ambience complete with rednecks and great food like red beans, those little red potatoes, ripe red tomatoes, and—oh wow—some red velvet cake! Say, what else is red and edible?" she asked with a big smile as she shrugged her shoulders.

We had barely finished one feast, and now she was planning the next. I was just about to pop. *Sommmebody help me!*

"Hey, while we're out here lying by the pool and digesting, why don't we take a short little visit back, okay, Maggs?"

"Oh great, I just love hearing myself talk, so fine by me. Can't wait to hear what I'm gonna say next, can you? Let's see—where did we get to before we lost our footing and fell into bed last night or this morning or whenever that was?" I questioned.

"Well, here, let me check the rolling machine, as you call it," she replied as she touched the rewind button on the recorder. "Okay, we stopped at my dear mother's funeral," she confirmed.

"All right now, Dr. Benis, if I remember correctly, your mother's death was actually harder on your daddy than you. At least, that's the way I remember it. Maybe it was a good thing you weren't able to attend your mother's funeral. Is that possible?

"Once you finally got outta the hospital, I remember that Grandma Bubbee stayed at your house with you and your daddy for several months.

"She was much like Aunt Lucy, ya know? Ya mess with the bull, you get the horns.

"She ran your house and took care of you and your daddy like our first-grade schoolteacher, Miss Reddy. The only difference was that Grandma Bubbee had a giant *red* heart—speaking of red—and it was so full of love that if you had pricked it, it would have burst with sugar 'n' spice and everything nice, *unlike* Miss Reddy's.

"Yes, Grandma Bubbee was your gift straight from heaven. I believe her mission here was to save your little life, missy. She sure loved you to pieces! She and Aunt Lucy got on very well with each other too, remember?"

CHAPTER 17

The Good Bad Deed

*There are times when each of us has to have some gumption to take a
stand as to what we wish to preserve or change in order to maintain
our self-respect and not be as "a reed shaken with the wind."*
—*John Milton, poet, quoting from Matthew 11:7*

THE NEXT YEAR PASSED BY mostly painfully and mostly slowly
for all of us.

According to Lu, though, apparently Aunt Lucy made Daddy one of those
offers he couldn't refuse. She sold her little house and moved into the big house
with us. The first thing she did was have her phone line moved to our house. That
was a good thing; ask the Browns. Aunt Lucy just couldn't accept the absence of
indoor plumbing, though; she was so civilized. She began looking for another
house to buy that would be suitable for all of us.

With the events of that tragic year of loss, Aunt Lucy had been dealt yet
another bad hand, and she was well aware of the wild card—our daddy, the
Monster, Mr. Hyde—and wasn't about to give him even one inch.

She had inherited an infant, a three-year-old, and seven more to look after
and bring up. It seemed that life never failed to pile just one more "little" thing
on this woman's proud but able-to-carry-only-so-much-at-one-time shoulders.
Aunt Lucy laid down her law with Daddy, with a zero tolerance for anything
alcohol-related. Her terms were simple: If he ever laid another hand on anyone
or anything in that house, it would be his last time laying a hand on anything.
And the first time he dared to show up there drinking would be the last time
he showed up period.

Mother had been buried almost one year to the day when Lu turned
eighteen and was about to graduate from high school. She had an old Ford that
Mr. Brown had gotten cheap and fixed up for her to help us after Mother died.
He let her fill up the gas tank every Sunday night over at his garage and refused
to take any money from Aunt Lucy. Yep, Mr. Brown was a keeper.

By then, P. C. was sixteen and worked curb service at the Starlite Drive-In, not too far from the house. He went straight from school to work every day, and Lu would pick him up at nine o'clock each night. On Saturdays, he worked from noon until ten o'clock at night, and he was off on Sundays. He was very lonely for Mother. He stayed away as much as possible because of Daddy, and he wanted to quit school and get out on his own. I didn't blame him; I sorta wanted to go with him—a serious change of scenery for my *own* little grieving heart. Fat chance of that happening. Anyway, P. C. was afraid of Daddy, as he should have been, but unfortunately, he was ashamed of himself and felt inadequate. Catch-22, right?

One Friday evening at about five o'clock—payday!—Daddy came home drinking. Could that be possible? After a whole year, the wild card, our daddy, had finally shown up again. Guess he was tired of playing it straight. Daddy really had no friends, because he was a mean drunk and predictably unpredictable. That type of personality tended to make people a little nervous.

That Melvin Bray was his only friend, and he'd long since been gone— lucky dog. The fact that it was Mother's one-year anniversary probably had something to do with the little celebration Daddy was drinking himself into. Even I could figure that out, and I didn't have two little letters after my name, as Dr. Benis, MD, did.

P. C. was at work, and Lu and Lainey had run back over to the schoolhouse to pick up Lu's cap and gown. Aunt Lucy and Ali had taken Fay and Mae with them to the Fancy Gap Market, and Lee, Paddy, and I had stayed at the house to do our chores, as usual. Well, the three little Chillton piggies were about to get a visit from the Big Bad Wolf—I mean, Lee's monster. We heard a horn blowing—*honk, honk, honk.*

"Oh brother, it's him!" Lee shouted as Daddy stopped the Chevy at the old well.

As we watched through the kitchen curtain, we could see he was throwing beer cans and liquor bottles down the well. Empty, no doubt. He certainly couldn't leave any incriminating evidence in his car for Aunt Lucy to find. Then he got back in the car and drove up the rest of the way to the house. Since his jail time that Easter when he had killed my little biddy, he had decided he sure didn't wanta go back there, for fear of being sent back to the ole alcoholic hospital. Nope, he sure didn't want any part of that place again. After Mother died, the sheriff actually came over to the house now and then just to check on him—more to check on *us* than *him*, certainly. As we watched him get back into the car, he tripped and fell.

"That's it; we're outta here!" Lee proclaimed.

She grabbed each of us by the hand, and we headed up the stairs. There was a curtain at the top of the stairs that created a door-like facade, and we all hid behind it, holding our breath. We could hear him loud and clear as he came in the back door, yelling our names and cursing maniacally.

"Where is everybody? You damn little brats can't hide from me!"

That's all Lee needed to hear.

"Be quiet; don't say a word. If he starts up those stairs and makes it to the top, we'll have to protect ourselves. He can't see us, 'cause we're behind this curtain. Breathe only when you have to. We can't let him know we're up here!" she whispered.

We could hear him stomping and yelling all through the house downstairs. He wouldn't give up and just pass out—no, he just had to come up those stairs.

"Here he comes; get ready. If he gets to this curtain, just push as hard as you can!" she whispered again.

Somehow he made it to the top, and as he pulled at the curtain, we all pushed against him as hard as we could, and thankfully, down went Daddy.

I remember the famous sportscaster Howard Cosell calling that famous fight between Joe Frazier and George Foreman. Foreman knocked Frazier out, and Cosell yelled in that famous voice of his, "Down ... goes ... Frazier!"—one of the all-time great lines in sports history. To this day, when I think of the horror at the top of the stairs, with three young kids fearing for their little lives—at the hands of their own father, no less—I think of that line, and over the years, it became "Down goes Daddy." I love it.

We heard every single bump as Daddy rolled and tumbled down to the bottom of the stairs one step at a time—in slow motion, it seemed. We didn't dare look; we just listened. Once Daddy landed, that was it. The only sound we could hear was our little hearts beating like the drums in an old Tarzan movie. We wanted to scream but froze in our tracks instead.

Finally, Lee whispered precise instructions. We were to back up and stay behind the curtain as she looked out to make sure Daddy was still there and not moving. She looked out, quickly closed the curtain again, took us by the hand, led us to her room, and then closed the door. We followed her over to her bed; then she took our hands in hers, and we all sat down.

"I'm pretty sure he's dead, and we've just committed a good *bad* deed, but we had to take a stand," she said calmly.

I was not familiar with the look on her face. Grief, sadness, relief, and joy were all mixed together, speaking loudly through her courageous, big brown eyes, the path to her righteous young soul.

Paddy and I just sat there with our hands over our mouths as if we didn't trust ourselves not to shout out at the top of our lungs that we had just killed our daddy.

I don't know how long we sat there in total silence, but then Lee took a deep breath and calmly said, "Okay, somebody had to do it. He killed Mother; we killed him. Besides, if he'd gotten us at the top of the stairs, he probably woulda thrown us all down the stairs one by one, and of course we'd all be dead now. Then when our bodies were found, the liar in chief would tell the sheriff, 'Hell, boys, I don't have any idea what happened to those kids. I just got home and found 'em laying there dead, just like that.' He wouldn't get away with it, though, 'cause in his case, he's always guilty till proven innocent. But as it is right now, only one person had to die, not three. And another thing: we didn't deserve to die, but *he* did!"

"Yeah, but what are we gonna do now?" Paddy asked.

"We're gonna climb out the window onto the roof, cross over to the oak, shinny down, and go sit on the front porch until Lu or Aunt Lucy gets home," she answered matter-of-factly.

"We're going to jail, aren't we?" Paddy asked boldly.

"Nah, I don't know where we're going, but it won't be jail," Lee answered confidently.

"Why not?" I asked.

"Because they don't put kids in jail, Magg-Pie—that's why," she assured me with resolve.

"Oh, thank goodness—this must be our lucky day!" I proclaimed with joy. Just what planet was I on anyway—the Pretender Planet? Of course.

We all climbed out the window and onto the roof, grabbed on to the old oak limbs, and shinnied down the tree to the ground. If there was one thing we Chillton kids could do, it was shinny up 'n' down a tree. That was a good thing.

I realized later why Lee chose to take us out the window. She had no intention of going down the stairs and having to step over Daddy's body with Paddy 'n' me in tow.

Once we were on the ground, we headed around to the front of the house and sat down on the old raised porch next to the steps at the front door. Again we sat in silence, just swinging our little legs as we waited, as though we didn't have a care in the world.

All of a sudden, the front door flung open. We looked behind us, and lo and behold, there stood Daddy! Actually, he was more leaning than standing, but he was shouting, "Where you brats been? I've been lookin' all over this place!"

Just then, it registered in our little frightened brains that he was actually not dead but quite alive—and standing there, towering over us. We figured we were in big trouble and were scared out of our wits. We jumped up off that porch and took off runnin' down through the tall grass as if we'd been shot out of a cannon, heading once again toward Mrs. Brown's. For some reason, Daddy didn't follow us. Oh, it really *was* our lucky day, I thought.

Once we got to Mrs. Brown's front door, Lee appeared calm and took charge as usual and asked Mrs. Brown if we could sit 'n' swing on her front porch and watch out for Lu and Aunt Lucy to get home; she didn't say a word about Daddy.

"Of course you can, kids, and I've just made some cherry Kool-Aid and peanut butter crackers," she told us. *Yum!* Dear Mrs. Brown—our hero.

As we sat there, now swinging our legs from Mrs. Brown's big porch swing, sipping and munching, Lee told us that, in a way, she was glad we hadn't killed Daddy.

"You don't want us to grow up to be killers, do ya?" Paddy asked her rather consolingly.

"Well, no, of course not, you silly-willy. But the real reason is that I know Mother wouldn't want us to kill anybody, including *him*. He got lucky today, and so did we. It's probably best if we just keep this to ourselves for now, okay?" she instructed. She swore us to secrecy and made us promise to never discuss what had happened that day except with each other.

What had happened that day was simple. Lee had been in a situation in which she was the oldest and had the responsibility of protecting Paddy and me. That was Mother's one hard and fast rule, and that's what Lee the Lion did—she made the best decision she could under horrific circumstances, she honored Mother's rule to protect us, and she did her job.

That same day, she also made us promise to never get in the car with Daddy unless Aunt Lucy or Lu was with us. Lee was very wise for her young age, and she made straight As, too! So did Paddy.

I didn't; I just got check marks at that age.

As we sat on the big swing on Mrs. Brown's front porch, just a swinging in the slight breeze, we could see the Chevy sitting at the house, meaning Daddy was still there. Lee decided to go down to the main road to watch out for Aunt Lucy and the girls and to warn Aunt Lucy that our daddy, the Monster, Mr. Hyde, was officially back. Aunt Lucy must have known it was just a matter of time, but still, the day would prove to be another disappointment to her. But seriously now, how could ole Chill possibly have celebrated the first anniversary of Mother's death without alcohol?

Lee made Paddy and me stay there in the swing and told us she'd come back for us when Aunt Lucy got there. We watched her as far as we could from Mrs. Brown's porch; then she disappeared into the trees. She had said she'd cross the road from Mrs. Brown's and wait by our old mailbox at the bottom of the drive. She knew Aunt Lucy would be there any minute, so she just waited patiently.

She saw Daddy coming toward her down the drive from the house in the Chevy, and she thought, *That's great—he's leaving!* As he passed her, she gave him her trademark I'm-not-afraid-of-you look, turned around, and started walking back up toward the house.

When Daddy got to the end of the long drive, he turned around and headed full speed back up the road to the house. Lee was almost to the back door when she turned, saw Daddy, and realized her predicament. She ran into the house, up the stairs, and into Lu's room and hid under Lu's bed. Hiding had worked before, so why not now? Only less than an hour before, she had been upstairs, hiding from Daddy with Paddy and me, and now there she was again, upstairs, hiding from Daddy—all alone.

She heard the screen door slam as he entered the kitchen through the back door. He was back in the house, and as she once again listened to the scary, awful, familiar sounds of him ranting and raving, stomping all around downstairs, and cursing her name, she positioned herself as far under Lu's bed as she possibly could, against the wall. She knew he would search the house for her until he found her, unless, of course, he passed out first—if only. She was hoping for a miracle—like Aunt Lucy arriving at the very moment she would need to be saved from her monster.

Daddy finally gave up on finding her downstairs and headed up the stairs, and Lee just lay there like a mummy under the bed, once again holding her breath.

A house of horrors—that's what it was.

Lu's room was the last room down the hall from the top of the stairs. Lee could hear Daddy as he barged in and out of each room, slammin' doors, pushin' stuff around, and gettin' closer and closer to her by the second as he yelled and cursed her name.

When he finally made it to Lu's room, he checked out the closet, turned to walk out, and then turned back around and walked toward the bed. Lying under the bed, her little body pressed against the back wall, Lee could see each step he took as he made his way over to the bed and then stopped abruptly. He didn't say a word. He just bent down on all fours and pulled up the bed skirt, and the next thing Lee saw was Daddy's crazed, wild-eyed, drunken glare.

At that point, she knew she was probably, at the very least, pretty close to death, but the little lion intended to put up a good fight.

One tough little cookie—that was Lee. What a frightful, mad frenzy must have taken place from that moment on. Daddy, who was six foot two and crazy-drunk, then went from his all-fours position to a lying-flat position.

In an angry rage, he deliberately turned his body around so that he could fully stretch his legs out under the bed, and he began kicking Lee with all his brute strength.

Yeah, that was our daddy—he was the man.

He kicked and kicked and kicked, and Lee screamed and screamed and screamed.

I'm sure she used every cuss word she and Barry Snyder *both* knew and then some. Then, sure enough, that miracle moment happened. Aunt Lucy arrived with one of Mother's big iron skillets in her hands and whacked Daddy so hard on the head that he didn't wake up for two days—seriously.

Yeah, Aunt Lucy sure knocked the fire out of him!

With the strength of Sampson, she pulled Lee's monster outta the way and then pulled Lee out from under the bed. She knew immediately that Lee was seriously injured.

Ali had both Fay and baby Mae downstairs with her, and she knew by Lee's screaming and Daddy's cussing that Aunt Lucy had gone upstairs to save Lee's life. Aunt Lucy urgently yelled instructions downstairs for Ali to call the sheriff to send an ambulance and some deputies to the house immediately.

Aunt Lucy then picked Lee up in her arms, carried her down the stairs, and laid her carefully on the couch. Lee was barely conscious but kept mumbling over and over, "Thank you, Aunt Lucy. Thank you, Aunt Lucy." Poor little Lee.

Then Aunt Lucy called Mrs. Brown and asked her to come over right away to help her. Mrs. Brown called Mr. Brown and told him to get to the Chilltons' to stand watch over Daddy until the sheriff arrived.

We all knew to expect the unexpected from Lee's monster, and we just couldn't take a chance on anything normal comin' outta him. *Lay there and die, you bastard!*

Daddy simply couldn't be trusted to do the right thing—ever.

Paddy and I were still swingin' on Mrs. Brown's front porch when the screen door flung open and Mrs. Brown popped out and told us to follow her and get in the car. She said Aunt Lucy had called her for help because our daddy was "carrying on again." We weren't that surprised, but we immediately thought of Lee and ran to Mrs. Brown's car and jumped in. She drove us across the road to the big house, and we all got out of the car and wasted no time gettin' into the house. Paddy and I freaked out when we saw Lee. Less than an hour ago, she had been just fine. All of a sudden, a vivid image of Daddy lying at the bottom of the stairs reappeared in my mind. We had thought he was dead. Why did he have to get up? Why couldn't he have just been dead and left us kids alone?

Well, evidently Daddy had landed a couple of brutal blows to Lee's little face, and she was covered in blood. She looked the way P. C. had on the night Daddy had almost killed him.

Paddy and I started crying, and then Ali started crying. Mrs. Brown immediately took her baby goddaughter, Mae, in her arms and then guided little Fay into the kitchen, away from all the tears and fears that were rapidly filling the room. It seemed as though Mr. Brown miraculously appeared, read Mrs. Brown's eyes, and pretty much teleported up the stairs to assess the situation with Daddy.

Just then, the ambulance arrived, along with the sheriff and two deputies. Oh, the humanity and shame of it all. It was just sick, the whole damn thing—pathetic, too.

Oh, don't be shy; please take another bow, Mr. Hyde, you monster.

The sheriff, the two deputies, and one of the emergency techs went upstairs to hell's den to attend to Lee's monster while the emergency crew hastily began working on Lee.

The crew immediately placed Lee on a stretcher and loaded her into the ambulance with Aunt Lucy by her side, and—*zoom, zoom*—they roared off toward Grace Chapel Regional Hospital.

Apparently, Daddy was still unconscious from Aunt Lucy's major head-boppin' with the iron skillet. That was a good thing. But they checked his vitals, and sure enough, he was alive. *Damn!* That was a bad thing. As they proceeded to load Daddy into the sheriff's car and roar off to the hospital, I wondered, *Why?*

About that time, Lu and Lainey drove up to the house and saw the sheriff's car door being closed on the unconscious Mr. Hyde. Mr. Brown was going to follow the sheriff, and he asked Lu to take Lainey inside and said that Mrs. Brown would explain everything. The scene was horribly chaotic, of course, but we kids always took our cue from Aunt Lucy, and she always remained calm and in control, no matter what the situation. Actually, Mrs. Brown and Aunt Lucy were much alike in that regard—so at least we had that going for us.

I was thankful that P. C. got to miss the whole fiasco; it was P. C.'s good fortune but, sadly, Lee's *mis*fortune. And for *what*? What did they ever do to deserve such cruelty from him, their own father? That just sucked.

Once Mrs. Brown had told the whole story to Lu, she asked Ali to watch Lainey, Fay, and Mae downstairs while the rest of us went up to Lu's room.

Once Lu surveyed the aftermath, she was absolutely livid, and her adrenaline was just a-pumpin'. She valiantly pulled her old iron bed away from the wall and pushed it across the room with little effort.

The scene was sickeningly disturbing. The old hardwood floor under Lu's bed was splattered with Lee's blood from one end to the other. The wall where Lee had huddled under the bed was covered in blood and had some clumps of her hair stuck to it. The floor was battered in several places, where Daddy had slammed his work boots into the wooden floor as he kicked Lee's small body over and over again. Mrs. Brown grabbed Paddy and me by our arms and rushed us back down the stairs. I was sure she was wishing she'd never taken us up there. Ali went up to join Lu, and the young investigative team remained upstairs for a while. Lord only knows what long-term effects that scene, that day, had on the two of them!

I got only a short glimpse, but to me, the floor and wall resembled the setting of a gruesome dogfight—a fight that both animals had lost. The scene reminded me of a vision I had been forced to witness about two years earlier. Daddy had been drinking and had taken me with him in the old Chevy without anyone's knowledge. I guess that wasn't too hard to do—with five or six kids running around all evening, you might not miss one here or there.

As I recall, I was almost five, and he took me to one of those dogfights. I had to stay and watch the whole dreadful thing because he had a bet on one of the dogs. Talk about cruelty to animals—but hey, what about cruelty to a little kid? Well, Lu's room looked a lot like the aftermath of that dogfight—blood everywhere, just horrific.

Lu and Ali stayed up in Lu's room "investigating" for a short while and then came back down and asked Mrs. Brown if we could all go to the hospital to check on Lee and Aunt Lucy. Mrs. Brown agreed of course, but before we left, Lu called P. C. at the restaurant and told him what had happened. He insisted that she come by and pick him up on the way to the hospital. Lu took Paddy and Lainey with her and headed over to the Starlite to pick up P. C., and Mrs. Brown took the rest of us to the hospital in her car.

When we all got to the hospital, we found Aunt Lucy sitting there all by herself in the ER, patiently waiting for some reassuring news from Dr. Cheek, who was in the OR with two surgeons who were performing emergency surgery on Lee. The whole experience was just too damn familiar, insane, and sick!

As we walked over to Aunt Lucy, I thought, *Boy, Lee's really gonna be mad when she wakes up!* She really prided herself on being the only one of nine children who had never had a broken bone, a stitch, or even a bloody nose. She was almost twelve years old at the time, and considering what a tomboy she was, that really was a pretty good record. She had had measles with the rest of us a few years before, but we didn't make her count that. Lee could pretty much do anything she set her mind to, and she could do it well, including her cussing.

That day was the first anniversary of my dear mother's death, and that was how we memorialized it. Frankly, it became an *awful* special day, because now we Chillton kids would have *two* dreadful events to honor each year on the anniversary of our mother's death.

ᏩᎢᎢᎢᏬ

"Oh yeah, I'm seriously feeling the forgiveness thing right about now. I'm literally filled with it, and it's about the size of my little fingernail. Well, maybe not that big. Can you tell? Yeah, I'll take that cigarette now. I'm not gonna smoke it; I'm just gonna chew on it. Do you have any more Tums?"

ᏩᎢᎢᎢᏬ

While we all were waiting in the ER, I noticed Lu dig in her jeans pocket and hand something to Aunt Lucy that looked like a folded-up handkerchief. Aunt Lucy unfolded it, and there were Lee's two front teeth. Lu and Lainey had found them on the floor at the unfair-fight scene. It was just like that horrible night with P. C.—déjà vu all over again. My daddy, Lee's monster, had knocked out both P. C. *and* Lee's front teeth!

It was at least three hours before Dr. Cheek came back to the ER, and none of us really expected good news; we all just needed *some* news. Finally, Dr. Cheek came out and gave us the lowdown. Lee had been seriously hurt. She'd suffered several broken ribs, and those not broken were cracked. One of the broken ribs had punctured her right lung. She had some incredibly serious bruising over her entire body—head to toe, front to back. She had broken both her tibia bones while kicking back at Daddy in her mighty efforts to deflect the blows from his huge feet during the fight.

I couldn't help but think, *Let's kill the bastard.*

In addition to all those injuries, Lee had several facial issues: both eyelids had been dangerously split open, and the cornea in her right eye had suffered a corneal abrasion. Luckily, no injuries were life-threatening; all her injuries had been addressed in the OR. Lee would be all right eventually—mostly—and hopefully by Christmas. Later on, she would often chuckle and remind all her "Pity-Party Club" members, "Hey, what's six months out of a girl's life when she's got everybody runnin' around in circles for her?"

Lee told Lu she'd sure rather be *her* than that monster!

"Why?" Lu asked her.

"Because Aunt Lucy's gonna whip his sorry ass!" she answered with a huge smile on her face.

It was funny to watch Lee envisioning the whole scene. As it turned out, Lee was absolutely correct; however, Aunt Lucy wouldn't whip Daddy in the literal sense. Truth was, though, before Aunt Lucy was through with Lee's monster, he'd wish Aunt Lucy would have just thrown him under a big, long yellow school bus—literally.

Daddy had also been taken to the hospital, and as I said, he didn't wake up for two days. Other than the big bump on his head, he didn't have a scratch on him. What a surprise, huh? And of course, as usual, he "didn't remember a thing." Regardless, though, his sorry ass left the hospital and went to jail, and this time, Aunt Lucy made sure he wouldn't be back—ever!

Apparently, the scene with Judge Bering in the courtroom that day went something like this:

Judge Bering: What do you have to say for yourself, Mr. Chillton?

Daddy: Judge, everybody knows I have a drinking problem. I'm an alcoholic.

Judge Bering: So you're not guilty of the charge that you almost killed your young daughter?

Daddy: No, Judge, I'm just saying I wouldn't have done it if I wasn't an alcoholic.

Judge Bering: Are you saying that because you're an alcoholic, you're not responsible for what you did to your daughter?

Daddy: Yes, that's it, Judge; I'm not responsible.

Judge Bering: Mr. Chillton, I definitely agree with you on that one point. You are definitely *not* responsible. Furthermore, no one makes you drink alcohol. It's *your* choice, *your* decision, and *you're guilty*. Amen, and court's adjourned.

After court, Aunt Lucy came home and said, "Children, your daddy is in the good Lord's mighty hands now, so you don't have to be afraid of him anymore. He won't be back."

Lee remained in the hospital for five weeks. She was such a courageous little lion, all bound and determined to bounce back "in five minutes," as she would say. During those five weeks, she was able to brush up on her cussin' and enjoy lots of cuddlin'. She collected a treasure chest of trinkets from months of divin' into Cracker Jack boxes and smoked all the candy cigarettes she could stand. She loved those things, and back then, they were cute and edible, too. They were a hot item at the Fancy Gap Curb Market.

While Lee was doing her S&R (smokin' and recuperatin'), Aunt Lucy got busy 'n' found us a great big new house. For the Chillton kids, it was simply out of this world—a big two-story brick home with two and a half baths, a huge canary-yellow country kitchen, and a giant screened-in porch, all on a beautiful corner lot! It was truly a bunch to take in, and we were just the bunch to do it. Shoot, we didn't just *take* it in; we *moved* in! In fact, we were all moved in before Lee got out of the hospital. Since both of Lee's legs were broken, she obviously couldn't walk upstairs to her fancy new room, so Aunt Lucy converted the dining room downstairs into a temporary bedroom for her. The kitchen was so large that it had a built-in dining area, eliminating the need for a separate dining room anyway.

Aunt Lucy made it all work like a beautiful, finely tuned music box. She was indeed incredible. I've said that many times, but it's just so true.

Another great thing about that new house: it was only two miles from the Browns' and was even closer to Lizzy in that nice little neighborhood. It was Mother's kind of house, and with all the new furnishings, she would have been delighted.

One Christmas, Papa and Miss Libby bought Mother and us a new couch, and she was so proud of it that she made us keep it covered all week with sheets. On the weekends, she'd take off the sheets but wouldn't allow us to sit on it unless our clothes were clean. Mother had such respect for the smallest things and was so grateful for what little she had.

At the end of May, we all attended Lu's graduation—except for Lee, of course. We decided to wait a couple more weeks to properly celebrate Lu's twelve-year program so that Lee could be a part of it. That was a great day, too. Aunt Lucy and P. C. went to the hospital to get Lee, and the rest of us stayed at the new house. We'd decorated the whole downstairs and had all kinds of party favors and food galore. Lizzy, her daddy, Grandma Bubbee, the Browns, Miss Libby, the uncles, the cousins, Dr. and Mrs. Cheek, Pastor and Mrs. Meyers, and Miss Cherry were all there. It was a wonderful graduation party for Lu and a great welcome-home party for Lee.

That evening when Lee first came into the house on her crutches and still wearing a black eye patch, she sorta reminded us all of a pirate. She didn't have a peg leg, but with the crutches and eye patch, she did resemble a little stowaway on the high seas, and we all were calling her Pixie Pirate before the evening was over. She had totally mastered those crutches and couldn't be stopped. However, the upstairs was off-limits to her, so she sweet-talked the sweet Mr. Brown into carrying her upstairs to see her *real* new room. She said something like "I'll race ya upstairs, Mr. Brown!" That's all it took to tug on Mr. Brown's tender heartstrings. He picked her up in those strong, loving arms of his and carried her upstairs to her official new room, and she was simply overwhelmed. Her monster had happened to her, but she had taken the experience and run with it—on crutches, no less. She was thrilled by the party and all the love, but that new room was the icing on the party cake. And as the saying goes, "a good time was had by all."

Yes, indeed, there *is* a God!

⟊⟊⟊

"Here, take these Tums, Maggs," Lizzy suggested as she handed me the little bottle. I took a few, and before I could get the top back on, she grabbed the bottle back from me and shook out several for herself.

"What's up with *you*?" I asked.

"Oh, probably the little jaunt to gay Paris this morning, where I consumed twenty pounds of incredibly rich food, remember?" she moaned.

"Oh sure, it was the food. It certainly has nothing to do with my startling but all-too-true oral biography, huh? The fact that you were actually living it right there along with me doesn't turn *your* stomach just a little too?" I questioned with conviction.

"I don't want to admit it, Maggs, but sometimes I feel myself *feeling*."

"What the heck does *that* mean?" I asked curiously.

"I'm the doctor. I'm not supposed to *feel* your pain. I'm just supposed to *hear* your pain and try to *heal* it. Trust me, there's a big difference in feeling and hearing one's pain. And in this case, the *one* is *you*! Obviously, the key word there is *you*, Maggs. We've been at this for what—three days now? I guess I'm just emotionally reeling a little myself, and it's a bit odd for me. As I listen to you relive all this, I can't help but visually imagine what your life was really like behind that sweet little smile you wore around all the time. You never gave the slightest hint of sadness or fear, but it was there—hidden behind that smile. I was aware of your sadness over your mother's death, but I too was sad for the loss of my own mother. I could relate to that emotion, and it didn't seem odd. But other than that, you gave the impression that life was big and wonderful for you in spite of what happened to Lee and P. C. and all the cruelty of your father in general. Of course, now I understand you were simply saving yourself psychologically until you could properly deal with your pain and sorrow. But as I said earlier, you weren't even aware of this." She paused and took a deep breath as if waiting for some defensive counter.

"Hey, I've thought a lot about this, Lizzy, and I think if Mother hadn't been so passive, I might have responded less like Lu and more like the rest. I mean, it seems to me that P. C, Ali, and Lee saw the situation crystal clear, but Paddy and I inherited Lu's interpretations of Daddy. Lu being the firstborn and our surrogate mother didn't bode very well for her *or* Paddy and me.

"Ya know, to this day, Lu has a difficult time discussing Daddy, even though she knows the ugly truth. It took Mother's death for her to join the Hate Club along with the rest of us, but it was very painful for her, and as I said, it still is. I can understand it, though, because sometimes I have flashbacks of that one year we were a happy family. Of course, I know *that* was a lie too, but Daddy did show inklings of feelings for us during that short-lived dry spell of his.

"Then I jerk myself back to reality and tell myself, *Wake up and smell the java, spacewalker; Daddy didn't mean it—not really.* It was never about Mother or us kids. It was always about him and his needs in that immediate moment. Lu lets the truth *lay*; I let it *lie*."

"Maggie, the truth doesn't lie; people lie. They refuse to face the truth, because it's just too painful. That's where Lu is. She has a need to hang on to a certain image of your daddy. It's her image of him before he was A A—alcoholic and absent. With the alcoholism came the absence, then the gambling, and then the physical and emotional abuse. It's an image that, to her, is worth her love and loyalty to him. That's Lu's choice, Lu's truth—and she lets it *lay*. So be it.

"But, Maggs, you too have a choice as well. In your case, you do know the score—what he was guilty of—and you accept it. Your image is actually somewhat different than Lu's. Your *lie* is manifested by pretending that it—your daddy—didn't bother you that much. Wrong—it *did*.

"We lie the loudest when we lie to ourselves, Maggie. I believe that because of that lie or pretense, you're angrier with *yourself* than with that ole grudge you've been weighted down with for so damn long now.

"You know, Maggs, the heaviest thing we can carry is a grudge. This grudge is like a big black spot on your heart! Oops, I feel a word about to form on my big, luscious, logical lips! You know what's coming, Maggs. Can you say *forgive*—"

"Stop!" I interrupted her as I covered my ears. "I know, I know, and I'm trying," I pleaded.

"Good. I believe you, and I'm proud of you, Maggie! I'm fully aware of the struggle here—honestly, I am, dear—but you simply must wipe out that perilous black spot so you can start letting go of your own suffering," Lizzy told me in a firm yet loving tone.

Just then, we heard Lizzy's private office line ringing from inside the house.

"Well, who could that be before noon on Sunday?" she asked rhetorically. She let the call go to voice mail and suggested we both sweat out all traces of the previous night's blonde binger in the sauna and then take relaxing bubble baths. No argument there.

"Oh my, what a splendid idea," I agreed, and we left the poolside and headed for the sauna. On the way, I thought about the first time I had ever gotten in a sauna. The visual popping in my head made me laugh out loud.

"What's so funny?" Lizzy asked.

"Oh, just the image of myself with you in the sauna for the first time, remember?" I answered her as I continued to laugh.

"Oh, damn, that *was* funny, Maggs," she answered, laughing back at me. "You spent the first five minutes convinced you were suffocating and the next twenty minutes going in and out to make sure you *didn't* suffocate! I think you lost five pounds, though, and it had nothing to do with sweating in the sauna. Actually, I think I lost a coupla pounds just laughing at ya."

We spent the next few hours relaxing and pampering ourselves. While we were sitting in the sauna, Lizzy suggested that when we finished our pamper party, we should get dressed and go over to the Antique Bazaar to see her appraiser friend. She really wanted to get his expert eyes on our little box and frame. I was all for it, and we both got excited at the thought of the possibility of having found a real treasure. We got dressed, and as we were heading out the door, she asked me to grab our gifts while she checked her voice mail from the earlier caller. I got the little treasure bags, went out to the garage, and raised the garage door. Lizzy came out the back door and told me the message was from the Mother, who wanted to cancel her appointment scheduled for Tuesday. Lizzy had called her back to reschedule and had discovered that the Mother was getting cold feet and didn't think she could handle what was probably in store for her emotionally through Lizzy's therapy. She'd been living a slow death— slowly dying for some peace and closure for years—but was simply afraid of her own feelings and couldn't imagine Lizzy's therapy making any real difference in her life after so long.

Yeah, I can relate to those fears for sure, I thought. *I got here on Friday after dreading coming for the last six months; it's now just Sunday, and I've been dragged through the painful past to the point of exhaustion, smokin', drinkin', 'n' thinkin'. I suppose thanks are in order? Maybe not yet, since the renowned Dr. Shrink is not quite finished performing my family discount. All I know is that I was alive when I got here, but I wouldn't swear to it today.*

Yeah, the truth does hurt, but does it really set ya free? I feel like I'm just goin' through the motions, like on autopilot—walking, talking, sleeping, eating, eating, eating ... Well, at least there's that! Shoot, I truly don't know if I'm alive or dead. According to Dr. Shrink, though, I've never really lived my own truth.

Lizzy insisted on ringing the Mother back to suggest that she seriously reconsider, keep the Tuesday appointment as planned, and then make a decision at that time about any future therapy. The Mother agreed. The good doctor was satisfied. She was convinced she could help the Mother and was determined to get inside her head.

If ya ask me, she's asking for it. What do I know? I'm just another head case myself!

CHAPTER 18

Lost Treasures

The human heart has hidden treasures, In secret kept, in silence sealed; The thoughts, the hopes, the dreams, the pleasures, whose charms were broken if revealed.
—Charlotte Bronte, English novelist

IT WAS LATE AFTERNOON, about four thirty on that beautiful Boston Sunday. Yet another sunny, brisk, 'n' breezy fall day, and we were once again top-down travelin', which I just loved. It took us a while to find a safe spot to park that fine joyridin' machine of hers. Parking was quite limited at the unique little Antique Bazaar, but based on the vehicles in the parking lot, one could only determine that this was definitely an upscale, wealth-driven enterprise. Once we parked and got inside the building, Lizzy led the way to her friend's shop. There were a couple customers ahead of us, and as we waited, we browsed and noticed some very expensive and curiously unique items for sale. A short time passed, and we heard an interestingly deep voice calling out to us.

"Miss Lizzy, how nice to see you again. How have you been?"

"Very well, thank you, Mr. Hobbs, and how are you today?" Lizzy replied as we walked over to the glass counter in front of Mr. Hobbs, who was perched on a stool.

"Oh, you know—at my age, *every* day's a great day, my dear," he responded with a warm smile as he took a big puff on his large-bowled ivory pipe.

"And for me as well, kind sir," Lizzy replied with her own warm smile. It was apparent the two of them were fond of each other, and Lizzy spoke to him in an endearing manner.

"Mr. Joshua Hobbs, I'd like you to meet Maggie. She's my oldest and dearest friend in the whole wide world, and she's visiting with me for a few weeks," she told him as she gave me a hug around the waist.

"It's my pleasure, Miss Maggie—so nice to meet you." He addressed me with kindness in that pure baritone voice of his.

I shook his hand with sincerity and responded likewise. He reminded me a lot of Mother's uncle Pink—short, round, and jolly. A lot like Santa, too.

"Well, what have you for me today, my dear Miss Lizzy?" he asked as Lizzy placed the two small brown bags on the counter in front of him.

"I don't know, but I'm hoping Maggie and I have found something with history and value—but not necessarily in that order," she teased as he opened the little bags, slowly took the box and frame out, and placed them both on a black velvet cloth on top of the glass counter. He put on a strange piece of headgear, complete with magnifying glass and tiny lightbulb. He resembled a coal miner preparing to lower himself into the mine to seek undiscovered bounty.

Next, he picked up the secret box and methodically began his examination. He too knew the magic formula for opening the little drawer and found the note. He unfolded the fragile paper, read it, and then placed it on the velvet cloth. He turned the little drawer over and readjusted his magnifying glass to get a closer look at the bottom of the drawer.

Lizzy and I watched curiously in absolute silence as the master intently worked; he appeared to be deep in thought.

The master nodded his head a few times as he mumbled to himself, and we didn't dare interrupt him.

As we stood there, we resembled the two little girls who used to stand at the candy counter at Eagle's Dime Store back home in Grace Chapel. During high school, Ali had worked there on Saturdays and had always given Lizzy and me a tiny little brown bag of cashews and chocolate-covered raisins. Oh, sweet memories!

I didn't know about Lizzy, but I felt myself holding my breath with both curiosity and excitement as Mr. Hobbs carefully laid the little drawer on the counter by the note and then picked up the small jeweled frame.

First, he dismantled the back and removed the tiny baby photo. He laid the photo on the counter; removed the small, aged, yellowed glass from the frame; and placed the glass on the counter as well. He picked up the photo, turned it over, readjusted his magnifying glass once more, and studied the back of the photo. Once again, he nodded and mumbled to himself as he examined each item in methodical detail. He placed the photo next to the drawer. Finally, he picked up the frame and diligently scanned the jeweled outline affixed to the frame. When finished, he laid the frame down and stood there for a few minutes in thought as he looked over the individual pieces in front of him.

"Where did you find these, Miss Lizzy?" he asked.

"At the Niceville Festival yesterday, Mr. Hobbs. Maggie found the box at one vendor's gazebo, and I found the frame at another. However, when we got home and examined them more closely, we realized that the jewels matched on both the box and the frame and apparently were designed as a set," she explained.

Mr. Hobbs picked up the little wooden drawer, turned it over, and pointed out some initials on the bottom. He handed Lizzy a small magnifying glass so that she could see the writing more clearly. There were three letters hand-carved in the wood: *SRL*. He then picked up the note and showed us the same letters.

"Yes, we did see the note, but we didn't notice the initials on the bottom of the drawer," Lizzy offered.

Mr. Hobbs then picked up the photo and turned it over so that Lizzy could see what was on the back of it as well:

My sweet baby boy—S. R. L.—1949, 2 years old
K. P. L.

"Oh my, that's interesting. We didn't take the photo out of the frame. We just thought it was one of those generic Gerber baby photos, you know? And, Mr. Hobbs, isn't that a little odd that we purchased the two items from two different vendors but both items obviously belong together?"

"Well, not really. The vendors at the festival shop all year from one year to the next for their inventory. Most of the items you'll find there at the festival are produced locally, especially the arts and crafts items such as these. However, from time to time, one will find something unique like you have here, where a vendor probably picked them up at an estate sale somewhere in the area and possibly sold them to other vendors. Those items could then end up on various vendors' tables all throughout the festival, and I think that's what you have here, Miss Lizzy," he explained.

"Well, at least now we know that SRL is a boy," Lizzy said, "because you can't tell if the baby is a boy or girl in the photo. Also, he was born in 1947 and was two years old in the photo, taken in 1949. We also know that based on his secret note, he loved his mom 'the most.'"

"Yes, Miss Lizzy, the human heart has hidden treasures," Mr. Hobbs said solemnly.

"So true, Mr. Hobbs, and if nothing else, Maggie and I have reunited the matching box and frame, which include SRL's love note to Mom and his baby picture. My goodness, Dr. Watson, we solved a mystery and didn't even know we had one!" Lizzy exclaimed as she nudged me.

"Yep, we sure have, Holmes." I nodded as I replied.

"Well, Miss Lizzy, when you came in today, you told me you wanted to determine history and value, correct?" Mr. Hobbs said.

"Yes, sir, and I believe we have confirmed the history part, but what about the value part, Mr. Hobbs?" Lizzy replied.

Mr. Hobbs carefully replaced the drawer in the box and the photo in the frame and returned them to the little brown bags—their temporary new homes. As he did, he explained that the only real value was of the sentimental kind. Further, he continued, since the secret box and matching frame, complete with the photo of the author of the note, had been reunited, the sentimental value would be realized only if the items were then reunited with their rightful owner. We all agreed and knew that wasn't gonna happen, so I suggested Lizzy give them a new home.

"By all means, Watson—splendid idea," she answered in kind. Just the thought of it seemed to make us both feel as if we were doing something good.

Mr. Hobbs handed Lizzy the brown bags, and she thanked him as they embraced each other. We said our good-byes and then wandered out into the main entrance hall of the bazaar, toward the big board proclaiming "You Are Here" with a red arrow.

I always used those maps to confirm whether or not I was lost, but Lizzy used it to direct us to the hotdog stand.

"I know—you're starving, and if you take another step without food, you're gonna fall on your face, right?" I grumbled.

"Wrong. We have to go to the hotdog stand to get a knockwurst with hot sauerkraut for Mr. Hobbs; now, aren't you ashamed?"

"Well, okay, but how in the whole wide world would I have even come close to that one?" I teased defensively.

"It's not *always* about me, ya know, Maggs—just *most* of the time." She giggled. "Actually, I always make sure I take Mr. Hobbs his special snack when I come out here to see him. In all the years I've known him, he's never allowed me to pay him, no matter how much time he spends with me when I bring an item out here for his opinion. I found out a long time ago that he loves these hotdogs, and this is my way of saying thanks, and he allows me to do it for him. It's just our little thing. He's a good man, Maggs."

"Do you know anybody who's *not* a good man, Lizzy?" I asked.

"Yes, a few," she said as her smile turned upside down. I didn't ask for names and just accepted her answer—for the time being, anyway.

Lizzy paid for the hotdog, and we walked back to Mr. Hobbs's shop. As we entered, the you-have-a-customer chime rang loudly, and Mr. Hobbs looked up from the busy counter to see Lizzy with his brown snack bag. He smiled his wise, loving smile as he winked at her and motioned her over to the counter, saying, "Thank ya there, Miss Lizzy. I was getting a little hungry, ya know?"

"I hope so, Mr. Hobbs, because this is just for you, ya know?" She smiled back with her own wink. She handed him his small goody bag, turned, and gracefully walked back toward me at the door, and once again, we waved good-bye to the very nice Mr. Hobbs.

"I feel like we really accomplished something here today, Maggs. How 'bout you?" she asked with a lift in her voice.

"Me too! I'm not sure just *what*, but I do feel good about it," I agreed. We were both in a moment of thought, pondering little SRL, his secret, and what life might have brought to him and the one he loved the most over the past forty years.

We got in the car, and Lizzy put the top down. The chilly fall night air was invigorating. We didn't talk. It seemed as though we were both riding along in another world—*our* world.

"What a wonderful day we've had, Magg-Pie. I can't remember one much better, can you?" she asked.

"No, I honestly can't. It was probably the sauna, ya think?" I asked.

"Yeah, that's it—the sauna," she mocked.

"Ah, I'm just pickin' at ya, honey. It's been a fabulous day, and I'll never, ever, never forget it—ever!" I assured her in my most ardent manner.

She looked over at me and smiled that same little Sarah Lizabeth Benis smile—the same loving expression of acceptance that had sealed our incredible relationship so long ago.

She was pulling into the driveway before I realized we were home. The garage door rose, and she slowly drove into the garage and turned off the ignition. She got out of the car and walked around to my side as I was getting out of the car. She put her arms around me and hugged me affectionately.

"Yeah, you're a pretty good date for an *ole* gal, Maggs." She chuckled at herself.

"Ya know, you're almost as funny as you *think* you are, *ole* wise one," I responded in kind as we walked arm 'n' arm into the house.

"Says you," she mumbled. "Hey, I've got a great idea, Maggs! My schedule is open tomorrow, so why don't we go to the office—after breakfast, of course—and you can help me choose some new colors for the walls? I'd like to cheer it up a bit, and you know I'm no good at this color stuff. Okay, Monet? Oh, and we'll spend a little time with the past too. What d'ya say, Monet?" she pleaded as she tugged on my sleeve.

"Fine, fine. I like the color part. Not too crazy about the past part, but okay, sure—like I have a choice in the matter, Doctor?" I grumbled.

As Lizzy got a bottle of pinot out of the wine cooler, I got two wine glasses from the butler's pantry, and without words, we strolled playfully out to the patio, where we resumed our earlier chaise positions by the pool. She poured the wine, and we made a toast of thanks for our beautiful day. We lifted our glasses once more and toasted each other in honor of our incomparable friendship. As we lounged back in our chairs, we reminisced about all our firsts: first boyfriends, first kisses, first dates, first proms, and first days of college. The only rule to our game of firsts was that the memory had to put a smile on our face. We both were intent on the remains of this day being nothing less than happy.

In no time at all, the clock was striking midnight.

"We gotta get inside or we'll turn really, really old, Maggs!" Lizzy laughed at herself as she checked her watch.

"Alrighty then, but I'm not turnin' out my light till I fall asleep, and I mean it, okay?" I stated my demands clearly.

"Yeah, that makes a whole lotta sense; you do just that, Merlin," she taunted as she rose from her chaise, motioning me to join her. We called it a night and headed into the house to reunite with Slumbertown, USA. And to all a good night!

CHAPTER 19

The Mother

My mind tells me to give up, but my heart won't let me.
                                              —Albert Smith, author

"**RISE 'N' SHINE, SUNSHINE!** It's another beautiful day in the neighborhood, as the nice man says," Lizzy said, cheerfully welcoming me to the new day.

"I know; it's Monday, and it's not raining, right?" I asked.

"No, it's not raining, it's not blue, and yes, it is Monday—why?" she answered.

"Oh, I just wanted to go top-down toolin' again if the weather's as nice as yesterday—that's all. Ya know how much I'm lovin' this Boston, MA, fall weather in that sweet convertible of yours. The plan's still to go by the paint store and pick up some color samples on the way to the office, right?" I asked.

"Oh yeah, that's right; we need to do that on the way in this morning."

"Hey, why don't I whip us up a great omelet while you get dressed, Doc?" I suggested as I lay there feeling cozy and comfortable.

"Well, you're obviously not awake yet, dear. Look, I *am* dressed, and your dark vitamins are roasting in the kitchen! Why don't *I* whip us up an omelet while *you* get dressed, and then we can go top-down toolin' around some more—ya like that picture, Dr. Artist?" she asked whimsically.

I sat up and smelled the coffee fragrance that was hovering over my head. "Yeah, I like that picture a whole lot, and look, I'm up too—see?" I teased as I put both feet on the floor and stood up as tall as my five-foot-three frame would allow. "I'll be dressed in a flash—just soon as I run 'n' grab a cup of those vitamins you keep forcin' down me."

"Oh yeah, I know that's the truth, fibber," she scolded as I headed for the kitchen. I got dressed quickly while the good doctor whipped up tasty omelets for us.

"Gosh, that was really a good omelet, Lizzy! I thought you said you didn't know how to cook!"

"Nah, I know how to cook; I just don't want to cook! As soon as you start cooking for people, next thing ya know, you'll be spending way too much life time in the damn kitchen. Forget that! Not me, man—no way, José. I got people around here to *see*, not to *feed*, remember?" She paused for a breath.

"Oh yeah," I taunted, "that's right, Dr. MD; you're a very important person. Excuse me, may I have your autograph? And then can we go get those paint samples already?"

"Funny girl, Maggs. Okay, let's go, but I know what you really want, and it ain't those paint samples. Hey, I feel the same way about that little baby of mine! She's not meant to be stuck in that garage all by her hot little self. Let's hit it, and then I'll be back on your nice list, right?"

"Pretty much," I agreed.

We had that top down in ten seconds and drove all over the parkway—the front way, the back way, the through way, every which way—and we had a blast, too. At one point, I had to tell ole bossy pants that she needed to keep it under 150 or I was gonna bail out. She told me to go ahead.

We finally got to the office and realized we'd forgotten the paint samples. We turned around in the parking lot and headed back out to the paint store. It didn't take us long at all to collect umpteen little color samples and head straight back to the office. As we were getting out of the car, Lizzy asked me to grab the treasure bags from the backseat, which we had left there from our excursion to Mr. Hobbs's shop the day before. I got the bags, and she managed the box of paint samples, including a few small cans of sample paint.

The first thing she did when we got inside the office was place the paint box down on the kitchen counter. Then she headed straight to her personal office and plopped down in one of the two beautiful, plush, Papa Bear–sized wingbacks. Those chairs were crazy-comfortable. I didn't know why she had to hypnotize people—all she would have had to do was sit 'em down in one of those chairs for less than five minutes and they'd have been out cold, no resistance!

The chairs sat in front of her awesome hand-carved cherry desk, which sat right in front of a matching credenza. She motioned for me to join her in the other wingback next to her. I sat down as she asked me where I felt would be a good place to officially reunite the little pair of treasures. Since we had already agreed they should not be separated again, one of us had to keep them both. Still holding the bags, and I got up from the chair, even though I didn't want to; I was already half asleep.

I walked a few feet over to the credenza, took the frame and the box out of the bags, and carefully placed them on the credenza. I walked back over and stood by Lizzy to get a proper look.

"Well, what about right there? They wouldn't mean anything to anyone but you and me, Lizzy, so why not keep them here in your office? We're not gonna split 'em up again, so this is just perfect. What d'ya think?"

She studied the little pair for a minute or so.

"I agree, Maggs, and I think they'll be very happy there, don't you?"

"I sure do, and so be it." I nodded as I took my place back in my comfy spot next to her. We both sat there for a few more minutes, gazing at and contemplating our sentimental-value-only purchases from Niceville. As we looked at them endearingly, we both agreed we had indeed found someone's treasure.

I was almost asleep, but she made me get up outta that fabulous chair and get busy with our decorating enterprise. As I continued to test some new colors on the walls in the reception area, Lizzy's office line rang, and we could hear the caller leaving a message. It was the Mother, confirming her two o'clock appointment with Lizzy for the next day. Lizzy was pleased, which prompted more conversation about the Mother and the still-missing little Ricky Lawrence.

"Her 'mind tells her to give up, but her heart won't let her,'" Lizzy pondered aloud as she played the message back a couple more times, hoping to glean something else from the Mother's voice.

"Maggs, we've done the color part, so let's get back to the past part." That machine of hers was documenting my *colorful past*—clever. She checked her rolling time machine to confirm exactly where we had left off last time.

Have you ever tried to eat and throw up at the same time? Well, that was the feeling I was getting right then as we began with Lizzy's "Oh, let's talk about the *past* good ole bad days some more" sessions. *Oh man, can I get a break here? I'm in hell; I can't take it anymore. Lizzy's got two new clients now: the Mother and the Misfit.*

⚭

After the Lee fiasco, there was no comin' back for ole Chill. He had finally done himself in. Of course, it was so long overdue that it was absurd. He no longer had Mother to forgive him and continue her "Okay, this is your last, last, last chance" mantra. This time, ole Chill was toast! Aunt Lucy quickly got into the filing business. She filed every complaint legally possible against Daddy.

Ali once said Aunt Lucy "threw the book at him," but Lee spoke up and said, "No, not quite—as I remember it, she clobbered him over the head with that damn big iron skillet and saved my life!" Lee was right and, no doubt, a grateful little cusser.

In no time, Aunt Lucy had filed for full custody of the entire O'Malley-Chillton clan—all nine of us! It *had* to be the luck of the Irish!

"May the good Lord take a liking to you—but not too soon!" That was an old Irish favorite of Aunt Lucy's and another expression of her fierce love of life, God's greatest gift. We were all doing quite well for the first time in our lives. We missed Mother terribly, though, and Aunt Lucy talked about her all the time—sorta like Miss Libby did after Papa died. It was just Aunt Lucy's way of keeping us all close to Mother and allowing us to feel our feelings out loud by talking about her anytime we felt like it. Looking back on it later, I realized it was just another therapy tactic Aunt Lucy used to help us with our grieving and healing.

P. C. suffered the loss of Mother the most. After she died, he was never the same, not really. P. C. was like the Mother, I realized. His heart was so broken and full of grief with his mother and best friend gone that life was mostly empty for him now, and that painful grief was taking an indelible, sad toll on him. I guess somehow he felt responsible for the crap Daddy pulled; he must have borrowed my cloak of dishonor without my knowing it. Whatever. All I knew was that Mother's absence forced him to buy a ticket on the wrong train—the train to Nowhere Fast, USA. Daddy was so cruel and had made life so emotionally dark for P. C. at such an early age that without Mother there to love him and encourage him, he was losing his way. Aunt Lucy was working on a plan for him, though.

Once we got moved into the new house and Lee got home from the hospital, life began to take on a new meaning for the rest of us. Yes, our dear mother was gone, but so was the monster, Mr. Hyde.

That fall, Lu's childhood dream came true, and she was packing for college. We were all excited for her. Mrs. Brown kept baby Mae, Fay, and Lainey while the rest of us went with Aunt Lucy to take Lu up to school. The college was two hours from home, so the ride gave us all a little more time with Lu before we had to say good-bye officially. Once we got to the campus, we helped her settle into her dorm.

Since it was Saturday and P. C. still had his job at the Starlite Drive-In, he didn't go with us. He was almost eighteen and had a few friends—if you could call 'em that. They were more like young hooligans. They were older and were always into mischief and hung out at the Starlite in their hot rod. I wished P. C. would find a darling little sweetheart, but so far, he hadn't. He didn't want to involve himself in anything that might require a heartfelt reaction, I supposed. Aunt Lucy was well aware of his wounded spirit, his broken and guarded heart, and his new associates. She had a plan to present to P. C. about college. It was his last year in high school, and he actually had shown some serious signs of interest in developing his artistic talents.

Actually, out of the nine of us, four of us showed promise in the field of art. As life's paths became more defined, though, I was the only one to pursue art as a career.

At that time, unfortunately, P. C. was more interested in hot rods and beer. I couldn't believe it. I could remember him saying he would never, ever, ever drink alcohol—I had heard him say that a hundred times!

About halfway home, we stopped at a little family restaurant on old Route 64 and had supper. We were already missing Lu. She was such a big part of all our lives, and now we had to start missing her, too, but at least she wasn't leaving us forever.

We finished eating and headed back to town and were about to pass the Starlite Drive-In, when Aunt Lucy suggested we stop to have milk shakes and say hi to P. C.

The Starlite still had curb service, so we didn't even have to get outta the car. We ordered our shakes, and Aunt Lucy asked the carhop to have P. C. come outside if he had a minute. The carhop told Aunt Lucy that P. C. had left early that evening. While we were waiting on our shakes, Aunt Lucy got out of the car and went inside to call Mrs. Brown and let her know to bring the girls on home 'cause we'd be there shortly. We all arrived at the house at the same time, and Ali and Paddy helped Mrs. Brown with the little girls. Lee was still on her crutches, so she pretty much was on her own, which meant very light chore duty for her—totally appropriate, of course, under the circumstances. Given a choice, I was certain Lee would have chosen the chores.

However, Lee had learned to do things with those crutches that amazed the rest of us. She also had become very adept at crawling up and down the stairs. Ever since Mr. Brown had carried her up to see her new room the night she had come home from the hospital for her welcome-home party, she was obsessed with getting up those stairs to that room.

Aunt Lucy had told her that when she was able to get up and down the stairs all by herself without the crutches, she could officially move into her new room permanently. About six weeks later, Lee was hauling butt up and down those stairs, with casts on both legs. It was pretty awesome to watch. She loved that room, and she was the only one who had her own private room in the new house. That was one of the bargaining tools Aunt Lucy had used on Lee to keep her spirits up during the first few weeks of her recovery in the hospital.

That was a rough time for Lee *and* Aunt Lucy. Lee would lie in her hospital bed with both legs in traction, and I'd sit by her bed with my little art pad in hand, sketching out her visions of what she wanted her new room to look like. Aunt Lucy had suggested Lee do that to help pass the time while she was in the hospital. When Lee had the room exactly the way she wanted it, Aunt Lucy promised she would take my drawings and would have the room ready for her by the time she was released from the hospital.

I'd say there was some serious psychology going on there, but Aunt Lucy would call it "just your common, everyday garden-variety-type bribery."

I must have drawn five hundred designs for that room for Lee. She really got into it and had so much fun that she didn't dwell on the dark side of what had happened to her. Lee finally made up her mind, and we gave the drawings to Aunt Lucy, who of course kept her promise and had the room professionally decorated exactly as Lee and I had designed it. The room had it all, and every single item was brand-spanking new; there was not one piece of secondhand charity, as Ali loved to boast.

Lee's new room was all about joy—the joy of giving and the joy of receiving—between Aunt Lucy and Lee. I'd have called her Lucky Lee, but under the circumstances, it didn't really sound quite right.

We all went into the house, and Aunt Lucy made some fresh coffee for herself and Mrs. Brown. While they sat at the kitchen table, chatting about a young visiting minister who was going to preach his first sermon ever at church the next day, we kids took our baths and got ready for bed. Aunt Lucy and Mrs. Brown had dibs on Fay and baby Mae, and the rest of us were on our own. With two and a half bathrooms, complete with real bathtubs and indoor plumbing, we had it made. What a way to live. The final chore for the evening was Ali's. She had to put all the Sunday church outfits together for the rest of us before she went to bed. She took this job very seriously, because it was the last thing she and Mother would do before they went to bed on Saturday nights after Mother got home from work. That was Ali's special time with Mother, and she didn't want to share it with anyone, even after Mother died. *Whatever works, do it,* I thought.

It was three o'clock in the morning when I looked over at the clock by the bed. The phone was ringing, and that's what had awakened me. We had a phone downstairs in the kitchen and an extension upstairs in Aunt Lucy's bedroom. If it was quiet, though, we could hear the phone ringing no matter where we were in the house. It stopped ringing, and I could hear Aunt Lucy talking.

I lay quietly in bed, straining to hear Aunt Lucy, wondering if this call could possibly be a good thing.

I had heard Aunt Lucy tell Mrs. Brown one time how she felt about phone calls in the middle of the night: "Unless somebody's dead, I'd just as soon you wait until morning to call me." Well, as fate would have it, that phone call was from Mrs. Brown, and somebody was dead.

Since Lee had her own room, P. C. and Paddy shared a room, Ali and I shared, Lainey and Fay shared, and baby Mae's crib was in Aunt Lucy's room. Aunt Lucy hung up the phone and went into P. C. and Paddy's room. She was looking for P. C. and discovered he wasn't in his bed, so she woke up Paddy and asked him if P. C. had ever come home. Paddy assured her he had not seen P. C. since P. C. had left for work that Saturday morning.

Aunt Lucy left Paddy and came into our room and woke up Ali. I was already sitting up in the bed and asked her what was up. She didn't answer but gently patted me on my head instead. Ali sat up in the bed, and Aunt Lucy explained to both of us that Mrs. Brown had called and was on her way over to the house to pick Aunt Lucy up to go to the hospital. She told us there had been an accident, but that was all she knew. Aunt Lucy told Ali to get up and go get in Aunt Lucy's bed and look after baby Mae and the rest of us until she got back. Aunt Lucy kissed us and went back to her room to get dressed, and a few minutes later, she went downstairs to wait for the Browns.

Ali went down the hall and got in Aunt Lucy's bed, and I got up and went to Lee's room and slipped into bed with her. I woke her up and told her what was going on, and she was quick to say she was sure that somehow, some way that the damn monster was involved. I told her I thought she was wrong, 'cause he was in jail. We lay there in the dark, betting each other back 'n' forth on various scenarios until we fell asleep.

Apparently, P. C. and two of his bad-boy friends had gone out on a little wild spree that night. That's why P. C. had left the Starlite early and hadn't been there when we'd stopped by for milk shakes. For some reason, P. C. had tagged along with the other two, and they had all ended up on a stranger's back porch at two in the morning.

The two young hooligans had picked a house at random to rob. They hot-rodded over to the Starlite and told P. C. they had a surprise for him and convinced him to leave work early and hang out with 'em. Both boys had handguns; P. C. didn't.

The random house they had chosen was none other than the house of the young visiting preacher Aunt Lucy and Mrs. Brown had discussed earlier that evening. The preacher, his wife, and their three small children had moved into that house less than two weeks prior to that horrible, fateful night. The two bad boys pulled the screens off the double windows on the back porch and raised the windows. The young preacher and his family were all asleep in their beds, as one would expect, and the preacher was awakened by the robbers. He went to the kitchen with his own gun in hand, and he could see moonlit images through the side of the window shades. He saw two guys stooped down under the windows and a third just standing on the porch behind them with his hands in his pockets. The preacher called out to them and told them he had a gun aimed at them and commanded them to back down off the porch. He had startled them, and the two bad boys pulled their guns and immediately started shooting right through the windows.

The preacher was startled even more, and he returned the gunfire.

It was over in a few flashes. The preacher didn't have a scratch on him. He'd fired all of his six bullets in the process of protecting himself and his young family. The first bullet had hit the younger of the two bad boys in the leg, and the other five had hit P. C. The ringleader hooligan fled the scene into the pitch-dark night and hid in the neighborhood.

His approach sounded a bit like That Melvin Bray's MO—never hang around the crime scene. The preacher ran inside, called the sheriff's office, and pleaded with them to send an ambulance, because he knew he had hit at least two of the three would-be intruders. He rushed back out to the porch to see if he could help them in any way while waiting for the ambulance. The hooligan boy was lying by P. C. when the preacher got to them. He bent down and could see more clearly just how young they were. He could also see that the bad boy had been hit in the leg and was alive. He checked P. C., but because it was so dark, he couldn't see all the blood. He knew P. C. had been shot, but he had no idea that five of his six bullets had found their way into P. C.'s innocent and unsuspecting young body. He could see P. C. was struggling to breathe, and he began performing CPR right away.

When the ambulance crew finally arrived, the young preacher was still performing CPR on P. C. through a wall of tears. Hard as he tried, and loud as he prayed over P. C.'s lifeless body, he couldn't save him.

Our darling P. C.—he was gone forever.

The preacher wasn't much older than P. C., and he was devastated. He sat down on the porch, gently pulled P. C. up onto his lap, and then cradled him in his arms as if P. C. were one of his own little children. He rocked P. C. back and forth, and as he wept, he kept whispering, "I'm so sorry. I'm so sorry."

One of the ambulance crew members bent down and tried to free P. C. from his arms, but the preacher wouldn't let go of P. C. He told them that P. C. didn't have a gun and had been just standing on the porch as the other two boys both had pulled guns and fired first. The emergency rescue tech said it sounded like a case of "wrong place, wrong time." He recognized P. C. but didn't say anything. The preacher just sat there and held P. C. until they loaded the other injured boy into the ambulance and then returned with a stretcher for P. C.

The preacher's young wife came out onto the porch and guided her weeping husband back into the house.

By then, the sheriff had arrived, and of course he recognized P. C. immediately and was pretty shaken up himself. He called Mr. Brown instead of Aunt Lucy, because he figured under the circumstances, that particular call just might be too much for Aunt Lucy to deal with alone. Mr. Brown assured the sheriff that he and Mrs. Brown would handle it, and he had Mrs. Brown call Aunt Lucy. That was the phone call that woke me up. Mrs. Brown told Aunt Lucy that P. C. had been involved in an accident and told her to get dressed; the Browns were on their way to pick her up to go to the hospital, Mrs. Brown said. Wisely, Mrs. Brown didn't tell her P. C. had been killed. They would deal with that once they picked her up and were on the way to the hospital.

Daddy wasn't at the scene of that tragic event, but he was involved all right. Direct culpability—Daddy was the *real* hooligan in P. C.'s life.

I'd lost the bet with Lee, 'cause she had been right when she'd said, "Somehow, some way that damn monster was involved."

Take another bow, Mr. Hyde.

CHAPTER 20

Peace, Brother

Death leaves a heartache no one can heal, Love
leaves a memory no one can steal.
—From a headstone in Ireland

I THOUGHT IT WAS HARD on Aunt Lucy when Mother died, but this was something else. She had such empathy for P. C. because of Daddy's cruelty toward him all those years, and she had plans for a much better life for P. C. now that Daddy was out of our lives for good. None of us could have known that P. C. was in such danger with those lost bad boys, not even him! The emergency tech had been right when he'd said it was a case of "wrong place, wrong time." P. C. had his problems, but I just couldn't believe he wanted to die that night. No way. He couldn't have been that messed up on *any* psychological level.

P. C. was Mother's second child and first boy, and Aunt Lucy loved him dearly. With Mother gone, she tried to be his shoulder and confidant but still let him have his space. She was trying to help him rebuild his self-esteem with every accomplishment. She blamed herself for a long time for what happened to P. C. that night. It seemed that some sort of tragedy entity had somehow attached itself to Aunt Lucy—but not to her righteous soul. She continued to carry the pieces of her broken heart with grace, somehow determined to strengthen her weakened heartstrings by being more diligent with the rest of us. Was that even possible?

The next morning was all too reminiscent of the morning not so long ago when Aunt Lucy had walked through the back door with the Chosen Three at her little house. I remembered it well. It was the number-one worst day of my life. Mother had died, and Aunt Lucy had the painful task of tellin' the rest of us. Then, less than a year and a half later, here was a new horror for the Chillton family to face.

Lee had survived her monster attack, had just gotten her two front teeth replaced, and was about to get her casts off that day; Lu had left for college; and, unbelievably and tragically, P. C. had left for heaven on the very same day! How cruel was that?

And once again, it was déjà' vu all over again. Once again, Aunt Lucy had the painful task of tellin' the rest of us.

It wasn't right. It couldn't be. It was just wrong!

So it was early Sunday morning, and we were all sittin' round the breakfast table, except for baby Mae, who was still asleep in her crib. Ali was makin' breakfast. Lu had been at college less than twenty-four hours. P. C. had never made it home the night before; Aunt Lucy had gotten an emergency phone call at three o'clock in the morning from Mrs. Brown and had gone to the hospital; and we were all just waitin' to hear from her.

As usual, the Chillton kids each had a theory, and we were all just sittin' there bettin' on the outcome, never even imagining what we were about to hear. A few minutes later, Aunt Lucy walked through the back door and into the kitchen. The minute we saw the look on her face, we knew it wasn't good, and not one of us had come close in the bettin' pool. She pulled up a chair and sat down next to little Fay. Before she spoke a word, she reached over and took Fay from her chair and held her in her lap. I remembered that she had done the exact same thing the morning she had told us about Mother. I think I understand why now.

Well, this news was really bad too. It wasn't like the news of Mother's death, 'cause it was one of *us*—a different kind of bad but still really bad. Kids were supposed to live forever, unless they got some horrible disease like polio back then. We were all hopelessly stunned.

I needed Lu, but she wasn't there.

Lee jumped outta her chair and grabbed her crutches. I don't know how many times she walked back and forth the whole length of that huge kitchen, blaming her monster with every short breath.

Paddy wasn't "paralyzed," as he called it; however, once again, he was feeling the trauma of the huge blow to his little heart. He got up from the table, walked over to where Aunt Lucy was sitting with Fay, and stood by her, eye to eye. He framed her loving face in his small hands, and as he looked at her through his tears, he asked only one question this time: "Is P. C. with Mother in heaven, Aunt Lucy?" Once again, dear Paddy was desperate for the right answer, and this time, he got it.

"Yes, Paddy. Since P. C. can't be here with us, he's in the next-best place possible—right up there in heaven with Mother, Papa, and Jesus." Apparently that was all Paddy needed to hear. As she sat there in the chair, Aunt Lucy freed one arm from around Fay and put it around Paddy. She drew him in close to her, and Paddy held on to her tightly and allowed his waiting stream of tears to flow freely.

Lainey had turned six by then but thankfully couldn't quite grasp the depth of what this news really meant. But of course, as time went on, she would.

Ali was a little different, though. She had handled Mother's death more like Aunt Lucy had, which was certainly somewhat different from the rest of us kids. She did the same with P. C.'s death. It seemed she was able to go into some safe house within her little soul and deal with her grieving more inwardly.

In the awesome book *As a Man Thinketh*, James Allen wrote about serenity and said, "Calmness of the mind is one of the beautiful jewels of wisdom. It is the result of long and patient effort in self-control."

Well, those words described Aunt Lucy and Ali to a tee. That was how they dealt with everything. Only one time in my life did I see Aunt Lucy and Ali lose their self-control, and each incident related to Daddy. Aunt Lucy loved Mother and loathed Daddy, and Ali hated charity—certainly understandable.

Lu suffered the loss of P. C. the most. They'd been together the longest and were very close. Lu had always been there for P. C. no matter what. Sadly, though, he would never be able to tell Lu, "That's three," because this time, she hadn't been able to save his life. The last words they had spoken to each other had been somewhat serious, though. On Friday night, before we all went to bed, Lu had told P. C. that since he couldn't ride with us to take her to college on Saturday, she wanted him to come up the next weekend; she had promised to take him on a tour of the campus for a little college inspiration. She had teased him by saying that since he wouldn't be able to do without her, he might as well come on up and go to college with her next year, where she could look after 'em while they both got smarter. She had also told him he'd better drop a few bad habits and pick up some new friends. Can you say *divine prediction*?

As usual, P. C. had listened and nodded while hanging his head and shuffling his feet. Then he'd looked back up at Lu and agreed that if Ali could get off work at Eagle's Dime Store, he'd ask off at Starlite and they'd come up for the weekend. That had made Lu and Aunt Lucy very happy.

Except for Lee, who had propped herself up against the wall behind the table, we all just sat there at the breakfast table in some kind of stunned trance. There was no conversation at all—just weeping. Baby Mae woke up, and we could hear her crying.

Without speaking, Aunt Lucy let go of Paddy and guided him into Ali's loving arms. Aunt Lucy put Fay back in her chair and then went upstairs to get Mae out of her crib.

Lee mounted her crutches once again and made her way around the room, cussin' and cryin' as if she were the only one there. She was filled with anger and frustration and needed to let go, and that's exactly what she was doing. It wasn't as if she could light up one of her candy Lucky Strikes, hop in the car, and tool around the neighborhood until she calmed down. We all sure woulda liked to, though.

As I watched her and Paddy, I could feel their pain. I put my head down on the table and heard myself crying out loud for Mother to help us. Just then, the back door opened, and there stood Lu!

Sometime in the wee hours, Mr. Brown had gone up to Lu's school to get Lu. She came into the kitchen and sat down at the table with us. She had had the benefit of two hours on the ride home from school with Mr. Brown. He was the one go-to guy Lu had in her life on a regular basis whom she loved and trusted. He had always admired Lu and treated her with respect, love, and kindness— unlike her Mr. Hyde. That time alone with Mr. Brown that morning proved to be the emotional glue Lu needed to get her through this new nightmare facing the Chilltons.

The next two days were a blur. We all had become way too familiar with the formalities of death and its precise process. This time, though, we siblings decided P. C. would benefit more if we were proactive. We could move on once we'd sent P. C. off with a few of his treasured keepsakes for his heavenly trip. We all got busy, searching for endearing items we knew he had held close to his heart.

Aunt Lucy looked through his wallet and found a great picture of him and Mother sitting on the front porch with our sweet collie, Lucky.

Lu found the red Swiss army knife he'd had since he was about five.

Ali donated her prized fourteen-karat-gold good-luck star charm from the beloved charm bracelet Aunt Lucy had gotten her for Christmas one year. She confirmed its star quality, and if the opportunity arose, she said, P. C. might be able to use it as a conversation piece among all the other stars in heaven.

Lee added one of her and P. C.'s favorite comic books from the series about Will Eisner's the Spirit—the '50s mystery adventures of the infamous criminologist Denny Colt, believed to be dead, who operated out of his eerie headquarters under Wildwood Cemetery and secretly fought crime as the Spirit. Maybe Lee was onto somethin'. Maybe she and P. C. knew somethin' we didn't know.

Adorable Paddy was on a crusade to find the one item P. C. couldn't possibly have left town without, because he felt P. C. would surely need it on his relaxing days up there: his cherished sketchbook. He had written "Little Black Book" on the cover—who knows why, because the book was green. It had been a birthday gift from Mother, and P. C. had treasured it. He'd go off and sit in the backyard and just sketch for hours. He'd show the drawings to Mother but not the rest of us—not even Lu or Aunt Lucy. *His* book, *his* business, I guess.

Lainey had a little Howdy Doody doll she was very fond of, but she wanted P. C. to have it. He'd won it for himself at the state fair in Raleigh when Lainey was about two. When he'd brought it home, though, she had seen it and called it "my-doll," as if *my-doll* were one word. Of course he'd had to give it to her. So now Lainey wanted him to have "my-doll" back, to keep him company in heaven. Good girl, Lainey.

I searched the house, the cars, my heart, and my mind, but I couldn't think of anything of P. C.'s that I felt was significant enough to send him off with. Finally, I went into Aunt Lucy's room and sat down in the wonderful, giant new rocking chair she had bought for all of us to rock baby Mae in when necessary. I rocked gently back and forth, idling, just thinkin' of nothin', everything, nothin'. As I sat there, I noticed Aunt Lucy's big Bible that Mother had given to her. I reached over and picked it up off the dresser. I opened it and began flippin' through the pages, and there it was: the most beautiful color picture of Jesus sitting under a palm tree, with several small children all around him. Some were sitting, some were playing, and Jesus was holding a little one on each knee. The image reminded me of the Scriptures that Pastor Meyers's had read at Mother's funeral, and from that day on, I realized and appreciated just how important children were to Jesus. That was it! Even though the picture wasn't one of P. C.'s personal items, I just knew it had to go with him. So I took the Bible downstairs, showed the picture to Aunt Lucy, and asked her if I could cut it out as my gift to P. C. She thought it was a great idea, and I was grateful.

While we were all busy preparing P. C.'s mementos for his big trip, Mrs. Brown came over to help Aunt Lucy and told her that the young minister and his family were leaving town right away. Of course, that meant he wouldn't preach his first sermon that Sunday morning as planned. Actually, it would be over twenty-five years before he would reenter the seminary and stand before a congregation to preach that most-important first sermon.

Lizzy and Paddy were unable to come, but Aunt Lucy, Lu, Ali, Lee, Lainey, Fay, Mae, and I all went to church that special Sunday. Pastor Meyers began by introducing the preacher, who was then twenty-five years older. He finally stood in front of his peers in our still-quaint little town to preach his first sermon, and it was most memorable, too! He spoke about life and death and how to live with both. His message was about his personal struggle with what had happened that fateful Saturday night long ago, and he referred to it as his "circle of life." As he wove his extraordinary story into a powerful message that beautiful Sunday, there wasn't a dry eye in the house. God is good; God is great.

It was Tuesday, not Monday, and it wasn't even sprinklin' rain, thank the good Lord, when we all gathered in the church for P. C.'s funeral service.

Aunt Lucy, all the Chillton kids, and all our relatives stood in a line and went down the aisle toward the casket, which sat in front of the altar. Lizzy was in line with us kids and had two big, bright sunflowers as her gift to P. C. Grandma Bubbee had gotten the flowers after Aunt Lucy had told her they were P. C.'s favorite.

With Lu orchestrating, all the kids—except for Fay and Mae, of course—gathered around the casket, and one by one, we each said good-bye to P. C. and then placed our special gifts right by his side as he lay there in the casket, so peaceful and unafraid.

As the oldest, Lu was last, and as the rest of us kids stood right there with her, we heard her say her final good-bye to P. C. She approached the casket and just gazed at P. C.'s face. He was definitely at peace—finally. Then she leaned in close to him and rubbed his face ever so gently as she smiled at him. She leaned in even closer, kissed him on his cheek, and whispered in his ear, "Well, little brother, you were in a world of hurt, and now you're in a world of peace, but I'm sure gonna miss you. If you can take a break from your sketchin' and whittlin' up there now 'n' then, how 'bout checkin' on us down here, okay? Hey, and be sure 'n' give Mother a big kiss for all of us, too." She placed the small red Swiss army knife under his perfectly clasped hands and leaned in once more to whisper in his ear, "Remember this?" Lu had given the knife to P. C. when he was five, and obviously there was some inside story only the two of them shared. She turned away from P. C., tears trickling down her devoted, pained, youthful face, and led the rest of us back to join Aunt Lucy on the very same pew P. C. and the rest of us had sat on at Mother's funeral only a year and a half earlier.

Pastor Meyers began the service with a sincere but unusually somber welcome, followed by this awesome quote: "Death leaves a heartache no one can heal, Love leaves a memory no one can steal."

It was almost frightening to watch all the grown-ups weeping that day. Not the kids, the grown-ups. Even Pastor Meyers broke down. It was incredibly sad. Of course, I understand now; they were all parents, and the thought of losing a child was the worst possible thing for them to ever have to deal with. As adults, everyone knew kids could die too, but people were never ready when it happened to them; it was always someone *else's* child. This child was Miss Lillian's boy, not theirs, but everybody had known him and loved him; he'd grown up with all those grown-ups, for goodness' sake! They all knew how our family lived and how P. C. had suffered Daddy's abuse. Then, out of the blue, he had been faced with the tragic loss of his beloved mother; it had been just too much.

I had thought the church felt sorry for Aunt Lucy when Mother died; well, this was even worse. I understood that too. I think I cried more for Aunt Lucy's sorrow than I did for P. C.'s death.

Oh, the sins of the father. That was one sad funeral. As I sat there and listened to Pastor Meyers, again I was reminded of all the Scriptures he'd quoted at Mother's funeral about how important children were to Jesus. Once again, Pastor Meyers reminded everyone of Jesus' love for and devotion to all the children in the world. I would never forget the image of him walking down from behind the pulpit and standing by P. C.'s casket. He gazed around the congregation, lifted his arms, instructed us all to rise from our pews, and began singing "Jesus Loves the Little Children." Then he went right on into "Jesus Loves Me."

That was all it took. Everyone was cryin' and huggin' his or her children, each other's children, and each other—what a sight that was. Well, one thing was for sure: our dear, troubled P. C. definitely had to have felt the love that day!

෴

"It's been a long time since our dear P. C. made his heavenly trip, but I think of him at least once a day every single day. I sure miss him, Lizzy," I confided. "No, I don't want a cigarette, but have ya got any chocolate?"

CHAPTER 21

The Color of Mood

Don't be discouraged. It's often the last key in the bunch that opens the lock.
—Author unknown

"**HOW DO I FEEL RIGHT NOW**, you ask, Dr. Benis? Well, in the world of colors, I'm feeling darkish sad; it's a new, awfully dark color. Maybe I should take a little break and go jump off a big cliff. That should ease my pain, right?"

"Don't be discouraged, Magg-Pie. I'm sad and feeling a little *off*-color myself. P. C. was a good boy and hardly had a chance—in his mind, anyway. He was another one of life's tragedies just waiting for that perfect moment. We'll revisit P. C., Maggs, but I do hear ya, so we'll stop for now—okay with you?"

"You kiddin'? You're the one who's makin' me talk about all this sad stuff anyway!"

"Okay then. I got a great idea! How about let's change our dark moods by picking some really bright colors for the office walls? Where's your big ole color-the-mood book, anyway? I saw you with it somewhere around here the other day."

"I've got it right here, and I've already chosen two colors I'm certain will be mood perfect. While you're listening to your patients' pain, these colors will silently assist you in the magical healing process that goes on in this sometimes scary but always loving environment you've created here."

"Okay, the fixer in me likes it so far. Proceed with that MFA of yours, Maggs; it's show-off-'n'-tell time!"

"Great! The mighty fine artist in me is glad, so here goes. Considering the life forces you interact with here in your office, Dr. Psych, I've chosen colors based on three things: the physical life, the psychological life, and the emotional life.

"Let's start out in the reception area. This is where all your patients first begin their journey toward healing, once they arrive at your office. The fact

164

that they're here in the first place tells you they're in need of *something*, and it is related to their physical, psychological, or emotional life. It could actually be all of these or a combination. Either way, they've come to *you* to fix them. You've told me in previous conversations that you usually have Paula greet them and see to any needs, and then you allow them to sit and gather themselves for about ten minutes, right? Then you personally come out of your office to the reception area, greet them, and walk them into your office. During these ten minutes or so, as they sit and contemplate their circumstances, they'll be surrounded by walls that are secretly performing *another* kind of therapy on them. This is called color therapy and should work well in conjunction with your medical hypnosis therapy. I, of all people, know that color and the brain can be a dynamic duo—and quite effective if one knows how to use color. You, of all people, know the mind is a powerful thing. With this in mind—and certainly no pun intended—I've chosen olive green for the reception area. First of all, green is the color of nature. It symbolizes life—how profound, huh? Then there's growth, harmony, fertility, and well-being. Now, remember what I said earlier about the physical, psychological, and emotional life? Well, the color green encompasses all of these. And incidentally, *olive* green, specifically, is the traditional color of peace. From my own personal experience, I believe it's safe to say anyone sitting out here in your reception area, waiting to talk with you, is definitely searching for peace in some area of these three states of life, right? Of course.

"Now let's go into your office and define what happens in there. They enter your office in anticipation of you solving their problems or at least getting to the root of their specific problem in order for them to find that much-needed peace in their lives, agree? This is a pretty tall order, huh, Dr. Shrink, MD? Now, don't tell me. I know—you're just the one to do it, right? Okay, so it's for this reason I've chosen the color lavender for your office. Lavender actually comes under the color purple. Purple is the most intuitive and sensitive of all colors. It's spiritual and thoughtful and possesses the gift of feeling—and thus *healing*, hopefully—and stands for high values. It provides a peaceful environment; the key word there is *peaceful*. In addition to all this, as you know, the Purple Heart is a US military decoration given to soldiers wounded in battle. The key word *there* is *wounded*. Like myself, I assume every single one of your patients could be described as somewhat wounded, right? Of course."

"Man, you *are* good, Maggs. I'm really impressed! This is some good stuff! What took ya so long? Do you have any idea how beneficial this can be to me and my patients?"

"That's a big ten-four, Doc. This is the one area in my life where I trust myself with myself."

"Oh, I get it! Now that you're finally allowing me to get into that head of yours, you want to get it over with ASAP, right? Any little thing you can do to help move it right along—say, like color therapy? Yep! Oh, I see clearly the method to your madness."

"Oh, Lizzy-Girl, you're so silly to be so damn intelligent. I just never thought of it—that's all. Does everybody have to have an angle with you? Is that a form of denial or manipulating the good doctor? Is that what they taught ya in Big Brain School? Hey, aren't you the wise one who's always reminding me 'wine, wine, everything in its own time'? Gimme a break."

"Yes, that would be me. You're right, Maggs—not to be confused with me being wrong, though. Now is that time, so in fact, let's break out that wine and call those painters! Tell 'em to be here tomorrow at seven o'clock sharp! The Mother's gonna be here tomorrow afternoon, and I wanta see a lotta olive green and lavender before she arrives, okay—please? I think I'm gonna need all the help I can get with this patient. Ya know she's already tried to cancel two appointments with me."

"Are you whinin', bossin', or beggin'? I can't tell. Oh shoot, I'll have Paula call the painters right now—satisfied?"

"Indeed I am, Maggs. You're the man, woman!"

We finished up at the office and headed back to Lizzy's. We'd decided to take in a movie that evening and destress a little. It was a good idea; we needed it. Reliving P. C.'s death and the funeral had been hard on both of us, and the next day was a big day.

Lizzy was excited and a little anxious about her appointment with the Mother. Thank God! Now she'd be on *her* case for a while, and maybe I could get a break—if only.

Actually, I was hopin' to get a glimpse of the Mother myself. The mysterious aura around this woman had intrigued Lizzy, and that didn't happen very often. I trusted Lizzy's instincts, though, and felt she was onto something—who knew what, but I was pretty sure we were about to find out.

The painters would arrive at seven o'clock the next morning to apply the new color therapy to the walls, and the Mother was set to arrive later that afternoon.

CHAPTER 22

A Melodious Ray of Hope

Hope is the thing with feathers
That perches in the soul
And sings the tune without the words
And never stops at all
And sweetest in the Gale is heard
And sore must be the storm
That could abash the little bird
That kept so many warm.
—Emily Dickinson, American poet

WE ARRIVED AT LIZZY'S OFFICE bright and early, and the painters were already there waiting for us. The day was off to a good start. We all got busy moving the furniture to the center of the spacious reception area and rolling up the beautiful rugs, and then we moved into Lizzy's office and repeated the same chores. The painters carefully placed their huge drop cloths over the furniture to protect it all from the serious painting that was about to begin. Paula came in a little early that morning to help Lizzy and me remove the gazillion books from all the built-in floor-to-ceiling shelves throughout the office, which would require painting as well. The painters finished at about eleven o'clock, and together we all moved the furniture back to the original positions.

Lizzy and I then went back to the house to shower, change, and get back to the office before her appointment with the Mother.

By the time we got back, the shelves had dried, so Paula and I began replacing all the books. Lizzy went into her office to prepare for the Mother. It was all falling into place beautifully, and the new look was awesome. However, the new color therapy "feel" was yet to be felt.

The good doctor couldn't have been more pleased with her new working environment, for herself *and* her patients. Ta da.

When Paula and I were almost finished with the books, she suggested I put on a fresh pot of coffee and brew some tea as well. I headed to the kitchen, put on the pots, and sat down and waited while they brewed. I could hear voices coming from the reception area and assumed the Mother had arrived.

I looked at my watch; it was 2:05, and I knew the routine. The Mother would sit in the reception area for about ten minutes and gather herself. *Today, though,* I thought, *she'll do so in the welcoming arms of the doctor's newest addition to the staff, Ms. Olive Green. I think Olive Green should be a Ms. Welcome, dear Mother—meet your new best friend, Ms. Olive Green.*

A couple minutes later, Paula entered the kitchen and prepared a cup of my just-brewed, busting-with-aroma, all-powerful java for the Mother. *You're welcome!* As Paula left the kitchen to deliver the hot brew to the Mother, I visualized Holmes sitting in her office, just waiting for the Mother to enter, and then, as she said, it was on!

It was my turn then, so I got up and poured myself a nice cup of java and sat back down in my comfortable, pillowed cane-backed chair and commenced to sippin' away. I was just totally relaxing in the knowledge that we had done a humdinger of a job on the office, and I was elated that we had gotten it all done before the Mother had arrived. All of a sudden, I looked up, and there stood the good doctor.

"You're not gonna believe this, Maggie!" she exclaimed.

Oh dear Lord—she called me Maggie. That always made me nervous; I figured her news must be serious. I sat up straight in the chair.

"Believe what?" I replied, just as puzzled as she looked.

"Get up and come with me, Maggie. I'd like to introduce you to the Mother."

"All right, I'm up. What's going on?"

"Just come on. I'll let *her* tell you," she whispered as we walked down the hall.

Lizzy led the way back to her office, and as we entered, I saw the Mother standing behind Lizzy's desk by the credenza, with her back to us. She turned around, and I could see she was holding the little note from the secret box. I looked at her face and noticed she was crying.

She reminded me of Mother. Her skin looked like porcelain—smooth, with just a touch of pink on her cheeks and lips, just as I remembered Mother's. There was also a faint but ever so light 'n' sweet fragrance of perfume floating around the room, which also reminded me of Mother. I was feeling a little paralyzed, not traumatized—or maybe *mesmerized* was more like it. Let's put it this way: the Mother clearly had an effect on me immediately, and I felt that familiar old uncomfortable-in-my-own-skin feeling, although I didn't know why. I could feel the hair on the back of my neck wiggling. Eerily strange—that's what it was. I didn't know her and had never laid eyes on her, but something about her had a strange effect on me.

The three of us just stood there without speaking for a minute or so. Finally, Lizzy broke the somber silence by introducing the Mother and me.

"Katherine Patricia Lawrence, meet Maggie Chillton." Without words, we both simply nodded politely at each other.

The Mother was still very tearful, so I refrained from interrupting her feelings with words or a handshake. She held the note in one hand and picked up the framed baby picture in the other as she gazed over at Lizzy. She was desperate for direction and answers. So was I.

Lizzy motioned for her to have a seat in the always-captivating arms of the huge, purposeful wingback, and she then repeated the same motion to me. We both followed Lizzy's lead, just as I had on the playground the day we'd first met way back in the first grade; I was confused and a little timid but willingly trusted her.

Once we were seated, Lizzy asked the Mother to explain to me the connection between her and our little treasures, which we had just welcomed the night before to their new home in Lizzy's office. Through her tears, the Mother began by telling me that the child in the picture was her little boy and that the love note was from him. I was certain I had heard her correctly, and my mind raced to put this information somewhere where it would make sense—but *where*? I looked over at Lizzy. She looked right through me but remained silent, waiting for me to make the connection.

Then it hit me. Katherine Patricia Lawrence was KPL—the initials on the back of the baby photo! That meant SRL from the love note in the secret box had to be none other than Ricky—Ricky Lawrence, the little boy who had gone missing in 1953! The Mother was Ricky's mother!

I was filled with sorrow and instantly felt a need to cry myself. But I didn't, for fear I wouldn't be able to stop—just as the last four days had been emotionally draining nonstop as I'd relived my own lost-loved-ones feelings. I had to force back my tears. Intellectually, I knew my breaking down, even in honor of the Mother's loss of her young son, wouldn't be helpful for either of us. I forced myself back into the Great Pretender mode, which I was more proficient and comfortable in anyway.

The Mother continued, describing the day the movers had come to her house in North Carolina to move her and her husband to Boston. The search

169

for Ricky had gone on for over three years, and Mr. Lawrence had been offered an opportunity with the military to move into a new position in Boston. They had decided the move might be the best thing for them, in hopes of an attempt at rebuilding their broken lives. They had both agreed it had become unbearable to remain in the town where Ricky had disappeared, because each day was a reminder of the nightmare they were forced to live every waking moment. They made the decision, moving day came, and the movers loaded the truck for the long haul to the Northeast.

A few weeks later, the Mother had realized she was missing a large box that she had carefully, painstakingly packed—a box chock-full of special mementos of Ricky. She had contacted the movers, and they had tried for months, unsuccessfully, to locate the invaluable missing box. Now, thirty-five years later, she was actually holding in her own two loving hands these two precious items from that long-ago lost box that had so cruelly refused to be found.

This time, I laser-beamed straight to Lizzy's brain for some kind of verification of *something*. *Well, she's the doctor, right?* Again she was silent, but this time, she returned the light gaze with raised eyebrows and a little I-told-you-so nod. I thought, *Oh, I know—you're right about something, of course. But what, exactly?*

My mind rushed back to the little Italian restaurant the first night I had arrived. It was hard to believe, but that had been only five days earlier. That was when Lizzy had told me all about her intriguing new patient and had given her the code name "the Mother." She had expressed an odd feeling she had about the Mother, but she hadn't been able to explain it at the time. Well, it was all happening a little too fast for my average mind, but I was just damn glad I wasn't sittin' in the Mother's chair. Holmes's mind, on the other hand, was working overtime, as usual. I was certain there was a faint odor of brain smoke permeating the air in the room—yep, she was on fire! She simply wouldn't allow herself to be bogged down with something as trite and basic as mental confusion.

Mental confusion—I had grown up on it and still practiced it diligently daily. Later I started calling it the Realm of Chaos. That was why I was up there in Boston at forty years old, sittin' in the shrink's big ole too-comfortable-to-fight-it chair, waitin' on a psychological transplant. *Now that I think about it, she must have hypnotized that damn chair. That explains a lot; she is good!* But again, considering the present situation, I was just damn grateful and relieved to be sittin' in *my* chair and not the Mother's.

I continued to sit there right beside the Mother. The room was eerily silent. I held on to myself with all my emotional might. I wanted to cry—needed to cry—but I wouldn't allow myself even one tiny little tear. I couldn't let my true feelings out; this was the Mother's time, not mine.

I was well aware of what had happened and why in *my* past—at least I thought I was. I did need to know how to deal with it in a healthy way, though, which was why I was in Boston. The Mother, on the other hand, still needed many answers.

As I sat there and watched her body language, it was apparent to me that she was actually experiencing joy—or maybe she was feeling hope, and it appeared as joy on her face and in her eyes. In her first appointment with Lizzy, she had expressed that she longed for joy and peace but felt hopeless because she had lost all faith of ever knowing what had happened to her little boy.

As I sat there studying her face and watching her lovingly caress and kiss her treasures, I believed that for the first time in over thirty-five years, she truly felt hopeful in that moment. I was reminded of the Dickinson poem about birds of hope that Danny had found after we buried the robin that day: "Hope is the thing with feathers that perches on the soul, and sings the tune without the words, and never stops at all." We buried that little robin on Easter weekend in early April 1953, and less than two months earlier, in February of that same year, Ricky had gone missing on Valentine's Day.

I doubt the color therapy had much to do with Lizzy's success with the Mother that day. Shoot, if we'd had an amazing rainbow sitting on top of our heads right in Lizzy's office, it wouldn't have mattered. However, we had hit the jackpot of all rainbows when we'd found Ricky's treasures at the Niceville Festival that beautiful fall afternoon. I remembered how insistent Lizzy had been about going to the festival that day, and I had been certain her eagerness was all about the food. Who coulda known that on that no-big-deal day, we would be led to the path of a powerful secret hidden long ago? Apparently, Ricky and his mother had needed to be reunited. This time, Lizzy and I obviously had been the chosen ones to assist in a miracle—or divine inspiration. They were the same thing in my book.

CHAPTER 23

Take a Deep Breath, Close Your Eyes, Relax

If you have faith the size of a mustard seed,
you can move mountains and cast out demons.
—Matthew 17:14–21

LIZZY STOOD UP from behind her desk and suggested we all go out onto the patio for a breath of fresh autumn air. That was a great idea, because when we got outside, it was obvious that life, the ultimate gift, was truly alive and well just on the other side of the walls of that awful, dreary room Lizzy called an office! Color therapy? I didn't care what color was embracing me that day; I was sad to the bone.

Being a mother myself, my heart was breaking into a million little pieces all around me as I observed the Mother's body language. It appeared the grief and sorrow inhabiting her body had slowly and painfully begun to detach themselves from that empty shell of a being her heart had been trapped in for so long. *Oh, if I could just cry out loud with her and for her.*

The distraction of Paula's perfect timing broke the melancholy mood a little when she opened the patio door and offered tea and cookies. Lizzy accepted for all of us while cleverly busying herself by patiently pulling aged brown leaves from several large golden mums. It was Sunday-sermon silent as I sat down at the patio table. The Mother stood by a matching mum, gazing out into space as a gentle breeze rustled her loosely coiffed hair. *A mum fest—how nice,* I thought as the silence continued.

The silence seemed to last an eternity, but only a few minutes later, Paula returned with our goodies, and both Lizzy and the Mother joined me at the table. The cautious but deliberate silence continued as we sipped our tea; then Lizzy spoke softly, asking Katherine if she was comfortable with me remaining with them. Of course, I had no idea where Lizzy was going with all this—how could I? I felt like one of the big mums next to me and remained silent.

Katherine politely agreed and was eager to know all the details surrounding the discovery of the secret box and the picture. Lizzy told her exactly what had happened and about our visit to Mr. Hobbs, the one who had put the two pieces together as a result of taking them apart.

A long, long time ago, this loving and devoted mother's life had changed in the most horrific way. Every parent's nightmare had come true and had made that unforgivable, cruel visit to her heart—and on Valentine's Day, no less. In her heart, life was over, and at the very best, it would never be the same. Until that day, the Mother, Katherine Lawrence, had had to continue to live out that nightmare without a single concrete piece of evidence to answer even one of her desperate questions: How? Why? Who?

With fierce intensity, she listened to every word Lizzy said. She leaned back in her chair and then leaned forward once again in a nervous demeanor, and she repeated the motion several times. It was obvious she was in an emotional state unfamiliar to her and found it hard to contain herself. It became apparent to me, though, that all of a sudden, she was very much alive, and hope was dancing all across her once adoring, happy face. I was right there with her and could feel both her pain and her joy.

I was also watching Lizzy and could almost read her incredible mind now. I was certain of one thing: the doctor had a plan, and it was just about to unfold. That thought was still resting on the edge of my brain when Lizzy spoke to Katherine.

"Have you ever been hypnotized, Katherine?"

"No. However, quite some time ago, my doctor suggested that it may be helpful and referred me to you."

"Would you allow me to use this technique in our therapy?" Lizzy asked.

Katherine leaned forward once again and answered, "My doctor told me of your success with this type of treatment, and if you believe it can help me, I'm willing to try, Dr. Benis. I'm not afraid anymore."

The Mother was showing signs of faith—maybe only "the size of a mustard seed," but it was there all right and would prove to be mighty. Hey, I was feeling it too! Lizzy didn't waste a minute, possibly for fear Katherine might change her mind. She immediately got up from the table and, as we took her cue, said, "Well, let's all go back into my office and discuss the best way to proceed."

I thought, *Okay, here we go,* and we all headed back into Lizzy's office.

Katherine and I took our original positions in the inviting, take-me-I'm-yours wingbacks.

Lizzy stood in front of us, leaning on her desk as she began explaining her methods of therapy. "Primarily, I use hypnosis to improve the memory—for the purpose of relieving stress, anger, and anxiety. The area of the brain known as the visual cortex processes information, registers it, and actually holds it in the subconscious mind. This holds true for visual subliminal messages as well. Katherine, I am particularly interested in possibly uncovering any visual information you may be holding in your subconscious mind—information that you are unaware of but that is there just the same." She quite naturally and disarmingly sat down on the edge of the desk as she continued to describe more specifically how hypnosis could work with an open and willing individual.

I was a willing individual, at least in that moment, but she didn't ask *me*. I realized I was just as intrigued as the Mother and hung on Lizzy's every word.

Lizzy gracefully wiggled off her perch on her desk, stood up, walked around behind the desk, and then sat down in her chair, obviously giving Katherine a moment to catch her emotional breath and ponder the information Lizzy had just given her.

I, the mum, remained silent and earnest. I also attempted to follow the doctor's professional theories. I began to wonder, *Could this actually work?*

By then, it was about four thirty, and Lizzy was ready to begin the magical process for which she was so famous. As I observed Katherine holding Ricky's little love note and baby picture, I sensed courage and determination—traits that had become foreign to her over the many years of gripping sadness and grief.

Even *I* had a sense of wonder and hope—as in, *I wonder if this is gonna work; I sure hope it does!*

Lizzy instructed Katherine to retire and relax on the large, stuffed chaise recliner resting beside Lizzy's desk. I was to retire to the reception area and relax. *Yeah, like that's gonna happen.*

I dutifully left Lizzy's office and went to the kitchen to make a cup of tea and work on some sketches I had started before I'd left Austin. My sketchbook was just like my American Express card—I *never* left home without it. As I waited for the tea to brew, I realized I was in some sort of odd place in my mind. *Okay,* I thought, *so pull out the Pretender card and move on, Magg-Pie.*

I forced myself to doodle for about half an hour but never fully engaged myself in the work, which was weird for me. I couldn't concentrate, but fortunately, the doctor appeared and asked me to rejoin her and Katherine.

"Bring your sketchbook, Maggie; I need your help."

My thought was *She's serious, and I'm back!*

"Yes, sir, ma'am, lead the way" was my trusty reply as I followed her with the tools of my trade in hand.

We reentered the office, and Katherine was lying on the recliner with her eyes closed as if she were asleep. Without conversation, Lizzy motioned for me to sit at her desk. I did, and I calmly waited for further instructions. Katherine was still "under," and Lizzy instructed her to describe in specific detail exactly what she had seen at the bus stop while waiting for the bus the day Ricky disappeared.

I looked at Lizzy but didn't need further instructions; I simply began to sketch the scenes as Katherine described them. The next couple of hours were quite an experience. I was finally seeing the Fixer at work. What she did for that loving mother that day was truly a beautiful thing.

As the Mother would remember an individual, Lizzy would direct her to look closely at everything about the person, including his or her style of clothes, the color of his or her clothes and hair, and especially anything that seemed odd or out of place compared to previous days at the bus stop.

I sketched furiously in black charcoal, noting precise colors by each individual's description. I felt like a forensic artist in a crime lab; it was very intriguing. Something else I found intriguing was the fact that although historically psychiatrists helped adults to find their inner child, in this case, the psychiatrist was trying to help the adult find her *outer* child—literally. Yes, it was quite intriguing.

Lizzy gave Katherine more specific instructions, and then Katherine opened her eyes and rejoined the two of us. She remained there on the recliner as Lizzy told her that while she had been under hypnosis, I had produced several sketches of individuals standing at Ricky's bus stop on the day he went missing, based on her memories of the day Ricky disappeared. Katherine had previously agreed that because of my professional talent as an artist, my specific involvement that day was to produce such sketches. She understood that this exercise would be an attempt to take her way back to the beginning, in hopes of uncovering even the smallest possible missed clue from that ominous, fateful day. Now I too understood my purpose.

Katherine was emotionally and physically drained, and Lizzy knew it. This had been a monumental day for the Mother—and for us too.

Lizzy asked Katherine if she would come back the next day for the purpose of identifying individuals in the sketches. She explained that the drawings were incomplete in their present form, as I had further work to do, and it would be premature to attempt to review them at that time. Katherine agreed, and Lizzy scheduled her for three o'clock the next day; then Lizzy walked her out of the office and to her car in order to ensure Katherine was emotionally stable enough to drive home.

Katherine was like a new person. The transformation she had experienced from two o'clock to five o'clock that afternoon had been nothing short of incredible. If I hadn't seen it with my own eyes, I wouldn't have believed it. When she had come into the office that day, she had been a sad, meek, withdrawn, and beaten human being. But she had left Lizzy's office a hopeful mother, standing proudly with shoulders back, with a conscious determination to make an all-out personal attempt to find out what had happened to her child. Ricky's love note and baby picture were the finds of her century, and finding those had set her cold heart on fire. She had left that day blazing mad that someone had taken her baby—and just as mad that she had given up on ever knowing what had happened to him. She couldn't get home fast enough to tell her husband and show him what we had found at the Niceville Festival only a few days earlier.

Lizzy came back into the office and sat down in a wingback. I was still sitting at her desk, completing the sketches based upon Katherine's descriptions and adding in the color. She took a long, deep breath as she leaned forward and put her face in her hands.

"What the hell just happened here today? Can you believe all this, Maggs? Am I dreaming?"

"Hey, I'm workin' here; don't confuse me anymore than I already am. And no, you're *not* dreamin', Lizzy! It really did happen just the way you lived it today—exactly. Well, you prefer quick results, right, Dr. Benis? How about frighteningly fast and furious? I can't explain it either, but your instincts were right on the other night at dinner at Ippilitto's, when you told me all about the Mother for the very first time."

"We were mentally dressed in our Holmes and Watson roles, and you told me somethin' like 'There's a plot here, and it's plenty thick,' remember? You also said that Ole Man Fate had something to do with it too. Well, Holmes, the plot thickens, and this mystery has just unfolded totally unexpectedly right before our very eyes. I think we're *all* in some state of disbelief, but I don't have time for it; I've got some serious colorin' to do here. Shoot, you're the doctor—what do *you* think?"

"I agree with you, Maggie. I *was* right."

"Oh wait, Ms. Benis. Please allow *me* to say it: 'right again,' right?"

"Yes, but that's not what I'm thinking right now, Maggie. I'm concerned that we may really be onto something out of my area of expertise. Katherine's too fragile, and I'd hate myself if I screwed this up. I don't know if I could ever forgive myself."

"Oh my, did you just use the *f* word? Remember now, dear, 'to err is human, to forgive is divine.' Maybe now ya know how *I've* been feelin' all these years! All that talk about forgiveness—it's hard, I tell ya."

"I hear you, Maggie. Forgiveness *is* hard. No matter who you're forgiving—yourself or someone else. But for *peace* sake, we must do it. The alternative is suffering, and you know that all too well. I'm just a little apprehensive with this whole curious situation with the Mother. I just may be in way over my head. Ya know, you're right too—I mean, I do like quick results, but this has happened a little too fast for even me. This whole thing with Katherine and Ricky is a mindblower!"

"Lizzy, listen to you—mindblower? Let's hope not. Get a grip, Doc; you're scarin' me!"

"Okay, then I have no choice but to trust my instincts, as usual. So are ya with me, Maggie?"

"Me? What have *I* got to do with this? I just draw and color. Why are you lookin' at me like that, Lizzy? Fine! Oh, let's see now … Let me think about it … *Yes!* I'm the one over here workin' and colorin' my butt off for ya, and you're the one over there in the big ole 'sleep, baby, sleep' chair, tryin' to get in the fetal position so that you can continue second-guessin' yourself! And what's up with that anyway, Dr. Freud?"

"I'm not sure, Maggie. I've got that eerie feeling again—like the one I had when I first met the Mother and she told me about Ricky. It's like an invisible red flag waving at me, sending me a message on a sixth-sense level. I've always known I possess an especially perceptive intuition. I'm not saying it's paranormal in nature, but it is, without a doubt, somewhat eerie."

"I get it. It's like when I get a tingling chill up my spine and the hair on the back of my neck stands up, and I stop in my tracks; when that happens to me, I'm aware that I need to pay special attention to the moment. I stop and feel the chills, and then the moment passes. But I really don't know what to do about it, if anything."

"Yeah, Maggs, like that! You're aware of something, but that's about it. That chilling or eerie feeling comes to us on a soul level, I think, and it's the heart's indicator that we need to take a moment to listen. The problem with us on the basic human level, though, is that most of us attribute this sixth sense simply to an overactive imagination. The mind rules the heart, and the end result is that we pass on that special moment and ignore a possibly crucial message being sent to us. For all we know, it's a cry for help."

Just then, the phone rang and zapped us both back to reality. As I listened, I realized by Lizzy's side of the conversation that the caller was Katherine's husband, Ballenger Lawrence. We would come to know him as Ballen. He told Lizzy that he was amazed at the story Katherine had come home with that evening. He said she had asked him to call Lizzy for permission to come to the three o'clock appointment scheduled for the next day. Lizzy told him he was certainly welcome and she looked forward to meeting him.

Based on the information Katherine had shared with Lizzy about her husband, it appeared he was a loving, gentle man. Naturally, he had to have been overwhelmed with the news of the day, just as Katherine was. Heck, they didn't know it, but we were almost as overwhelmed as they were! Ballen's call was a welcome sign to Lizzy. Katherine would need her husband's support.

As I continued to sit there filling in all of Katherine's scenes with color and tweaking the images, I realized that Lizzy's instincts were working overtime, and she probably was right with all her sixth-sense theory. Apparently, we had been given an assignment—Mission Impossible: A Cry for Help. Maybe, maybe not. One thing was for sure, though: Lizzy had accepted the challenge and made some kind of peace with herself. She was no longer confused or doubting herself about what she should do. She simply took the bull by the horns and doubled our efforts by keeping Holmes and Watson on the case. I guess she was convinced the four of us could actually unravel this mystery. Silly maybe, but our thinking process and powers of deduction did seem stronger when we donned our detective hats in addition to our respective professional ones—her doctor's hat and my artist's hat. We were counting on Katherine and Ballen, though, to possibly provide some long-hidden or forgotten clues.

As soon as she hung up the phone with Ballen, Lizzy started bossin' me around all over the place. It was crazy, scary, and exciting all at once. As we were moving into second gear, I had a thrilling thought: we had taken a detour from memory lane, and we were no longer talking about me!

We stayed at the office until midnight. We stopped only once, to order Chinese, and we ate while we worked. We were insanely focused. Well, maybe I wouldn't use *that* term.

Lizzy was on the computer, researching Ricky's disappearance and gathering info from any source available to her, while I remained artistically focused, sporting my new forensic-artist hat.

I was reminded of the time I sat with Lee in the hospital hour after hour, day after day, week after week, sketching her designs for her new room. I guess I was wearing my designer-artist hat back then. Lee had proclaimed more than once over the years that I owed my successful career to her. She was probably right, too.

CHAPTER 24

One Step at a Time

If we are facing in the right direction, all we have to do is keep walking.
—Buddhist proverb

THE NEXT DAY, when Katherine and Ballen arrived at Lizzy's office, they were so anxious to get started with the sketches that it was a little difficult for Lizzy to contain them. Katherine said they hadn't slept a wink the night before and didn't want to waste a minute.

Of course, Lizzy fully understood their reactions and the depth of the emotional impact that the discovery of Ricky's mementos had had on them.

It must have been ten minutes before Katherine realized she hadn't even introduced Ballen to us. She apologized, introduced Ballen, and, without taking a breath, urged Lizzy to show him the sketches depicting Katherine's unconscious recollections from the day Ricky went missing.

Katherine had told Lizzy the day before that during the three years of the ongoing investigation, neither she nor Ballen had ever been asked to work with a forensic artist at any time. Lizzy had explained to her that in the absence of any contradictory evidence, the investigators might have felt it wasn't necessary or, even more likely, did not have the resources to do so at the time.

Actually, at that point, all *we* knew about the case was that a little boy our age named Ricky had gone missing over thirty-five years ago and was still missing, and there were no clues from him or his abductor regarding the disappearance. But now, many years later, out of the blue, the Mother had identified her baby's missing treasures, which Lizzy and I had found out of the blue at an unlikely time and place. Lizzy and I believed without a doubt that there was an inexplicable force at work, so as always, I trusted Lizzy—and so did Lizzy.

Right on cue, Paula made her perfectly timed entrance and once again outdid herself, carrying a tray with elegant silver pots of hot coffee and tea, and a lovely array of assorted muffins and pastries. She methodically arranged her afternoon tea party on the buffet next to the round table at the floor-to-ceiling bay windows. That girl probably ran a five-star restaurant in a previous life.

Lizzy strolled with a confident posture to the round table, with the rest of us close behind. The sun was beaming so brightly through the giant windows that the room felt a bit ethereal. Paula's appearance seemed to distract Katherine and Ballen, which was a good thing. And once we all sat down at the table, their moods became calm. I guess the peace-promoting lavender color therapy had finally kicked in! *You're welcome.*

While we sat and sipped, Lizzy carefully explained her expectations to them. She and I had cleared the top of her desk and displayed all the sketches across the desk before they arrived. Lizzy asked the two of them to split the drawings up, study each one carefully, and then exchange them and repeat the process, searching all the sketches for any possible recognition or clues. They were not to discuss the sketches but to simply sit down, relax, and study them until Lizzy gave them further instructions. They agreed.

Lizzy and I made ourselves comfortable right where we were and continued to enjoy our tea party as Katherine and Ballen went to Lizzy's desk and gave the sketches a cursory once-over.

The evidence, as Lizzy and I referred to the sketches, consisted of six eleven-by-fourteen-inch full-color drawings with specific, detailed images, as described by Katherine.

Without conversation, Katherine picked up the sketches and divided them, and then the anxious, adoring parents quite naturally headed to the wingbacks. They sat down, and as the good doctor had instructed, they began slowly studying the sketches one at a time, with obvious intent and hopeful expectations.

About a half hour later, Lizzy said softly, "I'm certain we're headed in the right direction; all we have to do is keep walking, Maggs. I'll give them a few more minutes, and together we'll all examine each sketch in detail."

As we sat there and observed Katherine and Ballen, it was obvious to us that they were in fact making some discoveries. Exactly *what* and any implications were yet to unfold. Lizzy rose from the tea-party table and gracefully crossed the room to address the parents. She took the sketches from them, and then they all joined me at the table.

"As we drove over here today, Katherine and I were both concerned we may not be able to go through with this, Dr. Benis. For years now, we both have felt we let Ricky down. We never discussed it, but in our hearts, we were ashamed that we had lost all hope and just given up," Ballen said as he lowered his head and stared at the floor.

"You're being way too hard on yourselves. You did exactly what everyone does in a situation like this. You had no prior conscious knowledge or experience that could effectively aid in the outcome. You trusted the experts and followed the proper legal procedures of the due process of our legal system. You did what you were told. You trusted that process by putting Ricky, yourselves, and the outcome in the hopefully competent hands of those professionals who manage the process. I want you both to accept that and stop beating yourselves up over it. What's done is done, and from this point on, if you're open and willing, together we'll move forward one step at a time." Lizzy's explanation and encouragement seemed to comfort them both as they sat there clinging to her every hopeful word.

She had Katherine and Ballen's total trust and confidence, and it had nothing to do with hypnotism. Although, I felt certain that Lizzy's special technique and talent would prove invaluable before this unforeseen journey met its end.

We spent the next couple hours identifying the individuals and altering specific details in each sketch where necessary. Lizzy was both thorough and methodical as we moved through this engaging process, which she referred to as I&E, or identification and elimination. Incredibly, Katherine and Ballen identified each individual in each of the sketches. Then, with Ballen's help, we were even able to add a few extra physical details to a few of the individuals. As we deliberately covered each tiny detail in all but one of the sketches, we were able to eliminate almost every person as a suspect. The hefty file Lizzy was rapidly compiling resembled a major city's phone book. *The girl can take some notes,* I thought. We had one more sketch to go, and Ballen had it in his hands; he was staring at it. He pointed to a man and said that he recognized the person. He didn't know him, but he remembered seeing the man, who wore a baseball cap with a big *W* on it all the time.

Katherine had done well under hypnosis. She had remembered the *W* on a baseball cap of someone standing in the crowd at the bus stop that day.

Ballen said that it was a Washington Nationals cap and that he and his father were die-hard fans. In 1952, the team had ended an awful seven-year losing streak by finishing in fifth place. He and his dad had even attended several games in Washington, DC, so naturally, Ballen would notice anyone wearing his favorite team's baseball cap. He went on to say that the fella in the sketch had been the part-time groundskeeper at Ricky's school, and from time to time, Ballen had noticed him sitting on a huge mower at the school, mostly on Sunday afternoons.

Ballen asked me to adjust some of the facial features, though, and I followed his directions precisely. I was getting even more excited as these discoveries were made, and things were moving swiftly. It was amazing how the rough sketches I had prepared from Katherine's hypnotic state had transformed into actual, real, identifiable people from more than thirty-five years ago.

I continued with Ballen until he was satisfied with the likeness I had produced of the other Washington Nationals baseball fan, "Mr. W," a.k.a. the school groundskeeper. Katherine watched as the likeness unfolded. As I worked, she studied the sketch carefully. She couldn't place the face; however, she definitely remembered the big *W* on the hat. It was all right, though, that Katherine didn't remember Mr. W, since Ballen's memory was spot-on.

That sort of teamwork was what Lizzy was counting on; if Katherine didn't remember someone, hopefully Ballen would, and vice versa.

The sun was setting, and we were all pretty much ready to call it a day. In one word, Katherine and Ballen had been *phenomenal*, and Lizzy praised them joyfully. She suggested a one o'clock appointment for them on Friday afternoon, which would give us the rest of the day and the next to gather further evidence and compare notes from various police files. She was particularly interested in comparing our sketches to available police-file photos of all the individuals who had been questioned during the active investigation and the search for evidence.

Katherine and Ballen left the office with an even greater conviction. They were convinced that they were engaged in something that had the potential to provide them with some meaningful answers about Ricky. Lizzy and I felt the same.

We couldn't explain it, but we were all certain we were being led somewhere for the greater good. Unplanned consciously, but planned nevertheless, each one of us had been brought together through various circumstances, based on individual, specific needs. We didn't fully understand, but fate seemed to have orchestrated the whole scenario, and this little boy, Ricky, was now our primary focus.

Yes, Ole Man Fate was alive and well in Boston in the fall of 1989. To expect a happy ending to this newfound quest shrouded in mystery would be nothing short of fairy-tale, fantastical thinking—but maybe there would be an *acceptable* ending. The way this mother and father had spent the last thirty-five years was just *not* acceptable.

Once Katherine and Ballen had left, Lizzy and I returned to the tea table and enjoyed the last cup of tea and coffee and split a scone, agreeing we were both ready for some real food.

As we sat there, all of a sudden, I experienced a numbing chill creeping up my spine. I realized I was staring at the last sketch, which was sitting on the top of the table, where Ballen had left it. It was the one of Mr. W, a.k.a. the school groundskeeper. I mentally froze to acknowledge the sixth sense and the feeling in that moment. I felt so overwhelmed that I had to stand up.

I picked up the picture I had worked on so diligently with Ballen, perfecting each little detail to the nth degree, and then it hit me: *I know this guy!* I stooped down by Lizzy at the table, still holding the picture in my hand. I was stunned and tried to compose myself. Quivering, I placed the picture in front of her. I had to take a breath before speaking, as I was feeling physically overwhelmed. In a state of disbelief, I gasped in a soft whisper, "Lizzy ... Mr. W is That Melvin Bray!"

Stooping there on the floor, I almost lost my balance, so I got up and sat back down in the chair next to Lizzy. She took the sketch from me and was just as dumbfounded, trying to get her own thoughts together. We both just sat there and stared at the image; we were both speechless.

"Are you *sure* about this, Maggie?"

"Do you remember the chapter in memory lane when I told you about the time That Melvin Bray's uncle and father came to our house to talk to Daddy? Remember that they gave Daddy a photo of That Melvin Bray and had the sheriff post copies of it all over town, hoping someone would recognize him? Well, Mother saved that photo, and Aunt Lucy's probably still got it packed away in Mother's things. All I gotta do is call Aunt Lucy!"

"That's been over thirty-five years, Maggie. Why in the world would Aunt Lucy keep an old photo of someone she disliked?"

"Because that's just the way she was, Lizzy. She kept pictures of Daddy, too, and she despised him! I was probably twenty the last time I saw that photo of That Melvin Bray, and I know exactly where she kept it, too!"

"Well, call her then! What are ya waiting on—Christmas?"

I got Aunt Lucy on the phone and asked her if she still had the picture. She told me she was certain she did and would find it for me. I reminded her of where I thought she'd put it, but of course, that was a long time ago. She agreed with me, though, and said she'd look there first and call me back shortly. As always, I could count on Aunt Lucy.

Before we hung up, she reminded me to not forget the painting of Papa's

Smokey Mountains I had promised to paint for her for when the Fab Four came for Thanksgiving. She was still so clever and witty. Over the years, she'd renamed the Four Least Ones; they were now the Fab Four, and Lainey, Fay, Mae, and I got a kick out of it. I promised her she would have her painting—and framed, no less.

Now all we had to do was wait to hear back from Aunt Lucy. But for Lizzy and me, the next two hours felt like a life sentence. We lost our appetites but made a fresh pot of java and found a tin of cookies to munch on while we waited. Lizzy got back on the computer, looking for anything she might possibly find on That Melvin Bray.

"Pour me another cup, will ya, Maggs? I fear I'm fadin' fast—and strikin' out, to boot. Sure looks like our ole sheriff was correct way back then when he said, 'That boy doesn't wanta be found.'"

"Yeah, and I remember Mother tellin' Daddy they'd find him if they looked hard enough."

The scenarios Lizzy and I conjured up while we waited to hear back from Aunt Lucy were nothing short of Hollywood-movie material. We were focused, ready, and java-wired, but for what? The anticipation was exciting but scary.

"I wonder what Holmes and Dr. Watson would do right now, Maggs."

"Well, actually, the mystery would be solved by now, Lizzy. They only had an hour each week on TV, remember? It's been almost *two* hours now since I spoke with Aunt Lucy, and so far, we ain't got nothin'."

Just then, the phone rang.

"I got it, Doc. I'm sure it's Aunt Lucy!" I said as I dashed for the phone.

"All right, Maggs. Let's hope so," she answered as she went to the kitchen to find a file box for our inevitable trip south to Grace Chapel.

"Oh yeah, it was Aunt Lucy," I yelled out to her a few minutes later as I hung up the desk phone and headed out to the kitchen to tell her what Aunt Lucy had found.

"She found the photo, and it was in mint condition because she'd pressed it like a four-leaf clover in the middle of a big, fat *Encyclopedia Britannica*. However, it was not where we thought it was. She and I both thought it was in her big Bible—the beautiful Bible Mother had given her one Christmas. The same Bible Aunt Lucy had allowed me to cut that picture from—ya know, the one of Jesus and the little children—as my own personal send-off gift for P. C. But when she went to the Bible and looked for Melvin Bray's photo, she found that cut-out page of Jesus, the very one I had cut out and lovingly placed in P. C.'s casket—and trust me, I did cut it out. You were there, Lizzy, remember?

We *all*, including you, one by one, placed our little gifts in the casket with P. C. on the day of his funeral. But Aunt Lucy said there it was in the Bible—right where it was before I cut it out that day, complete with obvious, rough-cut edges, indicating that quite possibly a child had performed its removal from the precious Book.

"Aunt Lucy said she was shocked at first but then accepted it as P. C.'s gift back to her, because he knew how much she cherished that Bible since Mother had given it to her. Shoot, I sure hope P. C. at least gave me credit for my gift, Lizzy, ya know? Oh, I'm sure he did—that little stinker.

"I couldn't believe my ears when she told me she'd found that picture back in the Bible, so I asked her if *she* had taken the picture out of the casket at P. C.'s funeral and put it back in the Bible. She assured me she hadn't and said that when she realized that it was *that* picture, she sat down in baby Mae's old rocker and just had a good cry, talking to P. C., thanking him for being so thoughtful and loving her so much. If ya ask me, I'd say it was just another miracle for us to witness down here. Yep, that's what it was all right.

"Apparently, she'd moved Melvin Bray's photo from the Bible some time ago but was certain she hadn't thrown it away."

"Wow, that's pretty incredible about P. C.'s Jesus picture from the Bible though, Maggs! And Aunt Lucy still has That Melvin Bray's picture, too! If ya ask me, P. C. had a picture he wanted found, and so did That Melvin Bray. You agree, Magg-Pie? When's Aunt Lucy sending the photo?"

"I asked her to FedEx it to us tomorrow, assuring we'd have it by Friday morning before Katherine and Ballen get here."

"Perfect, Maggs. That'll give us time to compare your Mr. W sketch to the actual photo. If we can confirm without a reasonable doubt that the two match up and equal one infamous fella you call That Melvin Bray, then we'll just begin the process of pieces to puzzles."

"You realize we're no longer playin' a role here, right, Lizzy, a.k.a. Holmes?"

"Of course I do—ya think I'm nuts or something?"

"No, I wouldn't go *that* far. I'm just thinkin' out loud, and I'm feelin' a little strange ever since I recognized you-know-who in my sketch. I mean, what on earth was *he* doing in that crowd of folks waitin' on Ricky's school bus that day? That's just too damn strange, Lizzy!"

"I hear ya loud and clear, dear. Not to worry, though; we'll get to the bottom of it in due time. Hey, I got an even greater idea than I had earlier, Maggs— wanta hear it?"

"Oh sure, and I bet it involves food, right?"

"Yes, it does."

"Well, that's it—food?"

"Not quite, Magg-Pie. In the essence of time and fatigue, I thought we'd call in a dinner order to Ippilitto's before we leave here, and pick it up on our way home. I wanta get your opinion on a couple of ideas I have, and we can discuss it all over dinner at the house. That way, we can get right to bed, because if I get my way with ya, you're gonna need some serious sleep tonight, dear."

"Oh brother—coming from you, Lizzy, I know that's not meant to be kinky; plus, it sounds just like you, Dr. Benis. Yep, I know I'm right too, and I'm scared too, *right*?"

"Oh, stop it, little Magg-Pie—what a big baby! I'll tell you when we get home. What d'ya want for dinner? I'm calling the restaurant!"

"I'm not sure. I think I've just lost my appetite!"

CHAPTER 25

Big, Dark Panic Room

*The mind harbors the fear of the unknown and makes it
easy to get stuck in a rut, and scary to get out of it.*
—*Maureen Mayberry, artist*

THAT DR. BENIS, MD—she was a tough one all right. We left the office, stopped at Ippilitto's for the Italian food, and went to Lizzy's, and she set up dinner in the dining room. I thought, *Dinner's not the only thing being set up.* Yeah, something was up all right. Lizzy opened the pinot and poured us each a glass. We sat down, lifted our glasses toward heaven, and gave a mighty "Thank you, Lord" for the incredibly amazing day we'd had. Of course, we still didn't know exactly what was happening, but Lizzy convinced me we were onto something—more like she was *up* to something. I think she would have diagnosed me as a little paranoid. Oh well, it didn't do much good, but I switched to my auto-pretend mode. You know the key word there.

"I'm really starving; let's sit and have a little dinner before we talk any more theory and mystery, okay, Maggs?"

"Sure, but since when did we stop talkin' just because we're eatin'? Can't we do both at the same time like always and get this over with? I wanta know what's on your genius mind, especially if it involves me. Funny, but I've got this not-so-funny feeling, Doc."

"No, actually, Maggs, I sense a little fear and excess of caution, my dear."

"Hey, one toe in the water is quite enough for now, thank you very much, Dr. Freud. I'm beginning to understand how a little hamster becomes maniacal while running nonstop on that awful wheel."

"Maggs, you're conjuring up unnecessary demons, babe, and you're heading toward the anger zone. As a noted colleague of mine has stated, 'We are never angry for the reason we think we are.' Our conscious minds are part discriminating and part illusion, often causing us to cover up the actual basis for our behavior. Have I ever done one thing *ever* to cause you to fear or distrust me so much that you get angry at me?"

"No, of course not. I'm just sayin' I wanta know what your plans are for *me* in all this."

"Good Lord! Fine! I intend to use hypnosis with you tomorrow. Are you happy? Now can we just eat already?"

"Ya know, Liiii-za-beth, when you go totally analytical on me, you're bugged."

"Yeah, and when you call me Liiii-za-beth, *you're* angry. Truce?"

"Yes, and you just said you're gonna hypnotize me tomorrow. I knew it!"

"Look, Maggs, I love you, but I'm not going to love you to death! I'm more convinced now than ever that you need help—the kind of help I believe *I* can give you through hypnosis. So why *not* tomorrow, Maggs? And yes, that's what I wanted to discuss with you, but I didn't want to cause you any unnecessary anxiety—so much for that. I thought it would be a good idea to relax and have a little dinner, wine, and small talk before discussing the part about putting you under, as you say, as if it's the plague."

"Okay, but no matter *how* I say it, I know the key word there, Dr. Shrink!"

"Hold on, Maggie. Listen to me. Once you convinced me that Mr. W, the man standing at Ricky's bus stop in your sketch, and That Melvin Bray were in fact one and the same, I had to reevaluate the situation. Until all this unfolded today, I was in no hurry to use hypnosis on you. I was saving that option until you and I had finished our trip together down *your* memory lane, not Katherine's.

"Remember, dear, your visit with me this time was all about *you*—and accomplishing human completion, preferably while you're still here on Earth! I've been concerned about you for some time now, Maggie, and you've known that. But this visit was *not* about That Melvin Bray, certainly not about Ricky, and you didn't even know Katherine Lawrence. She was just a new patient of mine.

"As it stands right now, though, Maggs, That Melvin Bray just may possibly be connected in some crazy way to Ricky. And just as important, we may even unravel your own personal mystery hiding inside *you*! Look, my instincts tell me it's imperative I use hypnosis on you now. Hey, you're the artist, and I'm the shrink—I can't believe I just said that—and we're neither blind nor stupid. We're gonna trust *my* training and instincts and *your* artistry and memory, all right?

"I've said all along that Ole Man Fate has a hand in this—all these lives, circumstances, and discoveries attaching themselves to each other over a span of almost forty years in the most uncanny ways. There's no doubt in my genius mind, as you so eloquently put it, Maggs, that you and I are integral pieces of this puzzle. Just think about it. The two of us found Ricky's little treasures, and then my client, his mother, walked into my office a few days later and claimed them! That alone is miraculous. Yeah, we're exactly where the good Lord wants us. Right here, right now. This whole thing's like the perfect storm, and we can't ignore it. It's in the stars, the moon, the wind—and I also believe it's all God's perfect plan. I can't promise the outcome, but I can assure you we must follow its path and detour only when told to.

"Based on all you've told me, Maggs, we think *you* were the last person on Earth to see That Melvin Bray, right? So I want to use hypnosis to take you back to the last time you saw him. *That* was my even greater idea I was gonna tell you about before we sat down to eat, but that was so long ago now that I have a starving headache—thanks a lot!"

"Well, okay, fine then, so now I know, and that's all I wanted to know, ya know. So let's eat already, Doc."

"Yes, let's eat already, Magg-Pie."

We were exhausted both emotionally and physically. My anxiety was high, my nerves were raw, and my brooding was laced with a tinge of fear and anger. Oh, and let's not forget that Lizzy was starving. We sipped a little chilled wine and cooled off. We spiced up the spaghetti 'n' meatballs with a little playful conversation, which thankfully had zip to do with hypnosis.

Yeah, Lizzy was right. I'm a big baby. We cleared the table, and then we each carried a glass of wine off to bed, chanting, "Tomorrow, tomorrow, the sun'll come out tomorrow ... You're always a day away." *Next stop: the little, sleepy town of REM. Good night, Annie.*

"Relax, take a deep breath, and close your eyes" were the last words I heard before I forced myself to wake up. It wasn't even daylight, but I was glad to be awake. All that talk about hypnosis at dinner had made me dream about it. I had dreamed Lizzy was about to put me under. *Help!* Just dreaming about it caused me to hold my breath. *I mean, really, does she have to be so nonchalant about it? She obviously overestimates my power to pretend.*

"Open your eyes; wake up, Maggs!"

"Oh Lord, I'm *not* awake—I'm *under!*"

"Get up, Maggs. Your other best friend, java, is brewing in the kitchen. Get up; let's make some breakfast!"

"Oh Lizzy, you scared the hell outta me. I thought I was *under!*"

"Hey, I'm not *that* good—not yet, anyway. I can't put you to sleep unless you're *awake*. Come on now, silly—get up and make yourself useful, and *then* maybe I'll put ya under."

"Okay, boss, I'm up. Take me to your java—and crumpets."

"There's one for you, Maggs, one for me, half for you, and half for me. Let's see now—oh yeah, yogurt for you, and yogurt for me. I think that just about does it. Let's eat!"

"Well, thanks, Maggs, and can ya pass the jam over my way, please, ma'am? Say, what about that dream you were having when I woke you?"

"Sure, here's your jam—and I wasn't asleep. I was awake, but then I heard your voice and *thought* I was asleep. I was dreamin' I was under."

"Thanks—good jam, huh? I'm confused."

"Ah, Lizzy, let's just face it. I'm really feelin' freaky about goin' under."

"Oh really? Ya think I don't know that by now, Maggs? I *do* know—and it can be scary. Katherine's a perfect example. She was frightened of hypnosis too, remember? Then, thirty-five years later, she agreed to go under, and forty-eight hours later, her life had changed immeasurably—all because she finally had the courage to face her fears. So how about you tell me what's bothering you the most about my best professional tool—so *you* can face *your* fears also?"

"Well, I'm afraid I won't wake up and will be stuck in another type of hell in Somewhere Out There Land."

"Maggie, the mind *can* be a terrible thing sometimes. It has a way of pulling you into a dark, scary place that harbors the fear of the unknown, closing the door behind you. I'd say you've been seduced by an obsession with that fear. However, I don't see an appealing side to this seduction. Do you?"

"No, I don't. But how do ya overcome the fear of the unknown? Seems to me, the key word there is *unknown*, so just how do ya overcome the unknown?"

"It's a real brainteaser, huh, Maggs? But in your specific case—and everyone's a little different—my instincts tell me it's not the unknown but, rather, the known that has you frightened."

"Okay, so I *know* something I *don't* know, and it scares me, right?"

"Yes, Maggie—basically, that's it."

"So simple, Doc. How'd I miss that? That solves everything."

"Hey, Maggs, hold on a minute. I don't want to confuse you, but in a way, it's like you're forbidden to remember but terrified to forget. Try to follow me here, okay? We can't recover memories of a *missing* event—that means it never happened, so it can't be in your memory, period. However, we *can* recover memories. Those are events that *did* occur. Regarding the known/unknown factor I was referring to, I believe you have a memory of something that did indeed happen. Therefore, it's known to you and *is* in your memory bank, but doubt and fear are attached to it, and that's what has you walking around robotically, psychologically bummed—that is, you're forbidden to remember yet terrified to forget.

"It's a jungle in there, Maggie—an emotional jungle running wild inside you. You don't realize it, but I do, because that's what I do.

"Remember, Maggs, your most recent memories of That Melvin Bray were at the ripe young age of five. At that age, most of us are blessed with so little mental intellect that we don't possess the ability to discern or fully understand right from wrong as it relates to our behavior in a given situation. That part of the brain doesn't fully develop until the late teens.

"Further, if life starts out abnormal, it can actually become normal to us if we're faced with it day in and day out over a period of time. Your mother was a perfect example, and the rest of you were as well—other than Aunt Lucy and Lee, of course. They seemed to be able to see and accept people and their behavior more clearly. The key word there is *behavior*. But watching your daddy repeatedly do the awful things he did actually became the norm for most of the Chilltons, right? Dysfunction became normal. Now, I know it wasn't any fun, Maggs, but the fact that dysfunction was a regular thing in your family life forced it to become a normal way to live for your family. Sad, sick, and true.

"So now we're back to the unknown part of the known. I think something happened to you involving That Melvin Bray—something that may even concern your father—but for some reason, you've chosen to hide it. You've psychologically told a white lie to yourself, so to speak—you've blocked it out as if it never happened. It happened so long ago you don't even consciously realize you're hiding it. So coming from that perspective, it has in fact become unknown to you.

"You see, Maggs, as I explained, at five years old, we can't truly know the importance of what we experience or witness, since that part of the brain doesn't develop until the age of eight. Generally, we're not fully aware of the right, wrong, real, or make-believe aspects attached to a particular event at such a young age—what it could mean literally or whom it could affect. In your case, as you grew older, though, you figured it out but refused to allow yourself to acknowledge it, because quite possibly in your older, mature mind, you knew it was wrong for you to conceal that information. Perhaps you were ashamed, so you just buried it—both psychologically and emotionally. To this day, you've spent your whole life—so far, anyway—hard at work psychologically, making sure the memory stayed buried deep in your subconscious mind. I believe you need to go back to what you experienced at age five, because you may have been the last to see That Melvin Bray, and you may have information you don't realize you have about him and your father. So here we are now. Your subconscious mind knows the truth and is struggling to be heard, yet your conscious mind doesn't want to have anything to do with it. So what we have here, dear, is the mystery of the known/unknown event, created by you and you alone. Therefore, only *you* can solve it! But fortunately, as you know, **I** can assist you with this if you'll let me.

"Over the past several days, as I've listened to you relive what anyone would consider to be a traumatic childhood, Maggie, I've had a few of those chills of yours run up and down my spine as well, and my own sixth sense is on red alert. In particular, I'm focused on That Melvin Bray's sudden disappearance. I feel like the sheriff—I don't buy it. You know the sheriff and That Melvin Bray's uncle and father all thought your daddy was involved in some way, right? We'll definitely focus more on that later.

"But for now, Maggs, getting back to you, it's not really all that strange you may have chosen to conceal something that happened back then. Whether one is five or fifty-five doesn't really matter. It's the *why* that matters, and it's always attached to a fear of some kind—the fear of something happening to us or someone we love, should we tell or expose what we know or saw. After all, we all tell little white lies during the course of living our daily lives, right? Sometimes the reason is as small as the fear of just hurting someone's feelings. The point is, we all sometimes choose to tell one of those little white lies, depending on the situation. This allows us to be able to justify these little lies, since we're doing it out of some measure of kindness or good deed—at least in our own minds. We may harbor these lies for a short period, or we may carry them with us for the rest of our lives, depending on the degree of importance we place on the lie and the persons involved. Some of these little white lies may become insignificant as time goes by, but others may become a noose around our necks if we don't acknowledge them and cut them loose. I believe *your* white lie was never little and, thus, could never become insignificant in impacting your life.

"So here we are, babe, and as simply as I can put it, you need help cutting the noose loose, and I've got *help* written all over me!"

"I understand, Lizzy. You mean help as in hypnotherapy?"

"Yes, hypnosis can be very effective for capturing lost memories. You've just witnessed this with Katherine. And you don't lose control or reveal personal secrets under hypnosis unless you *want* to. Hypnotism is always healing and just basically deals with the natural abilities of the human mind to solve problems. It's a method of speeding up the process. When you're under, as you refer to it, you're actually in a calm, trancelike state of mind, but you're still conscious and able to access the subconscious mind.

"But, Maggs, my methods don't include psychological force. In order for me to perform hypnosis successfully, you must be open and willing. But you can't be open, willing, and *fearful*, because that creates a mental block. So this can present a problem for us, Maggie."

"So that's it, Doc?"

"Well, it's a little more complicated than that, Maggs, of course, but I'm certainly sensitive to the fears you have attached to hypnosis, so my explanation is a much-less-complicated interpretation and description of the process. However, in psychological essence, yes, that's it. And of course there's no Somewhere Out There Land to get stuck in. This is impossible. No one has ever been stuck in a hypnotic trance. Even without the assistance of a hypnotherapist, your own mind will return you to a conscious state of mind. And besides, think about it: you're already stuck in your own mind and heart! Wouldn't you agree, my dear?

"Also, there's one more crucial detail involved here that maybe you're not considering. *You're* not in charge of the hypnosis; *I* am. We're down to a matter of trust now. Katherine Lawrence's known me for what, two months? And you've known me for over thirty-six years. What is your problem, my dearest friend?"

As I sat there listening to Lizzy, I realized that she might be right—as always. I didn't trust myself, but I did trust her. Was I harboring a little white lie? Was it really hurting me or someone else—and who? How bad could it be?

As I pondered these thoughts at the breakfast table, in the necessary silence Lizzy was so willing to allow me, I remembered a special Sunday in church when I was eleven years old. That was the day I put all my trust in Jesus Christ and knew from that day forward, I had to have Him in my life forever and ever. The ever-so-wonderful Pastor Meyers explained to me how trust worked. It was so simple. It had to be; I was only eleven.

Pastor Meyers prayed with me, saying, "Accept the Lord with all your heart. Believe in Him, trust in Him, and listen to Him. If you believe in Him, trust in Him, and listen to Him, He'll always be there for you. He loves you because of who *He* is, not because of something *you* did or didn't do." Then he hugged me gently and kissed me on the top of my little head. I loved and trusted Pastor Meyers, too.

"Okay, put me under, Lizzy. I trust you and our almighty Savior, Jesus Christ!"

"Well, now, that's my girl, Maggs. When we've got Jesus on our side, we can't go wrong! So how about we shower, get dressed, head over to the office, and get on with the good deed?"

"Sounds like a great plan, Dr. Doc. Ya know, I think I'm comin' to the conclusion that pain is inevitable in life, but misery is an option, and you've finally convinced me I don't *have* to be miserable. Hallelujah!"

With a knot in my stomach, I rushed to get dressed—nervous anticipation, I suppose. We arrived at the office and didn't waste a minute other than to make a pot of hot tea, which was always soothing and calming—quite different from the java buzz. No matter how crazy my world was, afternoon tea 'n' cookies always hit the spot. Paula had hidden a tin of wonderful butter cookies that simply melted in your mouth, and Lizzy wouldn't stop until she found 'em. We fussed around in the kitchen, getting our little tea party arranged on the perfectly polished silver tray, and then headed to Lizzy's office. We set up the tea table, poured ourselves cups of tea to sip, and chatted for a few minutes—really just to relax and unwind before we plunged into the abyss of my subconscious, the underworld.

Lizzy was devoted to me and was insistent on observing my comfort and anxiety levels. I assured her I was not afraid anymore and actually felt relieved. When I realized my anxieties and fears had vanished, I felt so uplifted that I no longer feared the process would be one of those "the operation went fine, but the patient died" situations. Thank heaven!

Oh, I can only imagine the benefits if Lizzy's right. Did I say if? Well, of course she's right! I'm gonna be free! Finally, that awful, empty, life-sucking feeling that is alive at my perilous expense is about to experience a serious exorcism. So I gave the Fixer the green light.

CHAPTER 26

It's Over; I'm Under

Maybe it's up in the hills, under the leaves, in a ditch somewhere.
Maybe it's never found. But what you find is always only part of the missing.
—Paul Engle, American poet

"**OKAY, MAGGS,** I'm gonna set up the rolling machine, and here's the part you're gonna like: go lie down on the leather chaise over by my desk, and get ready for a nice little snooze. Now, isn't that wonderful? See? I told ya you'd like that part."

"Wow, this *is* nice! Ya know, I don't think you're gonna have to 'tool' me after all. This baby-soft leather is as sleep-invoking as those fabulous wingbacks, so … *gooood* night."

"Hold on! Wait for me! I gotta find my little chain with the shiny gold star—ya know, so I can dangle it in front of ya and say, 'Watch the shiny star … You're getting sleepy … very sleepy.'"

"Oh, that's funny—very funny. How 'bout we just do it already, Dr. Joker?"

"Maggs, relax. Where's that sense of humor, little sister? This is all good, remember? Relax. Take a few deep breaths. That's better. Now take another long, deep breath and exhale slowly. That's it. Now close your eyes. Breeeeathe … sloooowly."

"Wake up, Maggie. You can wake up now, Maggie" was all I heard. I woke up and felt calm and totally rested. I knew exactly where I was and didn't feel the least bit weird—which I found weird. How could I feel so good and as light as an angel wing's feather? I felt as if I coulda gotten up and flown right through the ceiling. It had been done before. *Oh my!* I realized I'd just been given a new perspective, a renewed life. That heavy anchor holding me down all that time had been set free. We both had.

"What was I so afraid of, Lizzy? Wait a minute! What day is it? I *am* really here right now with you, right?"

"Oh good Lord, Maggs. You're gonna drive me crazy, and then we're both

196

gonna need psychological help! *Yes*, you're definitely here right now with me—and you were magnificent! I'm so proud of you I can hardly contain myself! Maggs, this has been a process of intelligence, guided by experience—*my* intelligence and *your* experience.

"It's a carpe diem moment, baby! Please just lie there, relax, close your mouth, and breathe through your nose slowly. Everything's going to fall into its proper place, my dear. We have just opened up Pandora's box. Not to fear, though, because the evil inside it can't hurt us—rather, just the opposite! You see, 'what you often find is always only part of the missing,' but we're definitely much closer to finding the whole truth now.

"I'm confused, though, Maggs. I thought this was all about *your* truth, but apparently it's much, much more. How do you feel right now, my dear?"

"I'm just fine, really. I feel so good, and I'm even hungry, too!"

"Oh yes! You know that's beautiful music to *my* ears, Maggs! Okay, I want you to get up. Let's go out to the kitchen, and I'll make a pot of tea and call the Italians. Sound good?"

"Yep, and I'm dyin' to *hear* me, Lizzy!"

"I know you are, Maggs, but let's take a break and get some food in us, and then we'll both settle into a wingback and hear you on the tape together!"

We went on out to the kitchen, and she made the tea. While it was steeping, she called Ippilitto's and placed our order for delivery.

"Please, help us; we're starving!" were her exact words.

She hung up the phone and poured our tea. She wouldn't let me do a thing and insisted I sit there and relax. I sipped the warm, soothing tea, reflecting in silence. I anxiously pondered what my childhood secrets would reveal. What had I not revealed to anyone before?

"Maggs, I'm going to start the recorder. We're going to sit here and listen to it together. It's just you and me—verbatim. I'm asking the questions; you're providing the answers. Are you ready?"

"Of course, Lizzy, but I wanta hear it for myself. Remember, *I'm* the one who needs to figure this thing out in order to deal with it."

"Alrighty then, pick a wingback. Here we go!"

We both comfortably settled into the mighty wingbacks, and she pressed the start button. I knew my life would never be the same. I truly was going to have a new life—maybe even that second childhood Lizzy had spoken of a few days ago.

I was truly hopeful that this process would release me from my hidden fears and Daddy's cloak of dishonor. I was finally ready to accept the truth, come what may—and, hopefully, to finally cut that invisible noose around my neck. With just a tad of guarded confidence, I knew Lizzy was right, which meant I'd soon be changing my handle.

"Maggie, I want you to go back to that Easter weekend in 1953, when you were five years old. It was Good Friday, and your mother had the day off from work. She had had the Easter bunny bring you that sweet little biddy the night before, and you were so happy. It had been raining for days, and the sky was dark gray from all the rain. Your mother was in the kitchen with baby Fay on her hip. You and Lainey were there too, and your mother was cooking supper. It was about four o'clock in the afternoon, and you were all waiting for Lu and the rest of the kids to get home from school. The school bus would be dropping them off any time now. Are you there in the kitchen, Magg-Pie?"

"Yes."

"Can you see your mother at the stove, with baby Fay on her hip?"

"Yes."

"Do you see your daddy?"

"Yes."

"Is he there in the house? Can you see him?"

"Yes, I can see him, but he's not in the house."

"Where is he?"

"He's drivin' the old Chevy up the dirt drive to the house."

"Is he alone?"

"No."

"Who's with him?"

"That Melvin Bray."

"Okay, Magg-Pie, tell me exactly what you see right now."

"We're all standin' at the back door against the screen—Mother, with Fay on her hip, Lainey, and me. It's rainin' so hard we're gettin' wet through the screen. We're watchin' Daddy and That Melvin Bray drive up the muddy road toward the house. They're stopped at the old well, and That Melvin Bray is gettin' outta the car and goin' behind it to push. He keeps fallin' down in the mud, and it's rainin' like crazy. Mother says the car's stuck, and she closes the screen door to keep the rain out. Daddy's gettin' outta the car, and now they're both walkin' on up to the house. That Melvin Bray sits down on the porch. Daddy opens the screen door, and he's in the kitchen. He sees us but doesn't speak to us. He's soakin' wet, and he's sayin' bad words to Mother. Mother asks him to take off his wet clothes because he might catch a bad cold. He won't take off his wet clothes, and he's still yellin' at her. Now he's walkin' back out on the porch to talk to That Melvin Bray, and they're walkin' out to the woodshed."

"What are they doing at the woodshed, Maggie?"

"They're smokin' cigarettes."

"Is it still raining?"

"Yes, and now That Melvin Bray's walkin' back down the muddy road."

"Is he walking back down the muddy driveway toward the old Chevy?"

"Yes."

"Is your daddy with him, Magg-Pie?"

"No. Daddy's in the house, puttin' on a jacket 'cause he's so wet."

"What is he doing now?"

"Daddy falls down on the wet kitchen floor."

"Is he hurt?"

"No. He just gets up, and he's yellin' at Mother again."

"Is he still in the kitchen?"

"No. Daddy's standing on the porch right now, and he's yellin' at That Melvin Bray."

"Can you hear what your daddy is yelling to him, Magg-Pie?"

"Yes. He's hollerin' for him to get the whiskey out of the backseat of the car."

"That's very good, Maggie. Now I want you to tell me how you feel right this minute."

"I feel cold."

"Why are you cold?"

"It's cold in here in the kitchen because Daddy left the door open."

"Is he still on the porch?"

"No."

"Where is he right now, Maggie?"

"He's in the kitchen, pullin' dishes off the shelf, and he's callin' Mother and That Melvin Bray bad names."

"Where is your mother?"

"She's standin' in the kitchen doorway to the hall."

"Are you and Lainey with her?"

"Yes. We're standin' right beside her, and Lainey's cryin' a little bit."

"Does your mother still have baby Fay on her hip?"

"Yes."

"What are *you* doing, Maggie? Are *you* crying?"

"No, I'm not cryin'. I'm holdin' on to Mother's dress."

"Where is your daddy right now, Maggie?"

"He's walkin' back out to the woodshed."

"Where is your mother?"

"She's got the broom, and she's sweepin' up the broken dishes."

"What are *you* doing?"

"I'm holdin' baby Fay in the hallway."

"Where's Lainey?"

"She's right here with me, holding my dress, and she's still cryin'."

"What is your mother doing now?"

"She has taken baby Fay back and is telling Lainey to stop cryin'."

"Where is your daddy now, Maggie?"

"He's at the woodshed."

"Are you at the window?"

"Yes, we're all at the window, watchin' out for Daddy."

"Where is That Melvin Bray right now? Can you see him?"

"Yes, I can see him. He has fallen down in the mud at the old well."

"Can you still see your daddy at the woodshed?"

"Yes."

"Are you and your little sisters still in the kitchen with your mother?"

"Yes."

"Okay, Magg-Pie, I want you to tell me *exactly* what you see right now. Are you sure your daddy is *not* at the well with That Melvin Bray?"

"Yes, 'cause he's out at the woodshed, and I can see him smokin'."

"Did That Melvin Bray get up out of the mud and walk down the muddy driveway to the big road?"

"No."

"What is That Melvin Bray doing right now, Magg-Pie?"

"He's still sittin' in the mud, and he's pullin' himself up and leanin' against the old well."

"Okay, Magg-Pie, that's good. Now I want you to look very closely at That Melvin Bray. Can you still see him at the old well through all the rain?"

"Yes."

"What is That Melvin Bray doing right now?"

"He's pullin' himself up onto the well, and he's just sittin' there."

"Is he standing *by* the well or sitting *on* the well, Magg-Pie?"

"He's sitting on top of the well."

"Now look very closely again, Magg-Pie. What is he doing now?"

"He has fallen down the well."

"*Where* did he fall, Magg-Pie?"

"He fell down in the well."

"Are you sure he fell *in* the well, Magg-Pie?"

"Yes."

"You're sure that's what happened, even though it's raining and it's hard to see?"

"Yes."

"How can you be so sure he fell down *in* the well, Maggie?"

"Because when he pulled himself up out of the mud and climbed up to sit on top of the well, I could see his legs hangin' down just like they do when he sits on the front porch."

"Okay, Magg-Pie, but why do you say he fell down *in* the well?"

"Because he did."

"Is that the last time you ever saw That Melvin Bray?"

"Yes."

"Did you tell your mother?"

"No."

"Why didn't you tell your mother, Magg-Pie?"

"Because then she'd have to tell Daddy."

"Wouldn't that be the best thing to do? So your daddy could go help That Melvin Bray get out of the well?"

"Yes, it would be good for That Melvin Bray but not good for Mother."

"Why not, Magg-Pie?"

"Because if Mother told Daddy, then he'd be mad at her, and he might hurt her."

"But your mother didn't do anything to That Melvin Bray. Why do you think your daddy would hurt your mother if she told him to go help That Melvin Bray get out of the well? Wouldn't your daddy want your mother to tell him?"

"Yes, but Daddy would say it was her fault anyway, and he'd be really mad at her."

"Okay, Magg-Pie, I understand. You didn't ever tell your mother about That Melvin Bray falling in the well, so that she wouldn't have to tell your daddy. But *who* was going to help That Melvin Bray get out of the well?"

"That Melvin Bray could do it; he was tall and big like Daddy, and he could even drive a car, too."

"All right, little Magg-Pie, I understand. Now I'm going to ask you some more questions. Did you ever tell *anyone* that you saw That Melvin Bray fall down in the well?"

"No."

"So you *never* told your mother or Aunt Lucy?"

"No."

"Did you ever tell any of your brothers or sisters?"

"No."

"Why not, Magg-Pie?"

"Because if I told anybody, they'd tell Mother, and she'd tell Daddy, and then she'd be in a lotta trouble with Daddy."

"Did you ever see your daddy hurt your mother?"

"Yes."

"When?"

"Sometimes when Daddy was drinkin', he was mad at Mother, and he'd hurt her."

"How would he hurt her, Magg-Pie?"

"Daddy would scream at Mother, and then he'd hit her and make her cry."

"Okay, Maggie. Right now, I want you to think about the times when you saw your daddy hurt your mother and tell me about them—right now."

"One time, they were on the porch, and Daddy pulled her hair and pushed her off the porch, and she hurt her foot."

"Was your daddy drinking when that happened?"

"Yes."

"How do you know he was drinking?"

"Because Daddy was holding a can of beer."

"Were there any grown-ups there besides your mother and daddy when she fell off the porch?"

"No."

"Who was there?"

"Me 'n' Lainey 'n' baby Fay."

"Did your mother know that you knew your daddy hurt her the day she fell off the porch?"

"Yes."

"How did she know?"

"She asked me why I was cryin', and I told her 'cause Daddy hurt her foot."

"What did she say?"

"She said for me not to worry about it, because it was an accident."

"Magg-Pie, did you see your daddy hurt your mother any other time?"

"Yes."

"What happened?"

"I saw him hit her and push her on the floor in the kitchen when she was

202

cookin'. One time, he pushed her against the pear trees in the backyard, and she fell on an old bucket and cut her arm."

"Was he always drinking when he hurt your mother?"

"I think so."

"Why, Magg-Pie?"

"Because that was when Daddy shouted bad words and got mad at Mother."

"Did he do that when he was *not* drinking, Maggie?"

"I don't think so, 'cause Mother and Lu said he had a drinkin' problem and only did bad things when he was drinkin'."

"Do you know if your mother ever told Aunt Lucy about your daddy hurting her?"

"No."

"Did That Melvin Bray ever see your daddy hurt your mother?"

"I don't know."

"Okay, Magg-Pie, I want you to go back into the kitchen, by the window, where you were standing when you saw That Melvin Bray fall down in the well. You're standing there, looking out the window, and you just saw him fall down in the well. What do you do next?"

"I turn around and tell Mother, 'That Melvin Bray is stuck in the mud just like the car. What a big mess!'"

"What is your mother doing?"

"She's coming over to the window and is looking down at the old well, but she can't see That Melvin Bray."

"What is she doing now, Magg-Pie?"

"She walks back to the stove and says, 'He's probably pulled himself outta that big mess and gone down to the big road to hitchhike home.'"

"All right, Magg-Pie. Now I want you think about the time *after* that day when you saw That Melvin Bray fall down in the well, okay?"

"Yes."

"It's Christmastime, and you're all at your house, decorating that really big tree. Did That Melvin Bray come to your house then?"

"No."

"Did you ever see him at your house again?"

"No."

"Do you know if *anybody* ever saw or talked to That Melvin Bray again after that rainy day when you saw him fall down in the well?"

"Yes."

"Who saw That Melvin Bray?"

"Daddy said a man from work thought he saw That Melvin Bray in a car with a lady at Charlie's Place."

"Magg-Pie, if a man saw That Melvin Bray at Charlie's, then That Melvin Bray must have gotten out of the well, right?"

"Yes, and I was glad, because Daddy was never mad at Mother."

"But the sheriff and That Melvin Bray's uncle and father all kept looking for That Melvin Bray anyway, didn't they, Magg-Pie?"

"Yes."

"Do you know why they kept on looking for him, Maggie?"

"Because they said That Melvin Bray ran away, and they didn't want him to run away, so they kept on lookin' for him."

"Did you like That Melvin Bray, Magg-Pie?"

"No, I don't think so."

"You're not sure if you liked him or not?"

"No."

"Why not?"

"Because I don't think Mother liked him."

"Why do you think she didn't like him, Maggie?"

"Because one time, I heard her tell Daddy she didn't want That Melvin Bray alone with her children."

"Were you afraid of That Melvin Bray, Magg-Pie?"

"No."

"Did your siblings like That Melvin Bray?"

"I don't think Lee liked him."

"Why not?"

"'Cause she told Mother he was sick 'n' sweet."

"Did Aunt Lucy like him?"

"No."

"Do you know why Aunt Lucy didn't like him?"

"Yes."

"Why didn't she like him?"

"Because when he was with Daddy, they were always drinkin' alcohol, and she told Lu, 'He must be lookin' for trouble if he hangs around with your daddy.'"

"Did you ever go down to the old well after that rainy day, Maggie?"

"No."

"Why not, Magg-Pie?"

"I was afraid."

"Why were you afraid?"

"I don't know; I just was."

"Okay, Magg-Pie, I want you to look at the old well. Can you see the old well right now?"

"Yes."

"Are you feeling afraid of the old well right now?"

"A little bit."

"Are you feeling afraid of That Melvin Bray right now?

"No."

"Did you *ever* feel afraid of That Melvin Bray?"

"No."

"All right, Magg-Pie, I want you to leave your old farmhouse. You're not five years old; you're all grown up now, Maggie, and you know exactly what happened to That Melvin Bray. You saw him fall down into the old well that rainy Friday on Easter weekend, way back in 1953. You are no longer afraid of that vision itself or the memory of that vision. It is perfectly all right for you to remember it and accept it, and you are *not* afraid of it. When you saw That Melvin Bray fall down into the well, you didn't equate death with falling in the well. You did not do anything wrong. That Melvin Bray did what he did, and it had *nothing* to do with you. You believed he could climb out of the well. You were *never* responsible for That Melvin Bray. I want you to release the secret you have held about That Melvin Bray falling into the old well right now, Maggie. Do you understand me, Maggie?"

"Yes."

"Maggie, I want you to relax now. It's just you and me, sitting in my office in Boston. When I tell you to wake up, you will do as I say, and you will feel rested and refreshed, as though you've had a nice, long nap. We will revisit everything we have talked about today, and you will *not* be afraid of what you know and understand about what happened to That Melvin Bray. You will be at peace with yourself and That Melvin Bray. You will feel rested and refreshed."

"Open your eyes, Maggie. Wake up, Maggie. *Wake up now, Maggie.*"

Lizzy pressed the stop button and leaned back in her chair. She didn't say a word. Obviously she was intensely watching me and my body language. The room was absolutely silent.

I was stunned, rewinding the tape in my head as Lizzy continued to observe me. I knew it was going to take me some time to sort out the incredible story I had just heard come out of my own mouth in my own words. Suddenly, I felt a lump in my throat; it was the first warning sign that I was about to begin weeping uncontrollably.

I was totally devastated. Not paralyzed, not traumatized—just plain ole absolutely devastated. I made a desperate but futile attempt to hold on to the new rested, refreshed, glad-to-be-alive feelin'; instead, I burst into tears. A flurry of good, bad, and ugly images flew through my mind and heart all at once. I wanted to scream. I wasn't afraid, just overwhelmed.

I needed Mother to hold me, Lu to console me, Aunt Lucy to assure me, and my best friend, Lizzy, to help heal me. Had I done the right thing that awful rainy day by not telling anyone that Melvin Bray had fallen into the well? I had been just a little child. All I had been concerned with was my daddy hurting my mother. Was that so bad? Of course not!

But let's face it: I should have told Mother what I saw. If I'd been older, I would have. I definitely would have "equated falling in the well with serious injury or death," as the good doctor had put it. *I was just a little child. I now understand what I did and why I did it. I accept that, but now what?*

Oh, poor Uncle Bray and poor Daddy Bray! They had looked everywhere for That Melvin Bray, and I had done nothing to help them.

Lizzy's prior explanation of the shame one felt made perfect sense to me now. I was ashamed—just part of my punishment for not ever telling Mother or anyone else what I really saw that day. Oh, and the known/unknown part of all this? Well, I got it—like a ton of bricks.

I couldn't stop weeping. I wanted to just sit there and cry myself to death. I felt I didn't deserve to live. *No wonder I've never been at peace with myself,* I thought. And in that moment, I hated myself. I realized it was no big surprise that I had become the Great Pretender so early on.

After all, just what was I anyway—a *murderer*? While I realized I hadn't pushed That Melvin Bray down the well, I hadn't helped get him out either. Was he still *there*—down at the bottom of that old well? Could that be? Heavens to Betsy, what had I done?

As I sat there, I could hear myself praying out loud through my tears: "Oh dear Lord, what have I done? I believe in you! I trust in you! I'm listening to you. Help me!"

Making a bold and timely stand, Lizzy's prayerful words of comfort found their way to my wounded heart as she spoke them: "Maggie, your help *is* here, dear. It's okay. Cry it out; cry it out."

I felt myself waking up again, and I was still comfortably cradled in the huge wingback. I realized that I'd just awakened from another one of my out-of-body experiences. Was it a good one or not? Whatever my present state of mind was, I was certain it wasn't real, not really, so at least I had that goin' for me.

"How's my girl?" Lizzy asked.

"Well, I'm not too aware of exactly *what* I'm aware of. What time is it anyway?"

"Let's see here—my watch says it's not a minute past 7:53, Magg-Pie."

"Well, what *day* is it then?"

"Still Thursday here in Boston. It's still the month of October; the year's still 1989. Hey, Earth to Maggie."

"Great, that helps a lot. I'm attempting a little mental clarity here, Doc. Yeah, just like that—Earth to Maggie. So how long *was* I out anyway?"

"Oh, not very long, dear, but long enough."

While I had been taking my out-of-it nap, Lizzy had been busy as a bee, working on our mystery puzzle, and she was well prepared when I woke.

As she explained it, once I heard the tape and fully understood what had happened to That Melvin Bray, I had begun to hyperventilate and had literally passed out from emotional and mental overload. Of course, that escape was the help I had prayed out loud for. There was no shame in passing out from an intense case of TMMS, or terminal moment of mental sobriety, as alcohol was *not* involved. TMMS was what my alter ego, the good Dr. Watson, diagnosed, but of course, I was certain Dr. Shrink, MD, had a long psychological term for it, even longer than *hyperventilation*—maybe like *my-mind-couldn't-get-over-the-matter*.

Maybe that was too simple of an explanation, but either way, once I came out from under, it all hit me at once. I simply knew too much in that stone-sober moment, and I couldn't handle it, and it was lights out!

CHAPTER 27

Chasing the Truth

The truth will set you free, but first it will make you miserable.
—James A. Garfield, twentieth US president

AS I SLOWLY MADE MY WAY back from the old well scene of my distant childhood memory, I accepted the notion that I wasn't dreaming, nor had I entered an altered dream state. It was real. That was a good thing, though, because for the first time in over thirty-five years, my mind and heart were in unison about the truth of what I had witnessed that dreary day so long ago.

If That Melvin Bray hadn't gotten himself out of the well that stormy night long ago and had experienced his unfortunate fate, I could not hold myself responsible for his death. Hopefully, with Lizzy's help, I would finally come to terms with what had happened—without guilt. However, the reality was that I had seen That Melvin Bray fall down in the old well!

Once again, my mind began to uncontrollably race, and my heart started beating like a thousand tom-toms! Lizzy gently grasped my hand and said softly, "Maggs, tell me what you're thinking, dear."

I was nearing the mental danger zone once again, but her thoughtful touch stabilized me. I settled down, and we began to discuss what my recollections meant. I thought I was having a total mental and emotional breakdown, but she convinced me it was in fact a break*through*. I was encouraged by her outlook as she emphatically stated, "The truth will set you free, but first it will make you miserable!"

After a lengthy heart-to-heart conversation, I was quite comfortable with the fact that I was not a murderer. I hadn't killed That Melvin Bray—or anyone else, for that matter, with the exception of me, myself, and I, who had suffered a collective, self-imposed, slow death for so long.

The revelation was even more comforting because it eased emotions I had surrounding an awful recurring dream I'd had for years. The scenes were never the same, but in every single one of the dreams, I killed someone. I was unable to see a face, so I never knew the victim. I was always deeply saddened in the dreams that I had taken another human life. The dreams were really frightening because I could actually see myself performing awfully cruel acts, causing another human being terrible pain until the person breathed his last breath. I always had the feeling, though, that I had no other choice; it was either him or me—like legal murder. What an oxymoron. I would always wake up sobbing, and I'd feel a deep sadness in my heart all day long. Now, that was some seriously twisted stuff, because I knew I would never, ever, never commit such cruelty to even my worst enemy, and I was pretty sure I didn't even *have* a worst enemy.

Lizzy explained how that nightmare was part of the known/unknown dilemma I had been harboring in my subconscious. Over the years, it had manifested itself in a mountain of sorrow and guilt within me, and that sorrow was what she had started picking up on over the past few years when we got together. I guess the smarter she got, the sicker I became. She assured me I would never have that nightmare again.

Lizzy also helped me come to the conclusion that what happened that day at the well just happened—just the way it happened. Period! End of scary, known/unknown memory, but *not* end of story!

"You know That Melvin Bray is probably at the bottom of that old well, don't ya, Lizzy?"

"Yes, Maggie, my instincts tell me it's certainly the logical conclusion. We have a lot to sort out here, though, before we take any kind of overt action. Remember Pandora's box? We've just now pried it open and gotten a glimpse of what may be inside, but we don't know anything for sure."

"Well, hopefully when we get the FedEx from Aunt Lucy tomorrow, I can confirm that the guy standing at Ricky's bus stop in my sketch and That Melvin Bray are one and the same, but if it *is* him, what exactly does that mean? What's the connection between That Melvin Bray and the Lawrence family? Even if he *is* at the bottom of the well, that doesn't necessarily connect him to Ricky."

"True, Maggs, but let's think through this. Ricky disappeared on the day before Valentine's Day—February 13, 1953. As far as we know, you were the last person to see That Melvin Bray, and that was on Friday, April 3, 1953—six weeks *after* Ricky went missing."

"Yeah, Lizzy, but don't forget that guy who said he thought he saw That Melvin Bray up at Charlie's Place several weeks *after* I saw him fall in the well."

"Right, but the key word there is *thought* he saw him. As far as we know, no one ever confirmed that, Maggs."

"Also true. Plus, That Melvin Bray's uncle and father continued to look for him for years. I'm sure of it. And the sheriff, the uncle, and the father all thought Daddy had something to do with his disappearance, but there just wasn't any proof.

"Ya know, Daddy was so drunk that night, anything coulda happened. I guess the sheriff figured even if Daddy had done anything to That Melvin Bray, he wouldn't necessarily even have remembered it the next day when they pulled him outta the old Chevy.

"And another thing still really puzzles me: Why in the world was That Melvin Bray standing in that crowd of people at Ricky's bus stop the afternoon that Ricky disappeared anyway?"

"Well, Maggs, let's work on this. We know Ricky was abducted on February 13—Friday the Thirteenth, no less—because Saturday was Valentine's Day, the fourteenth. Katherine and Ballen had planned a little valentine party for Ricky and a few of his friends. Remember her telling me that?"

"Yep, and that means That Melvin Bray was not at Collins Mill on that Friday the Thirteenth, where he should have been. Normally, he worked at the mill Monday through Friday, seven to three, on the first shift with Daddy. So just what *was* he doing fifteen miles away in Ricky's little town, standing in the crowd at Ricky's bus stop that afternoon?"

"That's just another part of the puzzle, Maggs, but we can't even confirm it was That Melvin Bray in the sketch until we get that old photo tomorrow from Aunt Lucy."

"Yeah, yeah, I know, but if it *is* him, I'm thinkin' we're gonna be packin' some bags and headin' south, right?"

"Yes, ma'am—that I can confirm. We're committed, and we're going!"

It was game on, and I could tell Lizzy was in her zone. I was amazed by her uncanny ability to focus so intensely with such discrimination and analytical ability. She was blessed with laser-like powers to hone in on the underlying truth of any issue and possessed innate psychological astuteness. I might not have understood it all, but I accepted it. My confidence was born out of the fact that somehow Lizzy always got to the real motivation for someone's behavior. What was she—a head doctor or something?

That said, waiting for the FedEx delivery was gonna seem like a lifetime. I could hear another verse of the song from *Annie* playing loudly on my recently hypnotically repaired TCR (transistor cranium radio): "Tomorrow, tomorrow … It's only a day away."

CHAPTER 28

Bittersweet Tears

Hope is definitely not the same as optimism.
It is not the conviction that something will turn out well, but the
certainty that something makes sense, regardless of how it turns out.
—Vaclav Havel, Czech playwright and politician

I LAY IN BED, staring a serious hole in the ceiling. *Oh no, don't say "hole"—that's the new scary word goin' on round here. The mere thought of that dark, damp hole at the bottom of that well … Well, it sorta gives me the creeps. One thing's for darn sure: I'm certainly not gonna make the first move today. Besides, confusion is her area of expertise, not mine. I strive in it; she thrives in it. Clearly, my job is simple: (1) eat, even if I'm not hungry, (2) take orders—or else, and (3) draw like crazy. So be it. We all have our strengths, and frankly, I've become quite proficient at mine and have no intentions of rocking her psychological boat or mine this morning. I'm simply gonna lie here "like a skinny celebrity," as she calls it, until she threatens me.*

"Rise 'n' shine, dearest friend of mine. I've had an epiphany already. I woke up with it, Magg-Pie. Ya wanta hear it?"

Oh, bro-thuuuur! I knew it was too good to be true. Damn, she's up!

"Ahhh, okay. I'm sorta scared 'cause as cheerful as you seem, I detect something more ominous in your voice, but go ahead 'n' tell me."

"Well, based on *your* instincts this time, your memories, and your artistic genius, I agree with you, Maggs. When that FedEx package gets here this morning, you're going to confirm that That Melvin Bray and Mr. W are the same person. What this means, dear, is that for over thirty-five years now, you, Katherine, and Ballen have unknowingly, on a subconscious level, held the key clues to That Melvin Bray's mystery and possibly even the disappearance of little Ricky!"

"Heck, I'm certain the photos are gonna match, Lizzy; I told ya that! That Melvin Bray and Mr. W *are* the same person! But what's happened that I don't know about to convince you that That Melvin Bray and Ricky are, in fact, connected?"

"Oh, that was my epiphany! We've all been brought together after all this time to solve the mystery of Ricky's disappearance. As we keep digging, though, it appears That Melvin Bray has been thrown into the mix as well. Remember, Maggs, Ole Man Fate—no coincidences, right? More like divine intervention, right? I feel it so strongly that I've already accepted it to be the truth, and now I'm open psychologically and can fearlessly take the next crucial step toward proving our suspicions. I've been waiting for that feeling, the one that tells us to hush and listen to our higher self—God in us?"

"Yes! And that's the same feeling I had, Lizzy, when I first saw that *W* hat in my sketch! Once I'd tweaked the drawing for Ballen, I knew without a doubt that the guy was none other than That Melvin Bray!"

"Well, as strongly as we both feel, though, Maggs, I'm reluctant to share this with Katherine and Ballen just yet. I believe we need to keep the two cases separate for now, for *their* sake. We'll proceed by ourselves on the path with That Melvin Bray, and if he does have anything to do with Ricky, it'll be revealed along the way, I'm certain! So let's get going; we gotta get to the office! I still want that FedEx photo for any doubters we may encounter as we finally unravel our uncannily woven mystery, okay?"

"I'm up, movin' fast as I can! Yeah, an unsolved and mysterious story—talk about memory lane! Man, you penned that one right, Holmes. I'm havin' those chills right now!"

We got dressed, jumped in the Benz, and arrived at the office at about eight thirty. Paula was already there, busy making the java—what a girl! I don't even remember the ride over to the office that morning. Lizzy and I both were mentally twirling in our thoughts, and our minds were racing with what-ifs. We greeted Paula and headed straight to Lizzy's office and began gathering our materials pertaining to both Ricky and That Melvin Bray. This would prove to be a most intriguing day.

Paula entered and cheerfully said, "Coffee, anyone? I've looked all over this place for those butter cookies I bought, and somehow they've mysteriously disappeared!"

"Thanks, Paula. We sure needed this. Oh, about those missing cookies— well, I confess. I found 'em, and we ate 'em—sorry! Think you can get some more?"

"Oh, sure, but for now, you guys are in luck. I've got some frozen goodies in the fridge. I'll bring them in shortly; I'm assuming no one's had breakfast?"

"You're all over it, girly! What on earth would this office do without you? Seriously! Oh, and one more thing, Paula: be on the lookout for the FedEx man. That package will be addressed to Maggie, okay?"

We continued methodically putting all our findings in the proper files for travel and preparing for a trip south. Lizzy placed a call to the sheriff's office in Grace Chapel. The fact that she made that call before the FedEx delivery even arrived convinced me she was definitely certain of at least half the mystery. I got busy with the airlines, checking available flights. We decided to wait until Katherine and Ballen arrived to discuss our next moves and how they'd be involved at that point, if at all.

Emotionally charged air floated all around us in Lizzy's office that day. We knew it was possible that we were onto something so huge that if we stopped our momentum, even for one moment—well, let's just say we remained in high gear for some time to come. Lizzy's resolve was apparent. She was just as driven as the finely tuned machine she drove, but unlike the machine, she had a giant heart. My incredible, indelible best friend—the gift that kept on giving. Thank you, Lord!

"Here we are, ladies—time for a little brain food."

As Paula served some bagels, she also placed the much-anticipated FedEx package down on the credenza in Lizzy's office. We stared at it, but neither of us went for it.

"You do the honors, Maggs," Lizzy suggested as she pointed to the infamous package.

"Sure, my pleasure, sister—sorta." I picked it up and painstakingly opened it, so as not to damage the photo in any way.

The anticipation was so intense that someone probably could have heard our hearts beatin' from the patio. I was holdin' my breath, thinkin', *Have thine own way, Lord.* I paused for what seemed like forever, but I finally pulled out the old eight-by-ten-inch photo and laid it on the table next to the Mr. W sketch. Lizzy was standing by me, patiently impatient, watching my every move.

"There! Now, look at that photo. If they're not the same person, then they're identical twins, Lizzy!"

She took only a minute, maybe less, to examine the two photos before responding. "Incredible, Maggie—without a doubt! You were right, little sister. And you trusted your instincts. See? It works!"

She put her arms around me and hugged me tightly. We both were in some peculiar state of euphoria, yet we were filled with an eerie apprehension in anticipation of what was next and, of course, the what-ifs.

Just then, the phone rang, reestablishing our earthly footing. It was the sheriff, returning Lizzy's call. He was only a couple years younger than us, and we'd all grown up together back in Grace Chapel. His father, who had been our little town's sheriff for over twenty years, was the same sheriff who always came to our house armed with a deputy or two to pick up Lu's Mr. Hyde, a.k.a. Lee's monster. *Why did I call him Daddy?*

It was only logical that Sheriff Todd would be aware of the disappearances of Ricky and That Melvin Bray, because his daddy had remained focused on both cases for quite some time. Todd and Ricky were about the same age, so no doubt, back then at Todd's house, these cases were often the topic of conversations around the supper table. Being a father as well as a sheriff, Todd's daddy had desperately wanted to find Ricky. It was no surprise that Todd jumped all over it when Lizzy made the first phone call to him and told him what we suspected. Because Ricky was a child, Ricky's case was widely publicized, but That Melvin Bray was an adult, and people did not scrutinize his disappearance in the same way. His disappearance certainly was not considered an unsolved crime; people figured he had just left town. Strange? Yes. A crime? No.

Sheriff Todd agreed with Lizzy that we had to get to the bottom of the old well—literally. He said he would contact the Jennings family, since they still owned the property. They both agreed it might be premature, even cruel, to contact That Melvin Bray's family. If our suspicions were correct, the past would not be altered by waiting a few more days to involve the Bray family. Confirming the facts first seemed the kindest way to pursue this awful but necessary deed.

Lizzy's logical theory connecting That Melvin Bray and Ricky was still disjointed, but Sheriff Todd assured her he would join forces with us and pursue the old cold case as if it had just happened, thus enabling us to come to a factual and provable conclusion. Before they hung up, Todd promised Lizzy he'd call back once he'd contacted the Jennings folks and had something solid arranged to get us on the property as soon as possible.

As I listened to Lizzy on the phone, I had another flashback to Mother telling Daddy if That Melvin Bray wanted to be found, he'd show up somewhere sometime. I guess he was ready to be found, because it sure was lookin' as if somewhere and sometime were upon us.

"The Lawrences are here. Shall I bring them on in, Lizzy?" Paula asked as she peeked into Lizzy's office.

"Sure, Paula, please do."

Katherine and Ballen entered the office, and we all greeted one another with affection. Right off the bat, Lizzy asked them to compare the FedEx photo of That Melvin Bray to the Mr. W sketch on the table. Ballen was ecstatic, and Katherine had to sit down.

There was no doubt in my mind that Katherine felt an intense, ice-cold chill run up her spine. As I sat there and watched her, I thought, "It is not the conviction that something will turn out well, but the certainty that something makes sense, regardless of how it turns out."

It became apparent to me as I watched the bittersweet tears trickle down her cheeks that Katherine was in the process of preparing herself for a possible what-if.

Lizzy was also observing Katherine's emotional state, and she sat down beside her at the tea table. She explained to both of them her sincere desire to resolve their hauntingly painful past, but as close as we were, we were not there yet.

I was convinced Lizzy was certain of That Melvin Bray's fate; but at the same time, we both were aware of the possibility, slight as it was, that That Melvin Bray and Ricky might not have been directly connected. *But they must be!* I felt it in my bones! That Melvin Bray had been standing at Ricky's bus stop the very same Friday afternoon that Ricky disappeared. But we still didn't know the *who, what,* and *why* surrounding Ricky's disappearance.

I began a silent prayer, asking for one of Pastor Meyers's earthly angels to come and guide us. Then I thought, *Hey, such an angel may already be here.* All of a sudden, I could hear myself thinking, *Hush and listen.*

CHAPTER 29

I Love You the Most

Hope for a great sea-change, on the far side of revenge.
Believe that a further shore, is reachable from here.
Believe in miracles, and cures and healing wells.
—Seamus Heaney, Irish poet and Nobel Prize recipient in literature

IT WAS OBVIOUS Katherine was trying her best to accept Lizzy's sincere plea for her and Ballen to patiently hold on just a little longer. A timely tap on the office door distracted us, and then Paula entered with a silver tray decorated with more delectable delights. As she placed the tray on the credenza, she softly suggested that Lizzy step out of the office with her for a moment. As they headed for the door, I immediately distracted the loving couple with my southern hostess skills and began to pour coffee and tea.

As we waited for Lizzy to return, they reviewed all the sketches once more, saving the FedEx photo of Mr. W for last. I figured Sheriff Todd was returning Lizzy's call and confirming our plan to get onto the Jennings property to open the old well.

As Ballen and Katherine both stared at the FedEx photo intensely, Ballen remarked how odd it was that during all the investigating that had gone on for almost three years after Ricky's disappearance, not one person, including Katherine and him, had even considered Mr. W a person of interest. He had definitely been there at the bus stop that day, but somehow he had gone completely unnoticed by everyone. "How could this have happened?" he pondered out loud to Katherine and me as our threesome sat there weighing the facts. I immediately readjusted my invisible psychological mum hat, with a "Mum's the Word" logo, and simply nodded curiously in response.

The old cold case was heating up rapidly, and the new investigation was being led by the one and only Holmes—or, as she was more widely known, Dr. Benis, MD. Any response on my part might have been inappropriate; my lips were sealed!

The office door opened, and Lizzy entered and gracefully rejoined us at the tea table. I watched her as she leaned over to pour herself a cup of my java. I thought, *She doesn't drink that stuff in here; she drinks her tea. What's goin' on here?* Her strange behavior continued as she poured a pint of cream in her cup as well. *A little coffee with your cream there, Doc?* It was obvious to me that Lizzy had something on her mind, so I just sat there wearing my mum hat as she mentally prepared to present her theory and plans for proceeding. She finished mixing her concoction and then, in an aristocratic fashion, slowly sat back down in her cane-backed chair. She began ever so calmly to sip her coffee and assess the present situation we were all facing. As I waited with bated breath, I leaned back and gazed upon her. You could have heard a pin drop. *This is gonna be interesting. Are they in or out?* I wondered.

"Since our last meeting here on Wednesday, Maggie and I may have discovered the whereabouts of the infamous Mr. W. I've just spoken with the sheriff in that town and made him aware of the fact that we have new information in reference to Mr. W that is possibly related to Ricky. The sheriff suggested Maggie and I catch a flight out tonight and meet him at his office first thing in the morning with our evidence."

Okay, they're out. As I listened, I realized she was doing exactly as she had proposed to me earlier. It was premature to contact the family of That Melvin Bray, a.k.a. Mr. W, and it was also premature to include Katherine and Ballen at that point. They were out and wouldn't be joining us on the trip south. Our immediate focus would be on That Melvin Bray and getting that old well opened, because it was imperative we confirm our suspicions regarding his disappearance. Once we achieved that, we'd bloodhound the trail and track for clues to a possible connection to Ricky's disappearance. We had our work cut out for us, but it was definitely *on*.

"Once we've met with the sheriff and hopefully located Mr. W, I'll call you at home, and we'll discuss the best way to proceed on Ricky's behalf, based on exactly what we discover, if anything. I want you both to know I understand the cruelty and torment of time, and the pain that's attached to waiting, but I trust you both know I'm dedicated to finding some answers for you as quickly as possible. I promise you'll not wait even one minute longer than is absolutely necessary for those answers, and I'll call you the very minute I have them."

It was all Katherine could do to hold back her tears as she listened to Lizzy's words. With her head bowed, she began to cry. Her loving protector, the kindhearted Ballen, put his arm around his cherished wife as he responded to Lizzy.

"We understand completely, Dr. Benis, and we'll do whatever you think is best."

Lizzy responded to Ballen with a sincere thank-you as she stood up and moved toward Katherine. Ballen followed her lead, and with his arm still around Katherine, he gently lifted her up from her chair. Katherine was gathering her emotions, and she spoke softly in agreement as Lizzy empathetically embraced her. The couple graciously accepted the fact that they could do nothing else at that time but go home and wait. As Lizzy led the way, we all walked out of the office together toward their car, and once again with obvious affection for each other, we all bid adieu.

Lizzy and I watched them drive away, our hearts breaking for them, and then we both turned and made a beeline back into the office, filled with a dogged focus to find out what had happened to their little boy. Back in high gear, we got busy loading up a large box of our files and photos—or, as Lizzy referred to them, our *incredible-without-a-doubt-credible* evidence. Paula got on the phone with the airlines and made our reservations to Charlotte, which had the closest airport to Grace Chapel—about an hour 'n' a half away. She also reserved a rental car and a hotel room, so all we had to do was go home, pack suitcases, and head to the airport.

"Well, here we go, Maggs," Lizzy said as we drove to the airport. "I'm really feeling good about this; how 'bout you?"

"I'm great, Mr. Petty, but ya think ya could slow this baby down a bit? This ain't the speedway, ya know."

"You're right, Maggs; I do need to slow down. I'm just so revved up. I'm not quite myself."

"Hey, now you know how I've felt all my life. Yeah, that not-quite-myself feeling is a little weird, huh?"

"Well, that's all behind you, Maggie. Nothing's standing in your way now, and you can definitely be 'quite yourself'—ya hear me?"

"Yes, sir, ma'am—loud 'n' clear. Thank ya, ma'am!"

"You're welcome, baby, but I'm only gonna take half the credit."

"No, seriously—thank you, Lizzy! I know what you're sayin', but I'd still be lost out there if not for you. I just wanta get to that old well and get the sweet, ugly truth out once and for all! Until I see him with my own *adult* eyes, I fear that the time tormentor you spoke of will just keep this madness up, and I'll be doomed to remain in my emotional limbo. Intellectually, I get this whole crazy picture, but emotionally, I know what seeing it through these very same eyes as a *child* did to me."

"Listen to you, Maggie! You do get it! The whole crazy, colorful, mixed-up picture—must have something to do with the artist in you. Frankly, I'm relieved to hear you express yourself on this level, because it tells me you're open to the healing, and frankly, I'd be more concerned if you didn't react this way. This is serious stuff we're dealing with, and I'm confident your grand finale is just waiting to happen, honey. Then, knowing the sweet, ugly truth, you'll also be able to finally shed that ill-fitting cloak of dishonor. Now, that's truly sweet and something to look forward to, huh, Maggs?"

"You know it, but I'll be sittin' on pins 'n' needles till this is over! And by the way, I'm assuming you have your reasons for not telling Katherine and Ballen about That Melvin Bray and the well?"

"Most definitely, Maggs. Katherine's in a very fragile psychological state. We can't cause her even one ounce of unnecessary grief. She's putting up a good front, but this is such an old, deep wound that I'm not going to take any risks with her emotions that I don't absolutely have to."

"I understand. I watched her today, and I totally agree. Thank God she's got Ballen, ya know?"

"Yeah, now, there's a good man, but he can't save her from herself. That's my job now, Maggs; therefore, we have to be mindful of her state of mind, okay?"

"Heavens, ya know ya don't need to be concerned about me. I'll always follow your lead with careful thought, Lizzy. Ya know that, right?"

"Indeed, I do. Shoot, you have no idea how impressed I am with you this very minute! You just stay grounded and connected to the moment you're experiencing. As all this unfolds, try to remember to breathe, remain calm, and, as you said earlier, watch and see through your *adult* eyes. You've served your time, Maggs, and your sentence is almost up. Praise the Lord! Hey, we're here. Now to find a parking spot! Look, Maggs, our ethereal number five—one of our favorite numbers! Right here at the crosswalk—that was too easy. This is it; I'm pullin' in!"

"Perfect—just perfect! Something tells me we'll be gifted with other ethereal assistance along this physical trip back down memory lane. I'm anxious but not afraid. And I can just *feel* an earthly angel close by, Lizzy—can you?"

"Yes, ma'am, I'm with ya. I've got some new feelings talking to me too, Maggs. Let's just trust in Him and expect some more miracles, okay?"

We went inside, checked our bags, and headed to the gate for a short wait before we could board. Only a few others were at the gate, so we had the pick of the perch.

As we sat quietly in a private corner, we got into a spiritual conversation about life and death. Because we'd been introduced to death by the loss of each of our mothers as young children, we both knew what death meant and how it felt on a personal level. Somehow, though, through His grace, God had a way of lifting his little children up 'n' out of a crisis, as he did with Lizzy and me way back then.

But on that particular day, Lizzy and I were involved in another painful situation: a mother and father had lost a child. We both agreed that loss might be even more devastating. As a mother myself, I personally couldn't imagine anything worse than losing a child, except maybe for the dreadful dilemma Katherine and Ballen were still facing—losing a child literally and physically without ever knowing what had happened to him. They'd suffered a desperately lonely life and had experienced every possible feeling, from disbelief to guilt, yet so many years later, they still had no answers. Now, that was truly devastating.

Lizzy and I loved the Lord with all our hearts. Sure, we were somewhat out-there characters sometimes—even disobedient characters sometimes. Regardless, we were His characters, and He loved us back with all His being. Our souls belonged to Him. He was our wonderful Counselor, everlasting Father, and Prince of Peace. That was just the natural way of things for us. We were both trusting in Him to light our way on the dark, ominous road we were traveling, and we were somehow certain this was His will, not ours.

As we waited for our flight to be called, we felt compelled to join hands and pray together. We asked for continued guidance, courage, and strength to do God's will, trusting that the hands of heavenly hosts were leading us. We finished praying with an amen, followed by a simultaneous, heartfelt "Obedience now" as we gazed into each other's eyes squarely with confidence, knowing we had to hold on tight to that heavenly grasp until it was safe to let go. We raised our heads as our flight was announced.

"Hey, that's us, Maggs; let's move it!"

"I'm right beside ya, Lizzy-Girl."

We got on the plane, got in our seats, and were on our way to something far greater than anything we could've ever possibly imagined. We tried to relax during the flight, but it was mighty difficult. We were both curious about the possible fateful end of That Melvin Bray at that old well. At the same time, we were so spiritually inspired to help Katherine and Ballen that we both had to remember to follow Lizzy's earlier sound advice to me to be calm, breathe, and, most of all, hush and listen.

The captain announced our landing. *Thank you, dear Lord.* I don't think we could have sat on the plane a minute longer!

Lizzy was at least as anxious as I was. She had always been the calm, patient one of the two of us, but obviously this was a whole new experience for her as well. I could understand her feelings, though, because so much and so many were depending on her, and she was well aware of that fact.

I was feeling the strength and power of my faith, and the "be calm and breathe" part must have slipped into autopilot, as I actually was calm and breathing.

Once we landed, Lizzy took on her normal "I'm in charge" role and proceeded to make things happen. We went straight to the rental car counter, got the keys, and then went back to baggage and had the porter follow us to the car with our bags. We drove to the hotel and checked in. Although we were truly exhausted, more emotionally than physically, we ordered room service because we hadn't eaten since the pastries that afternoon at the office. Unusual as it was, Lizzy never once mentioned that she was "starving"—further confirmation for me that she had personally entered a new psychological realm and, as impossible as it seemed, had lost her appetite. She was also about to spread some new deeply rooted, God-given wings, and food simply was not that important anymore—for once in her skinny life. Now, that was truly a miracle. No kiddin'!

Dinner came, and we both fussed over it with little enthusiasm; then I showered while she pulled out some of the reports that Todd had faxed her that afternoon at the office before we'd left. I willingly went on to bed, leaving her to her comfortable world of the psychological human mind. At least we weren't talking about *my* mind anymore.

Strangely, as I lay there, exhausted in that comfortable bed, my thoughts were rambling all over the place. *Good night, Dr. Benis, MD, and thanks for taking me and my subconscious back to that old well, with me kickin' and screamin' all the way.* The realization that I hadn't killed anybody had truly given me a new lease on life. And finally, with that awareness, I was able to logically consider the present situation we were in. Lizzy, on the other hand, had the presence of a logical mind even when she was sleeping probably.

Oh well, I've said it before, 'n' I'll say it again: we all have our strengths.

"Maggs, hit the deck! It's showtime; get up!"

"Hey, is it even daylight yet?"

"Almost—get up!"

"Shoot, last night was so short that I didn't even have time to dream! I'm up already; go away!"

We were dressed, packed, checked out, and in the rental car in a fuzzy blur. We'd be in good ole, bad ole Grace Chapel in about an hour. Of course, the drive would have taken most people about an hour and a half, but not my friend Speed Racer.

We stopped about halfway there for gas and java. Lizzy chose something a little stronger, though: a humongous Mountain Dew. Now, that'll wake you up at seven thirty in the morning and keep ya up till seven thirty at night.

It was a little after eight o'clock when we pulled into the same small but remodeled sheriff's office in our still-quaint little childhood town. We both commented on how odd the circumstance was that had brought us both back there to our little town together. Yes, very odd, strange, weird, and scary—it was all of those things!

We parked, got out, and went into the building, where we found our childhood friend Todd sitting behind his desk, holding an open file. He realized we had arrived and immediately stood up and came around from behind his desk to greet us. We all hugged and reminisced about the last time we'd seen each other, almost four years ago. He pulled two chairs up to his desk for us and buzzed his assistant, Kalah, for fresh coffee.

We sat down together and wasted no time getting to the possibly morbid task we were facing. The good thing about this whole awful business was that all three of us had our own personal reasons for wanting to get to the truth, no matter what it might be.

Todd's reason was to resolve unfinished business for his father.

Lizzy's reason was to find out what had happened to That Melvin Bray for me and, of course, Ricky for Katherine and Ballen.

My reason was to find That Melvin Bray at the bottom of that well. Had he really fallen into it as I had remembered while under hypnosis?

I didn't push him; he fell, I reminded myself. *I wasn't even at the well!* That Melvin Bray might have lost his life that day, but so had I. It had taken me almost thirty-five years to pull a part of me out of that well too!

The three of us spent the next several hours reviewing all the evidence: the interviews, sketches, photos, testimonies, possible suspects. We reviewed each detail with keen enthusiasm, and we were all eager and willing to do whatever it took to find the one tiny clue that might be hiding. A fresh set of eyes, or three, just might solve the mystery.

Todd had already told us that Ole Man Jennings's son, Sydney, whom we also had gone to school with, would be calling us that afternoon to confirm the day and time we'd be able to come out to the property to start the excavation. Todd had told Sydney that it would be necessary for him to prevent anyone from coming onto the property until he was able to release the property back to him and that he was legally bound to remain silent about the investigation until further notice. Since Sydney and Todd were lifelong friends, Todd had no concerns about Sydney's reliability.

In addition to quarantining the property, based on all the facts and possible scenarios surrounding That Melvin Bray, legally, Todd was required to contact the local district's medical examiner. The fact that the old well might actually have been an unmarked human burial site—coupled with the fact that if there *was* a body at the bottom of the well, the deceased might also have been involved in an ongoing crime investigation, the unsolved case of Ricky Lawrence—required certain legal protocols. Therefore, the district medical examiner had to assume jurisdiction over the whole process.

Todd had already notified the ME after his first phone call with Lizzy two days earlier, and with the ME's direction, he had contacted the state archaeologist. Todd was waiting on Sydney Jennings, the ME was waiting on Sheriff Todd, and the state archaeologist was waiting on the ME; therefore, we all were waiting on Sydney! The crucial phone call came in at five o'clock that afternoon. *There's that special number five again,* I thought. *Have thine own way, Lord. It has been a very long thirty-five-year wait—so yes, by all means, have thine own way, Lord; we're all in your competent hands.*

Sydney told Todd we could start the next morning at nine o'clock, and Todd immediately called the ME. The ME said he would make the final call to the state archaeologist. Our plan was in place.

Todd invited Lizzy and me to his house for dinner that night. He'd married Lori Davis, who had been a good friend to Lizzy and me all through school. The fact that both our mothers were taken from us so abruptly at such a young age naturally sorta made all our friends feel sorry for us, but it also brought us all closer together. We gladly accepted Todd's dinner invitation and were excited to see Lori again. It had been almost four years since Lizzy and I'd gone back to Grace Chapel for our twentieth high school reunion. That was the last time we'd seen Lori and Todd. Sydney Jennings was a year younger than all of us, and he'd married Lori's younger sister, Deborah. The two families were very close, and it truly was a sweet family affair. We suggested Todd call Lori and ask her to invite Deborah and Sydney to join us.

Once those plans were in place, Todd called the Comfort Inn and got us the "Sheriff's Special," which was a suite consisting of a parlor in the middle of two king bedrooms. Perfect. We were set for the duration of our mission. We headed over to Todd's charming old renovated farmhouse, which his grandmother had left him. With Lori's sense of style and Todd's love for creating with a hammer, the two of them had transformed that old house into a beautiful, loving home to enjoy and raise their family in. In spite of the circumstances, we all had a lotta fun that night, and it was great to be together again. Rather than discussing the cases, we spent the evening dissing each other in the spirit of friendship. Our small reunion was filled with joy and laughter, which was the emotional nourishment we all needed on that momentous occasion.

Before I went to sleep that night, I decided I was going to be up and dressed the next morning before Lizzy. The truth was, I slept very little that night; I was too anxious. I was full of prayer and hope but still anxious. I reasoned with the Lord and myself that my anxiousness had nothing to do with trust or fear. I just wanted to get the adventure over with—and quickly. *Please, dear Lord. Ya know, He has such a great sense of humor,* I thought. *He created me, right? He knows me so well and puts up with all my shenanigans. I do love Him to heaven and back!*

The next morning popped in on me at six fifteen. I tried but couldn't lie there another moment. I got up and hit the shower. I was almost dressed and about to dry my hair, when that skinny blonde walked in, completely dressed and coiffed; if she hadn't been armed with a giant java, I woulda been tempted to trip her as she entered my room. Instead, with a big, grateful smile from ear to ear, I carefully relieved her of my favorite morning beverage.

"You know, I was trying to beat you up this morning—not literally, of course. Ya know what I mean."

"Of course. I couldn't sleep either, Maggs—just too much going on here. I promise you when this is over, you can beat me up anytime you want."

"Okay, I'll remember you said that."

"I'm sure you will. Hey, when you're done here, meet me in the lobby, will ya?"

Lizzy left me to finish getting dressed; then I headed down to the lobby. When I got there, Todd and Lizzy were chatting. He suggested that since we had a little time, we should grab a quick bite of breakfast since it might be a while before we ate again. As we grazed over the breakfast buffet, Todd told us Sydney had called to let him know that the team from the state archaeologist's office was already out at the property, setting up their equipment. We finished our breakfast and followed Todd out to the parking lot. Like the gentleman he was, he opened the doors of his souped-up sheriff's RV for us ladies.

As we rode out to the Jennings property, the three of us were all about the what-ifs. We couldn't help ourselves.

We arrived at the property and took the long road up to the house, passing the old well on our right. It looked so different. Todd parked under the even older and more mature pear trees in the side yard—the same old pear trees that Mother had walked under each night at about eleven fifteen, when her ride would drop her off from work. As we got out of the car, I could feel her presence, and for a moment, I noticed a wonderfully familiar, powdery fragrance floating around my head.

As we walked down to the well on that old driveway, I realized something was different. I looked down and noticed the road had been paved all the way from the main road up to the house. *Oh my, how nice.* Then another thought occurred to me: if that road had been paved back then, the old Chevy wouldn't have gotten stuck in the mud, That Melvin Bray wouldn't have gotten himself stuck in the mud and fallen in the well, I wouldn't have seen what I saw, and none of us would have been there that day, looking for That Melvin Bray! Life for many could have been so different if only that old gravel 'n' dirt—mostly dirt—road had been paved. It really was that simple.

I was about to jump outta my body and scream insanely as these thoughts screamed back at me. All of a sudden, peace came over me, and I felt calm; I felt Mother's presence.

Once we got to the well, where the excavation team had set up a big tent, none of us really had a clue what to expect, but we found out quickly that *patience* would be the new word of the day around that old well. It would be mostly slow going but, fortunately, not thirty-five-years slow. At least we had that goin' for us.

First, they would dig down about fifty feet, and then the slow part would begin. One promising factor that worked in the team's favor was that Mr. Jennings's entire estate of several hundred acres had not been touched since my family had left the property. About twenty years ago, he'd given a long-term lease to a farmer who grew mostly corn and a few other soil-friendly vegetables. The old house and barn were still there, which the farmer used for utility purposes, not his personal use. The barn was still in pretty good shape, although I was sure it had had a face-lift or two over the years. The house was a different story. It looked like something right outta that old movie *House on Haunted Hill.*

The well was about one hundred feet deep when originally drilled for Mr. Jennings in 1946. The minimum required depth back then was about forty feet, but obviously, the deeper the well, the less chance for contamination and bacteria to infiltrate the water supply.

In 1924, Mother and Aunt Lucy's water supply came from a natural spring, not a protected well. They shared the spring not only with all the wildlife in that neck of the woods but also with other people in that hollow who did more than just drink from that spring. The others contaminated it, and that's how Mother and Aunt Lucy ended up gravely ill with typhoid fever. What a way to live.

As we stood around the tent, we noticed an elderly gentleman driving up the driveway.

Todd told us it was the medical examiner, Dr. Alfred Maness. Over the next few days, I would come to realize that Lizzy had an older twin. She and Dr. Maness had so much in common that I was gonna have to order *two* of those plaques that read "To save time, let's just assume I know everything." He was disarming, charming, and quite intelligent, just like Lizzy. They bonded instantly, and it was interesting to watch the two of them "decipher stuff," as Dr. Maness would say. And Lizzy would say, "Let's think this through." He was a handsome fella of about sixty, was in fine physical shape, and was nothing but seriously confident when it came to his expertise and knowledge of his profession, just as Lizzy was.

It was about noon before the team finally had everything in place to begin the initial dig. There really wasn't much the rest of us could do but be there and continue the ongoing discussion of the facts and all the evidence, or the lack of it. Of course, we all had our opinions. But based on all the information that Lizzy and I could provide about the Lawrences, That Melvin Bray, and Ricky and my own revealing session with Lizzy, Todd and Dr. Maness came to the same conclusion: That Melvin Bray was probably at the bottom of that old well.

If I could have, I would have patted myself on the back, but since I couldn't, I felt a big smile spread across my face, and I just went with it. I was feeling pretty good, and about that time, Lizzy walked over to me and patted me on the back. Wouldn't ya know it?

"Hey, thanks—I needed that!"

"You're welcome. Todd called Lori, and she's bringing us out some sandwiches and a couple of gallons of her famous sweet iced tea—how 'bout *them* apples, Johnny?"

"Was I singin' out loud?"

"Yep, and right on key."

"Well, Me, Myself, and I were all over here just rehashing all that's happened from one Friday to the next. It's pretty incredible, ya know, Lizzy! And I was thinkin'—"

"Maggs, you know I know what you're thinking. I'm all over it. You're calm, you're breathing, you're happy, and you're singing. Most importantly, though, I do believe you've experienced forgiveness. You have finally forgiven yourself of a very old debt. Have I missed anything?"

"No. I know I'm in good hands, so you don't have to worry about *me* anymore. And yes, I do believe that I have finally begun to forgive myself. So I think we've just about come to the end of ole memory lane, ya know?"

"Yes, and thank God we have, Magg-Pie. I couldn't be happier—certainly for *you* but for *me* too, 'cause you're right. I don't have to worry about you anymore! You, my dear, are on your own! Now that you've forgiven yourself, you're going to see how much easier it is to forgive your daddy! Can I get a hallelujah?"

"You know it! Hallelujah!"

"You ladies havin' your own private revival over here, or is it open to the public?"

"Hey, Todd. Nah, it's not private, but if it was, we'd still let *you* in, dearie," Lizzy said.

"Actually," I said, "Lizzy and I were just discussing how in only one week, we've covered the past thirty-five years and then some! Now here we are, standing out in the middle of this old pasture, waiting to uncover a huge missing part of that thirty-five years."

"Well, Maggs, I'd sure like to know how ya did it—time machine?" Todd asked.

"If only, but no. However, she has her methods—trust me, Todd."

"Hey now, don't be givin' out any o' my secrets, Magg-Pie! Ole Sheriff Toddy here may *need* my tools and methods someday. Ya never know, right?"

"Todd, the truth is the Lizzy-Girl's right—for the *most* part, *most* of the time."

"Well, let's just hope she's right *this* time. Shoot, talk about turnin' over in his grave. Heck, my daddy'll be doing backflips when we get to the bottom of this old well!"

We all felt as if we'd just been to one of Pastor Meyers's Tuesday night prayer meetings and were seriously enjoying ourselves in spite of the circumstances, when Lori came drivin' up the driveway. We headed to the old pear trees to meet her. Todd took the two wicker picnic baskets filled with sandwiches and all kinds of other tasty goodies, Lizzy grabbed the two jugs of tea, and Lori and I divided the rest of her haul. We set up a coupla folding tables and chairs to aid in everyone's comfort. We weren't being irreverent, and maybe we all shoulda been walkin' around morbid and sad, but it was just impossible—right then, anyway. Truth was, we were all aware that the doom 'n' gloom would set in soon enough, so for just a little while, we would picnic joyfully and eat, drink, and be thankful.

It took a few hours for the excavation team to reach their first forty feet down. Lunch was the first break they had taken since they'd started early that morning. They ate and rested for about an hour and then went right back to their work. They went down another twenty feet or so before dusk was upon them, forcing them to shut off the noisemakers. Did I say *noise*? I thought, *There's really gonna be plenty of that before we leave this place, and it'll have zip to do with weird-looking post-hole diggers!* The team took the rest of the day's light to gear down and close up for the night. The excavation would resume bright 'n' early the next morning, which was Sunday. As I said before, Sunday was always my favorite day, because that was the only day my siblings and I could get up, go to church, and spend the whole day with Mother. I suspected, though, that this particular Sunday out there at that old well would most likely create a whole new meaning of Sunday for me. *What will be, will be.*

"Well, that's about all that's gonna happen out here today, folks," Dr. Maness said. "It was a mighty good start, though, I tell ya. I've worked with this team on a number of digs, and they're as good as they come. They don't take any chances regardless of their personal opinions. They work real tight and think as one. There're no egos here, except for mine, of course."

"Aw, now, Dr. Maness, you're just pickin', and I know it. You're as good as they come too," said Todd.

"See there, Sheriff Toddy, my boy—you just walked right into that one and fed that old ego o' mine without even thinkin'. Thank you, son."

"Dr. Maness, I saw that one coming a mile away," Lizzy said.

"Call me Alfred, Miss Lizzy."

"How about Alf?"

"If that pleases you, Miss Lizzy, Alf it is."

"Perfect, and you can call me Miss Lizzy."

If you'd asked me, I'd have said there was a bit o' flirtin' going on between the two of them. Just then, I grabbed a big red apple off the table and interrupted the potential lovebirds with a personal gesture toward the newly named Miss Lizzy.

"Here, take this. I know you're hungry, and you can call me ..."

She was so smooth that she just politely took the apple as an impish little grin formed on her pretty face, indicating she got my message. I just wanted to get credit for being so perceptive in observing the possibility of one of those ever-lasting relationships that began with an apple and the words "you can call me."

By then, it was dark and everybody was packing up to head out to his or her sleeping quarters for the evening. Todd dropped Lizzy and me off at the hotel; then he, Alf, and Dr. Bernard "Bernie" Childress, the state archaeologist, were meeting for dinner, which was mixed with plenty of criminal justice talk, I was sure.

"Man, I'd just love to be a fly on that wall, Maggs!"

"Or even better, sitting at the table, huh, Miss Piggy—I mean, Miss Lizzy?"

"Hey, *he* started it."

"Now, now, no need to be defensive, Doc. I'm just considering your new captivating colleague."

"He is rather, isn't he, Maggs?"

We strolled through the lobby and hopped on the elevator up to our sweet little suite. As I unlocked the door for us, I noticed the number on the door. I didn't know how we'd missed it before, but we had. The number on our door was 555. We took showers, dressed, and went back down to the restaurant for a quiet but certainly interesting conversation.

We both agreed this case was in the most competent hands, and we had no doubts that the decision to wait to notify That Melvin Bray's family had been the right one. I couldn't imagine them standing around out there, painfully waiting and waiting for something horrible, but needing desperately to do it. Then there was Ricky's family, which really couldn't move forward until we had dealt with That Melvin Bray. The conversation went on and on until one of us finally shouted, "Uncle! I'm going to bed!" I think it was me. So Lizzy signed the check to our room, and we left the table and went back to our suite and settled down for the night. I was lyin' there half asleep, not half awake, when Lizzy came in and sat down on the foot of my bed.

"Hey, what did we have for supper, Maggs?"

"Uh, let's see now ... We had ... iced tea and ... rolls 'n' butter and ... Did I say iced tea?"

"Yeah, I couldn't remember either. Hope I didn't wake ya, babe. Good night."

"Good night, Miss Lizzy, and sweet dreams to you too."

As she disappeared into the dark of the room, I lay there thinking of the next day, Sunday, the Sabbath. I then realized that Lizzy couldn't find the off button on the side of her brain either. I tossed and turned, considering the possibilities of the next day. It would be Sunday, the Sabbath, a day of worship. Over the years, though, I had realized that Sunday had come to represent different things for different people—posturing for some, prayer for many, penance for all, and peace for God only knows who. I finally drifted off with a peace of my own when the word *healing* sat firmly on top of the off button on the side of *my* brain.

The next morning, when daylight was crowing, as tired as I was, I began the process of crawling outta bed. Then I realized I wasn't so tired after all, and my mind was filled with wonderful thoughts of Mother. I lay back down on my pillow and closed my eyes in an attempt to reconnect with my thoughts. I recalled the dream I had had the night before.

I could see her—my wonderful, sweet mother. She was standing out by the old pear trees by the side of the house. *I knew it! She* was *there the day before*! She was holding her arms out to me, with that beautiful, endearing smile of hers. In the dream, I walked over to her, and she put her loving arms around me and held me so tightly that I could actually feel her embrace. It felt so wonderful and so real. She led the way as we walked down to the old well. We sat down on the ground, but it wasn't hard; it was as soft as a down pillow. She continued to hold me in her arms as we sat there. She was so beautiful. She had on the lovely white lace gown that Aunt Lucy had bought her—the one she was wearing the last time I saw her alive. She took my hands and held them in hers, and then she kissed them. I felt her soft lips on my hands, and I could smell the light, powdery fragrance she wore to church on Sundays. She never spoke a word, nor did I. It was the purest act of love and affection I'd ever felt—that was the only way I could describe it. I wasn't sure how long we sat there, but she never left me.

I guess I woke up when the daylight peeked through the drapes in my room. I rose back up off the pillow, realizing how rested and renewed I felt. It was awesome! I couldn't wait to get outta bed to tell Lizzy about my wonderful dream. As soon as my feet hit the floor, there stood Lizzy in my doorway, with an unusual look on her face.

"Okay, Miss Lizzy, that's a peculiar look even for you, so just what do you know that I don't know this early already?"

"Well, Maggs, I just had the most wonderful dream experience I've ever had since Grandma Bubbee died. Remember when I was lying in bed next to her the night she died, and I had my heavenly flight experience?"

"Yes, of course, honey. I remember it very well."

"Well, last night I dreamed Grandma Bubbee, my mother, and I were all out there at the farm at your old well!"

"No way! Are you serious?"

"Of course I'm serious! Would I kid about a thing like this, Maggs?"

Well, I immediately sat back down on my big king-sized bed and patted it, inviting her to sit 'n' join me. The two of us had some serious dreamin' out loud to do. We sat there for a while, reliving our angel experiences, and came to the same conclusion. Both of our dear mothers and Grandma Bubbee had come to "ground" us, as Lizzy put it—and she had always had a way with them.

In this case, we weren't in trouble, though. Both our mothers and Grandma Bubbee had come to us in our dreams to reveal themselves as the hands of our heavenly hosts, to assist us here on the earthly ground as we trudged our way through this difficult mission.

In both our dreams, Lizzy and I were led to the old well. This was our confirmation that all our answers would be in the hole at the bottom of that well. Only Grandma Bubbee had spoken; she had told Lizzy to "believe in miracles and cures and healing wells."

We couldn't get dressed and outta that hotel fast enough. As we were leaving the suite, I pulled the door closed, and this time I noticed the gold-plated room number on the door—the 555. We both noticed that the numbers were clearly much brighter than they had been just the night before—actually, they were shining! We stopped for a moment and pondered the idea that this was yet another sign from our heavenly hosts. There were three fives: one for my mother, one for Lizzy's mother, and one for Grandma Bubbee. We had a triple dose of the Lord's will about to be done, and we couldn't have been more grounded!

Thank you, dear heavenly hosts!

Lizzy and I drove out to the property to meet everyone there. As we drove, we revisited our previous night's dreams and agreed there was no doubt the Lord was all around us and all we had to do was be obedient. The paths our lives were traveling that day had begun a long, long time ago. As painful as some of the years had been, Lizzy and I understood that we were precisely where we were supposed to be in that moment: in that car, eating a brown-bag breakfast on our way to find the one and only Melvin Bray.

The awareness of our heavenly hosts provided us with a welcome yet unfamiliar comfort and encouragement to fearlessly forge on and down into the well. After our mothers died, I had had Aunt Lucy, and Lizzy had had Grandma Bubbee. It seemed only appropriate for wise and wonderful Grandma Bubbee to accompany Lizzy's mother in the dream. *God is good; God is great.*

As we approached my old driveway, I noticed the Browns' house on our left. Among my many memories of them, one thing stood out vividly: *their* driveway was always paved! *Oh bro-thuuur, why do I torture myself so?* The Browns' house was as lovely and manicured as always. It had been remodeled, though, and appeared to be twice its original size. Danny; his wife, Andrea; and their little girl, Erin, lived there now, and he was the pastor at our old church. Surprise, surprise! He certainly had grown up with a great mentor. Yep, Danny-Boy sure did love Pastor Meyers, just as we all did.

"Oh gosh, Lizzy, when we get finished here, we'll have to see Danny and his family. Heavens to Betsy, I haven't even called Aunt Lucy either; she's gonna get me! Shoot, I promised her we'd call her once we had the FedEx photo and figured out what we were gonna do!"

"And we will, Maggs. We'll call her and Danny tonight when we get back to the hotel, okay?"

We turned into the driveway, and about halfway up the drive, Lizzy stopped at the old well. Her new fella, Dr. Alf, Dr. Bernie, and Todd were all standing back from the excavating team, observing and deliberating. It was about nine thirty in the morning by then, and it was obvious that the team had already been at it for a while. The three watchers-in-waiting waved at us as we slowly passed by them, heading up to the pear trees to park the rental car.

As we got out of the car, Lizzy looked up at the pear trees for a minute and then mentioned that when she had first seen her mother and Grandma Bubbee in her dream, they were standing right there in that exact spot under those old pear trees. As we took our time walking on down to the well to join the deliberators, she told me, "Today is going to be a day of plenty." I sure hoped she was right—and of course, she was.

The three experts in their fields warmly greeted us, and Dr. Bernie explained the process that would take place once the excavation reached a depth of eighty-five feet. They had roughly twenty-five feet to go that morning before they'd stop. The last fifteen down would be mighty slow going, and the process would change somewhat. He explained that the earth changed over time and that we couldn't risk destroying any possible remains that might be there, because every time someone dug something up from the past, it gave more meaning to the present. The whole archaeological excavation process had always intrigued me, and there I was, right in the thick of one! It was a sight to see! At the rate they were going, it was possible we could know something concrete before Mr. Sun turned into Miss Moon that night, forcing the dark upon us. When that happened, we'd have to stop again. We just had to accept the fact that it would take as long as it took, and that was that.

We filled in the waiting with more interesting conversation as we all stood by and observed the team's progress. A couple more hours passed, and Dr.

Bernie called our attention to the fact that the eighty-five-foot depth had been reached, and from that point on, the team would switch equipment for the rest of the excavation. We watched them as they assembled a huge machine that looked like a giant post-hole digger. At least that was what we called them back then.

Paddy and I had helped P. C. replace our old mailbox once after Daddy knocked it down one night when he and That Melvin Bray were coming in from one of Daddy's potion parties. P. C. used a post-hole digger to dig a new hole for the mailbox post. This excavating digger looked much like ours, except it was huge. Instead of a two-sided shovel at the bottom of two thin four-foot-long wooden posts, this one was automatic and had a four-sided steel shovel-type scooper bucket at the end of a steel extension pole that could extend to 150 feet. A man was sitting on top of the machine, guiding it with perfect precision. Okay, actually, it really didn't look a thing like our old post-hole digger, but heck, I was just six or seven at the time—what did I know?

Actually, the two diggers would produce the same result, since they both were capable of removing a specific amount of dirt from the ground. This digger's scooper bucket was massive, though, and could remove an eight-by-eight-foot square piece of earth in increments of five feet deep at a time. Once the operator lowered the bucket into the hole, the machine would take a huge bite out of the ground underneath it. Once the operator raised the bucket out of the hole, he would swivel the huge steel arm around away from the well and gently lower and release the big bite of dirt onto a huge plastic sheet laid out on the ground. Once the excavation of the last fifteen to twenty feet was complete and all the removed dirt was on the plastic sheet, the crew would raise a circus-sized tent over the plastic sheet to keep the dirt and all that had come out of the ground with it safe and protected from the outside elements and weather. The tent would also serve as the team's work space, since they would perform the most critical portion of the excavation right there inside the tent.

About that time, we spotted Lori as she drove up the driveway with lunch. Lizzy and I left the men and made our way over to the pear trees to greet her and help set up the table and chairs. A few minutes later, Todd and Alf joined us, but Dr. Bernie remained with his team. Lori had prepared a lovely Sunday meal for us, with fried chicken and all the usual fixin's to accompany it. As I was enjoying her fried chicken, I couldn't help but be reminded of those Saturday evenings when Paddy would chase Mr. Jennings's plump hens all over the place and P. C. would perform the dirty duty of preparing them for plucking. Early on Sunday mornings, before church, Mother would fry up the chickens so they'd be ready for Sunday dinner after church. In the summer, on many Sundays, we'd spread blankets and have a picnic right there under those same old pear trees with Mother and Aunt Lucy. We kids would lie back on the blankets and create all kinds of images in the clouds. Such innocence and fond memories.

A short while later, Todd and Alf rejoined Dr. Bernie to check the progress at the old well. Lori, Lizzy, and I packed up the leftovers for a possible snack to be enjoyed later on in the day. Lori had also made banana pudding, which was almost as good as Mother's, and the three of us shared it with coffee over some playful memories we had shared as teenagers at our beloved Grace Chapel High School. Lori was aware of the seriousness of the day's mission, and she left us with a big hug and a sweet "See y'all later, girls." Lizzy and I stood at the top of the drive, waved until she was out of sight, and then walked to the dig site to join the rest.

About three o'clock that afternoon, the sun was as bright as I'd ever seen it, except for maybe at the beach, and the air was unseasonably warm. It felt more like spring than fall. Dr. Bernie stood by the big plastic sheet as the giant post-hole digger carefully lowered the last scoop of dirt and placed it on the sheet. It looked sorta like a two- or three-foot-high pile of dirt 'n' debris, pretty evenly distributed over a fifty-by-fifty-foot square area. Once the driver-in-the-box had released the last bucket of dirt onto the plastic sheet, he backed his machine out of the way, and the team immediately began to raise the tent over the huge plastic sheet.

The tent had only one opening for both entering and exiting. Large strobe-type lights were attached to tall posts throughout the interior of the tent. The plastic sheet was centered in the middle of the tent, and there was a four-foot-wide walking border around the sheet, which would serve as the team's work space. Several waist-high, skinny tables set up all around the walking border would serve as shelves for the artifacts. This whole process was remarkably impressive, and watching the team work with such incredible focus and precision with every move was both exciting and tense. They would not miss one little speck of anything. Whatever was in that dirt, Dr. Bernie and his team would find it.

Todd had assembled a few folding chairs to the right of the opening, just inside the tent, and that's where he, Lizzy, and I would remain throughout the final search for That Melvin Bray.

It wasn't long before Dr. Bernie motioned for Alf to join him on the far left side of the tent. Alf left us to ourselves to speak with Dr. Bernie at one of the skinny tables about the objects before them. As the team uncovered object after object and placed them on the tables, Dr. Bernie and Alf continued to examine each item one by one. Alf called out to Todd and signaled for him to join them, and Todd left us in our seats—but not for long.

Lizzy and I were in a trancelike state as we watched their every move; then Todd waved his hand for us to join them. We rose from out seats slowly and, with more than a little trepidation, walked to the other side of the tent, where the three men were standing. They were blocking the table, so we couldn't really see anything. Todd asked me to examine an object visually only and tell him what I thought it was, and then the three of them stepped aside.

As I moved in closer, visually scouring the dirt for "it" among several items on the table, my eyes locked onto it, and I knew exactly what it was. There, as plain as day to me, was That Melvin Bray's hat—at least portions of the fabric. On one large two-by-two-inch piece, the now-infamous embroidered *W* was still quite discernible. It was the same *W* hat he had worn from time to time at my house, and the same one he had on in my sketch of him standing at Ricky's bus stop the fateful Friday afternoon when Ricky disappeared. I looked up at Lizzy and nodded. My mind was racing, and my heart was trying to catch up, when Todd jumped into my head, asking me what I thought it was.

"That looks like a portion of his hat, Todd! The one he always wore and the one he had on in the drawing I sketched for Lizzy based upon Katherine's description of the bus stop that day."

"Okay, Maggs, I'm going to the car to get the photos; I'll be right back."

Dr. Bernie and Alf asked us if we would kindly return to our chairs until further notice, and of course, we did. When we got back to the front of the tent and sat down, Todd poked his head in through the tent opening, carrying the file Lizzy and I had prepared for him. He sat down with us and opened the file. He found my sketch showing That Melvin Bray at the bus stop, wearing his *W* hat. Then Todd pulled out the FedEx photo of That Melvin Bray that Aunt Lucy had sent, and he studied them both for a few minutes.

"Well, there's no doubt in my mind the photos match. It's the same person all right, and I'm in agreement with you, Maggie. What you identified over there at the table are the decayed remnants of his hat, the very hat in this photo. Now we just gotta find his remains."

He got up and rejoined the men on the other side of the tent. They were totally engrossed in the work in front of them. Lizzy and I sat there in a stunned state of mixed emotions, but we mostly felt relief, pride, and even joy. We no longer had even a hint of doubt. We were certain it was only a matter of time before we had evidence to prove the answer to that thirty-five-year-old haunting and lingering question: What happened to That Melvin Bray?

Dr. Bernie and a couple of his crew continued working in the same area where the several pieces of fabric had been found. The next time they stopped and called us over, we all gathered once again and viewed even more revealing objects that caused us to believe we had, in fact, found the remains of That Melvin Bray. There were many bones of all shapes and sizes, teeth, portions of a shoe, a brass belt buckle, a plastic pen with an illegible logo on it, some coins, and several more pieces of fabric. It was just believably unbelievable!

As the district medical examiner, Dr. Alf Maness felt compelled to tell us he also was confident of the identity based on all that Todd, Lizzy, and I had told him. However, he also cautioned us to reserve final judgment, because obviously he hadn't performed the proper forensics to confirm the true identity of the remains. He made it clear that the process would take a while once he transported all the findings to the state lab, and then legal protocol would require that Todd notify the next of kin once he had made a positive ID. He reminded us that we'd waited over thirty-five years for this, so we could certainly sit tight a little longer. Of course he was right, and so were we. We had the answer to the question. We knew what had happened to That Melvin Bray, and soon everyone else would know too!

While all this had been going on, Dr. Bernie Childress's team had all gathered directly opposite us on the other side of the plastic sheet. His team leader appeared before us and asked Dr. Bernie to join him and the crew on the other side of the tent. The two of them left us, and we continued to inspect That Melvin Bray—visually only, of course. As we stood there, Todd and Dr. Alf were speaking in full forensic jargon, while Lizzy and I were full of shock and awe. The discovery was a lot to grasp, and it was more than a little hard to breathe.

This was way more than we had anticipated. We'd had no idea that we'd have a backstage pass to this process and information. The up-close-and-personal view was a little tough to witness. Of course, Lizzy could handle anything; if asked, she'd tell people she had a PhD in perfection. I, on the other hand, was a horse of a different color. I was into colors, primarily ones that were vibrant, alive, bright, 'n' beautiful; dark brown dirt and death were not on my color palette. Frankly, I was shocked that I didn't have another TMMS attack. Lights out and there I'd be, lying on the floor under the big top in front of everyone.

As I think back on that day out there under the big top, I realize we had my mother, Lizzy's mother, and Grandma Bubbee all standing beside us, propping us up, for our own good sake.

Thank you, angels.

Dr. Bernie called out rather excitedly to Alf and Todd and waved his arms for them to join him and the others on the other side of the tent.

"Man, I guess they've found something pretty interesting over there too, Dr. Maness."

"Yes, sir, Toddy, my boy—let's go check it out."

Todd and Alf headed over to the group, who were all gathered around an area of dirt still on the plastic sheet. It didn't appear they were doing anything but looking and pointing at the dirt. They were not disturbing it in any way; they were just staring and nodding. Lizzy and I were curious, of course, but didn't move or take our eyes off the sight before us. When Todd and Alf got over there, all the others moved back except Dr. Bernie and his lead man. We could see the surprise on both Todd's and Alf's faces from where we were standing. It was obvious the crew had discovered even more credible evidence to prove our suspicions about That Melvin Bray.

"Damn, Maggie. What the ...?"

"Me too! What in the ...?"

"I have no idea, Maggie, and until they allow us over there, we're not gonna know!"

Just then, Todd looked up at us and sorta galloped back over to where we stood. We could tell he was excited.

"Here we go, Maggs. Breathe. Looks like all heaven's gonna break loose!"

"I am breathin'; can't ya hear me?"

"Well, you two," Todd said, "I've got some pretty amazing news, so hold on, okay? They found Ricky."

"What did you say, Todd?"

"Ya heard me right, Lizzy. They've uncovered Ricky's body, and it's in near-perfect condition, too!"

"But how can that be, Todd?"

"Well, Maggs, if ya can handle it, you can both see for yourselves. Dr. Bernie says it's a case of something called adipocere, and it's common in drowning deaths. I've studied it, but I've never actually seen the effects of it, not personally."

"I've studied this also, Todd. I'm familiar with it. It's a soapy substance that can grow on the body after death and actually can preserve the body."

"That's right, Lizzy, and quoting Dr. Maness: 'This could potentially help us in the search for evidence.' Y'all wanta see this child? Heck, if it wasn't for you two, we wouldn't even be here! This little boy may never've been found—or Melvin Bray either, for that matter!"

"We wouldn't miss this for the world, Todd. Come on, Maggie."

"You were right, Lizzy; all heaven just broke loose!"

"It sure looks that way, Maggie."

The turn of events was hard to believe, but Lizzy had told me it would be "a day of plenty." *The Lord gives, someone else takes, and then the Lord gives back even more!* I had a few other noteworthy observations about that day of plenty, too. It was Sunday, the Sabbath, the day of prayer and penance. It was also an amazingly beautiful, unseasonably warm day. The sun was gloriously bright, so much so that it felt more like spring or summer—seasons of new life, new beginnings, innocence, and discovery. It certainly didn't feel or look like the chilly fall—the season of dormancy and dying. No, this incredible Sabbath would prove to be all about forgiveness and healing.

That was what was happening all around us, and that old well would come to be known as "the healing well," and rightfully so.

"You gonna be all right, Maggs?"

"Yes, I'm fine, Lizzy-Girl. I just can't help but think of Katherine and Ballen right now—and the Bray family too, of course. But it's Katherine and Ballen my heart aches for the most, because Ricky was just a little child."

"I know what you're saying, Maggie, so let's go see their little boy and get them here ASAP, okay?"

"Yes, let's."

Todd stopped us just short of where Ricky was lying in the dirt 'n' debris, because Dr. Bernie and Alf wanted to talk with us before we saw Ricky.

"Ladies, we believe we've found Ricky Lawrence, the little boy who disappeared from his home back in February 1953. Dr. Maness and Sheriff Todd have explained the possible connection between him and Melvin Bray. Of course, we can't be certain until further forensic work is performed on the bodies, especially the remains of the first body, whom we do believe is Melvin Bray. We have photos here of the child, and we're certain this is in fact the body of Ricky Lawrence. As you will observe, he is in a remarkable physical state, as his body has been preserved with stunning detail due to adipocere.

"Adipocere is a waxy, soap-like postmortem product that forms from the fat and soft tissue of a deceased person. When the flesh of a deceased body turns waxy and soap-like, a person exhumed after being dead for decades may show minimal signs of decay. The timing of the formation and degradation of adipocere depends largely on the environmental circumstances. The changes occur rather quickly, usually within the first month after death, and can accompany a form of natural mummification. Adipocere can actually persist for hundreds of years, acting as a preservative for the body. Another interesting note: adipocerous formation is regarded by some as being a holy sign of incorruptibility."

"Yes, Dr. Childress, and this type of preservation can be most useful in a forensic context since it can preserve not only the body but evidence as well!"

"That is correct, Dr. Maness, and a very good point, especially considering where *your* expertise comes into the process, which, as you know, will need to begin quickly.

"Essentially, adipocere itself is a naturally occurring substance under the right circumstances and is a normal part of decomposition. A high-moisture, low-oxygen environment is the perfect place for adipocere to form on a body. I believe the well provided that perfect place, as I understand it had been closed up for a few years prior to the disappearance of this child. Sadly, the well kept the body hidden, but it also preserved it remarkably. One other factor I find interesting: unlike the child, the body of the older man was *not* protected by this remarkable process."

"That is interesting, Dr. Childress. Maybe there *is* something to that 'holy sign of incorruptibility' myth you mentioned earlier," Lizzy said.

"Yes, Dr. Benis. It sure makes you think when you consider the unusual circumstances surrounding these two cases, now, doesn't it?"

"Well, I've seen only one other case like this in all my years of forensic work, and that was also a drowning victim. Of course, I won't be able to determine the actual cause of Ricky's death until I've transported the body to the labs in Raleigh and completed the autopsy.

"However, Melvin Bray is a whole other story. Although his body hasn't been preserved, I don't believe the cause of death is a big mystery. But of course, that too is yet to be determined."

"May we see Ricky now, Alf?"

"Oh, by all means, Miss Lizzy, but please don't touch him."

Lizzy and I nodded in agreement, and as we moved forward, everyone else moved back so that Lizzy and I could get closer to Ricky. We stood right over his perfect little body without breathing; it was impossible to breathe—or even move, for that matter. This truly was a miracle, and I was certain of God's intention. It might have been five seconds or five minutes—it was impossible to tell—before we both exhaled and broke down and wept for the loss of his young life. As euphoric as we felt at the mere site of Ricky, seeing his small, lifeless body lying there so peacefully confirmed that he was in fact not alive—he only looked as though he were. He was no longer that happy-go-lucky, carefree little boy enjoying his wonderful life, just loving and being loved.

Ricky's adoring mother was left now without even the tiniest hope of ever finding her little boy alive. My heart ached with such pain that I could feel it all the way down to my toes, and it really did hurt. I wanted to pick him up in my arms and hold him tenderly, and I thought, *If only I could breathe precious life back into him—if only.*

We just stood there and spoke to the little fella in the language of heartfelt tears for him, his grieving mother, and his devoted father. Before we could stop crying, the others all joined in, as though our tears had given them permission to weep. The big tent was filled with amazement, emotions, and uncontrollable tears. It was an incredible experience for every single person out there at that old well that night.

What had started out as a search for That Melvin Bray in an attempt to find some possible connection to Ricky that would lead us to him had paid off in abundance. We had uncovered That Melvin Bray, literally, which had led us right to Ricky in all his young, lifeless, angelic splendor. A coincidence? Of course not. A miracle? Of course. Thank God that old road had not been paved! If it had, the old Chevy wouldn't have gotten stuck in the mud, That Melvin Bray wouldn't have gone to the car to get Daddy's alcohol, he would never have fallen in the well, and I would never have seen him fall. Of course, Ricky had already been in the well at the time, and That Melvin Bray had actually fallen in on top of him. That, of course, I couldn't possibly have ever known. So the bottom line was, if that old road had been paved, Ricky might never have been found. *Oh, forgive me, Lord! I'll never complain about that old dirt 'n' gravel road again—ever!*

I have no idea how I was able to stand there and gaze upon that little fella without going smack-dab crazy right there in my own skin—just by the grace of God, I'm sure. I felt Lizzy pull on my sleeve as she turned around to face the other mourners, and I joined her as we both gathered our emotions, turning away from Ricky. We both were in a state of shock, but we thanked the workers for what they'd made possible. They understood that at the end of all the tears of sadness for both families involved, hopefully a day of joy could emerge and some measure of closure would be possible for all of them.

Dr. Bernie and his team would begin dismantling the work site once Todd and Alf could get Alf's forensic team out to the site. This would have to happen immediately to properly prepare the remains for travel to the state labs, and time was indeed a serious factor in order to protect Ricky's body. Alf would see to Ricky, and Dr. Bernie was still in charge of collecting all the remains of That Melvin Bray and preparing them for travel as well.

Lizzy asked Todd if he would allow her to call Katherine and Ballen with the news before he spoke to them. He agreed without hesitation, since he was well aware of Katherine's fragile state. Todd was an educated country boy—a big fish in a little pond, just like his daddy. He had a big heart too, just as his daddy had. The magnitude of what had happened that day was beyond reality, and he was grateful to us for our role in ending his dad's relentless search for both Ricky and That Melvin Bray. Todd told us that his dad had never put those files in the cold-case drawer. Both cases had remained open and active until his dad retired, and he'd made Todd promise that he would not forget them either. What happened out there that day was historical, and no one would ever forget.

It was about nine o'clock at night before Alf's crew arrived to transport Ricky. Lizzy didn't want to call Katherine and Ballen until Ricky's body was safe in the vehicle and on the way to Raleigh. Alf had no intention of leaving Ricky's side and had a member of his team drive his car back to the lab so that he could ride in the medical van with Ricky. Dr. Bernie said he would remain with his crew at the site until he was certain they hadn't missed a thing and had collected everything belonging to That Melvin Bray. Todd was planning on staying at the site with Dr. Bernie, and as it turned out, they stayed and worked into the wee hours of the next morning. Todd later told us that Dr. Bernie was exceptionally impressive and, of course, didn't miss a thing.

Once Alf had left with Ricky, Lizzy wanted to call Katherine and Ballen while we were still there with Todd. He needed to speak with them also to explain what they could expect and when. Katherine and Ballen would make the positive identification for Todd, and he wanted them to get there as soon as possible. Lizzy knew she had to make that phone call, but she was concerned for Katherine and prayed that Ballen, not Katherine, would answer the phone. Lizzy dialed their number on her cell phone, and thank goodness, Ballen answered. Katherine had gone to bed a little earlier that evening and was resting.

Lizzy broke the news to Ballen in a way that only she could. As expected, he was unable to conceal his grief and broke down in sorrow. I had been certain I had no tears left in my entire body, but I had been wrong. I stood there by Lizzy and cried with Ballen. It was all Lizzy could do to hold back her own tears. I felt so helpless and could do nothing for either of them. Ballen told Lizzy he would wait until morning to tell Katherine. Lizzy agreed that was for the best and made him promise he'd call her back once he had told Katherine the next morning. Ballen understood that Katherine might need Lizzy's calm guidance. His own grief would fill his sleepless night. After all, Ricky was his little boy too.

Lizzy then explained that Todd needed to speak with him also and handed the phone over to Todd. She took a few steps back from Todd, and I moved with her, as if we were attached at the hip. She leaned against my back with her head between my shoulders and started sobbing. I think she surprised herself, and I was glad she allowed herself to express her feelings so openly.

Seeing Ricky as we had earlier had set the tone for our emotions. Before we'd even had time to adjust our minds and hearts to the realization that we had found That Melvin Bray, we had immediately found ourselves standing in front of Ricky's little body. There was just no way the mind was designed to absorb shock that quickly. Emotion *had* to follow in some form or another. After all, I was not a robot, and neither was Lizzy, notwithstanding all of her professional robot training and experience focused toward helping others deal with *their* emotions. Todd was kind and sensitive to Ballen's pain and communicated with him as well as possible. When he said good-bye, he looked over in our direction. We walked back over to him, and he asked if we were all right as he handed me the cell phone. I told him we were going back to the hotel if he didn't need us. He was well aware of our emotional fatigue and hugged us both, offering to drive us back. I assured him we could manage and promised we'd talk to him in the morning.

Back at Lizzy's car, which was still parked by the old pear trees, I got behind the steering wheel, and for once, Lizzy accepted her role as passenger. She was drained, and I knew it. I put the key in the ignition, started the car, and turned on the headlights. As I was backing up with my head turned around so as not to run into a ditch, Lizzy was looking forward. She asked me what was up in the pear tree. I hit the brakes and turned back around to look up at the old trees. Sure enough, there was something faintly reflecting light in the middle tree.

I put the car in Park, left the motor running, got out of the car, and walked over to the old three-tree pear orchard. I saw a single pear dangling through the scraggly old limbs and realized the headlights from the car were making it appear as though it were glowing—at least that's what I thought. However, as I reached for the pear, I realized it *was* illuminated by its own power.

It was a huge, ripe pear—one huge, ripe pear. It was hanging low on a leafless branch of an otherwise fruitless tree—in late fall. Further, I knew those old pear trees had stopped bearing fruit many years ago.

I carefully plucked the pear from the branch and walked back to the car and showed it to Lizzy. I could tell that the reflection of light was actually a soft halo hugging what was obviously a divine specimen of fruit. Lizzy didn't say anything. The fruit was still glowing as she took it from me and looked back up at the pear trees. Other than the illuminated halo from the pear and a soft-shadowed moon, the only light in the otherwise pitch-dark grassy knoll was coming from my headlights.

Lizzy looked at the pear and then pressed it to her face and smelled it.

"Maggie, I believe it's the dears again—your dear mother, my dear mother, and dear Bubbee."

With both hands, she lifted the giant, juicy pear up to her mouth and took a huge bite out of it. "Here, Maggs, take a bite; it's delicious!"

She handed the pear back to me, and I took a big, juicy bite too. It *was* delicious!

Instantly, we both looked up at the old pear trees, and this time, the moon shown so brightly that we could make out all three trees. We each savored our keen awareness of the Holy Spirit all around us through a mouthful of that divine, juicy pear!

It was obvious to us that this unusual pear was a gift from our mothers and Grandma Bubbee. It all seemed so natural, but actually, it was more than that— the *five* of us had all just enjoyed a celestial moment together. They knew our hearts were heavy and wanted us to know we were not alone on this heavenly mission.

We were still eating that divine pear when we arrived at the hotel. I parked the car, and we went straight to our suite. The three shiny fives on our door were all but shoutin' at us as Lizzy unlocked the door. She gently ran her fingers across them as she looked at me, smiled, and said, "Our dears, the angels." We walked into the parlor and plopped down on the couches. We sat there for a few minutes and realized that, amazingly, we weren't the least bit hungry. That pear had fed us not only spiritually but physically as well. Plus, we had a sense of peace and calm about us, and the profound sadness that had stabbed right through our hearts the moment we saw Ricky's face was already healing.

Angels can perform miracles too, I guess. Even stranger, after that night, those old pear trees began to bear fruit again, and they still do to this day. A miracle? Of course.

As kind and sensitive as all the folks Katherine and Ballen would soon meet were, they would be total strangers, so it was up to Lizzy and me to comfort Ricky's parents. We were going to have to rise above our own pain to help Katherine and Ballen, who certainly would be stricken with immeasurable grief when they arrived the next day.

As we sat there reliving the last few hours, we realized that a handful of people had solved a thirty-five-year-old mystery in just a couple days, and we were *all* grief stricken and deeply affected. It would be a while before any of us, and certainly Katherine and Ballen, would be able to truly realize the blessings of what had been hidden all that time at the bottom of that old well.

As we considered various scenarios of what the next day would bring, we stretched out on the couches and were so exhausted that we never even made it to our beds. As I watched her lying there, I knew Lizzy was still troubled by her own reactions to the last few hours. I reminded her that she was, after all, human and that there were some things she couldn't control, even with that big ole brain of hers. I think she was finally discovering that big ole heart of hers as well.

As our slumber was beginning to embrace our challenged hearts and minds, I heard her saying something about the number five and the Lord's will being done.

Amen, sister. Good night.

I woke with a start and checked the clock immediately. It was 6:45 a.m., and my first thought was of Aunt Lucy. Lizzy was still asleep, so I rolled over on the couch and quietly got up to go to my room to call Aunt Lucy. Aunt Lucy still got up with the chickens even though she didn't have any anymore, so there was no threat of my waking her too early. I had to get ahold of her that morning before she felt the need to track us down. I really didn't want to worry her another day. After all, I'd promised I'd call her days ago! She answered cheerfully on the second ring.

"I knew that was you, young lady! So tell me some good news, little Magg-Pie!"

"Oh my gosh, Aunt Lucy, it's bigger than we coulda ever imagined ever in our wildest dreams ever!"

"Honey, slow down. I'm trying to follow you, but slow down. Are you all right?"

"Yes, Aunt Lucy, but first, please forgive me for not callin' until now. We've been fast-trackin' back thirty-five years, and our heads are still spinnin' like crazy!"

"It's all right, honey. Where's the Lizzy-Girl? Is she okay, honey?"

"Well, believe it or not, she's still sleepin' in the other room. We never even made it to our beds last night. We got back here about ten o'clock and just fell asleep on the couches, and somehow I woke up first. As you know, Lizzy just won't allow ya to beat her outta bed, so this is a rare occasion. Yesterday was close to unbelievable, and she took it pretty hard. I really didn't wanta wake her, so I slipped in here to my room to call ya. I'm certain I too am in some kind of shocked state myself, so I'll need ya to be my voice of reason, okay?

"We really aren't gonna have much time to catch our breath. We've still got another huge day ahead of us, and unfortunately, the unique circumstances require the ole Lizzy-Girl's expertise, so she's gotta carry most of the load herself. I've just never witnessed her in a serious, emotional state, as I did last night, Aunt Lucy. Ya know she's just not one to show her true emotions. She says it's the shrink in her—ya think?"

"Well, Magg-Pie, that's probably got a lot to do with it, sweetie. You just ask the dear Lord to protect her and give her the courage she needs to do His will, okay? And considering what still lies ahead of you two, just tell me if you found That Melvin Bray, and let's plan for you girls to come stay with me tonight. Is that a good plan, honey? Only *you* know what's before you, and I don't want you to spend your energy on me right now, but I sure would like to know if you have any news on That Melvin Bray."

"Oh gosh, Aunt Lucy, I have so many incredible things to tell you, especially about Mother and her involvement in all this—plus Mrs. Benis and Grandma Bubbee, too!

"But as to That Melvin Bray—yes! We found him at the bottom of that old well, and even more astounding, we also found that little boy, Ricky Lawrence, too! It's all just incredible, Aunt Lucy!"

"Oh … my … dear … Lord! Praise His sweet name, Magg-Pie! Praise His sweet name! Well, no wonder you girls are out of it, honey! Is there anything your ole Aunt Lucy can do for you all? You just tell me, honey, and I'll do it; you know I will."

"Dear Aunt Lucy, you're doing it right now. Just having you there on the other end of this phone and hearing your courageous heart speak to me is like a steel lightnin' rod keepin' me grounded! As I've told you before, you're my rock, and I love you so much. Oh Aunt Lucy, here's Lizzy; she wants to speak to ya."

"Good morning, Aunt Lucy. How's my favorite aunt?"

"Oh, honey, I'm just fine, but I'm more concerned with you—you all right?"

"Well, I must admit I've been better, Aunt Lucy, but don't worry about me. I'm *almost* as strong as you, ya know? But seriously, though, the last nine days have been brewing up the perfect storm, and yesterday the impact of it all resulted in a flood of uncontrolled emotions; the proverbial dam broke. As prepared as I thought I was, well, to put it simply, I wasn't."

"Lizzy, honey, I understand—I really do. Now, don't be so hard on yourself. Magg-Pie tells me there's a lot more to accomplish before this day's over, and it looks like you've been chosen to do it. I just want you to try to remember that when the good Lord has a big, important job to get done, He's very particular about whom He gives that job to, okay? You're very special, Lizzy, and that's why He gave this one to *you*. You thank Him and see this thing through, sweetheart, okay?"

"Yes, ma'am, I will; I promise. Thank you, Aunt Lucy. I love you so much. You're just wonderful—you know that? I appreciate the way you love me and are always there for me. I know I've told you before, but Grandma Bubbee sure did love you a whole bunch too, and we all know Grandma Bubbee was awfully fussy about those she loved *special*."

"Well, I sure loved her special too, honey. Now listen to me: I told Magg-Pie that you two should come stay with me tonight if that would work out for y'all. I want to hear all about everything, but if it doesn't work out for tonight, I'll just expect to hear from you girls when the time is right, okay, honey? Y'all just do what you have to do, and know your ole Aunt Lucy's right here if you need me. Oh, and I guess yesterday's discovery is not for public knowledge yet, right?"

"Yes, ma'am, that's probably best for now, Aunt Lucy, and we'll call you as soon as we know what's what. Ya wanta speak to Maggs before we hang up?"

"Aw, honey, y'all got a lot to do, so just tell her I love her, and you girls be careful. I'm praying for you both. I'll wait to hear from ya. Bye for now, sweet pea."

"Boy, the good Lord sure gave us an awesome gift when he gave us Aunt Lucy, ya know, Maggs?"

"No kiddin', babe. Thank you, Lord! So you all right? I was a little concerned when ya didn't wake me up this mornin'. That's not like you."

"Oh, I'm okay. I've just got a heavy load of sadness on my heart, and I'm well aware of it. I've got to get myself in check here before we pick up Katherine and Ballen today, though. I fear the worst for her, and I must be at my best, Maggs. I just can't get the sight of that little child lying there out of my mind's eye. I admit it; I wasn't prepared for that, ya know?"

"Oh brooo-thuur! Where were you when all those grown men were weepin' like babies out there last night? It wasn't just you 'n' me, Lizzy. No one was prepared for that! Hey, I'm so filled with sadness that I could throw up right now this minute! Do you see yourself as some kind of robot or machine-like being? You're human just like the rest of us, Lizzy—aren't ya?"

"Yes, of course I'm human. It's just that in my line of work, I'm not supposed to show that side of myself."

"Okay, I understand that, but at the same time, you gotta be willing to allow yourself a release when something so devastating is right in front of you, as was the case last night with Ricky. Surely you know that. That's what *you* told *me* once I fully realized what had happened to That Melvin Bray. I was devastated too! You can't possibly plan for something like that. If it happens, you deal with it and don't question or punish yourself for your reaction—that's called emotion. Didn't they teach you that at the Big Brain School?"

"All right, all right, I get it already! Thanks for setting me straight, little sister. I'll try to behave like a *normal* person, okay? And just look at who's shrinkin' who."

"You're welcome. I love you too, so let's get dressed. Ya know that phone's gonna be ringin' any minute, and *you've* gotta answer it!"

"Yep, don't I know it."

No sooner had we gotten showered and dressed than the phone rang. It was Ballen. He spoke briefly to Lizzy and then put Katherine on the phone. Katherine must have turned both her soul and Ricky's over to the Lord—that was the only thing we could surmise from her calm, resolved demeanor with Lizzy on the phone. The first words out of her mouth were "I want to thank you both from the bottom of my heart, and praise the Lord." Not once did she break down or lose her composure on the phone. And drugs were *not* involved. We were joyfully stunned but of course knew the power of our almighty Lord and Savior.

In that moment, we didn't know what Ballen had done, but we figured that since we were certain he hadn't slept a wink, he had obviously stayed up all night praying the Twenty-third Psalm and asking the Lord to lift Katherine up in His strong arms, to comfort her, and to restore her soul. Then he must have asked the Lord to walk beside her and hold her sweet hands the rest of the way through what must have seemed to her like the valley of the shadow of death. The Lord certainly had a purpose for the condition of Ricky's holy body, and that would prove to be a great blessing to the long-suffering parents.

Ballen gave all their flight information to Lizzy, and we agreed to pick them up at the Charlotte airport. This arrangement was a good move on Lizzy's part, since we'd all have at least an hour together on the ride back to Grace Chapel to meet with Todd—a precious hour for Lizzy to prepare Katherine and Ballen for what they were about to experience when Alf and Todd would return their little boy to them later that evening. Yes, the great blessing.

We could only begin to imagine the frightening thoughts this mother had endured all those years, wondering what might have happened to her child and regretting that she hadn't been there to protect him. Katherine had been consumed with guilt about one specific point in particular. Her little boy had been safe at home with her, and then he had just disappeared right under her nose—she hadn't protected him! At least, that was the guilt she felt and couldn't resist clinging to all those years. What a heavy burden to carry around for the rest of her life, especially without ever getting the answer to that terrifying question: What happened?

I could also only imagine the blessed peace and resolve in her heart when she first saw Ricky. When I had first seen his face the night before, so peacefully perfect, I had realized one side of his mouth was turned up, forming a crooked little smile. It was almost as though he were prepared for the first time his mother would see him in a very long time, as if that little smile were saying, "See? I'm okay, Mom, and I love you the most!" How incredible was that?

Lizzy hung up the phone and quickly called Todd to let him know we'd be picking up Katherine and Ballen at the airport that afternoon at three thirty. Todd asked us to come straight to his office so that we could all drive together to Raleigh and said he'd call Alf to give him our ETA. It appeared everyone was in motion, headed in the same right direction. Lizzy was back in charge, even though she'd had to accept the fact that she was just a plain ole human, not a humanoid; it was all good and getting even better.

As we were standing at the gate, waiting for Katherine and Ballen, Lizzy bowed her head and softly offered a prayer of thanks for all that our sweet Lord had made possible for everyone. I thanked Him for not letting me lose my mind during all this. I felt a little bit selfish, so I immediately thanked Him for allowing Lizzy to hold on to *her* mind, and finally I gave special thanks for His great mercy and love for Katherine, Ballen, and the Bray family.

There they were, holding hands as they entered the gate area. We waved at them from across the room as they glanced around the waiting area, looking for us. Once they saw us, we all started walking toward each other. We got within arm's length, and without words, we all put our arms around each other and held on to each other tightly. The outpouring of emotion was just like at Mother's funeral. All kinds of emotions erupted from each of us all at once— sadness, happiness, joy, pain, laughter, tears. You name it, we felt it, and it was very special!

Those few minutes together were glorious, and I could feel the Lord all around us, loving us as we were loving each other through His grace. It was as though time stopped to allow me to remember the verse from Luke that Pastor Meyers had read at Mother's celebration of remembrance: "Let the little children come to me, and do not stop them; for it is to such as these that the kingdom of God belongs."

In that moment, I first realized what this whole mission the Lord had sent us on was all about. It was about the little children—in this case, a specific little child named Ricky. *Talk about the Lord's will being done, and here comes that word* obedient *again,* I thought. *We must be obedient and carry out our earthly mission.*

Katherine and Ballen might have lost their way, but they had not lost their faith. They were just tired and distraught in their human frailty from years and years of grief over the loss of Ricky. Ricky, for whatever reason—and only God knew why—had left them, but they had never left *him*, not really. As it was, their hearts and minds had been consumed with finding him since the day he went missing. Certainly God had never left them *or* Ricky. God's will was to be done on that special day, and He had led Katherine and Ballen to Ricky. "For all who are led by the Spirit of God are children of God"—another verse I remembered from Mother's funeral.

Once reunited, the four crusaders headed to baggage to get the luggage and continue to the final destination: Raleigh. It was going to be among the biggest days of all our lives—so far, anyway. We truly were on a mission from God, and we knew it!

Once we had the luggage, Ballen loaded it in the car, and we headed back to our first stop in Grace Chapel to meet with Todd. I drove, Ballen sat in the front with me, and Lizzy and Katherine sat in the back. This was the perfect arrangement since it allowed Lizzy and Katherine to be physically close to one another as Lizzy described precisely how we had found their little boy the day before. Certainly it was emotional, and we all shed a lotta tears while headin' south on old Highway 220 that afternoon.

At one point, as I was driving and wiping my eyes at the same time, I glanced over to my right, and wouldn't ya know it, there was Charlie's Place, doing business as usual. I remembered that a fella had told Todd's daddy that he thought he'd seen That Melvin Bray sitting in a car with a woman in the parking lot of Charlie's Place. Of course, we knew now that the fella had been mistaken, because That Melvin Bray had already fallen in the well about a month before the false sighting at Charlie's. However, that man's statement sure had created a false perception in the investigation and, at the same time, basically cleared ole Chill of any guilt in the strange disappearance of That Melvin Bray. In a flash, though, I had a comforting reality check: none of that mattered at all now. The wait and the worst were over, and the best was yet to come.

It was clearly apparent that Katherine had turned a righteous corner and had come to terms with herself and the reality of what was happening all around her. It was amazing and empowering to observe her transformation, which demonstrated that God was indeed an awesome God and that all things were possible through His grace. All we had to do was trust, obey, and get out of His way.

I knew from my own experiences, though, that sometimes surrendering to God was awfully hard to do. Somehow people tended to convince themselves that *they* were in charge and knew best. That was just wrong. What was up with that anyway? I believed we were just frightened and wouldn't let go because we didn't have the courage of God's convictions in our lives sometimes. God was so patient and loved us so much. He gave us free will to choose the paths we would travel. I wished sometimes He'd take my will away from me and just make all my decisions for me, because sometimes I could make a mess of things on my own. However, I was becoming increasingly more aware of the fact that courage was most definitely linked to obedience. Yes, I was learning.

By the time we arrived at Todd's office, Katherine and Ballen were ready to keep on moving and head straight on to Raleigh to see Ricky. Todd was standing at the door of his office, staring out the window, watching for us, just as anxious for sure. I parked the car, and we all got out and swiftly gathered at the door. Todd opened the door and welcomed us inside. It was a chilly day, nothing like the beautiful summerlike day we'd just experienced the day before out at the old well. Gosh, that seemed so long ago.

Lizzy made the introductions, and Todd expressed his heartfelt sympathy over Ricky and the long hardship they'd been through all these years. He was sincere and endearing. Katherine and Ballen graciously accepted his kindness. He was also sensitive to their sense of urgency and offered us all coffee for the road so that we could speed things up and get on our way quickly. Lizzy and I prepared several cups to go, and we headed out of the office to Todd's SUV. He drove, Ballen sat in the front with him, and Katherine sat between Lizzy and me in the back. We had her surrounded with love and affection if she needed it. The drive to Raleigh took a little over an hour, which was ample time for the Lawrences to get a feel for Todd's personality and expertise.

It was important to all of us that Katherine and Ballen felt comfortable and safe with the rest of their new family. Todd was a master at gaining their trust. He was so disarming and kind, but mostly, he was honest and sensitive. That could have been the longest hour in their lives, but Todd was comforting all of us and didn't even realize it. He explained to Katherine and Ballen that he'd been on the phone with Dr. Maness and Dr. Childress throughout the day and that both had made a great deal of progress. He was hopeful we'd have some answers to their long-unanswered questions that night—before we laid our heads down, as he put it. That news alone was comforting, but I wished I could do something more for Katherine and Ballen. In hindsight, I realized that more *was* being done, as the mystery was unfolding piece by piece, and we were almost there.

We pulled up to the security gate in front of the huge state crime labs center, where the competent Dr. Alf performed his forensic magic. The security guard checked Todd's ID and then made a phone call to Alf to approve our clearance. He opened the gate and motioned us through. Todd parked in an assigned space for law enforcement vehicles, and we got out and entered the building through the main entrance. Once at the reception desk, the rest of us had to be IDed for a clearance badge in order to move on to Alf's department. It was all serious and all business in that place, as it should be.

The agent at the desk buzzed Alf, and an attendant walked us to his department, where he was waiting for us. The minute he laid eyes on Katherine, he walked over to her and embraced her, which was thoughtful of him. Frankly, I hadn't expected it, but it was definitely the perfect gesture on his part. He was sincere, and Katherine felt it. He held her for a few minutes, expressing his condolences, and then gently let go of her. Without a pause, he then embraced Ballen similarly. Ballen was obviously touched and thanked him. Alf was so interesting and real. That was probably why he and Todd got along so well with each other. And of course, Alf had known Todd's daddy, since they had worked on cases together years ago when Todd's daddy was our sheriff.

Alf took us into a large conference room where we all seated ourselves. He offered us food and drinks, but we all declined his warm hospitality, and our refusal was his cue to proceed.

"Well, I understand how much you both need to know about your boy, and I'm not going to make you wait any longer than is absolutely necessary. Oftentimes, though, something can sound utterly crazy until you know all the facts. So I hope you'll trust me when I tell you that I believe it's best to talk with you first, and then I'll take you to him. Will that be all right with y'all?"

"Yes, Dr. Maness, whatever you feel is best," Ballen said. "My wife and I are so grateful for everything you're doing, and Sherriff Todd has assured us that Ricky is safe in your hands. We trust you. Of course we want to see him, but we'll follow your instructions."

"Well, I sure do appreciate that trust, because it means a lot to me. Now let's talk about what happened to your son. First, I'm aware that Dr. Benis here has told you of the condition we found Ricky in late yesterday evening. By that, I mean the condition of his body. So before we go any further, I'd like to answer any questions about that, if you have any."

"Yes, Dr. Benis did explain what happens to the body as a result of adipocere. My wife and I were not familiar with it, but we did some research of our own this morning, and we're now more educated on the subject and understand it. Dr. Benis also explained how sometimes we have to see something to believe it."

"Precisely. Dr. Benis is correct. I just wanted you both to be comfortable and to prepare you for when you see Ricky, because his body has, without a doubt, been remarkably preserved. And yes, this is in fact one of those situations where one must see it to believe it. Also, considering the other unique circumstances of Ricky's disappearance, I know it's been a living hell for you both all these years. The pain of not knowing what happened to him is nearly unimaginable, because one can think only of the most horrible scenarios in a situation like this. So until late this afternoon, we all could still only conjure up some of those horrible scenarios, but now I can tell you exactly what happened to Ricky.

"Keep in mind that going back over thirty-five years, even if we'd found Ricky right away, our tools and methods in forensic medicine were archaic compared to what we have today. Back then, we did the best we could with what we had to work with to identify the cause of death. Our knowledge and tools just hadn't caught up to science yet. It's quite possible that at that time, I may have only been able to give you some educated guesses of the actual cause of death.

"However, fast-forward thirty-five years to the present, and we find that modern medicine and technology in the world of forensic science are now quite different. Frankly, they're worlds apart. The fact that we were fortunate enough to find Ricky in an adipocerous state is even more incredible. When the body is in this state, it can be quite useful in the forensic context, because adipocere can preserve evidence, and that evidence is what we need to determine the actual cause of death, assuring no more educated guesses.

"When we arrived here late last night with Ricky, I immediately put my entire team to work. Because we found Ricky at the bottom of a wet well, my first thought was that he probably had drowned, as adipocere frequently occurs with drowning victims. It was logical, but we only decipher the evidence and what the evidence tells us. In Ricky's case, the evidence discovered during the autopsy proved Ricky did *not* drown. I can tell you conclusively that the cause of death was a cerebral aneurysm, commonly referred to as a brain aneurysm.

It's a fact that brain aneurysms can occur at any age. They are more common in adults than children, but Ricky did, most definitely, die of a special type of brain aneurysm called a berry aneurysm. Berry aneurysms are small, berry-shaped out-pouchings in the main arteries that supply the brain, and they are particularly dangerous since they are susceptible to rupture at any time, often leading to fatal bleeding within the brain and usually imminent death.

"I personally conducted the autopsy on Ricky, as well as the physical exterior body examination, assisted by some of my brightest forensic doctors. We are all in complete agreement. Ricky had absolutely no physical injuries. There was no evidence of any physical abuse or trauma to the body in any way. There were no bruises, cuts, burns, or even a broken bone—not a single one. That alone is astonishing when you consider the fact that he was pretty close to the bottom of a one-hundred-foot-deep well and didn't incur even one broken bone. There was no significant amount of water in his lungs, which positively ruled out death by drowning. All the evidence and how we interpret it confirm that Ricky was not alive when he entered the well. Your son died of a brain aneurysm, and that's what killed him. Apparently, he was put in the well *after* he died of the aneurysm. I'm absolutely certain that the cause of death and his abduction were totally unrelated. The evidence proves it. Truly, the abduction was an unfortunate tragedy in every possible way, but the individual who committed the abduction did not cause Ricky's death, nor could he have prevented Ricky's death.

"Hopefully Sheriff Todd here can put the rest of the pieces together for you as they relate to Ricky's abduction, with the assistance of our forensic archaeologist, Dr. Bernard Childress. He and his genius team are here as well, just down the hall. They too have been very busy, with the other young man we found down in the well first. They've literally put his body back together one bone at a time. They've worked nonstop around the clock to get you the evidence that hopefully will answer your unmerciful and tormenting questions: Who took your son, and why?

"Now, I know this is a lot to take in all at once. I just have to believe, though, that finding your son was your number-one concern. Lord knows you wanted to find him alive, but as it is, that wasn't to be. I can only hope that finding him finally, and now knowing what caused his death, is some kind of comfort to you both. If you'd like some time alone or if you want to go see Ricky now, just let me know; whatever you need is what we want to provide for you."

I was certain I didn't take more than half a breath from the first word out of Alf's mouth till the last. His explanation was like a mixture of both heaven 'n' hell all neatly packaged into this incredibly fabricated story. If only it had been just that. I agreed with his summation, though, and prayed silently that Katherine and Ballen could at least find comfort in the knowledge that their little boy had not been abused or killed by his abductor. That little fella would have died the way he did and when he did regardless of the abduction. Melvin Bray might have taken Ricky, but he hadn't taken his life!

"Dr. Maness, I can't tell you what hearing this means to me. As Ricky's mother, I'll never be able to express my deep appreciation for the peace you've given me today. Yes, certainly there is comfort in finally knowing what happened to Ricky. I thank you with all my heart, and I'll forever be in your debt. I also want you to know how much it means to me that you've taken such good care of our little boy since he was found yesterday. I'm especially grateful to you for that, and I really would like to see him now if that would be all right."

As Katherine stood up, Ballen joined her without speaking and gently took her hand in his. It appeared he was wrestling to comprehend the facts Alf had just delivered to him and was having a difficult time with it. The loving couple's roles had switched. Ballen the Strong was now sadly silent, and Katherine the Meek was unflappable and on a new mission—a mother's mission. It had been a long time coming, and she desperately needed to finally see her little boy again.

Alf remained reverently silent, nodded in acceptance of her wishes, and led them both out of the room and down a long hallway. We watched them as they walked the last few feet to be reunited with the love of their lives. My heart was filled with both joy and sadness.

About an hour later, the three of them returned to the conference room. Katherine and Ballen were in a blessed state of peace and calm. They looked as though the weight of the entire universe had been lifted off them. Although their lives wouldn't turn completely around that night, this closure was definitely the start of a new beginning for them, and possibly a renewed life. Their immediate need would surely be to take their son home and prepare for his big, long-overdue celebration of remembrance.

Ricky's disappearance had left many people with broken hearts and shattered lives. Both Katherine's and Ballen's parents were still living, and they had simply adored their little grandson. His disappearance had left giant holes in their hearts as well. Ricky also had several aunts, uncles, and cousins spread all over the country. This sudden news of Ricky was going to be utterly overwhelming for all of them, but in time, I was certain the good Lord would bless them all with divine inspiration and some glorious rejoicing.

Alf excused himself, saying he had something he needed to get out of his office for Katherine and Ballen. While he was gone, Todd left us to go check in with Dr. Bernie to let him know we were available to discuss That Melvin Bray. While Lizzy and I waited there with Katherine and Ballen, the four of us discussed how peaceful and angelic Ricky looked and how gracious it was that the Lord had taken such good care of him while he was missing all that time. Katherine even referenced the belief of the holy sign of incorruptibility.

Alf returned with a small metal box and presented it to Katherine; then he left us to go meet with Dr. Bernie and Todd. Katherine insisted on opening the curious container right then. She placed the box on the table and slowly lifted the latch to open it. I was reminded of Lizzy's statement only a few days earlier about Pandora's box, but I knew in my heart that this was no Pandora's box. This box could only be a precious treasure box straight from heaven.

The room was silent except for the faint, celestial strumming of a harp I was hearing in my own head, and once again, it was a little difficult to breathe. I was holding my breath—no wonder. I sat there as if in a trance as I watched Katherine reach inside the box and remove what appeared to be a small wrist bracelet or strap of some sort. However, a closer look revealed Ricky's Buster Brown wristwatch—the band only. It was a tan canvas strap covered in plastic, and the small buckle at the end of one strap was clearly broken.

Katherine laid the watchband on the table, reached back into the box, and removed another item. She held it in her hand, noting it was Ricky's small plastic wallet she had given him. He had never left home without it. His little metal Buster Brown button was still pinned to the top of it. Katherine carefully opened the wallet, and right there in its fold was Ricky's Washington Nationals baseball card that Ballen and Ballen's father had given him for his sixth birthday, just a few days before he disappeared. Katherine carefully removed the card and laid it on the table in front of her and Ballen.

She looked back inside the wallet and realized it contained something else. She removed the final object and placed it on the table next to the baseball card. She immediately recognized it as the small, colorful valentine she had given Ricky on their last day together in the kitchen, when they were taste-testing the cupcakes for his party, only an hour or so before he disappeared. Remarkably, both the cards had also been preserved.

She turned the valentine over and read aloud what she had written:

To my sweet valentine: I love you the most. Mom

That was all she had written—she had said it all.

As I sat there listening to her profession of love for her little boy, as a mother myself, I couldn't help but almost feel her pain. I was filled with emotion, and once again, my tears began to fall, landing in my lap. I wasn't by myself, though. We all just sat there, forced to feel our hearts breaking and mending at the same time through our selfless tears. It was necessary. The healing had begun.

While sitting there and experiencing that incredibly special, love-inspired valentine moment with everyone, I was delightfully reminded of the profound words of a wise little five-year-old known early on as Number Nine. This was her impression of love: "Anger gets in your heart, and the love beats it up." *Out of the mouths of babes, such insight. Thank you, Little One.*

Todd respectfully reentered the room and asked us if we'd all join him down the hall. He explained to Katherine and Ballen that we were going to meet with Dr. Bernie Childress and Dr. Maness in hopes of confirming the connection between Ricky and That Melvin Bray.

Katherine carefully returned her precious keepsakes to the box and closed it. She then stood up with a look of sheer confidence on her face and picked up her small treasure box and cradled it in her arms as if it were a newborn baby. She was taking charge, and we all fell in right behind her as Todd led the way down the hallway in hopes of ending her terrifying thirty-five-year-old nightmare.

Dr. Bernie and Alf were already seated at the large table and asked us to sit across the table from them. Todd chose the chair at the end of the table, centered between each side.

I couldn't help but notice another metal box, similar to the one Alf had given Katherine, sitting in the center of the table. Once we were all seated, Alf introduced Dr. Bernard Childress to Katherine and Ballen. Dr. Childress, like Alf, was renowned in his field, and Alf felt it appropriate and necessary to make this fact known to Katherine and Ballen, further assuring them that their son was in the most capable hands possible there at the state labs.

Dr. Bernie began with a kind statement of sympathy for their great loss and long, painful suffering, as his predecessors had. He immediately followed his expression of sorrow with an explanation of the conditions of the bodies when they were first discovered. Ricky's body was in such a condition that he was unmistakably identifiable, but they'd had to put That Melvin Bray back together one bone at a time. However, once that was done, he too was unmistakably identifiable. Of course, his identity had to be confirmed using other forensics and records. There was optimism in Dr. Bernie's voice as he said that being able to identify both Ricky and Melvin Bray so quickly had allowed them to move incredibly swiftly with the investigation—a real blessing, as he put it.

At that point, Alf spoke up, explaining the cause of death: "Melvin Bray had many broken and fractured bones, but the cause of death was clearly a cervical fracture—or, more simply, a broken neck. There are seven cervical vertebrae in the human neck, and the fracture of any one of these can be catastrophic. However, considerable force is needed to cause a cervical fracture. Motor vehicle collisions and falls are the most common causes. A severe, sudden twist of the neck can also cause a cervical fracture.

"Melvin Bray was over six feet tall and weighed about 165 pounds. It was a long fall, and he probably fought it. Based on information I have from Dr. Benis and Maggie, he didn't jump in the well; he fell in headfirst accidentally—allowing the probability of a sudden twist of the neck, causing the fracture and, ultimately, his death. Of course, having not been there at the well at the time of the fall, we can only speculate how he fell; we cannot know precisely. We do know for sure, though, what killed him and that it was most certainly an accident. At some point, Melvin Bray fell in that well, and between that point and when he came to a stop, he suffered a broken neck—of that I'm certain.

"We now know how Ricky died, how Melvin Bray died, and how Melvin Bray got in the well. What we don't know, though, is how Ricky got in the well. Sheriff Todd here has a very interesting and logical theory. Sheriff Todd, would you explain it, please?"

"Yes, thank you, Dr. Maness. Well, once I got the phone call from Lizzy several days ago, I began going over all the case files of both Ricky's disappearance and Melvin Bray's. Based on boxes of files, hundreds of opinions and interviews, and the small amount of actual evidence we had on Ricky, I still came up with a bunch of loose ends, as my predecessors had. Melvin Bray went missing about six weeks after Ricky, but his case was treated much differently. However, in both cases, the result was the same. They both seemed to have disappeared into thin air. When I spoke to Lizzy and Maggie, though, they convinced me that there was a great chance Melvin Bray was in the old well on the property where Maggie lived when both Ricky and Melvin Bray disappeared.

"Ricky disappeared on Friday, February 13, 1953, and Melvin Bray disappeared on Friday, April 3, 1953, exactly fifty days apart. I compared the old photo of Melvin Bray to the sketch Maggie did of him at the bus stop the day Ricky disappeared, and I was certain the two images were of the same man. At that point, there was still no evidence that Melvin Bray had any association with Ricky whatsoever. It just seemed curiously odd that he would be standing at that bus stop the very day Ricky disappeared, especially since he really didn't belong there. If he had fallen in the well, I sure hoped we'd find him—certainly for his loved ones, of course, but my other consideration was that if he was there at the bus stop and we were able to identify him, hopefully we could begin the search for clues to either connect him to Ricky in some way or to totally eliminate him as a suspect. I realized that even if he had fallen in the well, I already knew from Lizzy and Maggie that it was definitely an accident, and even if we did find him, that didn't mean we'd be able to link him to Ricky. It was a long shot but one worth taking. Then, when we actually found what we thought were the remains of Melvin Bray, I thought at least it was a start in the right direction. Plus, if it was indeed Melvin Bray, then at least one family would now know what had happened to their son.

"Once we'd recovered both Ricky and Melvin Bray, while I was waiting on Dr. Maness and Dr. Childress to conduct their examinations and the autopsy, I began working my way *back* from the well. Several of Dr. Childress's experts assisted me in carefully sifting through all the various personal items we'd found in the well. Once I was able to separate and define what belonged to Ricky and what was Melvin Bray's, I realized that we'd possibly finally found some crucial evidence that could speak to us for both Ricky *and* Melvin Bray. I believe Dr. Maness has already given Ricky's things to you, Mrs. Lawrence. This metal box sitting here on the table has the items belonging to Melvin Bray, and Dr. Maness will give those to the Bray family when they arrive tomorrow. However, there is one small item in the Bray box I would like you to look at, Mrs. Lawrence, if you will, please."

"Of course, Sheriff Todd. May I see it?"

Todd reached for the metal box and opened it. He removed a small item, but I couldn't make it out at first. Katherine, who was sitting next to Todd, extended her arm and opened her hand. Todd placed the object in her hand. With both hands, Katherine held the little object between her fingers. She took only a minute or so before she spoke, confirming it had belonged to Ricky, not Melvin Bray. Todd's expression remained the same as Katherine continued to examine the object. She said she had found the band that went with this trinket earlier, when Dr. Maness had given her Ricky's personal items. She confirmed that the item was the missing watch face belonging to Ricky's Buster Brown watch. She explained that she had noticed that the buckle on the watchband was also broken. She placed her metal box on the table and removed the little watchband. She handed both the band and the watch face to Todd. He placed the band on the table and then put the missing watch face in the center of the band, as it should be. There was no doubt the band and the watch belonged together.

258

Of course, Todd, Alf, and Dr. Bernie already knew this, but they were making a point. Apparently, they had found the watch face among Melvin Bray's things. They had found the watchband, however, with Ricky's things—nowhere near Melvin Bray's remains. This tiny metal-and-plastic watch face was the one crucial piece of evidence that would positively link Melvin Bray to Ricky Lawrence. It was conclusive. At that point, the room was so quiet that you coulda heard a pin drop. We were *all* holding our breath by then, and Katherine and Ballen both sat straight up in their chairs. Ballen reached over and took Katherine's hand in his as Todd continued his theory.

"While reviewing the files on Melvin Bray, I was able to put the pieces together, answering the big question of *why* he would be standing inside the base gate at Ricky's bus stop that fateful Friday afternoon. As Dr. Maness said earlier, this is only a theory, but it *is* logical.

"Mr. and Mrs. Lawrence, I believe Melvin Bray was at the bus stop simply because he'd been hired to mow the yard of the vacant house behind your house. Apparently, from time to time, he was just extra help at the army base. That's why he didn't stand out. He really wasn't a stranger. He'd been working there inside the gate off and on for over a year. His agreement with the base was that when he was going to be working at the school grounds, which was typically on the weekends, he would also tend to the yards of any vacant military houses there inside the base gate. They gave him a list each month of the vacant houses, and he was to mow those specific yards. They provided the push mower, and it was kept in a supply shed just inside the gate. So actually, I guess you could say he had just as much right to be there that day as anyone else, and I don't believe it's a big deal that he was there on a Friday afternoon instead of the weekend. So what! He played hooky from his regular job at Collins Mill that day, where he worked with Maggie's daddy. In hindsight, though, that was his first mistake. So the ominous question was what he was doing at that bus stop that day, right? Well, now we know.

"Before we go any further, I want you to know that I've confirmed the relationship between Melvin Bray and the army base. When I called Melvin Bray's uncle a little while ago to tell him we had indeed found the remains of his nephew, I asked him if he could give me any reason why his nephew would have been on that army base that day. His uncle told me what I just told you. Now, from this point forward, my logical theory begins.

"We know that Ricky was in your backyard, flying his kite. The kite may have flown over the back fence and into the yard behind your house, where Melvin Bray was mowing. In Ricky's FBI file, there was a notation of some string or thread tangled and dangling from the big oak tree in the backyard, but there was no mention of a kite. That same file also stated there was a push mower pressed firmly against the fence located directly under the oak tree, and it appeared that the yard was in the process of being mowed. This tells us Melvin Bray was most likely out there doing his job, just mowing the yard at that vacant house located directly behind your house.

"The evidence suggests that when the kite got stuck in the tree, Melvin Bray may have seen it and stopped mowing. He may have then gone to help the owner of that kite—Ricky. As Melvin Bray was over six feet tall and the fence was six feet tall, he could have quite easily grabbed the top of the fence and stuck his head over and offered to help Ricky with the kite. We already know from Maggie's sketch of the bus stop that Melvin Bray had on the infamous Washington Nationals *W* baseball hat of his. If Ricky saw that hat, they were probably instant friends, as the Washington Nationals was also Ricky's favorite baseball team. Certainly I can't prove all this, but it's a surefire, logical scenario that brought the two of them together that day.

"What happened next? Well, I can't prove this either, but again, it's logical based on how Ricky died. I don't believe Melvin Bray had any intentions at all of harming Ricky in the first place. That was not his motivation for being there that day. *What* I believe he did and *why* he did it do not make him a murderer. He did wrong—that's for sure—but I think I know why he did it.

"We all know Ricky was small for his age and weighed only about forty pounds. Melvin Bray could have easily helped Ricky over the fence. He then retrieved the kite, leaving a few strands of kite string stuck in the tree, but he dropped the kite back over into Ricky's yard, because that's where it was when Mrs. Lawrence went to check on Ricky and first realized he was gone. This scenario is consistent with the information in the investigation file, along with the half-mowed lawn and the mower parked against the fence.

"Melvin Bray was a young man in his midtwenties. He'd gotten into some trouble with the law back home in Virginia, involving a DUI offense. His father felt he was associating with some bad folks up there and asked his brother if Melvin could come down south to live with him for a while and maybe settle down in a different environment. The uncle agreed and even helped Melvin get a job at Collins Hosiery Mill. The uncle would allow him to use the car on the weekends when he needed to work at the schoolhouse and the army base, doing something productive and making a little extra money, too. Further conversation with the uncle convinced me that I have no reason to believe Melvin Bray's intentions were sinister. Once Dr. Maness confirmed how Ricky died, I was even more convinced of Melvin Bray's innocence, at least as it related to Ricky's cause of death.

"From this point forward, in all likelihood, this is probably pretty close to what happened that day. They were both on the other side of the fence in the vacant yard, and the two of them began talking about their favorite baseball team and simply lost track of time. Of course, Melvin Bray never should have taken Ricky out of his family's backyard to begin with. That was his second mistake. Then something totally unexpected and tragic occurred. Ricky suffered a brain aneurysm and died instantly. A situation such as this was not going to look good for Melvin Bray, as it was likely everyone was going to think he had kidnapped a little boy and killed him. At that point, Melvin Bray did the worst thing he could have possibly done. He took Ricky and put him in the old well, and he would just have to take his horrible secret to the grave with him. And he did just that—fifty days later, when he himself accidently fell in the old well and died.

"I believe when Melvin Bray realized Ricky had died, he panicked, and in his mind, he had no other choice but to hide Ricky. He was familiar with the old well because he worked with Maggie's daddy and had been out to Maggie's house many times with her daddy. So at some point on the very same day Ricky disappeared, the day he died, Melvin Bray put Ricky in the car, waited until dark that night, and then drove out to Maggie's house and put Ricky in the well. He went on home to his uncle's house, and no one had any reason to connect him to Ricky. The fact is that someone *could* have seen Melvin Bray and Ricky together—the opportunity was certainly there—but unfortunately, no one saw them or remembered seeing them.

"Later that night, when Melvin Bray got Ricky to the well, someone at Maggie's could have seen him putting something in the well, but it was dark, and apparently they'd seen Melvin Bray and Maggie's daddy throw things in the old well before. If anyone *had* seen him, they probably wouldn't have thought anything about it. The fact is that Ricky died, and Melvin Bray hid him. That was his third mistake. It was certainly a thoughtless, cruel, and selfish act borne out of fear, and it was wrong; we all know that. Who knows, though? Maybe someday Melvin Bray would have confessed to what he'd done, in an attempt to redeem himself. I'm certain you both would agree that would have been the right and most merciful thing for him to do. Of course, that could never happen once he fell and died in the well several weeks later.

"Another dilemma facing us was that even though we found them both in the well, there was still no evidence that the two were actually connected. The truth is, a third individual—or more—could have been involved with their disappearances. We still had to find something to connect the two. As we were going through all the personal items, we found a plastic ball-point pen with what was left of a logo on it. It turned out to be a special pen with indelible black ink that Melvin Bray used every day in his job, marking totals of daily inventory production, and the logo read Collins Hosiery Mill. Then we came upon that little watch face, which was nestled firmly in the dirt directly under Melvin Bray's brass belt buckle. I haven't figured out exactly how the watch face ended up with Melvin Bray, but I think the watchband probably broke and fell off Ricky's wrist while he was with Melvin Bray or when Melvin Bray was carrying him after he died. Regardless, at some point, the watch face got separated from the band, as indicated by the broken band on one end of the strap that was found next to Ricky. Melvin Bray must have kept the watch face, since it was located with *his* personal items when we found him, instead of with Ricky's remains. We could have been stuck at yet another fork in the road if it hadn't been for that little watch face. I tell y'all, I'm real grateful for that! That watch face is our conclusive evidence that the two of them were together at some point in time *before* Ricky was hidden in the well and *before* Melvin Bray fell into the well.

"Mr. and Mrs. Lawrence, a tragedy happened a long time ago. Your little boy and a young man both lost their lives. Based on the evidence—not just logical theory, but the evidence—I don't see how either death could have been prevented. What started out as one tragedy escalated into an unconscionable second tragedy as a result of the actions of a confused and frightened young man. As a result of his fears, it's taken over thirty-five years to uncover the contemptible and even pitiable truth. But here we are today, after all this time, and no one has ever connected the two cases until now. Mrs. Lawrence, it all started when you made an appointment with Dr. Benis all the way up there in Boston just a couple of months ago to talk about Ricky. It's been a nightmare for you, Mr. Lawrence, and all your loved ones—and the Bray family as well—but thankfully, it's over now. All of us here want to do whatever you need us to do to assist you in getting your son home now so that you can put him to a proper rest with the good Lord."

You coulda heard a feather drop. It was as though we'd all just sat through the saddest movie ever, and Todd had been the narrator, describing each scene in vivid detail. Todd's theory was probably as close to the truth as possible, and we all accepted it. One thing was certain: Melvin Bray hadn't killed Ricky; however, he had killed himself—accidently, of course. If he hadn't been drinking that awful rainy day with my daddy, he might not have fallen in the well.

Then I had that same thought from earlier: if he hadn't fallen in the well, I wouldn't have seen him fall, and we wouldn't have been looking for him in the well in the first place—and of course, we wouldn't have found Ricky. I could only think that That Melvin Bray's fall from grace down into the well that day was somehow his redemption—the deliverance from the sins of humanity, imposed by the good Lord since we could not redeem ourselves.

Ballen had gathered his composure and finally spoke. "'Thank you' just doesn't seem adequate for what each of you and your staff members have done for my wife, our son, and me here today. I just don't have the words to properly express how I feel right now."

Katherine added, "Yes, my husband and I are profoundly grateful, and as he said, we're touched beyond mere words. You found our little boy for us, and now we finally know what happened to him. We want to take him home and give him back to the Lord as soon as you'll let us have him."

Their strength and determination were also beyond mere words. But for the first time, I saw a deep emotion stirring in Ballen. As Katherine began to speak, it was she who reached for Ballen's hand this time. She held it tightly, as if she were returning his faithful love and devotion in that moment, when it was too difficult for him to speak his heart.

Before they could take Ricky home, there was a legal process that had to take place, and Alf had to prepare Ricky for the flight home to Boston. While all that was going on, Lizzy had some private time with Katherine and Ballen.

I went to a small waiting room and called Aunt Lucy and told her everything. She was absolutely shocked, of course, but I had learned a long time ago that Aunt Lucy could handle just about anything. She had proven it time and time again. Talk about courage and obedience!

Because of what I'd heard Mother say to Daddy once about That Melvin Bray, I asked Aunt Lucy if Mother had ever told her specifically that she didn't trust That Melvin Bray around us kids. She told me that Mother had said she "felt something about him," but it was more like concern that he was headed for trouble if he kept drinking and running around with Daddy.

Aunt Lucy was also quick to say that neither she nor Mother had ever felt we kids were in any danger, but they felt that because That Melvin Bray was young himself, he was possibly just one more bad influence on us kids. She said Mother had told him she feared something bad might happen to him or someone else if he didn't stay away from Daddy, and Mother had even tried to get him to go to church with us. That didn't surprise me a bit; of course she had.

Aunt Lucy wanted Lizzy and me to come spend the night with her, but it was going to be late by the time we got back to Grace Chapel from Raleigh, so I promised her we'd go by her house the next day before we headed to Charlotte to catch our flight back to Boston. She was fine with that, and before we hung up, she said, "Magg-Pie, you girls be sure to thank our sweet Lord for all these blessings, honey."

"Yes, ma'am, we will. I love ya, and we'll see ya in the mornin', Aunt Lucy."

A short while later, we all returned to the conference room, and Todd explained the legal protocol and process that would take place in getting Ricky to Boston. Katherine and Ballen would need to remain there in Raleigh for a couple of days while all the red tape was handled. Of course, they had no intention of leaving Ricky anyway. Todd said he would get them a hotel room right next door to the center, which would allow them some personal time to contact all their relatives with the news of Ricky. Todd, Alf, and Dr. Bernie were still on their own mission and would do everything within their power to make the process as painless and expedient as possible for Katherine and Ballen. In addition to the Lawrence family crisis, they were still facing Melvin Bray's family's loss as well. The Brays had lost a son too, and they had loved him no less than Katherine and Ballen had loved little Ricky. The kindness and humility of these three men was heartening. Thank heaven the good Lord knew exactly what we needed and when we needed it.

It was time for Lizzy and me to leave; our job was done. We were leaving the Lawrence family in the best hands possible, because these three men were, without a doubt, children of God. Lizzy and I knew this; thus, our departure was much easier. Alf had Cabel, one of his colleagues, drive Lizzy and me back to Grace Chapel to Todd's office to get our rental car.

The ride back with Cabel was enlightening. He told us this was the most unusual forensics case he had ever been involved in during his fifteen-year tenure with Dr. Maness. He also told us he had worked on Ricky's case personally a few years back and had been convinced Ricky was one of those lost children who would never be found. He also stated that most everyone figured That Melvin Bray had just left town on his own and had probably reunited with his family by now. He was visibly moved and probably had a renewed spirit and dedication toward the impossible and unbelievable. Man, could I tell him a few things about *that*!

Cabel drove into the parking lot at Todd's office and waited for us to get into the rental car and get on our way back to the hotel there in Grace Chapel before he drove off in the opposite direction back to Raleigh. It was a little past midnight by then, and we were half awake, not half asleep, as we should have been. Out of the blue, Lizzy suggested we go by Starlite Drive-In. She obviously had P. C. on her mind for some reason. The little late-night restaurant was still in business, but it no longer offered the once-popular curb service.

We parked the car and went into the little diner and sat down in a corner booth in the back. Lizzy began fiddling with the minijukebox that sat on the table. Although curb service was gone, the Starlite had kept the small tabletop jukeboxes for their customers' enjoyment. She finally made a selection, dropping a quarter in the little slot, and a familiar tune began to play.

Sometimes in our lives we all have pain and sorrow
But if we are wise,
We know that there's always tomorrow.
Lean on me, when you're not strong....

Sitting there at the Starlite and hearing that old Bill Withers tune was all too nostalgic, and I was taken back to a warm summer afternoon when Lizzy's mother took us to the Starlite for curb service. We were sitting in the car, when P. C. walked out carrying a tray with chocolate shakes for all of us and told Mrs. Benis they were on the house. Mrs. Benis told P. C. she would just have to pay him, and he told her, "Take the girls up to Eagle's and get 'em some dime stuff." He winked at Lizzy and me and headed over to the car beside us to take their order.

My darling, fond memory was interrupted by the waitress asking for our order. There were only four other customers, all sitting at the counter, drinking coffee and chatting about the three worlds—past, present, future—with the two late-night waitresses.

We placed our orders and leaned back against the old, worn-out leather booth seats.

"Maggs, as we were riding back from Raleigh and talking with Cabel about the unbelievable things that happen on this earth, I couldn't help but think of P. C."

"I can relate, Lizzy, and I'm glad we're here. Not a day goes by that I don't think of him. Ya know, as I was listening to the words of that song on the jukebox just now, I had a vision of that day when your mother brought us out here and

P. C. wouldn't let her pay him for our milk shakes. Remember? And she took us up to Eagle's Dime Store—remember that day?"

"Sure I do, Magg-Pie; you read my mind, little sister."

"It's still hard to believe what happened to him that night, ya know, Lizzy?"

"And why, Maggs? But of course, as Aunt Lucy would say, that's the good Lord's business—for him to know and us to accept."

We ate our chili dogs and drank our chocolate shakes in loving memory of the one and only P. C. We bid our neighbors at the counter goodnight and drove back to the hotel in silence. We needed to rest our hearts, our minds, and our bodies, for as the song goes, "Sometimes in our lives, we all have pain."

CHAPTER 30

Shedding the Cloak on the Road to Forgiveness

It is freeing to become aware that we do not have to be victims
of our past and can learn new ways of responding. But there is
a step beyond this recognition ... it is the step of forgiveness.
Forgiveness is love practiced among people who love poorly.
It sets us free without wanting anything in return.
—*Henri J. M. Nouwen, Catholic priest, author*

IS THAT A ROOSTER CROWIN'? *Yep, sure is.* There I was, tryin' my best to remain in slumber, but that ole cock-a-doodle-do was having no part o' that. The three of us—me, myself, and I—all agreed to just rise 'n' shine 'n' join 'im. Heck, it had to be every bit of six o'clock—why not?

There were no signs of "up 'n' at it" from the other quarters yet, so I decided to phone Aunt Lucy and make plans with her for the day, as we'd promised.

Naturally, she was up and on her second cup of coffee. First, she calmly asked me where we were and if we were all right. I assured her we were just fine. Then she asked me what we wanted for breakfast, and I told her to surprise us. She was delighted we were coming, not to mention anxious to hear the final outcome of the terribly sad thirty-five-year-old mystery. She made me promise we'd be there by nine thirty and plan to spend the night with her. I promised her we would. As I was hanging up the phone, Lizzy poked her head in with a hearty "Good morning, dearest—slept well, I hope."

"I sure did, Lizzy-Girl, and you?"

"Like a little baby, missy. Who was that on the phone?"

"Aunt Lucy. She's making a surprise breakfast for us, and we have to be there by nine thirty. Ya think ya can make that happen, Mr. Petty?"

"That's wonderful. Of course I can; I'm starving, Maggs!"

"That's just great, and I must say, I take that as a real good sign, ya know, babe?"

"Oh, I'm just fine, honey; no need to fret over me. I'm working through all this. As a matter of fact, the minute I opened my eyes this morning, I had this wonderful feeling, and it was slowly caressing my entire body. I felt light as a feather—strange but wonderful. Seriously, Maggs, for once in my life, I actually feel as though all is right with this world."

"Really? I want some o' *that*!"

"Well, all I can say is everything in its proper time, little Magg-Pie."

"Okay, so until then, I guess we'd better get dressed and packed and head on over to Aunt Lucy's for that surprise breakfast, 'cause ya know how she likes everything served hot!"

"I do know that, Maggs. Let's go; I'll race ya."

We checked out of the hotel and loaded our bags into the trunk of the rental car. Lizzy resumed her natural position behind the wheel with a renewed sense of excitement. Something was different about her; I just couldn't put my finger on it. Oh well, as she had explained, "everything in its proper time."

We arrived at Aunt Lucy's with not a minute to spare. We pulled into the driveway, and I was overcome with my *own* wonderful feelings as I took in all the fond memories of that big, beautiful yellow house and what it stood for in my life and the lives of my darling siblings—and Lizzy's too, of course. We were home. We jumped outta the car and raced up to the front door. We immediately started pounding on it, drumming out a little tune: "We're home, Aunt Lucy. Let us in, weeoooo. Let us in, weeeeeooooo."

The front door opened, and there stood our other mother—the awesome, wise, 'n' wonderful Aunt Lucy! The smile on her face was filled with that unconditional love of hers, and we couldn't have loved her back any more than we did in that very moment. We all burst into tears of joy and laughter. Aunt Lucy took us by the hands and pulled us into the foyer, and we made a little circle and danced around the room, experiencing the joy of being together again. As we were twirlin' around, deliriously happy in our little circle of love, I realized we weren't alone. The spacious foyer quickly filled with all my siblings: Lu, Ali, Lee, Paddy, Lainey, Fay, and Mae. It was quite a reunion. Well, I had told Aunt Lucy to surprise us. Our little love circle got much bigger as they all joined in, and we must have danced around for ten minutes before Aunt Lucy broke the circle first, leading us into the dining room for another one of her famous "Breakfast of Chilltons." That woman could sure cook good food *good*, like nobody's business! Oh, it wasn't fancy. Nothing from Paris, France, or even Paris, Georgia, and no Italians either—just good ole country cookin'!

We all sat down and joined hands, and naturally, Aunt Lucy started our reunion with a gracious prayer of thanks for all our many blessings and God's grace, love, and forgiveness, with a special reference to both the Lawrence and Bray families.

Aunt Lucy had hired a housekeeper a few years back, and Miss Lindy just happened to work on Tuesdays. Lucky us! She began to clear the table, and all of us "kids" playfully breathed a loud sigh of relief. Heck, *we* sure didn't wanta have to clean up that kitchen. Aunt Lucy led us all into the den, where she had a blazing fire going in the huge brick fireplace. It was so cozy, homey, and safe. We all sat for hours, reminiscing. This was the first time we had all been together, Lizzy included, since Christmas over five years ago. We'd see one family member or another on a short visit here or there, but it was difficult to get so many schedules together at once anymore. There were many tears, especially for our dear P. C., but there was much laughter too. As we were all bringing the family up to date on what had occurred in our specific lives over the past five years, we realized that the events of those five years didn't even come close to what had just happened in the past three *days* in our little ole Grace Chapel. And in just a few more days, our little town was going to be "on the map" like never before!

Ali the Honorable and the family journalist, who had married a writer and had three great kids, stood up and took center stage in front of the fireplace. She waved her arms in the air as if she were painting a rainbow and announced, "Oh, I can just see the *Tribune*'s front-page headline now: "Whatever Happened to That Melvin Bray and Little Ricky Lawrence?" Ya know, this is going to be huge, y'all—*huge!*"

Thirty-five years had gone by since Aunt Lucy and we Chillton kids had seen That Melvin Bray. As Lizzy and I recapped the past several days for them, they were all saddened for That Melvin Bray and his family, but at the same time, they couldn't help but be intrigued as they listened to the story unfold. Since everyone except Mae had known That Melvin Bray, this part of the story was certainly of particular interest to each of them. The part about Ricky, though, was just plain sad. None of us had known him, but we all sure did hurt for him.

"Children, sometimes a man meets his destiny on the road he took to avoid it. I think that's what happened to Melvin Bray when he took that little boy out to that old well that night."

"What insight, Aunt Lucy! You're the wisest person I know, ya know?"

"Aw, come here, Paddy-Lamb. Give your old aunt Lucy some sugar, baby."

"Okay, here I come, Aunt Lucy—move over."

After Mother died, followed by his big brother, P. C., little Paddy the Believer had clung to Aunt Lucy like a bee on honey. He used to say he "loved her to death," but when he grew older, he had changed it to "I love you to infinity and back." He didn't like the word *death*; plus, how could anyone be loved more than "to infinity and back"? It wasn't possible.

After college, Paddy had accepted a position in DC with the Supreme Court. He'd done quite well for himself, and Aunt Lucy was so proud of him. He was very devoted to her and visited her often. I was sure that made Mother happy. Actually, the Chillton kids and Lizzy were all close to each other and to Aunt Lucy. Aunt Lucy treated us all the same, except for Paddy. She had suffered the loss of P. C. deeply, and I believe it caused her to be more aware of Paddy, since he was also a boy.

The incredibly courageous and you-don't-wanta-make-me-roar Lee the Lion jumped up and joined Ali's floor show, confidently proclaiming, "I told y'all I didn't like That Melvin Bray. Shoot, I must have had a sixth sense about his sick scent. Maybe it was some kind of self-conscious scent of fear he wore—psychologically maybe, Dr. Lizzy? Whatever. All I remember is that when he walked in, I detected it, and none of y'all did, but it was there all right—I promise ya that! I'm not saying I think he intended to harm that little boy, but even as a child myself, I had a weird feeling about him, and now look what's happened to him!"

Lee was married, and she, her husband, and their two boys had land galore and a successful farm about twenty miles from Aunt Lucy. As Mother had told us long ago, Lee stood for justice. She was quite outspoken when a cause touched her heart. If she was on your side, you were fortunate, but if she wasn't, then you'd better switch sides or look out. Lee had started out as one righteous chick and never changed.

"You're right, Lee. Your mother felt sorry for that young man, and your daddy didn't do anything to help him, because he was a big mess himself. That Melvin Bray already had some problems when he came here, and once he attached himself to your daddy, he just continued on the wrong path and was headed for more trouble. However, what he did with that child was *his* decision, no one else's, not even your daddy's. The thing to remember, though, is that we are not his judge. That's the good Lord's business, not ours. You children remember that, too."

"You're so right, Aunt Lucy. I just wish I could have done something to help him."

"Now, Lu, as brave as you've always been, looking after this one and that one, mothering and protecting all these kids for your mother back then, just what exactly do you think you could have done for him, and when would you have had time to do it? He was also several years older than you. No, honey, you mustn't take that one on; it's not your cross to bear."

"I don't know, Aunt Lucy; it just seems such a shame for That Melvin Bray and that little boy to have had to leave this world the way they did. I was the oldest, and I was also aware that I felt sorry for him too, just like Mother. "

"Yes, ma'am, and just like your mother, there was nothing *you* could do to change that young man's path, Lu. You pray about it and let it go, honey."

A few days after P. C.'s funeral, Aunt Lucy had insisted Lu return to college. However, it had taken Lu the Brave Heart a long time to truly deal with the loss of her brother and best friend. She had remained deep in sorrow over P. C. for a long time, just as Aunt Lucy had. They had dealt with the loss in different ways, but for their own personal reasons, they both had felt responsible in some way for what happened to P. C.

Lu had left college after only two years and moved far away from our little town. Who could blame her? She had met a great fella, and they had gotten engaged, but she'd broken off the engagement after a year. She was very social and had many friends, but she'd never married. My feeling was that Mother and Daddy had tainted marriage for Lu. She worked hard at being strong and independent; of course, she'd had to develop those traits early in life. But the long-term suffering and psychological stress of her personal tragedies constrained her, resulting in an unfulfilled life. Lu had an awful lot of potential and a lust for life, but sadly, those gifts were never fully manifested. *I probably should suggest that she spend a few days in Boston with the good doctor. It couldn't hurt, right?* As I mentioned before, Lu's middle name was Luverta, and she hated that name and had agreed with Mother that she'd rather be called Lu and *never* Luverta. She and P. C. had their own unique notions about their names. Anyway, I figured out how Lu's name change happened. Of course, I had help from Ali, who kept up with all the family history. She would be the first one to tell people that she knew way too much, but that was what she got for snoopin' around. Ali was funny. She should have charged for that humor.

According to Ali, when Lu was born, Daddy insisted she be named Luverta. Mother really wanted to name her Christine, after a close cousin. They agreed on Christine Luverta, but Daddy insisted on calling her Luverta, not Christine. Obedient to her not-better half, Mother agreed, and Luverta it was—until Luverta became Lu at the ripe young age of six. Quite by mistake, Lu found out during one of Mr. Hyde's drunk 'n' disorderly outbursts just who Luverta was—and she was *not* a close cousin. She just happened to be one of ole Chill's mistresses, the one who broke Mother's heart—the *first* time. The knowledge was heartbreaking for both Mother and her firstborn, and the two of them agreed to change my eldest sister's name to Lu.

"Well, I guess you two are feeling like the good Lord's little helpers, huh, Maggs?"

"Ya know, Lainey, no one's more surprised here than Lizzy and me! Less than two weeks ago, I went up to Boston, and as we now describe it, all heaven broke loose! If we hadn't been there, we probably wouldn't believe a word of all this. I guess the more correct way to put it would be that the good Lord's been *our* helper! He has opened so many doors, walked beside us, and sent guardian angels to guide us, including our dear mother, Lizzy's mother, and Grandma Bubbee, to comfort us, feed us, and inspire us. I just wish you all could have been with us—you too, Aunt Lucy! Lizzy and I will never be the same."

"I guess we got to be the chosen ones *this* time, right, Lee? Maggie finally told me about your vision in the hospital that night your sweet mother went to heaven."

"Yes, you two did get lucky, Lizzy! Now you know how *I* felt, and you'll never forget it either!"

"Well, I guess Mae and I missed it all," Fay said. "We were just too young to remember anything. You guys know it's your responsibility to make sure you tell us everything, in case you haven't already. We need to know about our past too, ya know!"

"Yeah, that's right; don't leave us out, okay?" Mae agreed.

"Hey, Fay, Mae, you two have heard plenty of those terrible stories about ole Chill, but trust me, you didn't want to experience it firsthand like the rest of us. The best story of all about our daddy was the one about the day Aunt Lucy got Judge Bering to send him packing on a one-way ticket out of town. That, little sisters, was the best day of our lives—right, Lee?" Paddy said.

"Abso-damn-lutely, little brother!"

"Now, Lee, Paddy, don't y'all make it worse than it was," Aunt Lucy said.

"Aunt Lucy, how in the world could we do that? All we gotta do is tell the truth. Bad is bad, right, Paddy?"

"You know it, Lee! She's right, Aunt Lucy! It's another real shame, though, how he ended up finding another family to terrorize and abuse for years up north till he got sent away for good."

"Oh, children, let's not speak of your daddy anymore; this is a happy occasion, and we don't need to relive the bad, painful memories of the past, okay?"

"Aunt Lucy's right," Lu said. "Let's all be grateful. And most importantly, after all this time, we finally know what happened to That Melvin Bray and Ricky. Can y'all imagine what this means to those two families?"

"Right, Lu—that's what this is really all about now, honey. These two families, who each loved their child no more or less than the other, can now put them to rest with the good Lord. They can finally begin to find some peace in their own hearts and use that peace as comfort for the rest of their lives. They can also begin to take the step of forgiveness. 'It is freeing to become aware that we do not have to be victims of our past.' There's no doubt in my mind that both these families blame themselves in some way for what happened to their boys."

"You are so right, Aunt Lucy, and this forgiveness you speak of is imperative for these families to receive the peace they so desperately need and to go on and live with closure after all this time."

"Yes, Lizzy, and I think you'll agree with me when I say Katherine and Ballen are on *their* way to that peace, right?"

"Definitely, Maggs. I believe they are. I don't know the Bray family, but I think we'll all agree that we have two families now who are in need of some serious prayer."

"Amen, Lizzy-Girl! And I can't think of a better time than right now; let's pray, children."

Aunt Lucy led us all in a heartfelt prayer for both Melvin Bray's and Ricky's families, and out of the wild blue yonder, she asked God's forgiveness for Daddy! I couldn't help myself; I opened my eyes and peeked up at Aunt Lucy, only to realize everybody else was watching her too. Aunt Lucy went on to ask God to forgive *her* for her sinner's grudge against Daddy, which she had planted deep in her heart so long ago. As she prayed for God's forgiveness, I felt a warm feeling move through my body. I recited her words as my own. Forgiveness was alive and well, and we all felt it thanks to our heavenly Father. We all spent the rest of the day together, reliving the good ole *good* days and finding ways to poke fun at the bad ole *bad* days. We included Mother and P. C. in everything, and it was as though they were right there with us, sitting on the floor in front of that awesome fire.

Aunt Lucy reminded us that the happiest of people didn't have the best of everything; they just made the best of everything they had. Her words certainly rang true, too! I mean, there we were, just a mess o' grown-up siblings all sitting on the floor in front of a roaring fire, enjoying each other with popcorn and s'mores as our beloved aunt Lucy kept pots of coffee and hot chocolate flowing. Our spirits were renewed with joy as each hour passed. Were we one lucky family or what? Now, that was a way to live!

The next morning, we all had one more delightful meal together before we left in different directions. That morning was fabulous! Aunt Lucy was the best! She even surprised us by calling the one 'n' only Mrs. Brown to join us for breakfast. We were all still crazy about Mrs. Brown, and the feeling was mutual. Aunt Lucy and Mrs. Brown still fussed over Mae, Mae still thrived on it, and we all still enjoyed watching the three of them enjoy each other. *Isn't it great that some things never change?*

The parting was such sweet sorrow, because we loved each other so much and it was hard to leave each other. In her wisdom, though, Aunt Lucy reminded us that we'd all be back together in just a few weeks for Thanksgiving, and that made it easier. We hugged and kissed each other good-bye one last time. Lizzy and I were the first to leave, since we had to catch a noon flight out of Charlotte back to Boston. We got into the rental car as they all stood in the driveway, blowing kisses and waving at us until we were out of sight.

Once we turned in the rental car and got seated on the plane, we realized we were just plain tired and filled with every conceivable emotion possible. We'd experienced quite a lot in a short period of time. But *we* were the lucky ones. Aunt Lucy sure had pulled off a good surprise, and she had even provided us with the special gift of the incomparable Mrs. Brown! Apparently, our purpose there had been to bring families together again—several families, as a matter of fact! And that was exactly what we had done. Our holy mission from God was complete.

We slept through the whole flight and woke up to the captain announcing our arrival into Boston.

"I love it when that happens, Lizzy."

"Me too! We sure needed those z's, huh, Maggs? Let's get off this plane!"

"Hey, you're preachin' to the choir, sister. I'm outta here!"

We got off the plane and headed to baggage. It wasn't long before we had our bags and were in the parking lot, looking for our special parking space, divinely assigned to us just a few days earlier, marked by none other than the celestial number five. Lizzy unlocked the car, and we loaded the luggage in the trunk and hopped in. She started the engine on that fine pearly white flying machine of hers, and she had the top down before we got outta the parking lot.

It was almost five o'clock on that sunny but chilly fall afternoon. As Lizzy was rounding a sharp curve, I glanced over and observed her long blonde hair being tossed around in the light breeze of Moriah. I instantly reached back and loosened the ribbon that was holding back my own long blonde hair. We must have looked like two angels in that pearly white convertible, with our long blonde tresses dancing all around us, taking those curves like we knew what we were doing. We felt so free and exalted!

It felt good to just let go and be me. Of course, I didn't know just yet who *me* really was, but I was ready to find out. I was anxious to bid farewell to the Great Pretender and shed my cloak of dishonor once and for all. Love and forgiveness were running through my heart and mind, and I was innately aware of it.

We drove in silence for a few miles, and the ambience was simply divine. Lizzy was up to her usual flying antics as she took the twists and turns on the parkway, the long road home. There was a feeling of heaven in the air, and I was aware of that, too.

"You know, dear Maggie, at the proper time an angel will recognize another angel. At the proper time, an angel will also know when her work is finished. I believe our work is finished, and our time here is almost done."

As I listened to her words, I looked over at her, and a warm feeling came over me. It was the same feeling she had described to me that morning when she had first awakened. It was a wonderful feeling, and it slowly embraced my entire body. I felt as light as a feather—strange but wonderful!

Just then, for the first time in my life, I felt as though all was right in the world. I also remembered telling her that morning, rather playfully, "I want some o' *that*!"

In that moment, the proper time, it became crystal clear to me. I understood what she was saying, and once again, the Lizzy-Girl was right!

As I looked over at her, I recognized *her*, and I knew *me*. I too knew that our work was finished and our time here was done. I reached for her hand, and as she placed her hand in mine, I replied simply, "Yes, I know, dear Lizzy."

A multitude of memories flashed before me, including a vivid image of Daddy. An intense awareness of the fact that I had finally forgiven him uplifted my heart. I was euphoric and could hardly move. Lizzy was humming the great old tune by Etta James, "Something's Got a Hold on Me," and with her sweet hand still in mine, I leaned my head back on the headrest. I focused on the beautiful fall sky and then closed my eyes. Lizzy's humming had transformed into what sounded like a celestial choir accompanied by a symphony orchestra. I opened my eyes, and all heaven broke loose.

Something's got a hold on me
I've never felt like this before
Something's got a hold on me
I believe I'd die if I only could
I feel so strange, but I feel so good

Emily Johnson

Each of us leaves a thumbprint on this world,
a record that we were here,
who we were and what we did.
Your only choice is what kind of thumbprint to leave.
—Sidney B. Simon

'And suddenly a voice came from heaven, saying,
"This is My beloved Son, in whom I am well pleased."'
Matthew 3:17

Photo of the Author – Deborah Posso

Born in North Carolina, the author is a daughter, sister, wife, mother and grandmother. She considers life and forgiveness the ultimate gifts and writes about them in her first novel, sharing poignant memories of struggles and triumphs of some amazing people as they lived their gifts. She and her husband live in Atlanta.

CPSIA information can be obtained
at www.ICGtesting.com
Printed in the USA
BVHW071410021019
560007BV00003B/39/P

9 781458 212801